BY AUDREY HARTE

Audrey Harte ♡

Madisyn Harte ♡
Lindsay Cordero

Dedication

This book is deeply personal to me on many levels, but I had a lot of fun with it as well. I dedicate this to all of my friends who have stuck by my side and encouraged me to follow my dreams, whether it was acting, singing, writing, or making crocheted hangers! Haha. There are so many of you that I would never be able to remember all the names, but I'm pretty sure you know who you are.

And a special dedication to the memory of a karaoke buddy of mine that passed away at a very young age a little over a year ago. She was a beautiful soul, and I hope that including her in this book will help her memory live on forever. This is for _Dani Cali._

Table of CONTENTS

Chapter ONE

The moment I took my seat on the plane that was taking me to Las Vegas for my best friend's thirtieth birthday party, I had a sinking feeling in my stomach that the ten-year relationship I'd been in with the man sitting next to me was doomed. You'd think that traveling would be smooth sailing for a couple that had been together for such a long time, but nope, not with us. Every time we went somewhere together, there was bound to be drama.

Mike, my dear, beloved fiancé, hated to travel. Oh, don't get me wrong. He loved visiting other places, but he hated the actual act of having to travel to get there. Nine times of out ten, he'd be guaranteed to stand there, looking sullen and cranky; he was always on edge from the moment we stepped foot into the airport until the moment we finally checked into our hotel room. The last time we went back to visit my family, he lost his laptop because he'd gotten antsy after we made it through the TEA security check and didn't want to stop to put it back in his carry-on. Then he laid it down on a table next to where we were sitting at our gate and promptly forgot all about putting it back in his bag. Needless to say, by the time we checked into our hotel room in Hawaii and I asked where the laptop was, it was long gone.

This trip, I could sense something was different from all the other times before. This time I was fed up with the bullshit. I'd been traveling since I was a baby, having been born in Hawaii and then living there for the first eleven years of my life before my parents decided to uproot our life and move to Nebraska. Then starting in junior high, I joined my church's Bible Bowl team (i.e. kind of like college quiz bowl for Jesus Freaks in junior high and high school), which frequently took me all around the Midwest so I could compete in the monthly Round Robins and other tournaments. And finally, just before my eighteenth birthday, I moved to Los Angeles for a boy. Or more correctly, I moved to get the hell out of Nebraska. Consequently, I was a seasoned traveler, comfortable with the whole process, and the thought that I was stuck with someone who made that experience an unenjoyable one saddened me.

The shuttle ride that took us from the airport to where we were staying at the Signature at MGM Grand was long and tense, Mike snapping at me under his breath most of the way. Once we checked in and took our bags up to the room, he wanted to head downstairs to look for something to eat. Most men get cranky when they haven't eaten, and he was no exception. I trailed behind him as he stalked over to the food court, glancing from one fast food option to the other. Biting my lip, I hesitated before speaking up to remind him that we had a dinner reservation at Roy's Restaurant that night for Valentine's Day. Yep, not only was the next day my best friend's thirtieth birthday—the whole reason we were there in Sin City—but we'd also arrived on Valentine's Day. And of course I had to make our dinner reservation, because God knew he'd never do it himself.

Ignoring me, Mike finally settled on which place he wanted to grab food from—McDonalds. I shook my head in exasperation and mumbled that I was going to get something from the frozen yogurt place across the food court. Barely acknowledging me, he turned his attention to the cashier who asked to take his order. After perusing all of the choices, I chose my flavor of yogurt and opted to forgo adding any toppings, moving to the cash register to pay.

As I sat down in the small booth across from him, Mike glanced over at me and smirked. "Really, Erin? You couldn't get some real food? How much was that anyway?"

"Um, I dunno…like seven dollars, I think." Was he kidding me? McDonalds was what he considered *real food*? Who was he to give me shit over spending money on some frozen yogurt?

He laughed and sneered at me. "You'd better eat all of it then. That's freaking ridiculous for some yogurt."

"I'll eat all of it," I said defensively, digging my spoon into the quickly melting frozen yogurt that I had completely lost my appetite for. "It's Las Vegas… you know everything's more expensive here."

"That doesn't mean you have to buy into their bullshit. If you're going to spend that kind of money, you should've at least gotten something of more substance."

I stared at the tabletop as he bit into his cheap burger and stuffed some greasy fries into his mouth. This trip was supposed to be a fun little break from the real world, but instead, it felt like I'd been sentenced to the weekend from hell. I hated how often he belittled me and made me feel dumb. It seemed like it took an eternity for Mike to finish his meal, then we headed back up to the room.

Thankfully, now that he had some food in him, Mike had mellowed out, but I was still furious with him for making things so tense and awkward on what was supposed to be a fun little weekend trip. While he was now acting completely relaxed like nothing had happened, I was still upset and ready to pick a fight. He flopped onto the large hotel bed, grabbed the remote and turned on the TV, then stuffing a pillow under his head, he got comfortable as he flipped through the channels.

I seethed at the easy way he was able to let everything go and act like nothing at all had happened. Like he hadn't just acted like a total dick to me downstairs. Like he hadn't already ruined the entire trip for me with his shitty attitude. Sitting down on the bed beside him, I finally found my voice and said something.

"I don't want to be like this," I said to him quietly.

"What are you talking about?" he asked, quirking an eyebrow as he glanced sideways at me before returning his attention back to the TV.

"I don't want to fight with you like this every time we go somewhere together," I clarified, looking over at him.

"Erin, let it go. I'm already over it. You're just trying to create drama. You know you live for that shit," he said as he continued to flip through the channels.

"No, I'm not going to let it go. I hate living like this. I don't want to argue with you, and I'm not trying to create drama, but I don't want to be like this when we travel anymore." A sob hitched in my throat as a few tears started to leak from the corner of my eye.

Hearing me get all emotional, Mike groaned and rolled his eyes. "Don't start crying. See, you *are* just trying to create drama. There's no good reason for you to be crying right now."

"Yes, there is. I was in a perfectly good mood when we left our apartment this morning, and then you started bitching as soon as we got to the airport, and you got me all worked up and irritated, and now you're just lounging here like nothing's wrong at all while I'm tired and upset from you being a jerk to me all day!"

"I haven't been a jerk to you all day. Stop being dramatic." I hated it when he said those words. *Stop being dramatic.* I'll show him dramatic.

"I'm not being dramatic, and yes, you have been a total jerk to me all day for no good reason. I know you hate traveling, but that doesn't make it okay for you to go into asshole mode and take it out on me."

"Whatever, Erin, let's just drop it. We're here, so let's just enjoy the rest of the trip. I'm over it. Let it go."

Mike again returned his attention to the TV and finally settled on a re-run of *The Big Bang Theory* while I sat there fuming in silence. It never failed. If he did something shitty and it upset me and I then tried to confront him, he would turn it around completely so that it was my fault, blaming me of acting dramatic. I was sick of it.

I felt numb through the rest of our trip. I tried to keep the peace with Mike, even plastering on a big smile for my friend Allison when we met up with her and her friends and family the next evening for her birthday party. She'd chosen to go to the Minus Five Ice Lounge at the Monte Carlo, so after we'd all bundled ourselves into long blue winter coats, black boots and gloves—except for the birthday girl, who was given a luxurious looking fur coat—we headed into a freezing room completely made of ice.

Once inside, I knocked back fruity shot after fruity shot, enjoying the refreshing coolness of the ice glass in my gloved hand. Several drinks later, I didn't even care that Mike had acted like a dick when we'd first gotten to Vegas. I was feeling way too warm and fuzzy to be in a bad mood.

The rest of the weekend went smoothly, but exiting our plane after we landed at the Burbank Airport, I felt empty inside. My feet felt like lead as I trailed behind Mike down the long hallway and out of the airport terminal. We walked the short distance to where we'd left the car parked and put our luggage in the trunk. Mike said he'd drive home, which was more than fine by me, so I nodded in agreement and climbed in the passenger seat. Tilting the seat back, I closed my eyes and let myself drift off into my thoughts.

I was beginning to think I'd made a huge mistake. Maybe Mike wasn't the one for me. The thought terrified me. I had given him almost ten years of my life. Why was I only now realizing that I was never going to be happy and content with this man? I should have listened to him all of those years ago when he told me he just wanted to be friends.

When I first found Mike in the personals section on Craigslist, I was twenty-three and already tired of living the single, party lifestyle. I'd gone from one long-term relationship to another since I was sixteen, never really giving myself the chance to just have fun and casually date. So when I hit my early twenties, I finally let myself do just that. Only I let it get a little out of hand. The good girl brought up in a Christian home by devoutly religious parents went a little hog wild. If someone offered me drugs, I was down to experiment. I used several Internet dating sites to meet and hook up with guys. By the end of my two-year party spree, I felt dirty and used, like I'd slept with, fallen for and been rejected by half the male population of Los Angeles.

I was more than ready to meet a genuinely nice guy and settle down. No more partying for me. Well, I mean I still planned on occasionally hitting up a club with my girls (gotta get out and shake my moneymaker once in a while), but I was done with "dating" a new guy every few days. Mike was the answer to my prayers.

Responding to an ad I posted in the personals section, he said he just wanted to meet people and make some new friends, so the first time we met, I didn't put any effort into looking especially nice for him. If he wanted to be "just friends", why bother? I didn't fix my hair, didn't put on makeup, didn't wear anything dressy or fashion forward…I just showed up in baggy jeans and a t-shirt.

Tall and lanky with blond hair and blue eyes, he wore a white, long-sleeved shirt, a thick, knotted silver chain and stonewashed jeans. The first thing I thought when I saw him was that he was a total hottie and vaguely resembled Eminem with his buzzed haircut. He looked like a skater, which was right up my alley, but he said he was only looking for friends, so it didn't really matter what he looked like anyway.

We went to see a movie and then sat outside the theaters talking for hours. Well, I talked. He just listened for the most part. Since I didn't really care what he thought about me if we were just going to be friends, I decided not to hold anything back and told him everything about myself.

Over the next few weeks, we went to see two more movies. Each time after we got out of the theater, I would drive him to where he had parked his car. He would sit there awkwardly in my passenger seat for a moment and then just get out of the car and close the door without even saying good-bye or that he had a nice time. I thought it was a little weird, but I assumed he was probably just shy.

Eventually I invited him over to my place so I could cook him dinner while he watched the Laker game. I remember it clearly like it was yesterday. In an attempt to impress him with my mediocre cooking skills, I decided to make one of my grandmother's old recipes—cubed steak with a cream of mushroom sauce and mashed potatoes. It wasn't fancy, but to me it was yummy and filling. However, of course, I managed to burn the damn meat. And then I attempted to pick off the burnt pieces and salvage the dinner. If he noticed that the meal was less than perfectly cooked, he didn't give any indication that he thought so and only said it was delicious.

After dinner, I did what almost any girl would do if she wants to let a guy know she's interested in taking things to the next level: I jumped him. And he didn't stop me, so there went the whole "I just want to be friends" thing. The sex was kind of awkward at first. He was a virgin and had literally no experience with women before me. He hadn't even really kissed a girl before me.

I remember going to lunch with some of my friends who asked me how things were going with Mike. I told them that he seemed like a really nice guy and I was very attracted to him; however, I didn't really see things going anywhere long-term. The next week, we slept together again. This time the results were so different, I wasn't sure I had the same guy in my bed. It was like he had read a sex manual overnight. What an improvement! I felt so relieved. He may have been new to the game, but Mike was a fast learner. And I was completely appreciative of that fact.

Fast forward almost ten years later, and here we were. We'd grown up together. We'd learned together. We'd loved each other. And I was ready to strangle him most days.

Finally, the car came to a stop and Mike nudged me, letting me know we were home. I opened my eyes and grabbed my purse, taking my phone out to text my friend Cara, who had just moved into her own apartment after having to live with an ex-boyfriend for several months after they broke up.

Erin: *Hey girl.*

Cara: *Hey! Are you back from Vegas? How was it?*

Erin: *Yeah, we literally just got home. Need to unpack and get ready for work tomorrow. Vegas was eh.*

Cara: *Uh oh, did something happen?*

Erin: *Kinda. Dinner sometime this week?*

Cara: *Sure! You wanna come over and see the new place after you get off work on Tuesday night? I'll make something yummy for us and we can talk more.*

Erin: *Sounds perfect. See you there around 7:15?*
Cara: *See you then.*
Erin: *Yay! Can't wait to see you. :)*
Cara: *You too. :)*

Monday morning came way too quickly for my taste as usual. Returning to work after going out of town was always slightly depressing. I loved traveling so much—getting to explore new places and visiting some places I'd already been to as well. It was my dream to eventually quit my day job and support myself doing something creative full-time, and I fervently hoped that whatever I ended up doing, getting to travel frequently would be part of the package. But until that time came, at least my day job was one I enjoyed, and I loved the people I worked with.

"Well if it isn't my favorite person in the world," a male voice said behind me.

Quickly spinning around in my office chair, I squealed when I saw who it was. Bald, tan and tattooed with a lean build and always sporting his signature golf cap, Vinnie was easily one of the most attractive guys I worked with; however, since he worked for a branch of our company that was based in Australia, I only saw him on the rare occasion when work brought him to the L.A. office.

"Hey Vinnie," I said as I hopped up to give him a quick squeeze, blushing slightly as he came in for a cheek kiss greeting. Of course he had to smell sinfully good. Of course! Reluctantly I pulled back and plastered on a professional smile before sitting back down again. "So what can I do for you? Need some games? Got a flight for me to book?"

"Actually, yeah, can you hook me up with copies of the latest? Whatever's new would be awesome."

"Sure thing. For Xbox 360?"

"Yep. Can't believe you remember that."

"I have a good memory," I said, tapping my fingers against my temple as I flashed him a sweet smile. He was seriously swoon-worthy and seriously made me wish I was single.

"That you do," Vinnie said as he nodded at me with an appreciative smile. "And then yeah, I was supposed to be returning to Australia this weekend, but I need to push my flight to the following weekend. Also, I'm going to need to fly to Austin tomorrow and return on Thursday. Can you book the flights and hotel for me?"

"Consider it done. I'll book a room at the Renaissance Austin. Aisle seat?"

"Yes, please."

"No probs."

Vinnie fished a peppermint candy out of the crystal dish I had sitting on my ledge. "Thanks, Erin. You're a lifesaver." As he unwrapped the sweet and popped it in his mouth, I couldn't help thinking that he'd be minty fresh if I kissed him right now.

"Always happy to help. I'll email you the itinerary. Swing by later this afternoon for your travel folder."

"Will do, babe," he said and then flashed another charming smile at me. "Is Jerry in right now?"

"Yeah, he has a few minutes before his next meeting. Go ahead. I know he'll want to see you."

"Cool, thanks." I watched Vinnie pick up his bag and walk his fine ass down the short hallway to knock on the last door. That door belonged to Jerry Davis, who was the EVP of Production and had been my boss for the past three years. Our personalities gelled, but supporting him could be overwhelming.

Jerry's schedule was constantly changing, and there were many days I felt like I was drowning as I played Tetris with his calendar, trying to cram all of his meetings into the short amount of time available. A week into the job, I started chugging energy drinks and coffee to keep my energy level up as I alternated between phone calls and emails to schedule, confirm, reschedule and cancel meetings. From dawn until dusk, I was a meeting schedule machine. In three years, I had taken an actual lunch—and by "actual lunch", I mean like when you leave your desk and either eat somewhere else or you leave the premises and go out to eat—maybe a dozen times, and usually it was for birthday, new hire or goodbye lunches. Usually I ate at my desk, or sometimes I skipped it completely, opting to eat a big breakfast and dinner instead. And yeah sure, I'll admit that I've often snuck pieces of chocolate from my candy dish when I couldn't get away for lunch.

Just as Vinnie moved to knock on the door, he paused and then stood there for a moment, seeming to think about something before he turned back around and headed back towards me.

"What are your plans for lunch today?" he asked, quirking an eyebrow at me.

It wasn't the first time we'd gone to lunch together, but I felt slightly guiltier every time we did, because I always enjoyed myself so thoroughly that it made me regret the fact that I had a fiancé.

"Um, nothing special. Just some leftover spaghetti I made last night."

"Hmm…well since you just made it last night, it'll keep another day, right?"

My mouth twitched as I fought to keep from smiling and I nodded slowly in agreement. "Yes, I suppose it can."

"Great. Have sushi with me then? My treat."

"Sushi sounds great, but I don't know if I can get away. I have a last minute meeting I have to book for Jerry; there are thirteen guys I have to include from this office, and he wants all of them there. No exceptions."

"When's the meeting?"

"Tomorrow morning."

"Aw, that's plenty of time," Vinnie started to say, but then seeing the look on my face, he shook his head and laughed. "No? That's not enough time?"

"Not really when you consider how tight all of these guys' schedules are. Several of them have conflicting meetings, so now I get to play phone tag with all of the assistants today."

"Eesh. Well, better you than me. You're good at that kinda shit."

Good at that kinda shit? Okay. I'll take that.

"Thanks," I said, my lips quirking in a smile. "I think."

"Alright, well if you don't think you can get away for lunch, do you want me to bring something back for you? My treat?"

"That I will definitely take you up on. Get me something with avocado and spicy tuna."

"Done." Winking, Vinnie gave me one of his sexiest smiles and left me sitting there with a stupid grin on my face. Sometimes I really loved my job.

Chapter TWO

As soon as I got home from work, I pulled the ingredients needed to make a meatloaf out of the fridge and pantry. Ten minutes later, I shoved it in the oven and set the timer.

While I waited for dinner to cook, I started doing the laundry for both me and Mike, carting load after load back and forth between our apartment and the shared laundry room that was located all the way on the other side of the building. I put in the first load and then returned to our apartment and grabbed a trash bag so I could pick up the empty beer and water bottles that were scattered around Mike's computer area. He just ignored me and continued to play his game while I tidied up around him before moving on to the bedroom. I made the bed and picked up the rest of the laundry that was left scattered haphazardly around the room.

Just after I returned to the laundry room, the washing machine buzzed as it finished its last cycle. I turned to open the lid and got lost in my thoughts again as I mechanically shook out each piece before turning to toss them into one of the dryers behind me. I'd begun to have doubts about marrying Mike a few months ago when the sex started feeling weird—like I didn't want him to touch me anymore. The same thing happened with an ex of mine once before, so I have a hunch that our relationship has more than likely reached its expiration date.

This is a terrible realization for me to come to after all this time. Here I am living with this man, having invested the last ten years of my life, and now that I finally have his engagement ring on my finger after waiting for him to propose for eight out of those ten years, I just want out. Out before we exchange vows and start procreating, which will make splitting up all the more difficult and complicated. But still I also wonder if I should stay and try to make things work, or if I should cut my losses and move on.

I stared numbly at the neon digits displayed on the top of the dryer, chewing my lip. I didn't have a clue what to do about Mike, but I knew I had to do something. I put some quarters in the dryer and hit the start button, then headed back down the hallway to our apartment.

The delicious smell of meatloaf hit my face like a wall of deliciousness as I opened the door. I made a pretty damn good meatloaf, and my mouth was watering as I thought about taking the first bite of the juicy, meaty goodness. It took me about ten minutes to whip up some instant garlic mashed potatoes and steam some broccoli, then I made a plate for Mike and took it to him. He was in the middle of a game on *Starcraft 2*, so I set the food down beside him and returned to the kitchen to serve myself some dinner as well.

Starving, I devoured the meal, immensely enjoying the comfort it brought me as I ate each bite. When I got up to take my plate to the kitchen, I glanced over at Mike's plate and saw that it was still sitting there untouched.

"Babe, eat your dinner. It's getting cold," I said, sighing. "I really wish you would eat your dinner while it's still hot…you know, the way it's *meant* to be eaten."

Mike just grunted at me and waved his hand. "Later. I'm in the middle of a match. It'll still be good later."

I rolled my eyes and shook my head, turning back to the kitchen to clean up my mess and wash the dishes. After switching another load of laundry, I finally retreated to the couch to relax a little. I turned on the TV and checked my DVR to see what I had to watch. There were a couple new episodes of my favorite reality show, so I pressed play for the first one and reached for a plastic hanger and a ball of yarn.

I hated being idle, even if I was relaxing and watching TV. My mom had taught me how to make crocheted hangers when I was in high school, and it was a hobby that I had recently picked up again. I loved combining different colors to make them visually appealing. I wished for the hundredth time that

I could make my hobby into a profitable business, but there was just no way I could charge as much as I needed in order to make it worth the time I had to spend making them. The materials themselves weren't that costly, but each hanger took me a good twenty to thirty minutes to complete.

Mike always made fun of me when he saw me working on my hangers or making a new blanket. I just loved creating something with my own two hands, but he always teased me and called it my "old lady" hobby. But I was determined to make crochet hip and cool, so I ignored him and kept practicing my craft. They made great gifts, if nothing else.

When the first commercial break came, I glanced at the back of Mike's head. He'd been crouched over his keyboard in the same position for at least the past hour, wearing a large pair of headphones with a mic attached. He got off work before I did and was playing when I got home, so I'm assuming he'd probably been sitting there in the same position for more like three hours. This was not unusual for him. Nope, this was the norm. Sometimes I felt like throwing something at him, just to make him move from that spot for a minute. I was used to being ignored, but it didn't make it any less annoying.

"Oh, by the way, I have to go to Atlanta next weekend for work. We have our annual work conference on Friday and Saturday, with a big party on Saturday night—guess it's supposed to be like our holiday party since we didn't have one."

"Holiday party in February—that's weird. So no dates?"

"What?"

"No dates?" I repeated a little more loudly.

"What?" he asked again, not even bothering to take the headphones off or turn around.

Glaring at the back of his head, I grabbed a ball of yarn from the basket beside me and threw it at his head. That got his attention.

"Hey, what the hell?"

I huffed as I dropped my crochet and got up to march over to him and pull the headphones off before returning to the couch. "If you're going to talk to

22

me, then do me the courtesy of taking the headphones off so you can hear me respond to you."

"Sorry."

"So no dates are allowed?" I repeated one more time.

"Nah, it's for employees only."

I nodded. "Got it."

"Can you pack and iron some shirts and pants for me?"

Glaring at the back of his head, I imagined telling him to pack his own damn bag and do his own damn ironing, but the prideful woman in me couldn't allow my fiancé to show up in wrinkled clothes. Because if I refused, I knew that's exactly what would happen. He didn't care enough to do it himself, but he had no problem asking me to do it for him. When I would sometimes ask him why he didn't do it himself, his usual response was, "But honey, you do it so much better." Excuses. The boy was full of them.

"Yeah, I'll pack for you," I said grudgingly. I was tired of being his mother and his maid, but I preferred to avoid conflict as much as possible, because whenever I tried to talk to him about it, he would accuse me of trying to create drama. Was he crazy? I'm a Virgo. I hate confrontation. I'd rather smoke 'em peace pipe, like can't we all just get along?

But he would never take responsibility seriously. He would never understand that a person's actions are tied to how they feel about you. If he loved and respected me like he should, then he should show it more by doing things. Maybe clean up after himself once in a while, maybe pick up food for us, maybe pay attention to me instead of being glued to a video game all night, every night, seven days a week. Actually, on weekends, it was all day and night. I was desperate to find something in common with him again. I felt like I was losing the little connection we had left.

The next day, I couldn't wait to get off work and zoom over to Cara's new apartment. I was more than a little jealous of the fact that she had her own place, so I was looking forward to checking out her new pad and enjoying the single life vicariously through her. When I got to her floor in the parking garage, I spotted a compact spot on the end right by the elevator and stairs.

Score, I thought to myself as I slipped my full-size car into the tight space. Her apartment was conveniently located close to the parking structure entrance on her floor, and within a minute, I was standing in front of her door and ringing the doorbell.

"Hey girl, come on in," she said upon opening the door.

"I feel like I haven't seen you in forever," I said, giving her a quick hug. "Mmm, you smell good. What are you wearing?"

Cara laughed. "Nothing. I just got out of the shower, so maybe you smell my shampoo."

"Aha, that's probably it." I leaned forward and sniffed her hair. "Pantene?"

"But of course," she said with a giggle. "Can I get you something to drink? Want a glass of wine?"

"Mmm, sure. What you got?"

"I've got a Merlot and a Moscato."

"Is the Moscato chilled?"

"Duh," she said with a smirk.

I grinned back at her. "I guess that was a dumb question. I'll do that then."

"Coming right up," she said with a wink and a nod and retrieved two glasses from her wineglass rack. "So how's work been?"

"Oh the usual. Craziness with Jerry's schedule. But Vinnie was in the office yesterday and brought me sushi for lunch."

"Vinnie, Vinnie...I think you've mentioned him to me before. Who is he again?"

"Works in our Australia office. Tatted up and gorgeous. Smells like sin on a stick."

Cara nodded as she filled the first glass and handed it to me. "Oh yeah, I remember now. What about Mike?"

Taking a sip, I rolled my eyes at her. "Just because I have a fiancé doesn't mean I can't look and admire."

"Mmmhmm, but come on, girl. Let's be real. You'd love to do more than just look and admire."

"Well, duh. I am human after all. But nothing's going to happen, so you can relax."

Cara poured herself a glass and then came over to sit down with me, pulling her feet up on the couch as she got comfortable.

"Girl, I can't tell you how jealous I am. Your place looks amazing. What's it like living by yourself again?"

"So great," she said with the biggest smile. "I can't even tell you how good it feels to come home and not have to worry about having the place a certain way. Unless I'm having company over, it's just me."

"Do you miss Buddy?"

Buddy was a two-year-old English bulldog that Cara and her ex-boyfriend, Miguel, had adopted while they were still together. Miguel had insisted that he get the dog in the break-up while Cara had settled for the BMW they previously shared, but I knew how much she loved Buddy and wished Miguel had taken the car instead. Idly, I wondered to myself how Mike and I would split up our possessions if we ever broke up.

"I do, but Miguel is renting a room in a house with a yard, and he can give Buddy a better life than I can right now. If he stayed with me, he'd be cooped up in this apartment all day, and since I travel so much for work, I'd have to either put Buddy up at a kennel while I'm out of town, or I'd have to ask Miguel to dog-sit anyway. And since I'm not too keen on having to see my ex more than absolutely necessary, it seemed the wisest decision. But yeah, I miss him terribly." She paused and then added, "I miss Buddy—not Miguel—just to be clear."

"I knew what you meant, silly," I said and giggled. "You could always get another dog," I suggested.

"I know, but for the way my life is right now, I think it'd be selfish of me to try having another pet. Unless it's like a fish or something."

"How about a pet snake?"

"Aw hell no!" Cara said, wrinkling her nose at me. "You know I don't do scaly things."

"They're called reptiles."

"Whatever. If it has scales, I don't do it. Just like you don't do spiders."

"I fucking hate spiders. They are creepy, crawly, evil beings that need to DIE!"

"They aren't evil. They eat bugs, you know."

"I don't care. They are still evil and need to die!"

Cara chuckled and rolled her eyes at me. "Okay, they are evil and need to die. More wine?"

"Silly question," I said as I held my glass up for more. She smirked at me and got up to retrieve the bottle from the kitchen counter. I leaned back into the couch and glanced around the living room. "Looks a little bare in here. What's your vision for decorating the place? Or are you going to?"

"Yeah, I don't have an exact vision, yet, but I do want to fix the place up a bit. It'll be over time, though. Paying the security deposit and first month's rent on this place cleared me out. I am so broke. Thus my invite for you to come to dinner tonight instead of us going out somewhere."

"Totally understand. I was just asking, cuz I was thinking I could get something you want for your housewarming gift."

"Aw, you don't have to get me a housewarming gift."

"Shut up. Yes, I do. So better tell me what you want or you'll end up with whatever I decide to give you."

"Well, you have great taste, so it's not like that would be a bad thing. But okay…let me sleep on it tonight, and I'll let you know tomorrow. That work?"

"That totally works." I raised my glass to Cara and she smiled, clinking hers against mine. "To your new place! And to being a new single lady." I paused and thought for a moment before adding, "Now we just need to get you laid."

I said this as Cara was taking a sip of her wine, and she almost spit it right back out again when my words registered with her. "Erin!"

"What? It's true. You need to get laid."

"Ha, you make it sound so easy." Her lips twisted in a grimace.

"It is easy!" I insisted. "Just post an ad on Craigslist."

"I'm not posting an ad on Craigslist."

"Why not?"

"Because."

"Because why?"

"Because I'm not using Craigslist to get laid," she said in an exasperated tone.

"Look. It's super easy to use, and all the guys come to you. You don't have to post your picture or even send it to them unless you want to. So I just post the ad, have them email me with a few recent pictures—make sure they send you more than one—and then if I like what I see, I email them back with a couple recent pictures of my own. You can have them host so you don't have to reveal where you live or anything."

"I dunno. Craigslist is so sketchy. What about the Craigslist killer?"

"Girl, come on. I've used Craigslist too many times to count. I met some of my best friends on that site. Sure, there are crazy people out there, too. But just use your head and practice caution. There are regular people like you and me on there, too. Remember, I met Mike on Craigslist. And Corinne."

"Corinne, as in your best friend?"

"Yeah. I posted an ad for Justin Timberlake tickets like eleven years ago or so. Corinne answered my ad and told me she didn't have JT tickets, but she would love to go, so if I found a pair of tickets, she was totally down to pay me back for one of the tickets and go with me. I was new to town and didn't really have any friends, so I agreed. We ended up meeting first to see a movie—*The Italian Job* with Edward Norton, Mark Wahlberg and Charlize Theron?"

"That was such a good movie."

"Yeah, I love it. I watch it whenever I see it playing on TV. Anyway, so we met up for the movie first to make sure each other was cool, and then about a week later we went to the concert together. Been best friends ever since, and it's our tradition now. Whenever JT goes on a new concert tour, you can bet your ass we'll be there."

"Well, that's a great story. But still, finding someone to sleep with...on Craigslist?"

"Just trust me on this one. Post an ad tonight after I leave. I swear to God, you'll get like fifty responses in an hour. Look through them and see if anyone piques your interest. If not, no harm done. If nothing else, it'll provide you with a few hours of entertainment."

Cara nodded thoughtfully, like she was really starting to consider the possibilities. "True. I promise I'll think about it."

I grinned at her and drained the rest of my wine. "You won't regret it."

"I said I'll *think* about it. I didn't say I'm going to do it."

"Uh huh," was all I said, but I couldn't keep from smiling widely at her. "I'm so jelly. I want to live alone again and post ads on Craigslist for casual sex!"

"Then break up with Mike."

"I can't break up with Mike. We're engaged."

"Engagements can be broken," Cara insisted, ever so helpfully.

"I know that. But we've been together forever. I can't just throw that away."

"Are you seriously thinking about it?"

"No...I don't know. Not really. I mean..." I trailed off and stared at my feet. I'd been asking myself the same question for weeks now. Was I seriously thinking about breaking up with Mike? After all the time I'd invested in our relationship, did I really want to call it quits and start over again? The short answer? No, of course I didn't want to. But I was beginning to think that I'd be doing both him and me a disservice by continuing our relationship.

"It's not the end of the world if things don't work out between you two."

"I know that. Thanks, mom."

"Hey, I'm just trying to help."

I sighed. I knew she was just trying to help, but that didn't make the thoughts in my head feel any more justified. I felt so guilty, wanting out of my relationship after all these years. Mike and I had grown up together, experienced the beginning of adulthood together. I couldn't imagine my life without him. I tried to think what it'd be like if I never saw him or spoke to him again, and the thought made me so sad that I just wanted to stop thinking about it completely.

"It's just that…I guess the romantic in me wants more than we have. I want someone who gives a shit enough to do little things for me to show me he cares. They don't have to be grand gestures, but for example, helping me pick up the apartment, picking up take-out for dinner, making a dinner reservation on special occasions."

"What did you guys do for Valentine's Day?"

"We were in Vegas for Allison's birthday, so we had dinner at Roy's on Friday night, but I had to make the reservation."

"Did he get you flowers or anything?"

I just looked at her blandly and she winced.

"Guess not."

"Even when he has money in the bank, being sweet and romantic is never the first thing on Mike's mind."

"What is the first thing on his mind?"

"Smoking weed and playing video games. Oh, and saving up for the down payment on a house."

"Well that last part is good."

"Yeah, except he doesn't even talk about it being *our* house. He just talks about buying his own house. I feel like I'm not even part of the picture when he talks about the future."

"But you guys are getting married. You have his ring on your finger."

"I know, but I think that was his compromise. When he sold his car, he asked me what he should do with the money. Put a payment on a credit card? Add it to the house fund? I suggested he get me a ring. Bad idea. He blew up, and we had the worst fight ever. I almost thought we were going to break up then, but instead, a few weeks later he proposed."

"Maybe he was already planning on it and just wanted to throw you off so you'd be surprised."

"Maybe…or maybe he just thought I was getting too antsy and that was a way to shut me up and keep me waiting longer to actually get married."

"Have you guys set a date, yet?"

"I've been saying May of 2015, but now I don't know. Now maybe never."

"Why so far off?"

I looked at her and shook my head sadly. "I can't afford even a small wedding right now, and Mike doesn't care about frivolities, as he calls them. So if I want a nice little wedding, you better believe it will have to be me that ponies up for the bulk of the cost. And I need to keep saving for a couple of years before I'll be ready. Really, I feel like if Mike was truly the one I'm supposed to be with, that it wouldn't matter to me whether we have a nice wedding ceremony or whether we run off to Vegas and elope."

"That's true. So what are you going to do?"

"I don't know, yet. I just know I need to figure it out soon."

"Well, you know I support you no matter what you decide. I just want you to be happy."

"Thanks, girlfriend. So what's on the menu tonight?"

Just then a timer buzzed. "I made a quiche for us. I know you've been trying to watch your weight, and I am, too. So I made this egg white veggie quiche for us. There's a little bit of ham chopped up in there as well. Is that okay?" Cara asked as she got up to take a small casserole dish out of the oven.

"Sure, sounds good."

"Awesome. I have some fruit salad I made yesterday as well. I squeezed lemon juice on it, so it's still good. You can try it, and if you don't like it, my feelings won't be hurt if you don't want to finish it."

I nodded. "Sure, I'll try some. Thanks. Do you mind if I help myself to some more wine?"

"Not at all. There's another bottle in the wine fridge if you want to open a new one. I wouldn't mind another glass."

"Sure," I said, getting up to join her in the kitchen. I opened the wine fridge and retrieved the new bottle, then opened it to pour a new glass for both of us. I took a sip and watched her make our plates. The quiche smelled delicious, and my mouth was watering in anticipation. Lunch had been a cup of noodles at my desk, so I was starving. She added some fruit to each place and then handed me one with a napkin and fork.

"Looks yummy," I said as I lifted the plate to my nose to sniff my food appreciatively.

"Thanks, this is the first time I've made this, so you're my guinea pig. Hope you like it!" she said with a grin, then dug her fork in for the first bite. "Mmm, now that's good."

I followed suit and took my first bite as well. "Oh my god, Cara. This is so good."

"Right? Thank you. I think I will definitely be making this again."

I nodded vigorously, in complete agreement with her. "Yes, you should definitely make this again. And then invite me over to help you eat it again."

She laughed and nodded. "Deal. I'm glad you like it. And it's got lots of fresh veggies in it, and it's low fat."

"Yeah, that's great. I'll have to get the recipe from you and try it myself sometime. I've put on so much weight since I started dating Mike, and I can't believe how far I've let myself go. I need to start hitting the gym again. Maybe try running or something."

"Well, I'll go with you if you want company when you run."

"Really?"

"Sure, why not? I need to get back into shape."

I grinned, excited at the prospect of losing some weight. I wanted desperately to feel better about myself, and something told me that a good place to start with that was by focusing on my health.

When I left Cara's apartment an hour later, I felt reinvigorated. It was always good to be around my friends. They kept me grounded.

Chapter THREE

Mike and I didn't say a word to each other the entire drive to the airport the next morning. His company had booked everyone on an eight o'clock flight and was requiring them to check in two hours prior to their departure time, so here we were, driving to the airport at the butt crack of dawn on a Saturday morning. The plus side of being up at the butt crack of dawn is that there isn't much traffic. It wasn't until I pulled up to the departures curb at LAX twenty minutes later that either of us spoke.

"Did you pack socks and underwear?" Mike asked as he got his bag out of the trunk. I couldn't wait to get back in my car and drive home. I had the apartment all to myself for an entire weekend—something that hadn't happened in a few years—and I was eager to start enjoying the rare treat.

"It's a little late to be asking me that, don't you think? But yeah, of course I did. I remembered everything...as usual." I muttered that last bit under my breath as he moved to grab his jacket and laptop from the backseat.

He gave me a quick hug and kiss and said he'd see me later. I told him to have a safe flight and then got back into the car to merge back into the slow-moving airport traffic.

Half an hour later, I finally pulled into the gated parking lot of our building and headed inside to my blissfully empty apartment. Powering up my laptop, I sat down to smoke a bowl of weed while I checked my emails and got on Facebook. I'd recently self-published my first book, and one of the marketing tools I was trying out at the recommendation of some of my fellow indie authors was a street team. A street team basically consists of fans that want to help you market your books because they believe in your work. At least, that's what I'd been made to believe.

I had just posted on my author fan page, asking if anyone was interested in joining my street team. I had a few people who had commented on my posting, so I was now taking the time to get back to them and add them to the group. I didn't recognize any of the names as being one of my friends or readers, so I clicked on each person's profile to learn a little more about them.

There was one person who commented, and it happened to be a guy. All he said was, "I'm in." I squinted at the guy's profile picture, which was a little blurry and out of focus. His name was Jesse Williams, and his profile said he was twenty-two, but he looked about fifteen in his picture—if it was indeed him. I scrolled through the pictures on his profile, seeing some random pictures of guns and cash along with some Edgar Allen Poe quotes and a few photos of a young boy—the same boy who was in the profile picture. But there were also a few shots of an older boy who looked to be in his late teens. I suppose he could be twenty-two if that was actually him.

Nervous that I had almost invited an underage kid to join my street team when I was an author of erotic fiction, I decided to send a quick email to find out a little more about him. After introducing myself, I asked if he had read any romantic fiction before. I mentioned that I was just getting started and didn't know a whole lot about what I was doing. At the end of the message, I casually asked if his profile picture was a recent photo or if it had been taken when he was younger.

I didn't have to wait long for a reply. The notification popped up on my screen within a few minutes, telling me he had replied to my message. I opened his reply and smiled at his explanation that the profile picture he'd chosen was of his nephew, Jason. He confirmed that he was the older guy I'd seen in his pictures, and told me I was beautiful. I blushed a little, then laughed at myself for getting excited at a compliment from a twenty-two year old. Man, was I desperate for attention or what?

Jesse confirmed that he was a big fan of Edgar Allen Poe and offered to share some of his own poetry with me sometime if I was interested. I smiled to myself again. I used to write poetry all the time when I was younger, but I hadn't tried to write anything new in more years than I cared to count. I wasn't even sure where my old poems were anymore. I had a sneaking suspicion they were packed away in a dusty box, buried somewhere in my closet. I fired off a quick reply to Jesse, telling him I'd love to see some of his work sometime.

I was heading to the kitchen to scrounge around for some dinner when I heard the notification of a new private message again and headed back to my laptop to check it. It was a poem from Jesse, one he said he'd written when he first discovered he had a knack with words. It was dark and deep; it was hopeful and powerful. I was impressed with the simple poem. I knew he was young, but that didn't diminish the depth of emotion I felt in reading his words.

Impulsively, I headed to the bedroom and opened the closet doors. I dug through boxes, coughing as small dust clouds rose up. I noted to myself that I really needed to go through all of my boxes and do a cleansing—get rid of all of the junk I'd been hoarding for God knew how many years.

It only took me another minute to locate the stack of faded pages. Some were handwritten; some were printed pages. I sat there on my bedroom floor, flipping slowly through the stack of papers that were leading me on an emotional trip down memory lane. Some of the poems made me smile fondly, some made me grimace in embarrassment, but all of it made me miss writing poetry. There was just something so addicting about painting images with short phrases rather than telling a long story through hundreds of pages. I enjoyed both, but it'd been so long since I'd indulged in writing poetry.

Suddenly I felt like I was a teenager again—young, naïve, trusting and innocent, still eager and fresh and ready to take on the world. Suddenly I wanted more than anything to share some of my poetry with my new friend. I was drowning in my relationship with Mike. I couldn't breathe. I'd lost sight of who I was to the point where I didn't recognize myself anymore. Not just physically, but mentally and emotionally as well. Who had I let myself become? If I died today, what would I have to leave behind? What would I have to show for my thirty plus years on earth?

The humiliating realization that I would have next to nothing to show for all the many years I'd existed spurred me to return to the laptop and start typing a new message to Jesse. I wanted more. I deserved more. And I was desperate to have more. As I'd always feared, I had become like my mother: co-dependent and unable to be alone. All I knew was that I needed to have the kind of love you read about in romances and modern day fairy-tales. Otherwise, I knew I'd never be genuinely happy. I'd never be genuinely satisfied.

I shuffled through the pages on my lap, debating which poem I should send him first. My fingers trembled with excitement as I finally settled on one of my favorites in which I compared love to a rose…the petals representing happy memories of precious moments and the thorns, sadder memories of the difficult and rocky times. I transcribed the poem and hit send, nervous yet curious to hear what he would think of my work.

Somewhere outside, a door opened and slammed suddenly, making a loud crashing sound that echoed down the hallway. Then I heard a stampede of shrieking children just above me, sounding more like a herd of elephants. I frowned and grumbled under my breath about my inconsiderate neighbors while I sat there staring at my inbox, willing a response to come back quickly. I was a true product of my generation for sure—the generation of instant gratification. I stared for a good minute, but the status didn't change to "seen".

I was about to start transcribing another poem when I heard a loud pounding on a door down the hallway. Curious, I slowly opened my door and poked my head out. There were two police officers standing outside the apartment at the opposite end of the hallway from me.

The first officer tried to open the locked door to no avail. He then raised his fist to pound on the door again. "Police! Sir, we know you're in there. Please open the door."

I listened intently but could hear no response. Judging by the impatient look of annoyance on the officers' faces, they heard no response as well. "Sir, please stop wasting our time and open the door right now. We followed you for three miles. We saw you hit all those cars. Hello? Sir? Please don't make us break the door down, sir."

"Um, n-n-nobody's home," a stammering voice called out, making my mouth drop open in disbelief. Was this idiot seriously telling the cops that nobody was home? The first officer exchanged an exasperated look with his partner who shook his head and then jerked his head towards me.

Crap! My heart sank into the pit of my stomach. They'd noticed me. I was about to withdraw back into my apartment and close the door quietly, but it was too late. The first officer nodded and then removed the gun from his holster and stood back to watch the door and wait while the second officer turned and began to approach me.

I prepared to be chastised for standing in the hallway while they were pursuing a suspect or something along those lines as I mentally, and okay—I'll admit it—physically cringed back into the doorway of my apartment.

"Excuse me, ma'am, is there a manager or landlord on site? Someone who would have a key to all of the apartments?"

"Yeah, Shelly is the manager. She's just around the corner from here," I said, breathing a sigh of relief when all he did was thank me and nod politely before heading off towards the direction I had indicated.

I risked glancing back down the hallway toward the idiot's apartment and saw the first officer still standing there, watching the door. Deciding I could live without any further excitement, I slipped back into my apartment and closed the door, taking care to turn both locks and set the deadbolt chain as well.

Quietly I stood by the door and peered through the peephole, watching the second officer return only minutes later, followed by Shelly, who had a frazzled expression on her face, and understandably so. This was more action than our small building had seen in the entire five years Mike and I had lived here. Then to my dismay, he paused by my door and turned to face it directly, raising his hand to ring the doorbell. I nearly yelped as I stumbled backwards in surprise. Taking a quick moment to compose myself, I breathed deeply in and out a few times, then stepped forward to open the door.

"Yes?" I nearly squeaked, nervous that he would smell the marijuana that I had been smoking earlier and demand to see my prescription, or that my Shelly would smell it and evict me for doing it inside, which wasn't allowed in our building. Even though it was legal to obtain a prescription to smoke medical marijuana in the state of California, I had never motivated myself to get one. It was easy enough to get weed without one where I lived.

Either they didn't notice or just didn't say anything, but either way, I don't think I breathed at all for the next minute or so.

"Do you mind just keeping your door open for a bit so Ms. Johnson can step inside if things get ugly?"

"Oh, okay. Sure, I can do that," I said in as casual a tone as I could manage.

"Thank you. Ms. Johnson, as I said, for your own safety, please stay here and try not to interfere. We have justifiable cause to take Mr. Owens into custody."

"I understand. Just please try not to damage the property."

The cop nodded before returning down the hallway to join his partner. I watched in curious fascination as he unlocked the door and pushed it open, then pulled back to let his partner go in first as he pulled his own gun and followed closely behind him.

"This is so not how I expected to spent my Saturday morning," Shelly said, sighing as she leaned against the wall.

As we stood there waiting for them to reappear, I heard one of my neighbors come up behind us and ask what was going on.

I shrugged. "Not exactly sure. First I heard a door slam and then someone pounding on a door, so I stuck my head out and saw these two cops at the end of the hallway. From what I overheard, it sounded like the guy who lives in that apartment was involved in a hit and run with more than one car, and the idiot actually told the cops 'nobody is home'. Then one of them stayed to keep watch while the other went to get the key from Shelly. He told us to stay back here, and they haven't come back out of the apartment, yet."

No sooner had the words come out of my mouth than the two cops reappeared with a tall, brown-haired man in handcuffs. His eyes were bloodshot, and his hair looked like it hadn't been washed in at least a week, but he looked to be in his early thirties. I watched him get escorted out of the building, then Shelly told me to stay put and headed outside herself.

I retreated back into my apartment and ran to the window to continue watching the guy being walked out to the squad car that was parked in the red zone in front of my building. I spotted one of my next-door neighbors standing on the lawn, gesturing animatedly while talking to an older lady I didn't recognize. A few minutes later when I saw him head back inside, I returned to the hallway and poked my head back out again.

"Hey Josh, what's going on?" I called to him.

He shook his head as he moved down the hallway to join me. "Craziness. This son of a bitch just sideswiped like twenty cars that were parked on the street a few miles down from here in Tarzana. He just kept driving, so the cops followed him all the way here. Then he jumps out of the car and runs inside and tries to hide from them.

I laughed out loud. "When they were pounding on his door and calling out to them, he actually had the gall to shout back, 'Nobody's home'. Who does that? Was he drunk?"

"I'm assuming so, or maybe on drugs. Why else would he sideswipe twenty random cars? Unless he's just mad at the world or something. Regardless, it's reckless endangerment and damage of property."

"Right. Man, that's so crazy. Oh well. At least it provided us with a little excitement around here for once," I joked, but Josh just shook his head at me.

"Thanks, but I can live without that kind of excitement. Anyways, I'm going to get back to cooking my breakfast, so I'll catch you later."

"Okay, have a good day. I'll see you around."

Once back inside the apartment, I returned to my laptop. Transcribing the second poem took me less than five minutes, and off it went to sit in Jesse's inbox while I sat there staring at my own inbox again. I knew I was being ridiculous and acting half my age, but I couldn't stop myself. After so many years of being ignored, I was desperate for the attention. I longed more than anything to feel wanted and appreciated…to have someone curious about what was happening with me and want to know more about what made me tick.

A notification sound came from my laptop, announcing that I had just received a new message in my inbox. *Finally!* I eagerly opened the message.

Jesse: Wow, you really have a gift with words. Thank you for sharing that with me. Why did you stop writing poetry?

He liked my poetry. And he wanted to know why I stopped. Why *had* I stopped? If I was honest, I guess it was because I had gotten so caught up in life. And also because I was most inspired to write poetry when I was either in a new relationship or just breaking up with someone. Whenever my emotions were riding highest. I couldn't remember the last time I truly felt excited for my future with Mike.

It was just harmless flirtation is what I told myself as I tried to justify my increasingly frequent correspondence with Jesse.

Erin: I dunno why I stopped really...I guess I lost my inspiration. Some of the romantic in me died. I guess that's a bit of cynicism at work. Nobody wants to read poetry. People want to read books, novels, series. Nobody wants to read my mushy, romantic poetry.

Jesse: I want to read it. Send me another one.

Erin: Really?

Jesse: Yes, I want to read more. You are really talented.

I blushed at the compliment. It had been many years since anyone had read my poetry, let alone complimented me on it.

Erin: Okay, I'll send another, but I want to read some of yours, too.

Jesse: I'd love for you to. I have some posted on my blog.

Erin: Cool, I'll check it out.

*Jesse: ^.^*

D'aww, the guy made cute emoticons. For some reason, that made me like him even more. I looked up his blog and clicked on the *My Works* tab. Upon examining the page, I saw that there were indeed several poems listed. As I read each one, I realized that while the words were powerful and emotional, all of the imagery was dark and spoke of pain, depression and anguish. This guy was deep, but also disturbed. And more than likely damaged. And probably bad news for me, plain and simple. But as I looked at his picture again, something in his eyes…something in his eyes made me want to protect him.

Erin: *Wow, well so far I love everything you've written. You have a real gift…it's a natural talent for you. Seems very effortless.*

Jesse: *Thank you, that means a lot to me.*

Erin: *I only speak the truth. It sounds like you've gone through a lot…like you've experienced a lot of pain.*

Jesse: *I'm always in pain…every day of my fucking life.*

Erin: *Metaphorically speaking or literally?*

Jesse: *Football injury when I was 13. I was captain of the football team. Here in Podunk, Kentucky where I'm from, there's nothing in this fucking town other than football. If you play ball, you're a fucking god. If you don't, you're nobody. You don't exist. So once I broke my back, there went any chance I had to get the hell out of this piece of shit town. I should've slit my wrists then, but I didn't. My family needed me.*

Erin: *:(I'm very sorry to hear that. So you still have pain from the football injury?*

Jesse: *Yep. Been poppin' pain pills every day of my life ever since then.*

Erin: *No bueno. :(*

Jesse: *Nope, no bueno. But it helps me manage the pain and keep going when I have to work long hours. Pulling forty-eight hour days on the regular happens all the time.*

Erin: *Forty-eight? Shut up. That is crazy. What kind of job makes you do that? What do you do anyway?*

Jesse: *What do I do now or what do I WANT to do?*

Erin: *Um, both I guess?*

Jesse: *I want to go back to school so I can work in IT eventually.*

Erin: *Oh, that's cool. You like working with computers?*

Jesse: *I love it. Oh and I'd love to write and run a blog as well.*

Erin: *Nice! That all sounds great to me. :)*

Jesse: *^.^*

Erin: And what is it that you do now?

Jesse: I um, work for the family business.

Erin: Nothing wrong with that.

Jesse: They need me. And I don't have a whole lot of other options right now. I didn't finish high school, but I did get my GED. Had to start working in the family business early.

Erin: Sure, I get that. When I was a kid growing up in Hawaii, my parents owned a flower shop. I worked in the flower shop from about age four. As soon as I could hold a lei needle and a flower, I was making leis. By the time I was eight, I was running the cash register and chopping sugar cane for the tourists. Family businesses are like that. Everyone pitches in. I think most wouldn't survive—at least not at first—unless everyone did.

Jesse: You're from Hawaii? That's awesome. I've always wanted to go there. Someday.

Erin: Yep, born and raised. You definitely have to visit sometime. If you ever go, let me know and I'll tell you the good places to eat and shop.

Jesse: Dunno if I'll ever get to...tell you one thing, though...I ever go to Hawaii, I'll get arrested.

Erin: Arrested? Why?

Jesse: Yep, that's where Dog the Bounty Hunter lives, right?

Erin: Yeah?

Jesse: Then if I ever go to Hawaii, I'll get arrested, because I will hunt that son of a bitch down and kill him.

I laughed out loud, not taking him seriously. This guy fascinated me. I had no idea what would come out of his mouth next. Although I had a feeling he was bad news in big shouty caps, like BAD NEWS, I found him very interesting. And he seemed to find me interesting as well. I couldn't help myself. I couldn't stop talking to him.

Erin: lol...okay...I'll keep that in mind. But you should go to Hawaii to enjoy its beauty, its beaches, and its FOOD...not to hunt down Dog the Bounty Hunter.

Jesse: I've seen pictures. It does look beautiful.

Erin: It is. It was a great place to grow up.

Jesse: Do you miss living there?

Erin: I miss my family, I miss the culture, I miss the place...I just don't miss the humidity and the heat—although we've got plenty of heat here in SoCal—and I don't miss how high the cost of living is there.

Jesse: Yeah, I bet. I'm sorry that you miss your family. You were close to them?

Erin: Mmmhmm...me and my cousins...we were all pretty close in age and grew up more like siblings than cousins.

Jesse: Do you have any brothers or sisters?

Erin: I have a younger sister. You?

Jesse: Grew up in a house of women...I have one sister, three half sisters and one half brother, but he doesn't live with us. I had an older brother as well, but he died a few years ago.

Erin: Sorry to hear about your brother. :(

Jesse: Thanks.

Erin: You're lucky, though. I wish I had grown up with a bunch of sisters and brothers. Then again, the divorce would've been that much messier if more kids had been involved. Probably best it was just me and my sister.

Jesse was easy to talk to, and I'd been missing having someone to chat with. So I kept talking and talking until much more time had passed than I realized. By the time my stomach started growling at me, it was almost dinnertime.

Erin: Hey, I should probably let you go for now and find something to eat. I've been holed up in the apartment all day and I'm starving.

Jesse: Then go get something, silly. I should probably try to eat something myself...probably make a sandwich or something. Then I should get some sleep soon myself. Had to work late last night...didn't get home until this morning and I haven't been to bed, yet.

Erin: Oh geez, how long have you been up?

Jesse: Mmm, around 30 hours now, I guess.

Erin: Wow. Okay, no problem. I can let you go. I wish you would've said something.

Jesse: It's okay. I have insomnia a lot, so I didn't mind staying up. Not even sure I'll fall asleep now, but I feel tired. Since you need to find some food, I reckon it's as good a time as any to try to catch some shut-eye.

Erin: Okay...

Biting my lip, I hesitated before typing the next words. I didn't want to come off as desperate to talk to him again, but I *really* wanted to talk to him again. I didn't want to stop even now, but I needed to get out for some fresh air and find some food, and I needed to think for a bit. I mentally lectured myself for flirting with another guy when I had a fiancé living at home with me, my conscience having quite the battle with my heart. But ashamed or not, I couldn't deny the fact that I felt more alive just talking to Jesse online all day than I had in years of physically sitting in the same room as Mike. It was a sobering thought.

Erin: When can you chat again? It shouldn't take me too long to grab some food.

Jesse: Oh, well...I mean, I can come back and chat with you when you get back. I just thought you might need to get some other things done.

Erin: And you need to sleep.

Jesse: Eh, yeah, and I need to sleep, but I could stay up for a while longer...I like talking to you. I haven't really had anyone to talk to like this in a long time.

Erin: Me either. I like talking to you, too.

That was honest. I wasn't telling him anything I wouldn't tell any friend. But I had to be careful of leading this kid on. As much as I was enjoying talking to him, I knew it couldn't lead to more. This was a harmless flirtation and should remain as such.

Erin: However, just to be honest, I don't want to give you the wrong idea.

Jesse: How so?

Erin: Well, it's listed on my profile, so it's not like it's a big secret or anything.

Jesse: :) You're in a relationship. I know. I saw your relationship status. And I saw a picture of you with the dude that you posted from some party.

Erin: Oh, right...well then so yeah, you already know.

Jesse: So that means you can't have friends?

Erin: No! No, it doesn't mean that. I just didn't know if you knew for sure, and I didn't want to like...lead you on or anything.

Jesse: Erin...it's cool. I'd like to be your friend. I don't have a lot of those, and I could use one.

Erin: Me too. Well, then great! Um, I'll message you when I'm back. But seriously, if you need to get to sleep, please don't stay up just for me. Or I'll be up late tonight if you wanted to take a nap and get back up later or something.

Jesse: Message me when you get back and we'll see what happens.

Erin: Okay. :) Talk to you soon.

*Jesse: ^.^*

Erin: I'll try to hurry back.

Jesse: Go eat, woman!

Erin: I'm going, I'm going. ;) Go make your sandwich.

Jesse: I would if someone would stop talking to me.

Erin: lol...okay, bye...

Regretfully, I sighed as I closed the browser window. This was definitely not what I had anticipated happening this weekend, but I wasn't complaining. I'd forgotten how good it felt to be excited to talk to someone. Why couldn't I talk like this with Mike? I mean, sure, Jesse and I were just getting to know each other, so we had more things to talk about right now, but still. It bummed me out that Mike and I barely spoke to each other, and we'd lived together for five years, dated for almost five years longer than that.

I could remember back to the days when he insisted that he didn't really live with me since his name wasn't on the lease, yet pretty much all of his stuff was at my place. Once I decided to move to the valley to be closer to where he lived with his mom, he said he wouldn't be at my place as often since I'd be closer. That resolve of his lasted for exactly one night. He spent *one* night at his mom's, and every single night after that with me.

It had taken him eight years to do it, but he had finally proposed. And for so many years, I thought that was what I wanted. I thought I wanted to be with Mike for the rest of my life. Now I was terrified that I had been mistaken. I didn't want to hurt him. It was the very last thing I ever wanted to do. Even if I no longer felt like we were meant to be together, that didn't mean I wished ill for him at all. I wanted him to be happy, too. It wasn't fair to him if I stayed in a relationship that my heart was no longer in. We both deserved better than that.

Dinner was a meatball sub from an Italian joint down the street, since I didn't want to waste any time that could be spent chatting with my new friend. Jesse and I talked non-stop until past midnight. I told him more about myself, sharing my dreams of becoming a successful author and singer/songwriter. When I crawled into my bed alone for the first time in I couldn't remember how long and finally drifted off to sleep, it was with a smile on my lips as I thought about waking up in the morning and talking to him again. I wondered what new things I might learn about him next.

Chapter FOUR

10:05 AM THE NEXT MORNING

Jesse: Hey I'm online now and will be pretty much all day if you want to chat some more. I have to be somewhere around seven tonight my time, but I'll be back by ten. I'll just be working on a post for my blog, so message me when you get this. I really liked talking to you yesterday. It was nice falling asleep with a smile on my face for once. I don't do that very often.

When I woke up and stumbled into the living room to check my messages, a big yawn cracked my jaw as I stopped to rub the sleep from my eyes. Elated to find a message from Jesse waiting for me, I read it slowly as a big smile broke across my face. I immediately started typing.

Erin: Hey you, just woke up.

Jesse: Morning, sleepyhead. Sleep well?

Erin: I did. You?

Jesse: Eh, not great, but that's nothing unusual.

Erin: Oh? How come?

Jesse: I have a lot of bad dreams...makes me restless.

Erin: I'm sorry. Anything you wanna talk about?

Jesse: I can't really talk about it...

Erin: I'm sorry, I didn't mean to pry, but if you ever need someone to talk to...

Jesse: It's cool. I want to tell you, but...there are things that I am not allowed to discuss with outsiders.

Erin: Outsiders? You mean people who aren't in your family business?

Jesse: Yeah. But let's just say that the things I've seen are things that nobody should ever have to see.

Erin: :(You're just a kid yourself.

Jesse: I'm no kid. I'm the man of this family.

Erin: Okay, okay, you're not a kid. But you're a hell of a lot younger than me. Where's your dad?

Jesse: Age ain't nothin' but a number. Most people tell me I'm more mature...an old soul. My dad lives in California somewhere, but I've never met him.

Erin: Really? How come?

Jesse: He knocked my mom up for the third time and then took off before I was born. Bastard has never once come around to meet me. But he's tried to call a few times.

Erin: How'd that go?

Jesse: Dunno, I refuse to talk to him. I don't want anything to do with that asshole. He's had years to come back out here to Kentucky and see me.

Erin: When's the last time he tried to call?

Jesse: My eighteenth birthday.

Erin: I see...so you said that your older brother died?

Jesse: Yeah, Micah. He was only 26 when he was murdered.

Erin: OMG! That's horrible. I'm so sorry. :(We don't have to talk about it if you don't want.

Jesse: It's okay...I don't mind talking to you about him. It's kind of nice really.

Erin: How old were you when it happened?

Jesse: 13...after that, I had to step up and become the man of the family. So I dropped out of high school—my back was fucked anyway after I broke it, so there went my football scholarship and any chance I had at getting the hell out of Kentucky—and I started working. Someone had to put food on the table, and God knows my drugged-up mother wasn't going to do it.

Erin: Oh no, I'm so sorry. What was she addicted to, if you don't mind me asking?

Jesse: *Oxy.*

Erin: *Hmm, never heard of it.*

Jesse: *Oxycontin. It's a painkiller. Probably one of the best painkillers ever invented.*

Erin: *I see. So you've been working in the family business since you were 13? That's a long time. You're going to be ready for retirement by the time you're like 40.*

Jesse: *Heh, yeah. The shit my body has been through already—I'll be lucky if I live that long. I'm going to die young. I know it.*

Erin: *Don't say that!*

Jesse: *Why not? It's true. My body is falling apart and I'm not even twenty-two. I have a shitty job, no health insurance, I'm a drug addict, my mother's a drug addict. I got no hope of going anywhere, and no one who gives a shit.*

I didn't know what to say, but I felt so sad for him. I had no clue what it was he had been through. I only knew that I wanted to somehow bring comfort to him, make him feel better, put a smile on his face. How could I show him he wasn't alone in the world? How could I alleviate some of his pain? I couldn't imagine having such a sad, despondent outlook on life at such a tender, young age.

As long as I could remember, I'd always had a strong survival instinct. You have to be able to think positively in order to want to keep going day after day. Unbeknownst to my mother, she'd taught me how to look at the bright side of things. Observing the way she had let herself go and given up on trying for a better life, I'd learned there was no point in wallowing in despair so much that I'd get dragged deep into depression like she had. That alone was motivation enough for me to want to do the exact opposite, and to instead think positively and work hard to reach my goals. And to make sure that eventually I would never have to depend on anyone else ever again.

But I had grown up with loving parents, regardless of the sometimes questionable parenting choices they made, so I couldn't really compare anything I had experienced to Jesse's situation. From what he'd told me so far, it sounded like he had received very little love and definitely very little guidance on how to embrace and live your life and be an independent, self-sufficient human being, contributing your part to the world.

Erin: Well I give a shit.

Jesse: Heh...thanks...

Erin: I do, really. Please don't ever think you're all alone. I'm here for you whenever you need sometime to talk to, okay?

Jesse: I'm used to it...you don't need to worry about me. I can take care of myself.

Erin: Ha, telling me not to worry about someone I care about who is going through a hard time is like talking to a brick wall.

Jesse: I just wish I could get out of this town and make something of my life. If I could just get that chance...but I never will, so I should just shut up and quit fooling myself. I'll never get out of here. This is where I'll die.

Erin: Well if that's the way you keep thinking, then yeah, that's probably what will happen. You have to want more than that if you're ever going to do anything about it.

Jesse: I'm afraid to want more...

Erin: Why?

Jesse: Cuz I don't know if I could handle losing it.

Erin: I don't think you should be afraid to dream. That's what keeps me going. I dunno where I'd be now if I didn't ever dream of more.

Jesse: You shouldn't be afraid to dream. You're beautiful, talented, kind. You're going to go places someday.

Erin: I dunno about all that. But thank you.

Jesse: You will, and I'll be here cheering you on. I'll be like, "Erin Tanaka, the author? Oh yeah, I know her. We go way back."

I grinned and couldn't help feeling a little giddy at the thought. What if someday I really did become a well-known author? I'd already gotten my feet wet and self-published my first book earlier this year. It had done better than I had expected, although nowhere near as well as I'd secretly hoped. I thought it was a decent first attempt, but I had a lot to learn and so far to go still. Marketing isn't easy, nor is it cheap. I have so much respect for any independent artist, now that I have walked a bit in their shoes and experienced the frustration and self-doubt that can accompany you a good chunk of the time.

Erin: *Tell you what. I promise to keep dreaming if you promise to try to do the same. You never know what you are capable of if you want something badly enough.*

Jesse: *Oh I'm capable of plenty...but probably nothing you'd be too happy about.*

Erin: *Okay, you have to quit making these cryptic comments and then telling me you can't talk about it. If we're going to be friends, you need to tell me the truth. How else am I supposed to understand what's going on with you and offer advice?*

Jesse: **sigh**

Erin: **sigh back**

Jesse: *Heh, you're pretty stubborn, you know that?*

Erin: **grin* I may have been told that once or twice. :)*

Jesse: *Wench.*

Erin: *Hey, who are you callin' a wench?*

Jesse: *You.*

Erin: *Hmph! You can't avoid answering by calling me names, sir.*

Jesse: *Okay okay...I'll tell you a little more about what I do...but you have to promise to delete this conversation as soon as it's over, okay?*

Erin: *Seriously?*

Jesse: *Yes, seriously.*

Erin: *Alright alright. So? Spill. What is it that you do? What is this so-called "family business" you can't talk about?*

Jesse: *Okay...well...you ever watched Sons of Anarchy?*

Erin: *Mmm, nope.*

Jesse: *What?! That show is amazing. Well, do you even know what it's about then?*

Erin: *Nooo, not really. Anarchy?*

Jesse: *It's about a motorcycle club...it's supposed to be like their fictional version of Hells Angels.*

Erin: Now THAT I've heard of.

Jesse: Well, I'm the Captain of a motorcycle club. Like Hells Angels. I was going to tell you that I'm kind of like Jax in Sons of Anarchy, but you've never seen the show, so you wouldn't have a clue what that means.

Erin: Okay? So what's the big deal with that? What do you guys do? Ride around on motorcycles all day? Race against other motorcycle clubs?

Jesse: Look, I can't really talk about what we do, because that's club business, and I swore an oath. But I'll tell you what a typical day of my life is like. That's going to have to be good enough for now.

Erin: Got it.

Jesse: Alright...well, every morning when I wake up, there's a piece of paper on my chest with a list of things I need to do that day. It could be anything from picking up groceries for one of the old ladies whose man is in prison to working security at the clubhouse.

Erin: Wait, what? Prison?

Jesse: Yeah. Prison.

Erin: Uhh, okay? Look, I know you can't tell me club business, but you can't say something like that and then not tell me more.

Jesse: Ugh...fine. Delete this immediately, I mean it.

Erin: I will.

Jesse: Alright. Well, Kentucky has a big pipeline for illegal drug and firearm activity.

Erin: YOU RUN GUNS AND DRUGS?!?!

Jesse: Erin...

Erin: Sorry...sorry. Okay, deleting now.

Jesse: Me too. Thank you.

Erin: Sure...

Jesse: You probably don't want to talk to me anymore now, huh? It's not like I chose this life. This is not who I wanted to be, but this is the life I was born into. This is who I am.

Erin: Of course I still want to talk to you. I'm not judging you by what you do. You can't control who you were born to.

Jesse: I can't tell you how much it means to me to have you as a friend. You're pretty awesome.

Erin: Well, I'm happy to have you as a friend as well.

We kept talking the rest of the day until he had to leave to take care of some club business and I had to leave to pick up Mike. I chewed worriedly at my lip as I drove to the airport, my imagination running wild with the possibilities of what Jesse might be doing tonight. Was he picking up a shipment of cocaine? Was he getting more Oxy for himself and his mom? Was he gunning another club down for their AKs?

I had no idea what being a member of a motorcycle club entailed, but part of me was scandalized to even think of these things while the other part of me was intrigued. My life was so boring compared to his. I admittedly was finding a lot of thrill in the strangeness of learning about Jesse's world and what his life was really like. Sighing, I picked up my iPhone and selected the song he told me to listen to when I told him I loved dubstep: Krewella's remix of Fire Hive's *Knife Party*. I smiled as soon as the song started. Yup, this was definitely up my alley. As I continued to listen to the song, nodding my head and tapping my hand on the steering wheel in time with the beat, an image came to my mind of a hot make-out session with Jesse.

Wait. What?! Why am I thinking about making out with Jesse? We are just friends! And he's just a kid! I mentally lectured myself yet again. *Erin, get a grip. You are playing with fire, and you are going to get burned. Not only that, but you are going to hurt Mike.*

This was not good. This was not good at all.

By the time I picked up Mike, I'd gotten my thoughts under enough control that I was able to make light conversation on the drive home, asking if he had a safe flight, how the trip went, if he had enjoyed himself at the company dinner. His responses were short, and we soon fell back into our usual comfortable silence. Even though I felt sad that we didn't have more to talk about, at the same time I was relieved to be left to my thoughts, disturbing and confusing as they were.

When I got home and checked Facebook, I was disappointed to see that Jesse was not online and hadn't left me any messages. I did, however, have a message from my co-worker friend, Catherine. She and her husband Eric had invited us to go kayaking with them in Marina del Rey next weekend. After checking my calendar, I replied to her message, accepting their invitation. At this point, anything to get Mike and me out of the house would be a welcome distraction from the emotional gap that was widening between us every day.

Chapter FIVE

"Eep!" I exclaimed as a pair of hands slid over my eyes from behind me.

"Guess who!" a female voice exclaimed, then the hands disappeared from my eyes.

"Oh hey, Kristen," I said after swiveling my chair around, recognizing the tall girl with sparkling blue eyes who was grinning impishly at me.

"Hey girl hey! Just came by to see if you can sneak away for lunch today."

"Ugh, I dunno. I have so much crap to get done for Jerry. I really shouldn't."

"Aw come on. It's almost the weekend. Can't you get away just this once?"

"I'm really sorry, girlie girl, but I just can't. I have way too much to do today."

The bright smile on Kristen's face fell for a second, but it was so quick and then she was back to smiling widely again that I wasn't sure if I had imagined it. "Okay, no probs! Another time?"

"Another time for sure," I agreed. "Maybe next week? I could do Tuesday. Jerry's going out of town for another studio visit, so I should be able to sneak away for at least an hour—maybe even a little longer."

Kristen was one of the newer administrative assistants we'd hired, and we'd hit it off instantly. In her early twenties, she was cute in awkward sort of way, seeming to be all arms, legs and chestnut brown hair. She usually swung by my desk at least once a day to see if I wanted to join her for a quick smoke in the back of our building. I hadn't smoked regularly since my late teens, but I still indulged in the occasional cigarette—usually reserved for either social drinking situations or when I was having a particularly crazy day at work.

Whenever we stood outside smoking, I always felt like I was about to get into trouble—like I was back in high school and might get caught by a teacher.

"Tuesday works for me...okay, well, I guess I'll let you get back to it."

"Okay, enjoy your lunch."

"Thanks, I will," she said, then paused for a moment, looking like she wanted to say something else.

"Everything okay?" I asked, raising an eyebrow.

"Hmm? Oh yeah, everything's fine. I just...mmm, never mind. All good. I'll catch you later."

"Okay," I said as she smiled and waved and bounced off down the hallway and out the door. "That was a little weird," I muttered to myself after she disappeared, making a mental note to check on her later in the afternoon. She had definitely seemed like she needed to talk about something. I wanted to go after her and make sure she was okay, but first I had an entire day of meetings to reschedule as well as a fat stack of receipts to expense for Jerry in about five hours. I groaned out loud just thinking about it. *F me!*

This morning when Jerry came into the office, he announced that he was taking Friday off so he could take Amber, his new young wife, to Las Vegas for their one-month anniversary. Of course he wouldn't think about how hard it had been for me to get one of his meetings scheduled to begin with, and now he so casually decided to just not come to work that day, and I had to start all over again. Not only that, but the other assistants I'd been dealing with to get the meeting scheduled in the first place probably already hated me as it was.

I really couldn't wait until I could afford to never have to come to work again. I mean, of course I'd still be working, but not in an office. Impulsively, I checked my Amazon account. Zero sales for the day. *Lovely.* If I thought writing a book was difficult, selling one was even more so.

It had taken me a long time to even get to this point in my life—the point where I've started to really focus on building a career for myself. Not the nine to five desk job I currently held, but my new side career of being an author. I knew what I wanted, and although I wasn't completely sure yet as to how I would achieve all my goals, at least I could say that I was actively working on them.

It felt like the older I got, the more time I spent reflecting on life and what it is all about. Where did we come from? What makes us tick? What makes us keep going day after day? What makes us yearn for something more? After over thirty years of living, I still do not have any answers, but the jaded cynic in me has come to this conclusion.

Life is the difference between things you do for entertainment, because it makes you feel good, or things you do to survive and stay out of trouble. You work so you don't live on the street and don't starve. You cut your hair so you don't look like Cousin It. You wear deodorant so you don't offend anyone with your stench. You brush your teeth so they don't turn black and fall out of your mouth. You pick up your clothes, do your laundry and dishes so you don't look like you live in a pigsty. You eat healthy food and exercise regularly so your immune system stays strong and you don't get fat and disgusting.

You're nice to your boss and co-workers because you have to see them five days a week and you want them to like you and be nice to you and not fire your ass. You're nice to your mailman or other delivery person because you don't want them being careless with your packages. You make friends so you don't go insane from the lack of human contact. You stay away from the bad friends so you don't suffer from the consequences of their shenanigans.

You have children so you aren't alone and have someone to take care of you when you're old and incapable of caring for yourself anymore. You're good to your children so that they *will* take care of you instead of leaving your worthless carcass to rot on the street. You're good to your grandchildren so they'll send you cute pictures of them so you look cool to the other grannies and gramps when you're all sitting in some rest home, playing show and tell with your photo libraries on your iPads. And if you're really good to them, they might even come visit you once or twice a year in that smelly, overpriced shithole and smuggle you some high-grade Californian medical marijuana.

And so here I was, working this desk job, sitting in an office day after day, hating the monotony of my life and the lack of direction. But at least now

I've finally been motivated to do something about it. Tucking all my rambling thoughts away, I reluctantly turned my attention back to Jerry's schedule. First things first. Do the job I had now and do it well so I could keep living and keep pursuing my dreams.

"Earth to Erin." Kyle, one of the Project Managers, was waving his hand back and forth in front of my face.

Oh shit. Too late. I'd already zoned out too long. "Hey! Sorry. Got lost in thought."

"Obviously," he said.

"Trying to um—figure out how I'm going to get all of these meetings rescheduled by the end of the day. Jerry wants them all rescheduled for next week. Do you have any idea what a bitch it was to get all of the brand managers available and in town at the same time? And now I have to contact all of them and explain that Jerry has decided to take the day off and try to reschedule this stupid meeting ASAP. And all because Jerry's new wife has him by the balls. And since he's going to be out of town on Tuesday and Wednesday, that means it has to happen Monday or after he returns. And you know he's gonna give me shit if I can't get it scheduled for Monday. I'm predicting what will end up happening now. I'll finally get it scheduled for sometime late Monday afternoon. Then on Monday midday, he's gonna tell me to cancel and reschedule it after Austin. He won't have enough time to meet with them after all. That's right, I'm calling it now."

Kyle just raised his eyebrow at me and smirked. "Feel better now?"

I grunted. "Slightly." Then I sighed and shrugged my shoulders. "I'm sorry. It's just that sometimes he drives me absolutely cuckoo cachoo! Anyways, what can I do ya for?"

"Oh, I was just going to see if you wanted to maybe grab lunch and get out of here for awhile."

Kyle and I had been working together for years, but he had only more recently transferred to L.A. from our New York studio. The fact that he was married with two kids didn't keep him from flirting with me, but I wasn't the type of girl to cheat on my fiancé or sleep with a married man, so it remained a harmless flirtation. Though I sometimes wished it could be more and was pretty sure he felt the same.

"I wish," I said wistfully, "but as you can see, I'm a little swamped and a little crazy."

"And that's different from how you normally are how?"

I flicked a paper clip at him and missed. "I'm sorry. Rain check?"

"Sure, no problem. I'll catch you later, kay?"

"Yep. Enjoy your lunch!"

I swiveled back to my computer screen once again to search for the first number I needed to call to start rescheduling. I couldn't wait for the day to be over, and if people would stop interrupting and asking if I wanted to go to lunch, maybe I would get out of here at a decent time. Jesse would be waiting for me to get home so we could chat online as had already become our custom in the short time we'd known each other. I knew it was wrong, but I looked forward to our chats more and more each day. And the more I talked to him, the unhappier I felt in my current situation. I felt trapped and confused. I didn't want to hurt Mike, but I couldn't stay when my heart was no longer in it. What was I going to do?

"Babe, hurry up—we're going to be late. We're supposed to meet Catherine and Eric at the marina in half an hour."

It wasn't even noon and I was already on edge. I fingered the Hello Kitty Band-Aid that I'd put on because I'd bitten my nail down to the bed and made it bleed. I hadn't bitten my nails since I was in grade school, but that had changed this morning. Mike had tried to instigate sex last night, and I'd played the upset stomach card. The hurt look on his face told me I hadn't fooled him with my lame excuse. In the ten years we'd been together, I don't think I'd ever turned him down before—not that we were having sex that frequently these days. I wondered again how we had gotten to this point. How could I have been so blind as to have not seen years ago that we weren't meant to be together romantically?

He was still sitting on the couch and putting on his shoes as I stood there waiting for him, my fingers drumming impatiently against the doorframe.

"You know, you standing there yelling at me to hurry isn't going to get you anywhere," he said without looking up at me.

"I wasn't yelling," I snapped.

Finally glancing up, he just gave me a look. I rolled my eyes in frustration—not at him, but at myself. I knew I was being a royal bitch. It was my self-defense mechanism springing into action. Often when I became involved in an emotional situation that was particularly difficult for me to handle, I reacted this way. It was unfortunate, but I didn't know how else to act. Even though I would be the one who ended up doing the hurting, it killed me inside to think that I was actually going to go through with it. I would have given anything to avoid hurting Mike.

Finally he finished tying his shoes and then disappeared down the hallway and into the bedroom. I sighed again. What was taking him so long? He reappeared moments later, pulling on a hoodie.

"You ready now?" I asked, arching an eyebrow at him.

"Just go," he snapped, and gestured toward the door.

I shrugged and opened the door to leave. I just wanted to get this over and done with and come back home so I could get online and talk to Jesse.

Thankfully traffic wasn't too bad, so the drive down to Marina del Rey was fairly short. Catherine and Eric were waiting for us when we arrived. We spent a few minutes greeting each other and catching up, then turned to walk towards the small, weatherworn trailer that served as the rental office. After paying to rent two of their double kayaks for a couple of hours, we followed our guide back outside to the docks. He handed us each a life vest and instructed us on how to get into the kayak without capsizing the damn thing. I'd done this a few times before with my friends, but I still felt like I was going to land in the water every time I tried to board my kayak.

When we got out on the water, the current was so strong, it was hard to paddle. I kept splashing Mike every time I took a stroke with my oars, and he complained loudly and frequently. We couldn't seem to get into sync with our paddling. Ironically, I thought to myself that my attempt in rowing against the current was a metaphor for our struggling relationship.

The drive home was even worse. I was so irritated and on edge that I snapped at Mike and cursed at the ridiculous traffic that was currently holding us prisoner on the 405 like we were stuck in the middle of a parking lot. I was hot, sweaty, grumpy, and my arms and legs were caked with the salty grime of the marina, and then he tried to put a comforting hand on my knee. It made me want to cringe away. I didn't want him touching me. All I could think about was being with Jesse.

When we got home to our apartment, I couldn't get into the shower fast enough to wash all the ickiness of my body. I dried myself off, threw on some clean clothes and told Mike I had to run to the post office, but in actuality, I drove down the street to the nearest gas station and called Jesse.

I was already crying when he answered the phone. Explaining to him what happened, I recounted the events of the day. I told him I didn't know what to do, but I needed to tell Mike how I was feeling before he tried to touch me again. I didn't think I could bear to see the hurt look in his eyes if I pulled away from him again and make some lame excuse as to why I wasn't interested in his attentions.

Jesse was sympathetic, but he warned me to make absolute certain I was sure this was what I wanted before I made any drastic decisions that would change my life forever. But by that point, I was beyond rational thought. It was time to rip off the Band-Aid.

As I let myself back into the apartment that I had shared with my fiancé for the past five years, an overwhelming sense of dread came over me, and the breath caught in my chest. Glancing around the living room, I saw that Mike wasn't there and headed down the hall to our bedroom where I found him sitting on the bed. He had also showered and changed into clean clothes, and was now relaxing while he watched TV.

Clearing my throat nervously, I sat on the side of the bed and told Mike we needed to talk. With a concerned look on his face, he shut off the TV and shifted on the bed to look at me.

"Okay. What's up?" he asked, reaching out to rub my knee.

"Umm…I don't think I can do this anymore, Mike," I said lamely, unsure how to start breaking the heart of the man I had loved and cherished for the past ten years.

"What are you talking about? What's wrong?" he asked, his eyes searching mine for answers.

"I want to break up," I said as my breath hitched in my chest with a sob. I stared at the bed, trying to get myself back under control.

"What? What are you talking about? Why?" The questions tumbled from his mouth as he grabbed my hands frantically, trying to make me look up at him.

"I'm so sorry, Mike. I love you. I do. But I haven't been happy in a long time, and every time I've tried to talk to you, you just shut me down and tell me I'm trying to cause drama. I can't do this anymore, I'm sorry."

The sobs were coming fast and furiously now. I couldn't believe what I was doing to my best friend…to my family…the one I loved and had planned to marry. But even through the excruciating pain of breaking my man's heart, I reminded myself of the reasons that had brought me to this breaking point. I just had to get through this awful ordeal, and then I could move on with my life and start to heal. I could finally be free to be with Jesse, the man I thought I was falling in love with…who I thought I could finally truly be happy with.

"Why? Look, let's just talk about this. We can work things out. You can't leave me, Erin. I love you, and you love me. We're getting married!" The pained desperation and tears in his eyes were like multiple stab wounds to my heart. Even though part of me was furious with him for not listening to me all the previous times I'd tried in vain to get him to talk to me and to make more of an effort to contribute around the apartment, I never would have wished this pain on him or anyone else I loved.

I covered my face with my hands, the sobs still shaking my shoulders. "I'm sorry, I'm so sorry," I sobbed over and over again. "I just can't do this anymore."

I hadn't intended to tell him about Jesse. In my opinion, Jesse wasn't our problem. He had merely acted as a catalyst to bring this troubled relationship to the conclusion that was overdue by several years. But Mike was intent on finding out why I had decided to end our engagement, not that I blamed him in the slightest. If the situation had been reversed, I would have demanded to know the reasons why as well.

"Is there someone else?" he finally asked, his voice sounding lost and broken.

At first I shook my head. "No, this isn't about that," I insisted. "I haven't been feeling right about us in quite a while. I have begged you to help out more. I shouldn't have to do that. You're a grown-ass man! You're going to be thirty this year. I shouldn't have to ask you to take out the trash every day. I shouldn't have to beg you on Christmas Eve to go get me a present so I have *something* under the tree to open on Christmas morning. It's not like you can't afford it now. You're just lazy and never seem to think about doing something nice for me. I've told you so many times that it doesn't matter *what* you get me or how much you spend. It's about taking a bit of time out of your day to do something thoughtful for the woman you love to show me you give a shit. I do *everything* around here, and I'm exhausted, Mike. You've drained me completely, and I have nothing left to give you anymore."

He continued to cry and pleaded with me to reconsider my decision. "I'll change, I promise. Just give me one more chance. Please, Erin. Don't do this to me. Don't give up on us, yet. I can change. I love you so much." His grief rolled over me in waves as he clutched at my hands.

But I shook my head, tears still streaming down my face. I had already made up my mind. There was no going back now.

"I can't. I'm so sorry, but I just can't."

I stood up and headed for the living room to grab the box of Kleenex that was sitting on the coffee table. Mike followed me and stood there blocking the door like he thought I was going to leave or something. And I did want to leave. If he wasn't going to, I had to. I couldn't stay around him right now. The pain I saw in his eyes was killing me. If I stayed, I didn't know if I could remain strong and stick to my guns. He would talk me out of it and I would cave, too scared to end the longest romantic relationship I'd ever had with anyone.

"Come on, Erin. I love you. We can work this out. Do ten years mean nothing to you? You act like you don't even want to try."

Sitting down on the edge of the couch, I blew my nose and shook my head. I was going to have to tell him about Jesse. He wouldn't stop trying to convince me to try to work things out otherwise. He sat down on the armchair across from me, his eyes red and watery with unshed tears. I had never seen him like this before, and for a moment my resolve faltered as I questioned the intelligence of my decision.

I looked down at the ground as I gathered the courage to say the next words. "Look…I said there wasn't anyone else, but that was a lie. I just don't want you to thinking that is the reason for this. It actually has nothing to do with how I feel right now."

"I knew it. Who is he?" I could see the muscle in Mike's jaw tick as he ground his teeth together in silent anger.

"You don't know him. It's someone I met online through the author shit."

"What the fuck, Erin? How long have you been talking to this guy? Have you already met him? Have you been cheating on me?"

"No, nothing has happened. He lives in freaking Kentucky. I haven't met him, yet. I don't even really know why I like him, except he just seems to get me. He's made me happier in the past week than I've been in a really long time."

Mike just sat there and stared at the coffee table, shaking his head as the tears flowed down his face. "You're making a mistake. I love you. We should be able to try to work things out without some other guy in the picture. Please, Erin, I'm begging you."

"I'm sorry, Mike. I can't. It's over for me…for us."

Fresh tears brimmed in my eyes as a sob caught in my throat. Even though I knew I had to end our relationship, I was so scared of the thought that I might never see him again. I hoped that maybe someday we could still be friends, but I didn't know if he would ever forgive me.

"I don't know what exactly to do next. This wasn't something I was planning. Um..." I looked around the living room, at a total loss for words. I hadn't thought this far ahead. In all the times I'd imagined actually going through with it and breaking things off with Mike, I had never completely visualized it happening. I don't know that you really can prepare yourself for the devastation you feel when you rip your fiancé's heart out.

Mike just sat there and continued to stare at the coffee table, not saying a word. The occasional tear still trickling down his cheek. He was obviously in shock and not any better equipped to deal with our current situation. I had been his first love, his first girlfriend, his first kiss, and now I was his first ex, his first heartbreak.

"I need some time to think and figure things out, and I need to do it alone. I just need some space right now," I said, mumbling the last bit. "I know you've had no warning of this and probably have no clue what to do next, either. I'm going to get a hotel room and take a day or two to think."

He finally moved at that, his eyes rising up to meet mine. The sorrowful look he gave nearly undid me. I dropped my gaze quickly and cleared my throat. "Um, I'm going to get some things together and go. We'll talk later."

"Don't leave, Erin. Please. You can stay in the bedroom or I'll stay in there and you can stay out here. Just don't leave me right now."

I shook my head. "I have to. I can't stay here right now. This is just something I have to do, and I'm so very sorry that I'm hurting you right now. It's the very last thing I ever wanted to do." My voice cracked and I bit my lip, trying to sniffle back another sob. I quickly got to my feet and headed to the bedroom to pack a bag. I threw everything I'd need to survive in a hotel for a couple of days into my bag and grabbed my purse and keys.

Mike was standing by the front door when I returned to the living room.

"Mike, please don't," I started to say, but he moved forward and simply wrapped his arms around me in a tight hug. I stood there stiffly for a moment, then finally relaxed slightly and dropped my bag, raising both arms up to hug him in return. We held each other so tight, and with each passing moment, I felt the dagger twist deeper into my heart. I'm not sure how long we stood there like that, but I could feel the sobs shaking me as I thought about the fact that this might be the last time I ever held him like this. Finally I pulled back and bent down to pick up my bag, wiping my nose with the back of my sleeve, purposely not looking up at him.

"I'll call you later," I said, my voice already hoarse from all the tears.

He just nodded and stepped slowly to the side, allowing me to leave. I will never forget the defeated look I saw on his face just before I shut the door. His shoulders were slumped and his eyes red as he watched me hesitate once again. I gulped hard and tried to breathe through my stuffed up nose, but it was too clogged. My mouth opened in a slight gasp, and for a brief moment in the middle of all my self-inflicted pain, I thought how utterly awful I must look. How could he even want to be with a big mess like me? I nodded once to myself as I braced myself and finally shut the door. Someday he would thank me.

Chapter SIX

The drive to the hotel was quiet, which was weird for me. I almost always had music blasting in my car, but right now I couldn't handle the noise. My stomach churned in agitation as I tried to calm my racing heart, my thoughts racing wildly about in panic mode. I called Allison after I found parking in the lot next to the lobby. To my relief, she picked up after the second ring.

"Hey," I said, my voice already cracking.

"Hey," she said back. "What's up?"

"I um…I just left Mike."

"Left him where?"

"At home…I mean, Allison—I left him, left him. Like I broke up with him just now."

"You what?" her voice raised an octave as she responded in a shocked tone.

"I broke up with Mike. I've been unhappy for a while—you know that—and I started talking to that guy online. You know the one I told you about that joined my street team?"

"The teenager from Kentucky?"

"He's not a teenager, but he's only twenty-two."

"Uh huh. So what does this guy have to do with you breaking up with Mike?"

"We've been talking like every day for the past week, and I think I'm in love with him. He makes me feel more alive than I've felt in I don't know how long."

"Okay, Erin. You know I'm your friend and I love you and I support you one hundred percent in whatever you decide to do, but have you really thought this through? You're in love with this guy you've never met and have only been talking to online for a week?"

"We've been talking on the phone as well."

"You've been with Mike for ten years. That's a really long time. That's longer than Caleb and I have been together."

"I know and of course I've thought it through. This wasn't a decision I made lightly. It wasn't easy for me to do this, but it's something I had to do. I've known for a while that we weren't quite right for each other, but I'd already invested so many years into our relationship, and everyone says that the passion dies down after ten years, so I just figured it was normal and I should deal with it and try to be content. But random things kept happening… signs…I dunno. But things that made me stop and question my decision to remain with Mike.

"I just think I should feel more for the man I want to be with for the rest of my life, and I'm so, so tired of being Mike's mom. I know I signed up for this when we started dating. He's three years younger than me, but younger than that even, if we're speaking in years of maturity. I knew I'd be waiting longer for him to grow up and get his shit together, but it's been ten years now. How much longer am I supposed to wait around to see if he finally gets his thumb out of his ass, starts to grow up and starts to change?"

"Hey, like I said. I'm on your side, and I support whatever you decide to do. I'm just trying to make sure that you've considered everything. This is a huge, big deal."

"I know. I don't mean to snap at you. I just don't know what to do right now. I'm so scared, Allison."

"I know. Do you want to maybe come up here to San Jose and spend some time with me and Caleb?"

"Thank you, I appreciate that, but I can't. I have to work and can't take the time off right now. I'll be okay. It's just going to take some time before I feel normal again. God, how the hell am I going to deal with starting all over again?"

"You'll do it one day at a time."

"Yeah, I know."

There was a long pause before Allison finally spoke again. "So um, this younger guy. What's going on with him?"

"I'm not sure, yet. He wants to get the hell out of Kentucky, though."

"Didn't you say he's in some kind of motorcycle club?"

"Yeah, it's like Hells Angels."

"Aren't you scared, Erin? I watch *Sons of Anarchy*. That is *not* some shit you want to get tangled up in."

I paused as I thought about it before responding. I hadn't seen the show, but I remembered Jesse mentioning it to me as well. My knowledge of this motorcycle club world was sorely lacking.

"No, I haven't seen the show—just heard about it. But I've talked to him, and it's not the life he would have chosen for himself. He was born into it. It's all he's ever known. But he wants out, and he wants to move here and be with me."

"Oy. Is he coming there?"

"Yeah, we're trying to figure it out."

"Uhh, Erin, I really think you should take some time to yourself and think about what you're doing. Without any outside influences. This guy is clouding your judgment. You don't need him in the picture right now."

"I appreciate your concern, but I love Jesse. He's got such a good heart. He didn't ask me to do any of this. He questioned me himself and asked me to make sure that this was really what I wanted. I want him to get out of that hellhole and be here with me where I can help him, and he can help me. We'll be good for each other and help each other heal."

Allison sighed. "I still think you're making a mistake, but you're gonna do what you want to do, I guess. Just please be careful."

"Thank you. I love you, girl. I guess I'm gonna go check into my room now."

"Okay. Call me later. Everything will be okay. Okay?"

I sniffed back a sob and nodded. "I know. It just doesn't feel like that right now."

"Take a hot shower and try to eat something."

"There's no way I could eat something right now. I'd literally puke. But yeah, I'll probably take a hot shower. Always makes me feel better. That and sleep—although I don't think I could sleep a wink right now. Anyways…I'll talk to you soon."

"Okay. Love you."

"Love you. Bye."

I hung up the phone and sat in silence for several minutes, sniffling and rubbing the hot tears from my eyes, contemplating everything that had happened. What had I done? *Had* I really thought things through? Maybe Allison was right, but all I could think was that I wanted Jesse here with me. I wanted him here so badly I could taste it. I wanted him here to hold me and wipe my tears away and tell me everything would be okay…to tell me that I wasn't crazy loco for doing this, and that there was a light at the end of the tunnel, even if I couldn't see it right now. I needed his strength and his support, and he was over a thousand miles away from me. I needed to know that someone believed in me and believed I deserved better than what I had settled for when I agreed to marry Mike.

Taking a deep breath, I gathered my belongings and got out of the car, then moved to get my bag out of the trunk. I felt unsteady as I walked towards the elevator, wheeling my suitcase behind me. With each step that brought me closer to the hotel, the entire situation became more real. There was no turning back. It was time for a change, and it was happening now whether I liked it or not. I had instigated this entire thing and now it was time to start dealing with the consequences of my decision. Whether or not it was the right decision remained to be seen, but there would be consequences nonetheless.

If the girl who checked me in at the front desk noticed my puffy red eyes, she didn't give any indication of it. Her smile was warm and pleasant and never once faltered as she quickly and efficiently checked me in. Before I knew it, I was on my way to the elevator lobby with my room keycard in hand.

When I got to my room, I wheeled my suitcase inside and set it against the wall before turning to adjust the thermostat. It was freezing and I had been crying—never a good combo and a surefire way to get myself sick. What better way to spend the first week after I broke up with my fiancé of ten years than being miserable with a cold? I guess it'd be my penance. Even if I believed I was doing the right thing in leaving Mike, I didn't feel right about hurting him. How could I? I loved him and always would, even if I didn't want to be with him anymore.

I curled up on an armchair and called Jesse, rubbing my chilled fingers together and blowing on them for a little warmth. He answered immediately and asked if I was okay.

"No, not really. I just walked out on the guy I thought I was going to marry, so I feel pretty damn shitty."

"Aww, baby, I know. I'm so sorry. I wish I could be there with you right now. I would wrap my arms around you and hold you so tight. You could cry all you wanted."

"I wish you were here."

"I will be, as soon as I can."

"When is that going to be?"

"I'm not sure, yet. My bank accounts are still frozen. Fucking feds are trying to RICO my entire family and froze my accounts earlier this year. I haven't been able to touch a fucking cent since January."

"Oh my God, that's horrible."

"Yeah, fuckers."

I started to speak and then hesitated. Against my better instincts, I was about to offer to pay for his plane ticket—I was that desperate to have him here with me as soon as possible. Was this a stupid thing for me to do? Probably. But I couldn't help it. I wanted him to be in California so we could start our new life together as soon as possible. I wanted him away from the chaotic criminal life he'd led in Kentucky since he was old enough to hold a gun. I felt like I'd been sent to help him escape the prison of a life he never wanted.

"I don't mind buying your plane ticket here, babe. You can always pay me back later once your accounts are unfrozen again."

"Oh no, I couldn't ask you to do that. It'll take me a while, and I might have to do a job to get the cash, but trust me, one way or another, I will get there to you as soon as I can."

"Well, how soon is that going to be?" I know my voice was starting to sound petulant and whiny, but I was so scared, and I needed some reassurance that I wasn't alone in this.

"I'm not sure, yet, babe. Might be a few more months before I can make it happen. But you should take some time to yourself to figure things out, you know? This is a big change for you, and you don't really need me getting mixed up in the middle of everything right now."

Ugh. He sounded like Allison, and I didn't want to hear it. I hated when other people tried to tell me what I should or shouldn't do, think or feel.

"Babe, don't we love each other? Don't you want to be here with me?"

"Of course, I do. You know I do."

"Do I? Maybe all of this is too much for you and you're gonna change your mind and forget all about me."

"Fuck, no. I could never forget about you, Erin. You're the best thing that's ever happened to me. I feel like I can fucking breathe again. You've brought hope and light back into my life again. I was starting to believe that I was nothing but a worthless piece of shit and that I was never going to know anything better. And then you came along and now I believe. Now I believe in that little thing they call love. But I would be a selfish monster to not consider your feelings right now. I don't want you to regret leaving your man for me."

"I didn't leave him for you. You just gave me the strength to do what I should have done years ago, but was too scared to."

"Well, now you finally did it."

"Yep. Yep, I sure did." I drew in a deep breath as my heartbeat began to speed up again. I had done it. I had taken the plunge and left Mike. I had made the decision to change my life forever. Whether it was the right one was yet to be seen, but I was really hoping it was.

"Well, I was going to take a job that was going to take me out of town for a few days, but I don't want to leave you alone right now while you're going through this."

"A job? Like what kind of job?"

"I can't tell you the details, babe, but it was for good money. They were going to send me to the Middle East on a cargo plane, but I'm going to tell them I can't do it."

"Won't you get into trouble for that?"

"Probably. But you just let me worry about that, okay? You have enough to deal with right now."

I felt sick to my stomach. He was going to get into trouble because of me. I didn't know what kind of trouble exactly, but I didn't have a good feeling about it. And it was all my fault, because I couldn't handle one more day of living with Mike and having to pretend that everything was fine and that I didn't feel like tearing my hair out every single day. I knew I deserved better than what we had ended up with after ten years, and Mike deserved someone who would love him for him—everything he was, lacking or not. I knew I shouldn't have gotten involved with someone else before I had broken things off with him, but I hadn't gone into this with that intention. It had just happened. But deep down I knew that I had wanted it to happen.

"Okay, so then let me buy you a ticket here. You need to get out of there. That place is killing you, Jesse. You know it. It's slowly sucking you dry, and like you said, you're probably going to end up dead before you're thirty at this point."

"I dunno, Erin. Let me think about it, okay?"

"Okay," I agreed and wiped away a hot tear that had welled up in my eye. I tried hard not to feel so disappointed, but I couldn't stop the rising feeling of dread that was sweeping over me. The huge lump in my throat just wouldn't go away.

"Listen, you try to get some sleep. I gotta take care of something, but I'll call you tomorrow, okay?"

"Okay," I said again. "Good night." I quickly hung up the phone before I let the tears start to fall freely again. I pulled down the covers and crawled into the center of the bed, wrapping my arms around one of the pillows. Then I buried my face into the softness of that pillow and let the sobs shake my body. I cried and cried until I thought I must have drained all the water from my body through my eyes, and then I cried some more, finally drifting off to sleep from pure exhaustion.

It wasn't until hours later that my cell phone rang again, pulling me from my sleep. Groggily, I reached for my phone and looked to see who it was. Mike.

Sighing, I took a deep breath and debated whether I wanted to answer or not. In the end, guilt won out, and I answered.

"Hey," I said quietly.

"Erin?" Mike's voice was hoarse, like he had also been crying for hours. I was such a shitty person.

"Yes?"

"I've been sitting here for hours, thinking about everything you said, and I just can't let you go without a fight. Please...please think again about what you're doing. I don't want you to leave. I love you. So much. I know I haven't been the greatest at showing it, but I promise to try harder. We can see a therapist like you wanted. We can go out on more dates, you and me. We can try some new restaurants, wherever you want to go. I'd love to take you to the movies and get dinner tomorrow night. Will you let me take you out?"

"Mike, no...I can't. I told you I can't do this anymore with you. I love you—I'll always love you, but not the way you deserve. It's too late for us."

"It's not too late for us—you just don't want to try. You want this asshole from Kentucky to come out here and you don't even want to fight to save our life together. I don't even know who you are anymore, Erin."

"That makes two of us. I don't really know who I am anymore, either."

"Then you really shouldn't be making decisions like this right now. I'm worried about you. Forget what's between us, but this isn't like you, Erin. You're acting irrationally and making ridiculous decisions right now."

"You think they're ridiculous, but I don't. I think they're necessary." He was making me angry now, and I was dangerously close to hanging up, whether I felt bad for him or not. "Look, I don't want to keep arguing with you. I can't do this anymore right now. I'm exhausted and I need some sleep. We can talk some more tomorrow."

"No, please don't hang up, Erin. I can't sleep, either. Please keep talking to me. I love you so much. I don't know what I'm going to do without you. Please don't hang up." He kept pleading with me, and the emotion in his voice nearly undid me. The tears were coming fast and furiously now.

"I need to go. I'm so sorry," I said, my voice catching with sobs. I could still hear him begging me not to hang up as I ended the call. He immediately tried to call me back, but I ignored the call and turned the ringer off. After laying in the dark for another half hour or so, I finally drifted off to sleep.

When I woke again a few hours later, it took me a minute to realize that I wasn't waking up in my bed at home with Mike next to me. I was lying by myself in a cold hotel room. I had just broken up with my fiancé of ten years. I was in love with a criminal from Kentucky who was ten years my junior, and I had absolutely no idea what to do next. I wanted to stop time until I figured things out. I was obviously in over my head, caught in some kind of desperate quarter-life crisis. All I wanted right now was to get to the other side of this situation.

After lying in bed for another hour, thinking about what I was going to do next, I finally roused myself from my thoughts and got up to shower. I didn't linger, even though the hot water felt divine. I had a lot to do to get started on living my new life as a single woman. I wasn't sure what Jesse would decide—whether he would allow me to buy him a plane ticket or whether he would continue to remain stubborn and insist on waiting until he could afford to buy it himself or until I'd had a few more months to think things over and be by myself. I'd been with someone for ten years. I didn't know how to be alone.

Once I had dressed and dried my hair, I opened my laptop to look up some apartment listings on Craigslist. Encino was a great area, and I really enjoyed living there. If it was at all possible, I wanted to remain somewhere in Encino. To my delight, I found something that wasn't too far away from where Mike and I lived now. The rent was a little higher, but I figured it was worth taking a look, so I called the number listed and waited for someone to answer.

After a few rings, a woman with a heavy Russian accent answered.

"Hello."

"Hi, I'm calling about the ad I saw on Craigslist for a one-bedroom apartment in Encino. Is it still available?"

"Yes, it is."

"Oh great. Are you possibly available to show it to me sometime today?"

"Hmm, what time you want to come? You free now?"

"Oh um," I hesitated briefly, the whole thing becoming so very real again. I swallowed hard before answering, but I knew I had to keep putting one foot in front of the other if I was going to get through this in one piece. "Sure, yes. I could come by now. I'm about fifteen minutes away."

"Okay, I see you then. I'm Sylvia."

"My name is Erin."

"Okay, Erin, I see you soon."

"Thank you, Sylvia," I said before hanging up.

When I looked up the address of the apartment building on my Maps app, I realized that it literally was just down the block from where we lived now. I chewed on my lip as I drove, thinking that on one hand it would be awesome to be able to stay in the same neighborhood, but at the same time it might be awkward. If we still lived on the same block, chances were we might run into each other at any given time. At the grocery store, at the gas station, at my favorite restaurants. And once we both started seeing each other people, it could become even more awkward if we ran into each other. But this was one of the best options for places located close to where I worked that were safe and pleasant to live, yet still affordable.

In no time at all, I was pulling up in front of a small apartment building. I could literally see my building from where I stood on the sidewalk. I loved the look of the place. It was well maintained and had almost a cottage feel to it.

An older woman dressed in a gauzy white blouse and skinny sky blue jeans and wearing a pair of sunglasses was standing in front of the gate to the building. When she saw me, she smiled and waved.

"Hello, are you Erin?"

"Yes, I assume you're Sylvia?" I said as I shook the hand she offered me.

"Yes, hi, nice to meet you," she said as beckoned me to follow her through the gate that she had just unlocked. "So you are looking for an apartment for yourself, yes?"

"Yes, I um…well, I just broke up with my fiancé and we live together in an apartment down the street from here. So I may need to move, depending on what we end up agreeing on, and I saw this place listed on Craigslist and wanted to check it out. I love this neighborhood and would like to stay in it, if at all possible."

"Ah, I'm so sorry to hear that, but yes. This is a great neighborhood and I love it as well."

"Do you live here in this building?" I asked.

"No, I live in the neighborhood, though. I manage this building and one other—the one I live in."

"Oh that's cool."

"Okay, so I actually have two units I can show you. One is on the second level, and one is on the first. Both have been updated, so you're getting a great deal whichever you decide to go. One of them is slightly more than the other, so keep that in mind as I show them to you."

She unlocked the door of the first unit, which was located on the second level towards the back of the building. I almost gasped out loud as I walked into the living room. It had obviously recently been remodeled and upgraded, and it looked fantastic. Immediately I could see myself living there. After perusing the entire apartment, I turned and asked how much it was; she told me it was thirteen hundred. Yikes. I wasn't sure I could really justify paying that much rent on my own. Mike and I had been splitting the rent on our place, which was a little under twelve hundred, for the past six years. I was a little nervous at the thought of having to pay the entire rent on my own.

I asked to see the second unit, which she said was fifty dollars cheaper. It was also very pleasant looking, but she said it didn't come with a parking spot in the back of the building, so I would have to deal with street parking. That in and of itself wasn't really a big deal, since street parking was way less stressful and much more available than it was in Hollywood and the west side, where everything is permit parking and they have a zillion signs listed. I absolutely detested having to read through six freaking signs just to be able to tell if I could park somewhere. In the valley, all you had to worry about was which side of the street was street cleaning on which day of the week. I'd take that any day over having to deal with living in Hollywood or the west side with all their permit parking.

Thanking Sylvia for taking the time to meet with me and show me the units, I assured her I would call and let her know as soon as possible. When I got back into my car, I pulled up the calculator on my phone and started doing some rough math to figure out what my nut was for my current lost of living. After a while, I sighed heavily. I could theoretically make it work, but I was going to be pretty strapped for quite a while, and I was going to have to take an advance against one of my credit cards to pay for the security deposit. Sighing, I shook my head. I was going to have to ask Mike to move back in with his mom. I just didn't have any choice right now.

When I got home and let myself in, Mike was right there to greet me. He pulled me into a tight hug and I stood there awkwardly with my arms at my sides. Why was he making this harder for himself and for me? I didn't want to be touched by him right now. After a few moments, he realized I wasn't hugging him back and released me, stepping back to get a good look at my face.

"We need to talk about what's going to happen," I said as I moved past him to sit down on the couch.

"Okay," he said finally in a defeated tone, moving to sit down on the armchair next to me.

"I went to see an apartment just now."

"You did?" he asked, looking a little surprised, then his eyebrows lowered and he looked angry. "Not wasting any time, are you?"

"Mike, we have to be realistic about this. We're over. We need to start figuring out our living situation and what we are going to do next. The apartment I just saw was nice and I'd love to take it, but I can't really afford a security deposit right now."

"Okay. So what are you going to do then?"

I bit my lip, afraid to say the next words, but I didn't have much choice. "Well, you have family around here. I don't. So I'm hoping that you can move back in with your mom until you can figure out what to do next and let me have the apartment."

He nodded slowly. "I see."

"Please, Mike. I'm so sorry, and I know it's not fair, but I don't have anyone else to fall back on out here. I don't really have much of a choice, and you never really liked this place anyway."

"Okay, Erin. You can have the apartment."

"Oh, okay. Well, thank you, Mike. I appreciate it." I was surprised that it had been this easy to get him to agree. I had been expecting much more of a fight from him, but I suspected things were finally starting to sink in with him, and while he may hate me for leaving him right now, I knew he still loved me.

"Yeah…well…I'm going to need a little time to get everything moved, so I would ask that you be considerate of that fact."

"Yes, yes of course," I assured him. "Take the time you need." I just hoped he didn't take too long, because I was still hoping to get Jesse to agree to coming out here to L.A. sooner than later.

"Alright…well, I'll probably take a few loads over there today, and then I'll have to do more during the week after work, but I'll try to be out of here by the end of next weekend."

"Sure, no problem. I was going to stay at the hotel again tonight anyway, so if you want to stay here tonight, that's fine. I'm just going to go straight to work from the hotel tomorrow morning."

"Okay," he said, nodding.

"Okay then. I guess that's settled." I got to my feet and moved toward the front door, but Mike got up as well and stopped me before I could open the door to leave.

"Can I please have one more hug," he asked pleadingly. I just nodded and let him wrap his arms around me one more time. As we stood there, I thought to myself how perfectly we fit together. That had never been our problem. When he held me, it had always felt so nice...so peaceful...so safe. But it wasn't enough for me.

Chapter SEVEN

Getting up for work the next morning was a challenge. I was so depressed that I didn't even feel like moving, let alone getting myself ready to head into the office. But I had bills to pay, so I didn't have much choice.

My appetite was still pretty much non-existent, so I was going on Day 3 of eating next to nothing. I'd managed to force down a little yogurt and granola fruit parfait the day before, but that was it. The plus side was that I'd already lost five pounds. The thought of that actually perked me up a little and I secretly prayed that my lack of appetite would persist for a little while longer, although I wasn't too keen on the depression that caused it continuing.

I honestly don't know how I managed to get through the day. At lunchtime, I actually did take my lunch break—something I rarely did—and went upstairs to see if my friend Lisa was available to steal away for a few minutes. Lisa was the executive assistant to the CEO of the publisher we both worked for. She'd been with the company for ten years and was one of my closest friends at work. Not only had she been a great friend to me, but sort of a guide and mentor. We decided to take a quick break and do a walk around our building. I quickly explained the events of the weekend to her and waited for her reaction.

Lisa took it all in stride as she listened, nodding and occasionally interrupting me to ask a question. At the end, she sighed and shrugged her shoulders.

"I can't tell you what to do, Erin. You have to make that decision for yourself. I'm not too sure what to think of this Jesse kid, but whatever you decide, just please be careful, okay? I don't want to see you get hurt. But you most definitely deserve to be happy. You deserve it more than anyone I know."

I blushed and shook my head. "No, I don't. Everyone deserves to love and be loved. And Mike deserves someone who will love him just as he is. Or maybe he will change for the right woman—I don't know. All I know is that I can't waste any more time waiting for him to change for me. I can't force him to do the things that I wish he would do of his own free will. I can't force him to be sensitive and thoughtful and do nice things for me just because he loves me and wants to put a smile on my face or make my life a little bit easier. Fuck, now that I say all of this out loud, he kinda sounds like a complete douchebag."

Giving me a wry smile, Lisa laughed. "Um, I've been telling you that for how many years now?"

I laughed with her. "Uh yeah, well…better late than never. Better now before we get married and have kids and complicate things any further."

We were nearing the front entrance of the building when Lisa stopped for a moment and turned to give me a hug.

"Alright, girlie girl. I have to get back to work now, but keep me posted. You're going to be okay."

I nodded and thanked her for the chat before turning to head back to my desk and another massive pile of expense reports. Thankfully I managed to keep myself busy, and the rest of the day felt as if it passed relatively quickly. I couldn't wait to get home and talk to Jesse. I wanted to sleep in my own bed tonight…alone at last.

I was just leaving work when Mike texted me saying that he was going by the apartment to pick up a load of stuff and would be gone in an hour. I decided to kill some time going to the grocery store and then stopped by the gas station on the way home to fill up my tank. I didn't think I could handle coming home and seeing him pack up his things. The break-up was still too fresh.

I was a little nervous that he might still be there when I got home, but when I opened the door to the apartment, my mouth dropped open in shock.

There were roses everywhere I looked. He'd pulled the leather ottoman right by the front door so it'd be the first thing I'd see when I entered the apartment, and he'd left his laptop sitting there, displaying a bear holding a heart saying "I love you", with fresh pink and white roses circling around the laptop. I walked further into the apartment and saw two-dozen red roses arranged in a vase sitting on the kitchen counter and another two dozen roses of various colors in another vase on the dining room table.

Muttering under my breath, I headed into the bedroom. He was extremely tardy—we're talking years here—in making a big gesture, and I was already over it. I stopped in my tracks when I looked at my bed. He had spelled out "I love you" with roses, but shortened it to an I, a heart and a U. At the head of the bed was a large bouquet of stargazer lilies.

I was at a complete loss for words. I was shocked that he had made the effort, saddened that I didn't want to let it change my mind, and angered by the fact that he had just strewn fresh-cut flowers all over my brand new fluffy white bedspread. I began to pick the flowers up off the bed, slowly at first, but quickly picking up speed as my level of anger increased. Yep, I could see green stains from the flowers on what used to be pristine white. The rational side of me knew he was just trying anything he could to get me back, but I was beyond rational at this point.

I stomped from the bedroom into the kitchen and threw the flowers down on the table, then went around the apartment to shut all the windows. Idiot. Why would he have left the windows open like that?

As I stood there seething, I shivered all of a sudden and finally realized something. The dumbass had left the central air on full-blast, but hadn't closed the apartment windows. So now I was paying to cool the entire outdoors. Wonderful. And God knows how long it'd been like that, because I had no clue when he'd done everything and left again.

I moved into the living room to retrieve the rest of the roses from the ottoman and carry them to the kitchen table. Then I made myself take a few deep breaths and just wait a minute before I picked up my phone to text Mike.

Erin: *The flowers are lovely, but they don't change anything. Sorry.*

He texted back immediately.

Mike: *I had to try. Bought out three flower shops of all the roses they had to get everything I needed. One of the florists asked what I'd done and I told* *her I was trying to get my fiancé back. She said this would work. Heh, guess she was wrong. I love you, Erin. I always will.*

I felt like a royal bitch, and I was amazed that he'd relieved three flower shops of their entire rose inventory, but I didn't have it in me to give him any other kind of response. The feelings I used to have for him were not the same. I had loved him for ten years and gave him everything, but in all those ten years, he hadn't loved me the way I deserved to be loved, and I was tired of settling. I deserved someone who would show me his love equally…maybe not in the same ways, but I would feel the depth of his love in his actions and in his words. I wouldn't ever have to question how he felt, because he would make it a point to always make sure I knew. I wouldn't doubt him, because he would never give me a reason to. I knew this man existed, and I was really hoping that it was Jesse. I was really hoping I wasn't wrong about him.

When I called Jesse to talk and told him what I'd come home to, he asked me how I felt about it and I told him what I'd told Mike. It didn't change anything for me. I was not in love with Mike, and it was time for me to move on and be with someone who wouldn't just *tell* me he loved me but would *show* me he loved me. I wanted this so badly, more than anything else.

I brought up the plane ticket again, offering to pay for it if he would only say the word and accept my offer to come be with me. This time he hesitated, and I began to feel hopeful. He said he'd think about it, and I began to feel giddy with excitement as I imagined picking him up from the airport and running to meet him, feeling his strong, tattooed arms circle around me in a tight hug. We would finally get to kiss, and it would be magic. Promising to let me know tomorrow, he wished me sweet dreams before ending the call.

Crawling into bed, I turned off the bedside lamp and snuggled down into the covers. Sleep eluded me as I lay there quietly, my eyes wide open and staring blindly into the darkness as the events of the past few days replayed through my mind. So much had happened…so much had changed. A small part of me wanted to freeze the moment until I could settle myself again. Everything was out of whack and I felt so…unsettled. I needed to feel balance again, but I knew it would take a while for the storm to calm. It was probably going to get a whole lot worse before it started to get better.

Eventually I sat back up in bed, reached to turn the light on, and opened the nightstand drawer to retrieve my pipe and lighter. I had packed it with a fresh bowl earlier in the evening, predicting that I might end up needing it to fall asleep. The scent of the marijuana burning soothed me as I puffed away until the bowl was finished. Then I returned everything to the nightstand drawer and shut the light off once again. Sighing softly, I tried to get comfortable, tucking one pillow between my legs and another close to my chest as I curled one arm under another pillow and used my other arm to pull a fourth pillow closer to my face. So there I was in pillow heaven as I finally drifted off to sleep, a small smile curving my lips as I remembered how nice it was to fall asleep alone once in a while.

I felt refreshed when I woke up the next morning. Even the sight of all those lovely wasted roses piled haphazardly on my kitchen table couldn't dampen my spirits. I brought my Bluetooth speakers into the bathroom and cranked up the volume so I could listen to music while I showered. Ariana Grande's song, *The Way*, featuring Mac Miller came on next, and I sang along, my heart feeling light and full with my love for Jesse. I felt so hopeful for our future together. As I shampooed my hair, I mused to myself that Ariana's song was kind of perfect for us. Jesse was my bad boy, and I most definitely loved the way he loved me. I couldn't wait to see and feel the way he would love me in person. If I felt this good already and we hadn't even met face to face, I surmised that it could only get better.

My phone rang just as I was getting out of the shower, and I grinned like an idiot when I saw that it was Jesse.

"Hey, baby," I nearly sang into the phone. "Good morning!"

"Hey, sugar," he drawled back. "Morning to you, too. Did you get to sleep okay last night? Sorry I had to get off so soon, but I was about ready to drop. Needed some sleep desperately."

"Eh, I had to smoke a bowl before I finally drifted off, but that worked like a charm."

"That's good."

"Yeah, the sleep felt good, and I'm glad you got some as well."

"So listen, sweetie, I've been thinking about your offer."

"Yeah?" I said, my voice hopeful.

"Yeah, and I still don't like having to ask you for this at all, but I want to be there for you. So okay. You can go ahead and get me that ticket."

"Yeah?" I said again, but with a lot more excitement. I could barely keep myself from bouncing up and down.

"Yeah. Go for it."

"Oh hurray, baby! Yayyy, I'm so happy. You have no idea. I can't wait for you to be here with me."

"I can't wait, either. I love you, baby girl."

"I love you, too. So so much." I made a big kissing noise into the phone, making him laugh.

"You're cute," he said as he chuckled.

"So when should I book it for? How soon can you come?"

"Well, I do need to get a few things in order before I leave, and I still have to deal with telling the club I'm leaving, and that ain't gonna be pretty."

"How come?"

He sighed. "Club membership is a lifetime kinda thing. You're not really supposed to quit. You're not supposed to walk away."

"Why? What will they do to you if you do?"

"I may get my ass kicked. I will definitely be stripped of my patches and my cut. And I'll never ever be able to show my face here in Kentucky again."

I whistled softly. "Wow, that seems pretty harsh."

"It's the way it is. But you don't need to worry about that, okay?"

"Okay," I said hesitantly, but I was definitely worried about him now. I didn't want Jesse getting hurt because of me. I wanted to protect him and save him from that life that was quickly killing him.

"Good girl. Now, I need probably a week to get everything in order, so why don't you check the flights and see what you can find for next Wednesday."

"Okay. Any particular time that works better for you?"

"Yeah, try to get something late morning, cuz my mom and brother will have to drive me to Lexington and they won't be thrilled if the flight is too early."

"Alrighty," I said happily. "I'll send you the itinerary once it's booked. Yay, honey! I'm so excited."

"Me too, baby girl, me too. Soon I'll be there with you, holding you in my arms, and I'm never ever gonna let go."

I felt so warm and fuzzy inside as he said those words. Even my cheeks were warm as I smiled. He made me feel so safe and loved already. Only one more week now until I would be in his arms.

"Promise?"

"I fuckin' swear it to you, Erin," he insisted. "Never gonna let my BG go."

"BG?"

"Yeah, for baby girl. In fact, that's what I'm gonna call you from now on. Kay, BG?"

My lips curled into another smile and I nodded. "Kay. Do you have a nickname you like to be called?" I asked curiously. "Not that I'll call you that, cuz I might want to make up my own for you, but do they—does the club call you Jesse?"

"Nah, they call me JJ."

"Is that what you want me to call you?"

"No, BG, you can call me Jesse."

"Okay." I wasn't sure whether to be pleased or not that he wanted me to call him Jesse instead of JJ, but I reminded myself that he was trying to leave that part of his life behind, so it only made sense that he'd not want to be called by the name given to him by his club anymore. This was his chance to leave all of that behind, wipe the slate clean and have a fresh new start in California. I would do anything in my power to help him get that second chance at life.

"I gotta run. Call you later, kay?"

"Kay. Love you."

"I love you, BG. Talk soon."

The call ended and I stood there staring dreamily into space for a minute before finally rousing myself from my daydreaming. I needed to finish getting ready for work or I was going to be late. And I still had to load all of those roses in the car. There was no way I was keeping them all, but it was a shame for them to just go to waste, so I figured I'd take them to work and make bouquets for some of the girls at work.

When I got into the office, I headed straight for the kitchen and retrieved a few vases from below the sink where I knew we kept some spares. It took me a good fifteen minutes, but I was able to make some very pretty looking arrangements with the roses Mike had given me. At least they'd make someone else happy.

I was just finishing up the last one when Jerry came into the kitchen and stopped in his tracks, raising an eyebrow. "Oh you shouldn't have!" he exclaimed, smirking at me.

I smirked back at him. "I didn't. Mike did. After I dumped him this weekend."

"What? You broke up with Mike? Are you okay?" Jerry looked genuinely concerned, which touched me. For all his bad taste in women, he was a good guy and a pretty good boss most of the time.

"Oh yeah, it was my choice. I'm fine."

"Okay, well if you need to take a day or anything, just say the word. I know you guys were together for a long time, so whatever you need."

"Thanks, Jerry. I appreciate that," I said, smiling warmly at him. "It was a long time, but you know, I think it's for the best. But I'll be fine, so don't worry about me. I promise I won't let this affect my work in any shape, form or fashion."

"Oh, I'm not worried about you, kiddo. You're always the utmost professional in any situation. But seriously, we are all human, so if you need a day—take it."

"I'm good, I promise. Thank you again, sir."

"So do I get some of those flowers?"

I laughed and shook my head. "I was going to give them to the other girls, but do you really want some?"

He laughed with me and grinned. "No, I'm only kidding. I'm sure the ladies will appreciate you sharing your good fortune."

"Good fortune—ha. Interesting way of putting it. Anyhow, let me take these to the girls and I'll be at my desk shortly."

"No rush," he insisted before turning to fill his mug with coffee before leaving the kitchen again. "See you in a bit."

I turned to the counter for the first two vases and took one upstairs to Lisa and then went back downstairs to drop one off with Kristen. When I had stopped by to check on her before leaving work the other day when she'd been acting weird, she'd been heading to The Blue Door Lounge with her boss and some of the other people in their department for happy hour. Many a drunken night had been spent at the Blue Door, our company's local watering hole. I'd asked her if she was okay or if she needed to talk to me about anything, but she had waved me off and insisted she was fine. Then she tried to convince me to join them for drinks, but I had just wanted to get home to talk to Jesse, so I declined.

Kristen wasn't at her desk when I came by, so I put the flowers down and scribbled a quick note on a hot pink sticky pad that was sitting there. I took the last vase to Melissa, our awesome receptionist who had just started at the beginning of the year after Meg, our former receptionist, decided she wanted to be a stay-at-home mom and left the company to have her first baby. Meg had been one of my favorite people at the company and one of the best receptionists I'd ever worked with, but Melissa was an excellent replacement. She had the brightest smile and a good energy about her that I loved. When I brought her the flowers, she squealed and jumped up to hug me and asked what the special occasion was. When I explained to her what happened with Mike, her mouth dropped open in shock and she asked if I was okay. I assured her I was and thanked her for asking, then told her I had to get back to Jerry, but that I hoped she enjoyed the flowers.

There was a voicemail message from Mike waiting for me on my cellphone when I got back to my desk. I wasn't sure I wanted to listen to it. In fact, I was pretty damn sure I didn't want to hear anything he had to say right now, but I supposed it could be something important, and I wasn't a complete bitch. I pressed play and listened.

"Hey, it's me. Sent you an email just now with a song I heard on my way to work today. Made me think of you. Listen, I'd really love to get together for coffee and talk. I miss you. Call me back."

My eyes shot to my inbox and I opened his email. Opening the link, I saw that the song was *When I Was Your Man* by Bruno Mars. Reluctantly, I pressed play and watched the video and listened to the familiar song. I was pretty shocked at Mike's sentiment as he normally wasn't much of a romantic, and as I listened to Bruno croon and wail the words, the tears began to trickle down my cheeks. I grabbed several Kleenex and dabbed furiously at my eyes. This was so not the time or place for this shit. I closed the window before the song finished playing, grabbed my make-up bag and got up to use the ladies room.

I headed straight for the mirror and wiped the remaining tears from my eyes, trying my best to repair my make-up. I was just reapplying my eyeliner when a toilet flushed and one of the bathroom stall doors opened. Kristen came out of the stall and glanced at me, then back down again as she moved to wash her hands at one of the sinks. Her reflection in the mirror showed that she'd been crying.

I turned to her and reached out a hand to touch her shoulder. "Hey girl, are you okay?"

She sniffled and glanced at me, then shrugged. "Yeah, I'll be okay. Just stupid hormones, you know—PMS shit."

I nodded. "Yeah, I hate that. Being a girl sucks."

Laughing, she nodded as well. "Yup, sure does. Looks like maybe I should be asking you the same question, though. Are *you* okay?"

"Yeah...or I will be anyway." I leaned into one of the bathrooms stalls to grab a wad of toilet paper, then blew my nose noisily. "Mike and I broke up."

"What?" she gasped, turning to face me with wide eyes.

"Yeah, on Saturday. I went to a hotel and stayed there this weekend, then asked him if he could move in with his mom and stay with her while he found a new place—let me keep the apartment. He said okay, so he started moving his things yesterday, but when I got off work, I came home to an apartment full of flowers.

"Shut up! He brought you flowers?"

"Yep. Said he bought out three flower shops of their entire rose inventory."

"Wow, that must have cost a fortune!"

"I know. I don't know what he was thinking."

"Guess he had to make the grand gesture."

"I guess, but it was a *little* too late. Anyways, I brought most of them to work to share with you and a couple of the other girls. I left some on your desk a little bit ago."

"Oh, thank you! Sorry, I haven't been back to my desk, yet. Stomach issues," she said, looking mildly embarrassed.

I nodded. "Yeah, no worries. I left you a note there so you'd know they were from me."

"Cool, well I'm sure I'll enjoy them." She leaned forward to give me a hug. "Anyways, I gotta get back to it. Let me know if you need to take a walk and vent later or anything."

"Yeah, I might be in need of a cigarette later."

"Oh, yeah...well um, I'm actually trying to quit, but I still have a couple left if you want them. I'll still walk with you."

"Good for you, Kristen! Okay, I'll let you know if I get desperate."

"Later," she said and waved as she left the ladies room.

I took a few more minutes to finish pulling myself together before I headed back to my desk. After checking flights from Lexington to Los Angeles, I booked the cheapest one I could find and sent the itinerary to Jesse. His flight was arriving in the evening, so I would be able to work a full day and swing by home first to clean up before I had to be at the airport to pick him up. Thankfully, for the rest of the day I managed to focus on the tasks I had scheduled for myself and get them all completed. I was a professional, and I always did my job to the best of my ability, so I wasn't about to let my personal life ruin my professional reputation. I couldn't afford it. There was nothing for me to fall back on. If I lost this job right now, I was fucked—plain and simple. I no longer had a fiancé to rescue me temporarily until I could find something new.

Jesse texted me just as I was getting ready to leave the office and said he'd gotten my email with his flights. He thanked me and said to call him later when I got home from work. I texted him back and said I would be home in half an hour and sent him a kissy face. When he sent a long string of kissy faces back to me, I giggled and sighed. Maybe I was over thirty now, but that didn't mean I couldn't still feel like a teenager.

Chapter EIGHT

To my surprise, the next seven days went by more quickly than I had anticipated. I had expected each day to just drag, but I was so busy getting ready to send my team to a seminar up north in San Francisco that the days were just flying by. Thankfully I had Kristen's help putting all the travel packets together. We were both there until eight or nine a few nights that week, printing boarding passes and flight itineraries, making sure each folder had all the pertinent information that each employee would need for the entirety of their stay.

On Wednesday morning, I went into work earlier than usual so I could get a head start on the day and make sure I left on time. Jesse's flight was getting in around eight-thirty, so I had a couple of hours to get cleaned up and leave for the airport, and I was hoping I could squeeze in a mani/pedi. I wanted to look sexy for my new man, from my fingers to my toes. I'd already gotten a bikini wax the day before. He'd better appreciate all the trouble I was going to.

As soon as the clock ticked five, I was out of my seat and heading for the exit. Traffic was light and the drive home was quick, so I was able to stop by the nail salon to get my mani/pedi. I decided to do gel French tips and then chose soft pink polish for my toes. It was amazing how something as simple as a trip to the nail salon could make you feel like a new woman.

When I got home, I jumped in the shower and shaved everywhere. Then spent ten minutes blow-drying my long hair. I kept looking at the clock to make sure I was good on time. I had about an hour left, and I still had to figure out what I was going to wear and do my hair and make-up. After perusing the entirety of my closet for a good five minutes, I finally settled on a flowy black cotton tank top and paired it with a faded pair of blue skinny jeans. The tank top showed off my cleavage and the skinny jeans fit my legs like a glove. I loved my legs—they were my best feature and I'd always gotten compliments on them from both men and women.

I curled my hair and did my make-up, getting more and more excited as each minute passed. Jesse had sent me a text earlier while he was on his layover in Chicago. He'd begged me to please bring him a pack of smokes to the airport as he hadn't had a cigarette since he ran out right before his flight out of Lexington. I told him not to worry—I would have a pack waiting for him when he got to L.A. So after I was finished getting ready, I left the apartment and stopped by the nearest gas station to pick up a pack of Marlboro Reds.

The music was blasting in my car as I made my way down the 405 to LAX. I felt pumped and ready to take on the world. Jesse was finally going to be here with me where he belonged. My heart felt like it was about to beat right out of my damn chest as I approached the passenger pick-up curb. Just then my phone started ringing. It was him calling. He was here. He was *really* here.

"Hello?" I said a little uncertainly. I was so freaking nervous. This was it. This was the moment of truth. I was about to meet the guy I'd been talking to for the past few weeks who had somehow made me fallen head over heels in love with him even though I had never set eyes on him before.

"BG, where are you? I need a smoke so bad."

"I'm right here by the curb. I just pulled up like literally five seconds ago. Where are you?"

"I'm over here by the first sign for terminal one. I came over here to smoke and the fucking TSA took my damn lighter. I just want to smoke a goddamn cigarette. Is that asking too much? Hey man, hey! Hey! Do you have a lighter? Fuck. Dammit. Erin, where the fuck are you?"

I was a little stunned at how Jesse was talking to me. "Um, I'm right here, like right past the first sign for terminal one. I'm getting out of the car now and I'm looking around for you. What are you wearing?" I asked as I got out of the car and stood to turn and scan the crowd for him.

"White t-shirt, black jeans," he said gruffly.

I smiled to myself, thinking of what Charlie Hunnam would look like in a white t-shirt and black jeans. I still hadn't watched the show, but I'd Googled *Sons of Anarchy* after both Jesse and Allison had mentioned it. Jesse had said he was like Jax, so that's kind of the picture I had in my mind combined with the few pictures I had seen of him.

"I still can't see you, baby."

"Fuck, I'm right here by this fuckin' stupid ass airport rent-a-cop who won't lend me his fuckin' lighter. Fuckin' selfish asshole. I just want to smoke my goddamn cigarette."

The smile on my face faltered for a moment at the anger in his voice. Just then, I saw a guy in a worn baggy shirt that looked kind of old and dirty, worn black jeans and dirty white sneakers. He looked like he was kind of stooped over, almost like he had a slight hunchback. He was yelling at some poor TSA officer who was clearly getting irritated at his tirade and looked like he was about ready to call for back up. I was stunned. No way in hell that was Jesse. No way in hell.

I blinked and shook my head and looked around wildly, convinced I was looking at the wrong person. My Jesse looked sweet and sexy…not like this hunched over guy who was yelling at an airport official because he hadn't had a cigarette in several hours. I was about ready to get back into the car and drive off and pretend like I hadn't seen him. But he knew my address. What if he showed up and tried something? It was too late to change my mind. What the hell had I gotten myself into? I swallowed hard as he finally looked up and saw me. Even then, I still wasn't sure it was him. He looked nothing like the pictures I had seen.

He made a rude gesture to the TSA officer and then stomped off to the side to grab his suitcase before dragging it over to the curb where I stood by my car. I mumbled hello and immediately turned away from him to open the trunk of the car. Avoiding eye contact with him, I grabbed his heavy suitcase and lifted it into the trunk. He didn't say a word and just opened the passenger door and got in.

As I got back into the car, I reached over to hand him a lighter. He took it and muttered thank you, immediately lighting up and rolling his car window down. I glanced sideways at him when I paused to buckle my seatbelt before merging my way back into traffic. To my relief and dismay—both at once—I saw the same tattoos on his hands that I'd seen on Jesse's in his pictures. I turned on my signal to merge left and glanced behind me before slowly pulling back into traffic.

Once I got us back onto the 405, I had relaxed enough to glance over at him again. Jesse didn't say a word as I drove—just sat there hunched over, smoking his cigarette. When he finished the first one, he asked for the pack of smokes he'd asked me to get. I silently reached into the backseat for my purse and got the pack of smokes out for him. He ripped the package open and quickly lit up another cigarette.

"Um, are you okay?" I asked quietly as we neared Sepulveda pass. I maybe wished I had never set eyes on this guy now that I had met him in person, but I wasn't a completely heartless bitch.

He didn't answer right away, so I finally asked him again, a little more loudly this time. "Hey, Jesse. Are you okay? You're kind of freaking me out right now. You're not saying anything, and I don't know what's wrong."

"No, I'm not fucking okay, okay? I haven't had any of my pain meds since I left Kentucky and I'm not feeling so hot right now. In fact my back is fucking killing me."

"I'm sorry…didn't you bring any with you?" I didn't know much about prescription pain meds, but he was obviously in pain. And I didn't think my Advil was going to help him.

"No. My mom and my sister fuckin' stole a bottle from me right before I left. But I was leaving them…leaving them to fend for themselves, so I figured they needed it worse than I did. Didn't really think the withdrawals would hit me so fast or so hard."

"I see. Well can you get some more? Do you want me to take you to a pharmacy in the morning?"

"No, because I don't have a fucking prescription."

95

"Oh...well, how do you usually get it then?"

"Erin, it's club business. I told you. I can't talk about it."

"Well, you fucking made it my business when you got into my car telling me you're going through withdrawals from drugs. I don't know what I'm supposed to do right now." I was tired of him cursing and snapping at me, so I was going to give it right back to him.

"I need to get into a pain clinic as soon as possible. I can start taking Suboxin to get off the Oxy."

"Okay. We'll figure it out in the morning. Let's just get you home and into bed."

Once we got back to my place, I had warmed towards him a bit and started to see a glimpse of the guy that Jesse was when he wasn't going through withdrawals from prescription painkillers. He was still nowhere close to what I had pictured in my head, and nowhere close to how he'd looked in any of the pictures he'd sent me.

I showed him around the apartment and then he sat down on the couch and just stared ahead.

"I'm just going to sleep here tonight. Okay? I probably won't be able to sleep much anyway, and I'll keep you up."

"Yep, totally cool." I was only too happy to agree and get the hell out of the room as soon as possible.

"Hey um, do you have anything to drink?"

"Oh yeah, I'm sorry. Water's in the fridge. I'll get you some, but feel free to help yourself."

"Not water...I mean, you got some vodka or something?"

"Oh." I hesitated before answering. I did have some vodka and tequila in the cabinet, but that was it. I wasn't a big drinker, so I didn't really keep much of it around. But I didn't know if it was a good idea to be giving him alcohol.

"Look, I don't have any Oxy, and I'm going through withdrawals. I'm hurtin' real bad right now, and it's gonna be hell trying to go to sleep. If I drink enough, I might be able to knock myself out so I can at least get a night of sleep. In the morning, I can go to the ER and see if I can get them to give me an MRI and prescribe me some Oxy."

"You can do that?" I asked skeptically. I was also wondering how he expected to get to the hospital when he had no car and no money. Or how he was going to pay for it when he had no insurance.

"Yeah, I have a letter signed by my old doctor who fuckin' went and died on me last year, so it's hit and miss. Sometimes the doctor will be sympathetic and take pity on me and give me the Oxy, and sometimes he's a dick and refuses to and tries to get me into rehab instead."

"Um okay…well, I have to work in the morning. I guess I can take you to the ER before I go into work."

"Thanks," he said and then gasped, his eyes squeezing shut as he grimaced and leaned forward, clutching his stomach.

I frowned and then went to get the vodka from the kitchen cabinet. I brought it out to him with a shot glass and set it down on the coffee table.

"Thank you," he said gruffly.

"Sure," I said. I didn't know what else to do at that point, so I said I was heading to bed and would wake him up in the morning when it was time to get ready to go to the hospital.

Once I was safe in my bedroom with the door shut, I dressed for bed and crawled in under the covers. I pulled a pillow to me and started to cry softly. What had I gotten myself into? I had traded in one bad situation for something even worse. I had not realized how bad his addiction was or what would happen if he didn't have any. Never once had it crossed my mind that he might come here without any at all. I was furious with him for keeping it from me.

I had a rough time falling asleep, but finally I managed to drift off. When I went into the living room to wake Jesse early the next morning, the bottle of vodka I'd left with him was empty. I shook my head and picked up the empty bottle and shot glass and took them to the kitchen. Then I discovered that Jesse wasn't an easy person to wake up once he did fall asleep. And this idiot had just drunk an entire bottle of vodka by himself in one evening to make himself pass out and avoid Oxy withdrawals. I was living in some kind of Twilight Zone, waiting to be woken up at any moment, realizing it was all a dream.

It took me half an hour to get him herded into my car and then we were on our way to the hospital. I had a huge knot in my stomach as I pulled into the mostly empty parking lot next to the hospital. I so did not want to be here. I wanted to be a million miles away right now, but instead I was stuck here taking this loser drug addict to the hospital so he could get more Oxy. Reluctantly I followed him over to the front entrance and tried to make sense of all the posted signs, finally figuring out which way to go.

After he spoke briefly with a woman sitting at a desk, Jesse nodded toward a little waiting room that was just off to the side. I went inside and took a seat, twiddling my thumbs nervously while we waited for his name to be called. He didn't have to wait too long before a kindly looking doctor came to retrieve him.

"I'll be right here," I said as Jesse looked at me before nodding and getting up to follow the doctor out of the room.

After he was gone I let out a big breath I didn't realize I'd been holding, then glanced around the small waiting room. A young woman with her two small children was sitting across the way from me. She looked tired and snapped at the little boy when he reached over and snatched a toy from the little girl who had been sitting there quietly playing with it. Immediately the little girl opened her mouth and began to wail, her little eyes scrunched up with tears as she cried bloody murder. The little boy just sat there and laughed at her until the mom took the toy away from him and gave it back to his sister, and then his lips began to tremble and he began to cry as well. Meantime the little girl was still sniffling, but seemed to be calming down now that she had her toy back.

I closed my eyes as the little boy's shrieking grew louder and louder. I wasn't one to be prone to headaches, but I had a massive one forming right now. Thankfully, the mom handed over a sippy cup to distract him, which seemed to work because he shut up right away. None of the magazines looked appealing, so I turned my attention to the flat screen TV that was playing a music video. It was some song I'd never heard, but it was almost over. I could only shake my head and laugh at the next song that came on. Talk about perfect timing. As I again listened to Bruno Mars sing *When I Was Your Man*, I began to imagine Mike driving to work and listening to the same song, the tears forming in his eyes as he realized that it was really over between us. In no time at all, I had tears running down my cheeks. I dug through my purse for some Kleenex, but couldn't find any. I resorted to using the sleeve of my sweater to dab at my eyes.

Just as I was getting ready to get up and walk outside to get some fresh air, Jesse returned. He shook his head and turned and headed outside.

"Fuckin' prick wouldn't give me any. Thinks I'm some kind of junkie addict and tried to talk to me about rehab centers in the area. There another hospital around here?"

I barely managed to keep myself from groaning out loud. I looked at my phone to check the time. I had less than an hour left until I had to be at work.

"Yeah, there's another hospital about fifteen minutes from here, but you may have to take a cab back home, because I can't be late for work."

"Really? You can't just wait for me?"

"Jesse, I need to get to work. I can't afford to lose my job."

"I know, but I don't have any money for a cab."

I sighed as I got into the car. "I'll give you some cash for a cab if I have to leave you there."

The drive to the next hospital was silent other than for the sound of Jesse rolling down his window and lighting up a cigarette. When I finally pulled up in front of the ER, he got out and went inside after I told him I'd be waiting in the car. As I sat there checking my work email on my phone, I kept a close eye on the time. I felt sick to my stomach. I was caught in a nightmare that I didn't know how to end, and it was my own damn fault. What the hell was I thinking bringing some guy I didn't know all the way to L.A.? How had I been so naïve as to think that it could possibly be a good idea?

Half an hour later, Jesse finally called me to come pick him up from outside the ER. Amazingly enough, this time he had found a sympathetic doctor who had given him the prescription for Oxy that he was hoping for. I drove him to the pharmacy to drop off the prescription and then took him home, promising to pick up his prescription on my lunch break and bring it by.

When I got home that evening, I found Jesse grinding up a tablet of Oxy on a small plate. He seemed much more alert than he had been, and he was sitting up straighter.

"What are you doing?" I asked curiously as he took a credit card out of his wallet and started dicing the crumbs of Oxy on the plate.

"Hits harder if I snort it," he explained.

Oh great. Just when I thought this couldn't get any worse. Rolling my eyes, I left the room to put my stuff down in the bedroom, then returned to the kitchen to start making dinner. I had everything I needed to make spaghetti and garlic bread, so I turned the oven on to preheat and started prepping the noodles and sauce. I could hear Jesse snorting the lines of Oxy as I filled a saucepan with water to boil the spaghetti.

I was just starting to brown the meat for the sauce when Jesse wandered into the kitchen and came up behind me, wrapping his arms around my waist. I tensed immediately, not really wanting him to touch me, but he squeezed me and said, "I love you, BG. I'm so glad I finally feel straight again. Withdrawals off Oxy are the worst."

I just nodded like I understood and continued to brown the meat, not saying a word. "Dinner will be ready in about fifteen minutes. I'll bring it out to you."

"Mmm, smells amazing."

"It's just spaghetti," I said with a shrug.

"Well, it looks and smells better than what I'm used to, so I'm sure it's going to be delicious."

"Thanks."

"Hey, Erin, look at me."

I glanced up at him then back down to the saucepan. "Yes?"

"Hey," he said again and put his hand on my arm until I stopped stirring the sauce and turned the burner off, turning to him. "I'm sorry I put you through that, Erin, but I'm straight now. Everything is gonna be okay. Your man is here now, and I'm gonna take care of you."

I looked at him skeptically and shrugged. He reached out and pulled me forward into his arms. At first I just stood there stiffly, not returning the embrace, but then I got a whiff of his cologne and my resolve weakened. He'd finally taken a shower and now that he wasn't going through withdrawals, he wasn't standing hunched over anymore, and he had cleaned himself up pretty well. Slowly my arms rose to circle his waist and I clung to him tightly as the tears began to fall. Jesse just stood there and held me, letting me cry, patting my back and murmuring that everything was going to be okay.

Later that night at my invitation, Jesse crawled into my bed and wrapped his arms around me, holding me as we drifted off to sleep. This was what I had been dreaming about for the past few weeks.

When I woke in the morning, I felt a hundred times more optimistic about the entire situation. Maybe Jesse was right and everything *would* be okay now.

"Hey babe," he said groggily when I woke him. "Can you do me a favor and bring me my pills?"

"Sure," I said and left the bedroom to retrieve them from the coffee table in the living room. When I returned and handed the bottle to him, he asked for the plate as well. I rolled my eyes, but brought him the plate. Then I watched as he took two tablets out and then closed the bottle and handed it back to me.

"Okay, the doctor only gave me a small prescription, so until I can get into a pain clinic, I'm going to have to make this last. I need you to hide these from me. I'm taking one for now, one for later today, and then you can give me the third one tonight when you get home from work."

I blinked and just looked at him. "Seriously?"

"Yes, seriously. Hide them from me, Erin. I need to pace myself and I can't trust myself to not take more than I truly need. I'm an addict."

Sighing, I took the bottle from him and left the room, muttering to myself as I looked around for a good hiding place. I finally settled on stashing it in

one of the drawers to my entertainment center. When I left for work, I was torn between feeling relieved that Jesse seemed to be back to normal and feeling stressed and worried that he was going to run out of the pain meds again.

The weekend was actually somewhat enjoyable, but when I came home from work on Monday, Jesse asked me for his third pill as soon as I set foot in the door. Of course he saw where I had hidden the bottle when I went to retrieve it, so yet another hiding place was out. It was already getting difficult to think of new places to hide his pill bottle, and I hated that he'd asked me to do this for him. I hated the fact that he even had to.

We actually attempted to have sex that night, which turned out to be a total disaster. Before I met Jesse, I didn't know it could be an issue, but apparently some guys had problems getting it up when taking medication such as Oxy. He apologized profusely to me, telling me it wasn't me and that he wished he could keep it up long enough that he could fuck the shit out of me. *So romantic.*

The next morning, I knew Jesse was already running low on the Oxy, which sent me into a state of panic. I didn't have the money to be sending him to a pain clinic, and I had told him so. He said he would ask his mom if she could help out a bit and send him some money via Western Union. What was I going to do if he couldn't get more Oxy or this other Suboxin stuff he'd mentioned before he ran out of his current prescription?

When I handed the bottle to him, he only took out one tablet and said he would split it and take one half now and one later, and then another when I got home from work. I was nervous when I got home that night because I knew he wouldn't have had his normal dosage, and I wasn't sure how bad his mood would be. But thankfully he seemed to be just fine and was in great spirits, so I was able to relax and enjoy a nice evening together with him. I even decided to take him out to BJ's for some deep-dish pizza, which he loved.

I had to fly to Las Vegas the next day to do some scouting for an event that we were going to have there later in the year. Rolling out of bed to get ready, I reached into the back of my closet to find the Jesse's pill bottle so I could take out another tab to leave for him. Only as my hand reached into the space, my fingers met nothing but empty space. Confused, I patted my hand up and down that area of the closet, feeling around for the hard plastic, but I couldn't find anything. As I began to realize that Jesse must have gone through my things looking for the bottle, I became furious. I woke him up and hissed at him as he looked at me through bleary eyes.

"Godfuckingdammit, Jesse. Why the fuck did you bother asking me to hide your pills if you were just going to end up going through my shit to find them? Now you have nothing left and you're going to start going through withdrawals again. I can't believe how selfish you are. I can't freaking believe you pulled this shit on me right when I have to leave town for work."

I didn't wait for him to answer me but stormed off to the bathroom to take a shower and get ready to leave for the airport. Before I walked out of the apartment, I returned to the bedroom where Jesse was still laying in bed.

"Look, Jesse, this is just not going to work. You and I are over. You need to get out. I don't care what you do, but you need to figure it out. I don't want you here when I get back from Las Vegas."

Before he could protest or say a word, I turned on my heel and stormed down the hallway to the front door. He called after me, but I was beyond caring. I had no use for his lies and worthless promises. I slammed the front door on my way out, pissed at Jesse and the entire fucked up situation, but also at myself for allowing it to happen.

As I stormed into the parking lot at the back of the apartment building, I ran into my neighbor friend Josh. He took one look at my face and asked me what was wrong. My lip trembled for a moment as I sniffed and fought to hold back the tears, but it was a doomed effort. Everything that was happening was just too much for me to handle gracefully at the moment.

Josh's face fell when I burst into tears, and he quickly moved forward to give me a big hug. "Aww, Erin, don't cry."

"I'm sorry, I just don't even know what to do right now. I have so royally fucked up my life, and I haven't got a clue how to start piecing it back together."

A little sob caught in my throat as I thought about how quickly I had gone from feeling on top of the world to wanting to die.

"Well, lady, I'm assuming this has something to do with you breaking up with Mike, and this new kid you've got visiting you?"

I sniffed again and nodded, wiping the tears from my eye with a napkin I'd found in my purse. "I plea momentary insanity and all I can deduce is that I'm currently suffering from some kind of quarter life crises."

"I see," he said, a half smile quirking his lips. "Well, what exactly is the issue right now? I mean, I'm taking it that things are not working out so well with the new guy?"

"Definitely not," I agreed. I didn't have a lot of time to spare as I needed to get to the airport soon or I was going to miss my flight, but I took a few minutes to explain the events of the past week. Josh's eyebrows rose higher and higher on his forehead as I told him everything. I even told him about some receipts for guns and bullets that Jesse had shown me on one of his better nights.

When I finished, he shook his head. "Damn, girl. That is quite the story, and very fucked up indeed. I hate to say this, but it sounds like you totally got Catfished."

"Come again?"

"Catfished…it's this stupid show on MTV about online dating. A catfish is someone who creates a fake profile on like Facebook, as an example, and pretends to be someone else. Usually they try to trick a person into falling in love with them. So the show investigates into each possible Catfish situation to find out if that's what's what's going on, or if the person is really who they say they are. It's pretty hilarious and sad at the same time. But yeah, dude, totally sounds like you got Catfished."

Was Josh right? Had I really let myself get Catfished? I shook my head as I thought about the possibility. I was so disappointed in myself for being so blind and foolish. This kid had probably been targeting me from day one. He found an unhappy woman in her early thirties who was dumb enough to fall for his shit and pay for him to get the hell out of Kentucky.

"Ugh, I hope you're wrong, but I guess it sounds like it's totally possible. What about the receipts for the guns and bullets, though?"

"You said he's from Kentucky. Probably everybody and their mother has a gun out there."

"Hmm, good point," I acknowledged. "Anyways, I really have to get on the freeway or I'm going to miss my flight."

"Oh shit, where are you going?"

"Vegas—just a day trip. It's for work."

"Oh man, talk about shitting timing."

"I know! Ughhh…do me a favor, will you? If you're around at home at all today, would you mind just keeping an eye on my apartment and let me know if you see him come out acting suspicious or if you hear anything crazy? I'm a little nervous leaving him here after I just ripped him a new one."

"Alright, but I'm not going near your apartment door. I kind of like being alive."

"Of course, like I said. Just if you happen to see or hear anything, give me a buzz."

"Will do. Have a safe flight, okay? And try not to stress out too much. You'll get it all figured out when you get back."

I sighed and nodded and leaned forward to give him another quick hug. "Thank you. I really appreciate it. Talk to you later, okay?"

"Yep," he agreed, nodding to me as he turned and headed back into the building.

My phone beeped with an incoming text message. Glancing down, I saw that it was from Jesse, but I was still too worked up to deal with him. I needed some time to calm down. I would talk to him when I got home from Vegas. Right now I needed to clear my mind and focus on work.

Chapter NINE

On my way to the airport, my mother called to tell me that my grandmother (her mother) had passed away. She had recently entered hospice and hadn't been doing too well. Numbly I thanked her for calling to let me know and mumbled my condolences. Then I apologized for not being able to talk to her longer, but I had a plane to catch for a business trip. She said it was okay and to call her later if I wanted to talk.

If I thought I couldn't feel any worse than I already did, I was wrong. My grandmother and I had never been as close as she may have wished, but that was because her main priority ever since I had moved to L.A. had been attempting to keep me on the straight and narrow by constantly nagging me to go to church again.

As I thought sadly about the fact that I'd never again hear her sing, "I love you, a bushel and a peck, a bushel and a peck and a hug around the neck," my eyes remained surprisingly dry. I didn't know if it was because I was in shock or if it was because I was still too pissed off by Jesse's betrayal, but I couldn't even will the tears to come at the moment.

When I got to the airport, I looked at the time and felt relieved that I'd arrived with a bit of time to spare. As I parked my car and started walking towards the terminal, I took a deep breath of the fresh morning air. It had rained recently, so the air actually felt pretty clean and crisp for L.A. In spite of everything, it was a beautiful day outside. I smiled to myself as I reminded myself to be grateful for all the good in my life, but the feeling quickly faded when my phone started ringing. It was Jesse. Pressing a button, I ignored the call and got in line for the TSA security check.

Clearing security didn't take long, and soon I was sitting at my gate waiting for my flight to board. My phone rang again, but I again ignored it and pulled out my laptop. We still had fifteen minutes until boarding time, so I figured I'd try to get some writing done. It'd been way too long since I'd spent any time on my latest book, with all the personal hullabaloo that'd been going on in my life. But I might as well saved the effort, because Jesse was relentless in his attempts to reach me. The phone would not stop ringing. He'd already left three voicemails, none of which I had listened to.

Against my better judgment, I finally relented and listened to the first message. It was a minute long tirade with Jesse going off at me, accusing me of not even wanting to try, of wanting him to fail, of not trusting him. He claimed he had told me that the reason he had taken the rest of the Oxy was that he had an appointment at a pain clinic today, and that if he was going to get off of the Oxy, he needed to get rid of it all before he started the Suboxin treatment.

Rolling my eyes, I listened to the next message, where he had calmed down a bit and was pleading with me to just call and talk to him. The third message, he was downright begging me not to send him back to Kentucky. He said he was a dead man if he set foot back in Corbin. Upon hearing that, I shook my head in disgust. I didn't know what to believe from him anymore.

He left a fourth message as I was listening to the third, saying that he would be getting on a bus to take him to some shelter in Compton if I didn't call him back soon. He said it was my last chance. *Ha.* Yes, please! He could get on that bus and let it take him anywhere but where I was. I didn't care anymore. But then he pleaded with me again, asking if I'd let him stay with me a little longer, just as a friend. He would sleep on the couch—he just needed that second chance at life. He would get a job ASAP and save up and move out and get his own place. He begged me to consider it and asked me to please call him. I sighed and turned my phone off as my group was called to board. This was so not what I needed to be focused on right now.

Regardless of the fact that I felt like I was developing an ulcer from dealing with all of the stress that had entered my life since I'd met Jesse, I managed to get through all of the site walks I had scheduled for myself when I'd started planning this venue scouting trip. It was my job to plan the holiday party for our department every year, but this was the first time we were taking everyone to Las Vegas. I was both terrified and excited at once by the challenge, but the pleasure I'd normally have taken from the entire process had been sullied by the aftershocks of the self-destruction of my personal life. My sanity was hanging on by a thread these days, but I knew I had to keep pushing through. The instinct to survive is what has driven me to keep keepin' on all my life. Life could throw whatever curveballs it wanted, and maybe I had to be hit with a few of them before I learn how to knock that shit out of the park, but I knew I would get there. Sometimes it's hard to see the light at the end of the tunnel, but I had to have faith that it was there, even if I couldn't see it, yet.

I was at the Neon Boneyard, my first appointment of the day, but I was half an hour early because it had only taken me twenty minutes to get there. I asked the security guard where the restrooms were and excused myself so I could freshen up. I nearly gasped when I took a good look at myself in the mirror. The Vegas heat combined with the exertion of getting around the airport had the make-up melting on my face, and I had three huge pimples on my nose! Ughhh…wonderful, just wonderful! I dug around in my oversized purse, frantically searching for some cover-up and powder. Finally I located the small tube and compact in the side pocket and began covering up the small patch of evil. I was so stressed out and had been eating like crap, so it was no wonder, but I felt so embarrassed anytime I broke out. It's like your skin is screaming, "I'm an unhealthy slob who eats fast food!"

Once I was satisfied with my appearance, I returned to the lobby area and waited for my contact to come retrieve me for our site walk. My phone buzzed with an incoming text message, but I ignored it after seeing that it was from Jesse. Nothing was more important than my job right now. A few moments later, a pleasant looking older woman with soft, wavy brown hair greeted me with a warm smile. I liked her immediately. She introduced herself as Teresa and beckoned me to follow her.

The tour didn't take long, and I didn't have a lot of questions for her. Everything would have to be rented separately and brought in if we wanted to have our event there, which would be a lot of hassle. I was already going to be very busy with booking everyone's flights, so I was hoping I thanked her for her time and then called a cab to pick me up. My next destination was Lavo at The Palazzo, and I ended up being early for that appointment as well. Fortunately my contact was available since she had a last minute cancellation right before me. She showed me both Lavo and Tao, which was right next door at The Venetian. I wasn't blown away by Lavo, which seemed kind of small, but I really loved Tao. The cleaning crew was still working on the remnants of the previous night's party, and silver confetti was strewn everywhere. I made a mental note to come back the next time I was in Vegas, regardless of which venue I ended up picking for our party.

Hyde at Bellagio was next up on my list, but my contact wasn't available until our scheduled time, so I wandered off into the slot machine area and found my favorite game—the Goldfish. It was my addiction. I didn't really understand all the mechanics of the possible ways to win, but I knew if I kept hitting the button with the fish food bonus, eventually I would get to play one of the bonus rounds. The person who invented this damn game was an evil genius who obviously knows how to cater to the inner child. Hi, my name is Erin. I'm over thirty and I get excited by the fish food bonus. Twenty minutes later I had twenty dollars less in my wallet, but I had gotten to play the fish food bonus twice. I was relatively happy, considering everything.

When I finally followed my contact into Hyde, a smile immediately broke out on my lips. Some guy with spiky brown hair who I assumed might be the DJ was doing a sound check and had just started playing *Crystallize* by Lindsey Stirling, one of my favorite songs ever. He winked at me as a major grin broke out on my lips. I freaking loved dubstep, and throw in the violin and it's just crazy good. I took it as a good Omen that this just might be the place.

Just then the water fountain show began right outside the window, and I had the most incredible front row view. Besides having Lindsey's blessing and my eye on the cute DJ, I loved the ambiance and the décor, and you couldn't beat the fabulous view with the fountain right outside. After I drilled the poor sales manager relentlessly for all the details, I said I'd get back to her when I returned to L.A.

On the way to the airport, I checked my messages and had a new one from Jesse. It was a final plea for me to give him one last chance to stay with me until he got on his feet. His voice was broken like he had been crying, and my resolve cracked a little as I listened to him beg. It was my fault that he was there after all. I had flown him out to L.A., promising to help him start his life over, and here I was kicking him to the curb. What kind of insensitive monster was I, regardless of the fact that I felt deceived and taken advantage of? I sighed to myself, knowing that I was going to cave and offer him my couch for the time being.

My plane was about to take off when I finally texted him, saying he could stay on the couch for a few months while he got back on his feet, but then he needed to move. He texted me back immediately, thanking me and swearing he wouldn't let me down. As I switched my phone to airplane mode and leaned back in my seat to wait for takeoff, I had a feeling I was going to regret my decision, but I wanted to believe he could still turn his life around and that bringing him to L.A. hadn't been a complete waste.

When I finally got home that night, I joined Jesse on the porch for a smoke. I'd picked up the nasty habit again when he'd arrived, as it was easier for me to stand being around cigarette smoke if I was also smoking myself. He'd gone to the pain clinic after his mom sent another money order and gotten more Oxy, so he was at least in a decent mood. We talked things over and I told him that things between us were over for good, but that I accepted responsibility for bringing him out to L.A., so I was letting him have the couch for now. I warned him that this was his last chance, then bid him good night and headed for bed.

By the time the weekend came, I was ready to change my mind again and send him straight back to Kentucky. He had ripped through his pills too quickly once again and started going through withdrawals on Friday night.

As I sat in my bedroom that Saturday afternoon with the door closed, huddled in bed with my laptop trying to work on my latest book, the tears began to fall. I couldn't do this. I couldn't save Jesse. I couldn't be that selfless person. I had to be selfish right now or I was going to lose my freaking mind.

I placed an ad on Craigslist to find someone to grab coffee with just to get me out of the apartment so I didn't have to listen to him going through the painful symptoms of withdrawal. He'd been vomiting all weekend and it sounded absolutely wretched. Feeling bad that he was suffering so much, I'd offered to bring him back some food when I got back, which he gratefully accepted. And then he promptly threw up everything again later that night.

When Monday morning came, I headed into the living room to give Jesse the news of my changed decision. I told him that since I took partial responsibility for him coming out to California, I would get him a plane or bus ticket anywhere he wanted, but he had to leave. He simply nodded, not looking surprised, then croaked that he had tore the lining of his throat from all the vomiting and asked if I could give him a little time to recover before he had to get on a plane back to Kentucky. I told him he had until Wednesday and then I headed to my laptop and booked his ticket, muttering under my breath that I knew he'd been full of shit when he said he could never return to Kentucky. He'd only been stalling, trying to convince me to let him stay.

I ended up lending him the money he needed to get his next prescription of Oxy that day. I couldn't in good conscience send him away feeling like he had coming off of it, so it was the last thing I agreed to do for Jesse other than driving him to the airport that Wednesday morning. When I got out to help him with his bags at the airport, he swore he would pay me back and said he hoped I'd remain friends with him, even if we weren't together anymore. I gave him a hug and told him of course I would continue to be his friend.

I felt a heavy weight lift from my chest as I drove away, watching him in my rearview mirror as he trudged forward into the terminal. I did care about him still, even if I wanted to get as far away from him as possible right now. But I was so glad it was over. I couldn't wait to walk into my apartment and have it completely to myself again.

That day at work was fantastic. Processing expense reports and booking meetings had never been that much fun, but right now, I was happy to be doing them. I was so relieved to have Jesse gone and have my life back to normal again. The fantasy of being with someone like MC President Jax Teller was dead.

I couldn't wait for my trip home to Hawaii to see my family. It was quickly coming up in a few weeks, and I needed to get my ass back into the gym so wearing a bathing suit wouldn't be quite so embarrassing. I had my very first book signing coming up next weekend in San Francisco, so I was flying up to San Jose to meet up with my friend Allison, who was also doing the same book signing. My life was about to get super busy, and I welcomed the return to normalcy with open arms.

When I got to San Jose the following week, Allison picked me up from the airport and I filled her in on all the gritty details of the past few weeks. She gave me an "I told you so" look, but wisely said nothing.

"So does this mean you're going to get back together with Mike?" she asked as she pulled into the parking lot of her apartment building.

I shook my head. "I don't know. I broke up with Mike for a reason, and that hasn't changed, but I do question whether I made the right decision. Maybe things would get better if we were both actively working on our issues."

"Have you talked to him at all?"

I shook my head. "No, he texted me once, asking if I wanted to get some coffee with him, but I declined. It's just too painful to see him right now. I feel just awful about the fact that I hurt him, even if it's partially his fault that it had to come to that."

Allison nodded as she pulled into the garage. As we got out of the car, she pointed to some boxes that were stacked against the wall. "The bottom two are my books for the signing tomorrow, and then your box that you shipped to me is right there on top."

"Oh awesome, thank you!"

"Brian is coming with us tomorrow. He's going to be my assistant."

"Putting him to work, eh? Sounds good. I hope I don't need an assistant."

"I'll share him." When I raised my eyebrows at her, she laughed. "You know what I meant. He can assist both of us."

I laughed and winked at her. "Yes, I know what you meant. It just sounded funny."

We didn't stay up late that night since we had to get up early and drive to San Francisco. Brian helped us load all of our shit into the car, and then we were off, swinging by Mickey D's on the way to pick up breakfast and by Starbucks to pick up coffee. I needed that sweet, sweet caffeine to help wake me up. The drive to San Francisco didn't take long, but I nearly had a heart attack when we arrived and I saw how expensive parking was around there.

Allison and I started unloading the car while Brian went in search of a bellhop trolley, then all three of us headed to the ballroom to start setting up our shared table for the very first time. It was fun to figure out how I wanted to set up my swag, and in no time at all, I had arranged everything in a satisfactory manner. As we both sat down in our chairs and got ready for them to open the doors, we exchanged nervous smiles.

"Here goes nothin'," Allison said.

"What happens if no one comes to see me?" I asked, gulping hard.

"People will come—don't worry."

She was right…people did come, but not to see me. They were all there to see her and most of the other authors, with the exception of maybe one or two people who had actually bought my book or who brought a photo book with pictures of everyone's book covers. And one blogger who had flown all the way from Australia that morning bought a copy of my book from me at Allison's encouragement. But I didn't feel too bad, because I saw one of the successful indie authors sitting at her table with practically no one there to see her either all afternoon.

All in all, it was an interesting experience. As I watched some of the other authors break down their tables after the signing was over, I took mental notes of other kinds of swag that I saw displayed. So far I only had bookmarks and postcards of the cover art for my first book, and I was curious as to what else I could do that wouldn't be too expensive but still fun for the readers.

The Cheesecake Factory was our restaurant of choice for dinner that night to celebrate surviving our first book signing together, but also because it was our tradition. We loved that place so much and had been going there whenever we visited each other as long as we'd been friends. With a Pomegranate Margarita in her hand and a Peach Bellini in mine, we toasted to what we both hoped was the beginning of our long and illustrious careers as romance authors.

The next day we were laying poolside trying to get a tan when a Facebook notification popped up on my phone. When I glanced down to see what it was for, I saw that some girl whose name I didn't recognize had liked one of my pictures. Curious, I logged into my account and pulled up the picture in question. It was a picture I had taken of Mike and his brother at Christmas the year before. I clicked on the girl's name and scrolled through her pictures and timeline. She didn't have her account set to private, so I was able to see a lot of what she had posted even though we weren't friends.

"Look at this," I said to Allison, who was laying back in her lounge chair with her sunglasses on and her eyes closed, her face tilted towards the sun.

Cracking one eye open she looked at me, then took my phone as I handed it to her. "What am I looking at?" she asked.

"Some chick I've never heard of before just liked a couple of my pictures of Mike, and she's Facebook friends with him. Her name is Anabelle Price."

"Maybe she's just a friend," Allison suggested, but I wasn't buying any of that bullshit.

Texting Mike, I asked if he was seeing anyone. He texted back a few minutes later saying he had gone out on a date with someone, if that's what I was asking. I texted back, asking if it was this Anabelle chick. His response was immediate with him demanding to know how I knew that. I told her she had liked my pictures on Facebook, so I'd gotten notifications for it. Muttering a string of colorful expletives, I shook my head in disgust as I tossed my phone on the table beside me.

"I can't freaking believe him. He tries to make me feel so guilty, like I broke his heart and ruined his world, and then he is already dating someone else?"

"You left *him* for someone else," Allison reminded me, but I just waved her off and continued my rant.

"Doesn't matter. He acted like I was *it* for him. I just want him to admit that I was right. We weren't right for each other. That's all."

"And that would solve everything and make you feel better?" Quirking an eyebrow at me, Allison stared me down until I squirmed uncomfortably in my lounge chair.

"No, it won't solve everything, but yes, it would make me feel better." I stuck my tongue out, making her laugh.

"Your trip to Hawaii is coming up soon, isn't it?"

"Yep, I leave two weeks from this coming Wednesday."

"Are you excited?"

"Yes and no...I still have Mike's ticket that I bought for him. You know this trip was supposed to be his thirtieth birthday present."

"Man, that sucks. And you can't transfer the ticket to someone else, like maybe your sister? Or me?"

I laughed and shook my head. "I wish! But no, it's non-transferable. Only he can use it. He'll have several months to reuse the credit if he wants."

"You're going to give him the credit?"

Shrugging, I nodded. "It's not that big of a deal. I cashed in my AMEX points for our tickets anyway, so in reality I only paid like sixty dollars total for both our tickets."

"Still, now you're out AMEX points that could have been applied to a plane ticket for one of your upcoming book signings."

"True."

"You could ask him to go with you...still use his ticket."

I nodded thoughtfully. "I could. I'm not really sure at this point if I made the right decision. Maybe it would be good for us to have the time along together and figure out if there is something still there."

"I think you should do it. Ask him to go."

I nodded again. "Yeah, I think I will. But I'll wait til I get back to L.A. and ask him to dinner so I can see him in person when I ask him to go."

"Good call. Then this Anabelle chick can take a hike."

"Yeah." Even though I'd been the one to break things off with Mike, and for another guy at that, I did feel jealous that he had moved on so quickly. After that grand gesture of filling my apartment with flowers, it seemed premature for him to have started dating someone else this soon. All of a sudden, I couldn't wait to get back home to L.A. I decided to go ahead and text Mike now to see if he could grab dinner the next night.

Erin: *Hey, wanna grab dinner tomorrow?*

Mike: *Sure. Where?*

Erin: *Sushi? 7 PM?*

Mike: *Okay.*

Well, that was easy. Now I just had to convince him to still come to Hawaii with me after I tore his world apart and broke his heart and moved some drug addict kid from Kentucky in with me for a couple of weeks. No big deal.

Chapter TEN

When I walked into our usual sushi restaurant, I felt little flutters of nerves in my stomach. That was a good sign. That meant I still felt something for Mike. But what if I didn't want to feel anything? Honestly, I wasn't sure what I wanted anymore. He wasn't there, yet, so I asked for a table for two and sat down to peruse the menu while I waited for him to arrive.

Mike showed up a few minutes later and said, "Hey," as he sat down in the chair across from me.

"Hey," I echoed.

He didn't look at all different than the last time I'd seen him. I don't know why I expected him to.

"So, how have you been?" I asked, trying to start up the conversation. Talking to him over meals had never been easy. He was a man of little words and prying a conversation out of him was like pulling teeth.

"Okay," he said simply, not giving any indication whether okay really meant okay.

"You going to see that Anabelle chick again?"

He just shrugged. "I dunno. Maybe."

I nodded, my throat feeling tight. To stall for some time before taking the plunge and asking him about Hawaii, I looked down at the menu again. "Should I order, or do you want to?"

"You can order."

"Okay." I waved at our waitress and she came over to take our order. "We'll have the rainbow roll, the Hiro's spicy tuna and the White Lightning," I rattled off, listing our usual favorites.

She nodded and asked Mike if he'd like anything to drink as she took our menus. He ordered a Sapporo, and then I asked if I could have another White Cranberry cocktail as well. I'd already sucked down the first one I'd ordered while I'd been waiting for him to get there. This request was going to take a little liquid courage. Especially if he turned me down. It was weird being there at the restaurant together, but yet not together. In one aspect, it felt like nothing had changed, like nothing had happened. Yet at the same time, everything had changed.

"So how's work?"

"Same."

"Gotcha…how are things going at home with your mom?"

"Okay."

Did I really want to take him to Hawaii with me? He was such a thrilling conversationalist. Again I questioned why I wanted to consider fixing things with him. But at this point, I kind of really just didn't want this other chick stepping into the picture before the dust had even settled. Mike was such a quiet guy—it had never occurred to me that he might find someone else to date so quickly. I guess I should have thought about that before I broke up with him.

"Your birthday is coming up soon," I said casually.

"Yeah."

"You gonna do anything? It's a big one for ya. Dirty Thirty!"

"I dunno, probably get some beers with the guys or something."

"Hmm…well," I paused uncertainly, afraid to hear his response as I was pretty sure it wasn't going to be what I wanted. "You know, you could be spending it in Hawaii with me."

He raised an eyebrow at me and didn't answer for a moment. "What happened to your new boy toy?"

"Went back to Kentucky. Turned out to be a drug addict and a liar."

"And now you want things with you and me to go back to normal?"

"I didn't say that. I just don't know if I made the right decision, and we've got a history—ten years is a long time." I gulped as he stared at me. "I just thought that maybe it might be good for us to get away and have some time along together and see if there's something there still. I guess I don't want to give up, yet."

"I didn't want to give up. I asked you to work things out. You still insisted on me leaving, and then you brought that drug addict out here, and now that things aren't working out with him, you just want me to go with you to Hawaii and pretend like nothing ever happened?"

"I don't expect that. I know we've got a lot of things to work out, but I've already got the ticket, and it's just going to go to waste if you don't use it. And like I said, we could use the time to reconnect and see if this relationship is worth saving."

"I dunno," he said, shaking his head. "I'm going to need some time to think about it."

"Okay, take your time. I mean, I'd like to know at least a few days before we leave, but you can take the time until then to think about it and let me know."

"Alright," he agreed as the waitress returned with our food.

Well, at least he'd agreed to think about it. That was better than a downright no, although it meant that I would spent the next week and a half agonizing over his impending answer.

That Saturday was Jesse's birthday, and because I did still give a shit about him, I texted and wished him a Happy Birthday. He thanked me and said that his family had a big dinner for him. I rolled my eyes as I thought again how stupid I'd been to believe him when he told me he could never go back to Kentucky. I had stayed in light contact with him since he'd left, mostly out of self-inflicted guilt. The first I'd hear from him, he said he had a needle in his hand and was staying with some friend. Now his family was throwing him a birthday party. Guess it hadn't been that difficult for him to return after all.

But Sunday night, I got a text from Jesse—only it wasn't from Jesse. It was from Billy, his half-brother. At least, that's who he said it was. He said that they had found Jesse unconscious next to a bottle of pills. He had overdosed and left a suicide note. In the note, he referenced a notebook in which he had written goodbye letters to the loved ones he was leaving behind.

Billy went on to say that Jesse was in the hospital on life support, and they were basically just waiting for his dad to get there before they pulled the plug. I was and wasn't surprised at the same time. Jesse had been a very mixed up and confused person who had been addicted to prescription painkillers since he was a teenager. Billy said he would keep me updated. I thanked him and sat there crying for a long time. I knew it wasn't my fault, but at the same time, I totally felt like it was all my fault. I had sent him back to Kentucky to die. What if everything he had told me had been true? But I reasoned with myself that it still didn't change the fact that he was a drug addict and a liar. I had to make the decision to send him back home out of self-preservation. In the two weeks he'd been with me, I'd felt a piece of me die every day. I felt myself resigning to a lifetime of despair and grief, and I knew I would be of no use to him or anyone else if I lost myself completely.

Another text came from Jesse's mother a few minutes later. She asked me if Jesse had been drinking while he was with me, and I told her that yes, he had. She claimed that they had had no idea that he'd been so depressed and drinking again. They did know about the Oxy, but they didn't know about the drinking. I told her he had drank an entire bottle of vodka the night he had arrived, because he was coming down off the Oxy and had no way to get anymore when he got here.

I could barely sleep that night, and then early the next morning, another text came from Billy. It was official. Jesse was dead. They had just pulled the plug late in the night when his dad got to the hospital and said his goodbyes.

I sat there feeling numb and empty, and oh so very guilty. Jesse was gone. Jesse was gone because of me. I had killed him. He had driven me crazy and turned out to be an unstable drug addict who lied and manipulated me to do what he needed, but he had also just been a boy. Just a boy who had loved me, and I had loved him for a little while. And I would never see him again. I would never speak to him again. He would never get that second chance at life. The tears came hot and heavy as I mourned the loss of a broken man who I had once loved. I had sent him back to Kentucky, and he had taken his life. Could I ever forgive myself?

I called out sick from work the next day. I was absolutely devastated and heartbroken and sick to my stomach, and there was no way I'd be able to focus and concentrate on anything when I felt like this.

The next day, I went into Jerry's office and asked him if he had a moment. Nodding his head, he indicated I should close the door and sit.

"What's up, Erin?" he asked, smiling warmly at me.

"Um, I just wanted to let you know that someone close to me just passed away, and I found out that it was due to suicide. So understandably, I'm a little upset, and just wanted to make you aware in case I seem a little off or anything. I apologize in advance and will make every effort to not let it affect my work, but I just wanted to let you know."

"Oh no, I'm so sorry to hear that. Please let me know if there is anything I can do."

"Thanks," I said as I nodded to him and got up to leave. When I was safely back at my desk, I let out a big breath and wiped away a tear.

Getting through the rest of the day was difficult, but I pushed on. When I got home that night, I texted Billy to let him know that I had Jesse's Facebook login and password, in case the family wanted to do some kind of memorial thing with his page. A minute later, my phone rang, displaying Jesse's number. Assuming Billy wanted to discuss the details, I answered the phone.

"Hello?" I said.

"Erin," was all he said in return.

My stomach dropped. Holy shit. There was no mistaking *that* voice. Jesse was still alive. That motherfucking liar was still alive. Are you kidding me?

"What? What the fuck? Jesse?" I yelled into the phone.

"Erin, calm down."

"What do you mean, calm down? You pretend to be your brother and text me and tell me you fucking overdosed and committed suicide and now I find out you're alive and you want me to calm down? What the fuck, Jesse?"

"Okay first of all, I didn't pretend to be my brother. That was really Billy texting you from my phone. Second of all, I had to do it, but it was a cover-up. Only Billy and my dad and the doctor were in on it. There was no other way for me to leave the club for good and not have them fuck with my family when I was gone."

"Still, I don't care. You could have told me. Who was I going to tell?"

"I'm telling you now."

"Yeah, it's a little late to be telling me now. After I thought you really killed yourself and thought it was all my fault 'cuz I sent you back home to Kentucky. I called out sick yesterday because I thought you were dead!"

"Well, I'm sorry about that, but I couldn't tell you before, and I shouldn't be telling you now. But I need a friend, Erin. I need someone to talk to."

"I dunno, I don't need friends who lie to me."

"Please, Erin. I'm begging. Just give me another chance. I need you to be there for me right now, just as a friend, I swear. It's going to be real lonely in the next several weeks, maybe months here. I'm holed up in a motel room in Lexington, and I have to stay out of sight, 'cuz if they see me and realize I'm still alive, I'm dead. They already suspect something's up, so I really have to be careful. And I'm going to need a friend to talk to while I'm going through this."

"Ugh, I swear, you are crazy. And I still wish you had just told me to begin with. But fine, yes, I'll be your friend. I'll keep your secret."

"I mean it, Erin. You can't tell anyone. Not your best friend, not your sister, no one."

"I get it. I won't tell anyone."

"Okay then. Well, I gotta git, but I'll give you a call soon, okay?"

"Okay," I muttered, still extremely pissed off that he had lied to me yet again and made me believe he was dead. And I couldn't even tell anyone! But on the bright side, at least that motherfucker wasn't dead, and it wasn't my fault. Ugh. Men!

The next morning I was just finishing up a call with a caterer for an event that Jerry had coming up the following week when Kristen came by and asked me if I could steal away for a quick smoke. I definitely needed the air, so I agreed to join her, but when we got to the back of the building, she said she didn't actually have any cigarettes.

"I'm sorry, I didn't really need to smoke, but I needed to talk to you."

"Okay, sure. What's up?"

Kristen's lip trembled and her eyes began to water immediately. "I'm in trouble, Erin. Like really bad trouble." Then she promptly burst into full-on tears, so I pulled her to me in a hug and patted her back to console her.

"What's wrong, girlie? Tell me. You can talk to me."

"I know, I'm just—I'm so messed up right now, and I have absolutely no clue what to do."

"What happened?"

"Well, I was at The Blue Door a few weeks ago, getting drinks with Evan and the other guys in my group, and we were all pretty schlitzed, and then Evan took me home."

Uh oh...I didn't have a good feeling about where this conversation was going. Evan was her boss, and he was married with a kid. I shook my head at her. "Kristen, please don't tell me you slept with Evan."

She just started crying harder, and I hugged her again and wished I had known this was going to turn into a sob-fest so I could have brought some Kleenex with me.

"Okay, so obviously you slept with your boss."

Kristen just nodded and sniffled again, looking at her feet.

"And I know you feel bad and will never do it again, right?"

"That's not the point," she sobbed. "I'm pregnant, Erin!"

"Oh God," I said, my mouth dropping open. This was no bueno. There were so many layers to this potential scandal, I didn't know where to start. A younger woman sleeping with her older boss—that was already a problem. Then throw in the fact that he's married with a kid that just complicated matters even further.

"Have you told him? What are you going to do?"

"I don't know. I can't get him alone long enough to really talk to me. We tried to go to lunch yesterday, but the mother of one of the kids his son goes to school with spotted us and came over to talk. So there went that chance."

"Well, what are you thinking of doing after you talk to him?"

"I don't know. Probably get an abortion. I just need to talk to him first."

"Okay, okay. Yeah, I definitely think you guys need to talk."

"Yeah, I'll keep trying. I need to make a decision soon. Anyways, thanks for coming to talk to me. I just needed to tell someone, and you're one of the few people I trust."

"Well, I'm glad you feel that way, and please let me know if there's anything I can do, okay?" I leaned forward and hugged her tightly.

"Love you, lady," she said. "You go on in. I just need another couple minutes to pull myself together before I go back to my desk."

"Okay." I headed back inside and let out another deep breath when I got to my desk. Man, it just didn't stop with the great news around here. I so didn't see that coming. I needed that vacation in Hawaii desperately right now.

Chapter ELEVEN

Two weeks later, I was on a plane to Hawaii…alone. After picking up my rental car, I started my drive to the North Shore. I was about halfway there and passing through Haleiwa when Jesse called me.

"Hello."

"Hey, baby girl. You in Hawaii, yet?"

"Yep, just got here. Driving to the vacation rental right now."

"That's cool."

"How are you?" I asked hesitantly. I didn't really have the time to get into a long, drawn-out conversation with him, but I knew he had no one else to talk to really.

"Been better. They found out I was still alive. Blew up my bike. I have pieces of shrapnel in my head, and my brother had to come stitch me up."

"Oh my God, are you okay?" I was genuinely horrified. No matter how badly he had hurt me, I hadn't wished *this* on the poor bastard.

"Yeah, I'll be okay. Always am." He laughed. "Or I won't be. Who knows."

"Okay. Well, I'm almost to the house, so I'm probably going to lose reception pretty soon." I didn't really know if I would lose reception, but I did want to get off of the phone. I was beginning to become very concerned for any association I had with him, whether in the past or not.

"You have a good time now."

"Thanks. Bye now."

"Bye, Erin."

Bye Erin. I used to love the way he said my name, but now it just made me cringe. About ten minutes later, I reached the Foodland that was at the foot of Pupukea Hills and called Maile, the caretaker, to let her know I was almost there so she could come out to the gate to meet me. I had booked my stay at The Mobius Villa, a vacation rental house I had found on VRBO.com.

Maile met me on the side of the road, right out in front of the gate. She was a young woman with short curly brown hair who appeared to be in her late twenties. After opening the gate, she gestured for me to drive through, then followed behind me. She called out, telling me to drive up to the house and she would meet me there. I drove up a long, dirt and gravel driveway through long green grasses and stems of bamboo until it suddenly opened into a large clearing.

My jaw dropped as I took in the giant, magnificent villa sprawled out in front of me. It was unique and artsy, and I loved it immediately. I got out of the car and stretched my legs, then turned to walk down the driveway a bit to wait for Maile to join me.

Welcoming me warmly as she walked up the driveway, she gave me the keys and gate opener and explained the rules of the house, then took me in to show me around. There was a large open living space that included a kitchen and dining area, then upstairs there was a large living room area where you could lounge and relax. After she showed me to The Ark, the room I had chosen which was located right off the main living space of the house, she told me to contact her if I needed anything during my stay. According to her, I had lucked out and just missed a big wedding party that had been staying there. No one else was booked while I was there, so I would have the entire place to myself. Awesome! If only I had come with someone to enjoy this big, empty house. Le sigh. Pushing that thought aside, I retrieved my bags from the car and began to unpack and settle in.

Halfway through unpacking, I lay down on the big king-sized canopy bed, draped in yards of off-white fabric and mosquito netting, and listened to the sounds of nature right outside my window. You could hear the tropical birds calling out to each other and the mist of the rain as it started and stopped. I had missed Hawaii so much, and it felt amazing to be home again. But the last time I had been there, Mike had been with me, so it didn't feel quite the same this time.

I wasn't here to just relax, I was here to work as well, so I pulled out my laptop and fiddled with setting up the new WiFi. Of course before I could start writing, I logged into Facebook to see if I had any new messages or notifications. I had several notifications from…Jesse? What.The.Fuck. Blinking for a moment, I finally jerked myself out of my dumb stupor and started clicking on each notification. He had liked and commented on several of my pictures. What the hell was he thinking? I messaged him as quickly as my fingers could type.

Erin: Hey um, could you maybe not like and comment on my shit anymore until I get back from my vacation? I didn't exactly know you were going to come back to life all of a sudden, and everyone still thinks you're dead. Now I get to spend the next couple of hours explaining to everyone how you're actually really still alive!

Jesse: Okay, sorry. Look it's probably better if I stay away from you for now.

And like that he unfriended me.

What the fuck? Like seriously, what was wrong with this guy's head? Well, other than the shrapnel that was hypothetically imbedded in it. I had remained his friend, I had kept his secret, and this was how he repaid me? Enough was enough. I no longer felt any remaining sympathy for this asshole that apparently only cared about himself.

And like I had told Jesse, indeed I spent the next two hours explaining to all my friends and family how Jesse had faked his suicide and wasn't really dead. After that, I needed a drink, so I headed down the hill to Foodland to pick up a bottle of Cabernet and a bottle opener and then came right back to the house. I drank my wine out of a coffee mug, but I wasn't picky. I turned on my Frou Frou station on Pandora and went outside to have a cigarette. I had almost kicked the habit again after Jesse's visit, but I still had an occasional craving, so I had picked up a pack to bring with me.

After my cigarette, I texted my cousin, letting her know I was on the way to the house to say hello to the family. I told her I was beat and couldn't stay long, but I would come spend more time at the house the following day.

It was always great to see my dad's side of the family. I loved them all so much and had been devastated when we moved to Nebraska. I hugged all my cousins, aunts, uncles, grandparents and second cousins, stopping to talk story for a bit with each one. Then I got to hold Jeremy, my baby second cousin, for a bit while his mom had some dinner. He was half Japanese and half Thai and so stinking cute! I wanted to squeeze his little chubby cheeks, but I doubt he would have appreciated that, so I contained myself and kept my oohing and aahing to a minimum.

The next morning when I woke up, I headed down to Ted's Bakery to pick up some breakfast to bring back to the house. I ordered Portuguese sausage with white rice, scrambled eggs and country potatoes and one of Ted's famous glazed donuts. Ted's glazed donuts were soft and fluffy on the inside. They were ridiculously good and one of the things I missed most about Hawaii.

When I got back up to the rental house with my breakfast, I took it outside on the lanai along with my laptop and set everything up on a little metal table that sat right outside my room. As I ate my delicious Hawaiian breakfast, relishing each bite, I decided to post an ad on Craigslist. I didn't want to spend my entire trip moping about, wishing Mike had come with me, so I figured that I might as well meet someone new and have a little fun.

SoCal Girl Coming Home to Hawaii

Hi there, I'm originally from North Shore on Oahu, but I have lived in Los Angeles for 15 years. I'm here visiting my family for a few days. I'm interested in possibly meeting someone in Hawaii while I'm on vacation. Not opposed to doing a long distance thing for a while with the possibility of either us relocating eventually. Little bit about me -- I'm 32, 5'9", hapa (half Japanese/ half Caucasian), work for a video game company and am an aspiring writer on the side. I love music, movies, dancing, concerts, traveling, cooking, hanging out with friends, trying new restaurants, etc. If you're interested in hanging out while I'm in town, please send me a recent pic and let me know your idea of what we might do together when we first meet. :) I'm up for an adventure!

I got a plethora of responses, just like I used to do when I had posted on Craigslist before I met Mike. One of the guys looked pretty damn cute, but he had sent me a naked picture with a towel held up in front of his crotch. I almost deleted the email without reading it, but he did have some mouthwatering abs and a really nice ass. So I ended up reading it anyway.

From: Mike Sanchez <10a0ccc868ad3b98867f245f1749ce00@reply.craigslist.org>

Subject: 6'0" 185 lbs green eyes for Socal Girl Coming Home to Hawaii

Just genuinely interested in you, read your post randomly and was intrigued.

Well, that had been short and sweet, but his name was Mike! I really didn't want to date someone who had the same name as my ex fiancé, but he was mighty fine to look at, so I decided to respond. Why not? I was on vacation. I should get to enjoy a yummy looking man, regardless what his name was. I couldn't hold something like that against the poor guy. Honestly, let's be real here… his name could have been something like Wilbert or Harold and I still would have been interested.

From: Erin Tanaka

Subject: Nice to meet you

Hi Mike…I'm Erin. Don't have much time here in Hawaii, but I don't have plans tonight and I have a bit of time tomorrow and Saturday before I leave. This is me. :)

I sent him a few recent pictures of myself and waited to see if he'd respond. I only had to wait about twenty minutes before he emailed me back.

From: Mike Sanchez <10a0ccc868ad3b98867f245f1749ce00@reply. craigslist.org>
Subject: Well hello there

Very pretty! Well tonight might not be good, but can still end up being free very late...what time tomorrow will you be free?

I was bummed that it sounded like he couldn't make it out that night, but I could be patient for a man as fine as him, so I emailed him back.

From: Erin Tanaka
Subject: Tomorrow

I'm supposed to be having lunch with an old friend, but I haven't gotten confirmation from her yet on what time or where, and then I'm supposed to be going out for drinks later at night with an old classmate, but you could maybe come along for that if you're interested. :) Or I can cancel on her completely— not a big deal either way. Here's my number. Hit me up if you want to hang.

I included my cell phone number, hit send, and waited. I killed time by checking my Facebook messages, emailing some bloggers about a blog tour I had coming up, and answering some emails from my day job, but to my disappointment, nothing else came from my potential suitor. It was almost lunchtime, so I drove down to Foodland to pick up some spam musubi and Hawaiian Sun Pass-O-Guava juice and munched on the Asian treat as I drove to the other side of the island to hit up the swap meet. I needed to get a bunch of snacks and other touristy shit to send back to my friends and family on the mainland, and the swap meet at Aloha Stadium was the best place to do that.

After I spent an hour there loading up on as many goodies and souvenirs that I could carry, I took everything back to the car and headed back to Haleiwa. I stopped at the post office and went inside to buy a large box and packing tape, then returned to my car to start packing everything up. As I was opening the trunk of my car, my phone buzzed with a text message. Glancing down, I didn't recognize the number, so I opened the message to see whom it was from.

Mike: *Good morning, Erin! :P*

Erin: *Hi, who's this? :)*

Mike: *This is Mike.*

Erin: *Oh hey :)*

Mike: *How are you?*

Erin: *I'm good :) just finished mailing a bunch of goodies back to myself for all my friends in Cali. What are you up to?*

Mike: *Nice! Working right now actually...whatcha send yourself?*

Erin: *Everything! Lol*

Mike: *Lmao*

Erin: *Chocolate macadamia nuts, regular macadamia nuts, Iso peanuts, cookies, cuttlefish, coffee, Li Hing mango, beach towels, Aloha cups, etc.*

Mike: *Wow, sounds good, lol.*

I finished loading the box with everything, taped it up, wrote the address to ship it to myself at work in California, then toted the heavy package inside where the post office cashier informed me it would cost seventy-five dollars to ship it. I nearly had a heart attack. When I got back in my car to head back to the villa, I texted Mike again.

Erin: *So what do you do for work?*

Mike: *I deliver the stuff you just sent actually*

Erin: *Oh nice!*

Mike: *Lol*

Erin: *So what time do you get off? Did you want to do something?*

Mike: *Who did you ship through?*

Erin: *Post office. I'm in Haleiwa.*

Mike: *I really do, I wanted to last night even, but random events happened yesterday, and I'm actually somewhat tied up. I am really trying to have free time before you leave though.*

Erin: Aw :(

Mike: *Ahh, I work for Fed Ex.*

Erin: *Oh, I gotcha.*

Mike: *And I have really bad service, so I apologize if my texts are sent all mixed up.*

Erin: *Yeah, I leave for the airport around 6 tomorrow and will be hanging out with my family from about 4 until then. :/ It's cool, I've had the same issue with service here.*

Mike: *Yeah, I'm from NY...service is horrendous here.*

Erin: *Haha...so you don't have any time tonight?*

Mike: *:P I'm trying to free it up. What did you have in mind?*

Erin: *I see. Nothing in particular...my girlfriend said she didn't mind if I cancelled on drinks tonight. So dinner? Drinks? I dunno! I haven't lived here in like 22 years, so I don't really know what there is to do.*

Mike: *Oh that's right...hmm that sucks actually.*

Erin: *What sucks?*

Mike: *I don't want you to jump ship on your friends and then I can't make it.*

Erin: *Oh, it's fine. She is flexible, so if you bail, we will still hang out.*

Mike: *Well, I've only been here 2 months so...whatever, lol.*

Erin: *Lol, aha still a newbie. What part of the island are you living?*

Mike: *Oh shytt, I forgot gamer girl here.*

Erin: *Lol yup.*

Mike: *Yeah, I'm a noob when it comes to the island.*

Erin: *I work for a video game publisher, so it's a pretty sweet gig. What would be the approximate time you can hang out tonight if you CAN free up tonight.*

Mike: *Beast! Sometime after 7 or 8, get out at 5, need time to clean up and stuff.*

Erin: *Okay.*

Mike: *I mean there is a slim chance I can skate out earlier, but I doubt that.*

Erin: *It's cool—I was just asking to see if I could fit in happy hour with my friend first.*

I didn't know for sure if this guy was trying to hang out with me or if he was just messing with me. He reached out to me, but then he sounds like he can't even make it. I wasn't sure what kind of game he was playing, but it kinda sucked. I didn't want to spend my entire vacation sitting in my rental car while I text some guy I might or might not hook up with, so I set my phone down and started to drive back to Pupukea. My phone buzzed again as I pulled into my driveway.

Mike: *So you leave tomorrow at 6 pm?*

Erin: *Well, I'm unavailable after 4 PM unless I say goodbye to my family earlier in the day and then could just head to the airport after hanging out. Bottom line, I have to drop the rental car at like 7:30. Where do you live? Honolulu?*

Mike: *Understood! We'll make this happen, lol. Yeah, I'm close to Waikiki.*

Erin: *Okay. Do you dance?*

Mike: *I've been known to dance, lol. Haven't in forever, though.*

Erin: *Just thinking we could hit up a club if you can get free tonight. It's been a while for me, too. Just an idea.*

I headed inside and changed into my bathing suit. It was running out of time to get a tan, so I wanted to go lay outside on the lawn and catch some rays while I texted with my new loverboy who maybe was or maybe wasn't available tonight. I was lying down on the towel I had just spread down on the lawn when my phone buzzed again.

Mike: *Honestly, this may seem a bit corny, but I haven't been to the movies since I moved here and missed so many hits that have been out. Think we can do that and grab a bite to eat?*

Erin: *Sure! When will you know if you can get free?*

Mike: *Probably more towards the end of the day.*

Erin: *I see.*

Mike: *I'm sorry. :-*

Erin: *You're a bit of a tease, lol.*

He didn't text back again for a few minutes, so I stretched out and soaked up the sun, peacefully dozing off. After a little while, I got up to use the restroom and then came back outside. I saw someone in the back yard as I came back onto the lanai. It was an older woman wearing jean shorts and a tank top. She was very tan and fit. She waved to me and smiled.

"Hello! How are you?" she called, then set down a watering can and walked over to me. "I'm Nodie, nice to meet you. My husband Sam and I own the Mobius."

"Erin. Nice to meet you as well. You have a lovely house."

"Thank you. We built it ourselves from the ground up. Our son also helped with some of the more artistic elements."

"Well, it's just beautiful. Thank you for letting me stay here."

"Of course. How are you enjoying your stay? You said in your email that you have family around here?"

"I'm having a great time, and yes, I grew up in this area, and my family lives across from Velzyland."

"Oh okay, well, aloha and welcome. Please make yourself at home and let me know if you need anything at all while you're here."

"Thanks so much, I really appreciate it."

It made me smile to know I had rented a room from such nice people. After she left me to my sunbathing, I checked my phone and saw that Mike had sent me another message twenty minutes ago.

Mike: Lmao! *Well maybe if I go to championship, I can visit you in Cali. ;-) If, of course, we hit it off.*

Then he'd sent another text ten minutes later.

Mike: *No? Bad idea? Lol*

Erin: *Sorry, I just saw your message! Yeah, that'd be cool. :) What championship?*

Mike: *League of Legends.*

Erin: *Ohh. I know someone who used to work at Riot, so I've just recently learned all about the e-sports events they do. I used to play WoW, lol.*

Mike: *Nice! Yeah, e-sports are awesome. I used to go so hard on WoW.*

Erin: *Yup, I played from Burning Crusade to Mists of Pandaria, but I only got my panda to like 54 when I stopped playing.*

Mike: *Sweet, I started right before BC into Mists. What was your main?*

Erin: *My fave was my Mage.*

Mike: *Nice.*

Erin: *You? Horde or Alliance? I played both, but mainly Alliance.*

Mike: *My fave was my Shaman.*

Erin: *Ah, Horde. Yeah, my Mage was a Dranaei.*

Mike: *Yeah, I started Ally with a Druid and then a Priest, then had multiple Shamans Ally and Horde.*

Erin: *Yeah, I liked my Druid second best, and then my priest. Oh, I thought only Horde had Shamans. What Ally race had Shamans?*

Mike: *My Ally Shaman was Draenei. They also have Dwarf Shamans now.*

Erin: *Oh that's right. God, it's been a while, lol. I played an Undead Shadow Priest for a long time. Her name was Assilemotias. So is that why you may be busy? Got League of Legends stuff happening?*

Mike: *I wish, I would just have you over so we could watch. Which would actually be an awesome evening imho.*

Erin: *Hehe. :)*

My hottie was such a nerd. I loved it!

Mike: *Imagine that…some drinks and a pretty lady by my side watching, lol. That's crazy.*

Erin: *Would be fun :)*

Mike: *So Encino, California, huh?*

Erin: *Yup. How'd you know that?*

All of a sudden, my senses went on high alert. I hadn't mentioned what city I lived in other than that I was from L.A.—had I? As I tried hard to remember, he texted again and said the first part of my address with the street number and name. I about freaked out when I remembered that he worked for Fed Ex. Ugh! *What* a brat!

Erin: *Oh my God! Stalker! Lol. Are you abusing your Fed Ex privileges?? :p*

Mike: *Lololol! My awesome skills of deduction.*

Erin: *Uh huh. :p*

Mike: *Lol. Did I scare you off? My bad!*

Erin: *Lol, no not yet.*

Mike: *Lmao. Okay, let's try then. To scare you, lol.*

Erin: *What!*

Mike: *Hahaha...don't trip. I'm just messing with ya.*

Erin: *Oh, hehe, okay. :)*

Mike: *What are you doing right now? Other than texting with me?*

Erin: *Just laying out getting some sun and reading Divergent.*

Mike: *What's that?*

Erin: *A book my friend recommended. One of those dystopian novels, kinda like Hunger Games.*

Mike: *Oh got it.*

Erin: *Yeah, it's really good so far.*

Mike: *Cool, I'll have to check it out. They have the e-book version, yeah? How many books are there?*

Erin: *Yep, they sure do. I think it's a trilogy, but I could be wrong. You know, I actually self-published my first book a little earlier this year and now I'm working on the sequel. It's going to be a trilogy as well.*

Mike: *Oh nice! That's badass.*

Erin: *It's not as cool as this series, though. I write romantic fiction. :P*

Mike: *Sweet, you can write about me in the next one.*

Erin: *You never know! ;) After all, my book WAS inspired by some of my online dating experiences. Hehehe...*

Mike: *Lmao!*

I couldn't stop grinning as our texts flew back and forth. He sure knew how to talk my language. I had no doubt in my mind that I would get along great with another serious gamer. Well, I should call myself an ex-serious gamer. I have no time these days! It's all work, work, work, and barely no room for play. Not play that can take hours upon hours per day anyway!

Erin: *I really hope I get to see you before I leave. But no worries. I do get at least one week and maybe two this year for Christmas. Maybe I'll come back to spend Christmas here.*

Prior to this, his texts had been coming quickly, but now they came to a grinding halt. Had I said too much? Pushed too far? We hadn't even met, yet, and I was already suggesting spending Christmas together? Crap. Well, it was too late to take it back now, so I decided to make a joke of it.

Erin: *Okay, my turn now...no? Bad idea?? Lol...*

Mike: *Lmao! Bad idea.*

Erin: *Kay :-(I go way now.*

Mike: *Lolol! I'm going back home to Brooklyn, so I won't be here :-*

Erin: *Oh :-\\ That sucks.*

Mike: *I'll come to the LoL championship in L.A.*

Erin: *When is that?*

Mike: *September, I think.*

Erin: *September?? That's a long ways away. :(*

Mike: *I know. I'm really trying to get free tonight, I promise. But yeah, I would be willing to fly out for at least two weekends during the championships.*

Erin: *You're such a nerd. :)*

Mike: *You love it. :)*

Erin: *I know, it's kinda hot, lol.*

Mike: *Alright, I gotta jet for a while, but I'll hit you up later.*

Erin: *Okay, ttyl.*

Chapter TWELVE

Never in a million years had I imagined I'd meet someone I'd hit it off with this well, and we hadn't even met, yet. I was so excited to meet this guy, and I was crossing my fingers and toes that he'd manage to get free for the evening. Deciding I'd had enough sunbathing, I picked up my towel and book to head back inside. My cousin Kylie texted me and asked if I wanted to go paddle boarding with her, her husband Jonathan, and their little boy, Kenny, so I said I'd meet them at their place in fifteen minutes. Throwing some shorts and a tank top on, I grabbed my purse and keys and filled a beach bag with a towel, suntan lotion, bottle of water and my copy of *Divergent*, then locked my room up and headed out to the driveway.

As I started the car, I reached over to tilt all the air vents towards me, the blast of chilly air a welcome respite from the dripping island humidity. My skin was so sticky, and my long brown hair had a mind of its own, refusing to do anything I actually wanted it to. I usually didn't even bother trying to do anything other than pull it into a bun or ponytail whenever I was here, and make-up pretty much melted right off your damn face. It was just too damn hot and it was completely pointless trying to be girlie here unless you just wanted to be laidback Hawaiian girlie who tans and surfs every day and doesn't bother with hair or make-up. When she accessorizes, all she's figuring out is which bikini top and puka shell necklace to wear with her cut-off jean shorts and slippahs, or what flower to stick in her hair. Well, when in Rome... guess I couldn't be like an L.A. Barbie doll all the time.

When I got to my family's house, Kylie was walking down the driveway, looking very pregnant as she held little Kenny's hand. He was toddling along next to her, his little baby legs so damn cute I just wanted to bite them. I felt a pang in my chest as I looked at them both and smiled, getting out of the car to greet them both. I missed my family here so much and regretted the fact that I didn't live closer to them every day.

I hugged Kylie and asked if I could pick Kenny up for a minute. She laughed and said I was welcome to try, so I grinned and eagerly picked up my adorable second cousin for a quick cuddle. He, of course, was having none of it and immediately squirmed right back out of my arms as he waved his hands and started to cry for his mommy.

"Kenny, it's okay," she crooned to him. "Don't you want to go to auntie? She never gets to see you, you know."

It was obvious that my little cousin was not interested in me holding him, regardless of how rarely I got to see him. I smiled a little sadly as I set him back down and watched him wrap his little arms tightly around his mom's leg.

"Where's Jeremy?" I asked, looking around.

"He's right there," she said, nodding towards the driveway next door. "He's loading all the paddleboard stuff in the truck."

"Eh, let's go," he called. "I wanna stop and get some breakfast from Ted's."

I laughed and shook my head. "Oh my God, I just ate the biggest breakfast from there a little bit ago. I couldn't fit another bite in."

Kylie laughed at me as she started heading for the truck, and I followed her, watching Kenny toddle along. "It's okay, you know. You're on vacation. Enjoy yourself."

"I know, but I really need to lose some pounds."

"Only if it'll make you happy."

"It will definitely make me happier."

"Still, you're on vacation right now. You can lose the pounds when you go back to Cali."

"I know, but I don't need to make it super difficult for myself, either," I argued back with her, laughing as I climbed into the back cab of the truck.

"Eh well, I'm eating for two right now, so that's my excuse," she said as she patted her belly before starting to lean down to pick Kenny up.

"Yeah, I don't have that kind of excuse right now." I shook my head and sighed.

Kylie stopped bending over and huffed, unable to reach Kenny over her large, protruding belly. "Babe, can you pick him up? I can't reach him over my belly."

Jonathan nodded and came over to pick his boy up and help him get situated in his car seat. Then he and Kylie both climbed into the truck, and we were ready to go. We took the short detour down the street to Ted's Bakery and waited in the truck while Jonathan went inside to get what he needed. Ten minutes later, we were back on the road and driving down to Kawela Bay.

When we arrived, we parked the truck by some palm trees and gathered our things before starting the short trek to the actual beach itself.

"Didn't they film *Lost* here?" I asked curiously as I walked down to the sand, throwing my beach bag on the ground after I dug my beach towel out of it.

"Yup," Kylie said, nodding. "Do you want a spam musubi?"

I groaned at her offer. I was a weak woman when it came to spam musubi. "Ugh, I really shouldn't, but eh—fuck it. Like you said, I'm on vacation. Thank you!" She grinned at me and handed one over, still warm and wrapped in plastic.

Stripping back down to my bathing suit, I sat down on my beach towel and dug around in my bag for the suntan spray. Watching his dad take the paddleboard down to the water, Kenny waved his arms around excitedly as he bounced up and down on the balls of his feet in the sand.

"You wanna go in the water with Daddy?" Kylie asked. Kenny nodded his head and raised his arms, waiting for his mom to pick him up.

Kylie made a soft, "Oof," as she slowly bent to pick him up. After she handed him over to his dad, she returned to where I was sitting on the beach and lowered herself down on the towel beside me.

"The sun feels so good," I murmured as I basked in the warm rays of sunlight on my face.

"So are you enjoying your vacation?" she asked. "Like the place where you're staying?"

"Yeah, it's nice up there, and yeah, of course I am having a great time seeing all the family…it's just tough being here without Mike."

"I bet. You said he is seeing someone new already?"

"Yep. Can't really blame him, though. I did break up with him."

"I can't believe that crazy story you told me about that motorcycle club guy from where was it? Arkansas?"

"Kentucky," I groaned. "Don't remind me."

"So he's really alive?"

"Yep."

"And you knew this whole time?"

"Yep…well, not the whole time. I thought he was dead when his brother supposedly texted me to tell me he committed suicide, but when I texted him back to ask if they wanted his Facebook login so they could do like a memorial thing with it if they wanted, that's when Jesse called me and confessed that he had faked it. He claims it was the only way he could leave the club for good and not have them mess with his family when he's gone. But yeah, after that, I knew. And he asked me to keep his secret, so I did."

"Wow. That's so fucked up."

"You can say that again. I thought he was dead! I was mourning him. I called out sick because I felt so devastated. I thought I had sent him to his death."

"Girl, you are not responsible for his actions."

"I know I'm not, but that didn't keep me from feeling partially responsible. So you can imagine how relieved I was to find out that he's still alive."

"Oh for sure, I get that. I definitely wouldn't want to feel responsible for someone else's death."

Shivering suddenly, I rubbed my arms briskly at the morbid thought. "Anyways! So on to lighter subjects…I decided to post an ad on Craigslist while I'm here and someone responded."

Kylie's eyebrows shot up as she looked at me askance. "What?! You're crazy."

"I met Mike on Craigslist, remember?"

"Oh yeah, I totally forgot about that. Alright…so? Who's the guy who responded?"

"Well, his name is Mike …"

Groaning, Kylie rolled her eyes and laughed. "Seriously?"

"I know, what are the odds? But it's not exactly like he has a unique name or anything."

"True. Okay, so what does the new Mike look like?"

"Lemme show you." I reached for my phone and scrolled through my emails to find his picture. "Here," I said as I handed my phone to her.

She lifted her sunglasses and squinted, tilting the phone screen around in different angles as she tried to get a good look at his pictures. "Damn, girl!"

"I know, right?" I laughed and shrugged. "And he's a total gamer nerd, too! We've been texting non-stop all day. We totally hit it off already and we haven't even met, yet."

"When are you going to see him? Aren't you leaving tomorrow already?"

"Well, he's trying to get free tonight, but I'm not sure if he'll be able to, yet. He said he would try to make it happen before I left."

"What are you guys going to do?"

"I suggested dancing, but he wants to see a movie and grab some dinner or something."

"That's cool. Well, have fun, but just be safe," she warned.

"Of course." I nodded.

"When is he supposed to let you know?"

"Honestly, no clue. It's driving me a little nuts. I really, *really* want to meet him before I go back to L.A."

Just then Jonathan called over to us. When we looked up, we saw Jonathan standing on the paddleboard with Kenny crouched down on his hands and knees in front of him. He was peering over the edge of the board and giggling as his dad paddled them around.

"Here, can you help me up?" Kylie pleaded with a puppy dog look.

I laughed as I jumped up to my feet and turned to help her up. She was so cute when she was pregnant, and I felt a little pang of jealousy as I wished for my own happy little family and a sweet baby growing in my belly. *One of these days*, I told myself. *Just be patient.* We walked down to the clear, green-blue water until we were up to our calves and watched the boys play. I took some pictures of them, catching the joy and laughter in Kenny's face as he rode around on the paddleboard. Kylie asked me to text them to her, and then I beckoned for her to come closer to me so I could take a selfie of both of us.

Jonathan finally paddled back to the shallow area where we were, and Kenny jumped off the board into Kylie's waiting arms. They were the picture perfect happy family, living in paradise. They looked so content and fulfilled, standing there together, the water all around them. I felt a comforting peace come over me. What they had was what I wanted, and right then and there, I made a promise to myself that I wouldn't settle until I found the same someday. And who knew? It could be with this guy I was hopefully meeting tonight. Stranger things had happened.

Kylie broke me out of my brooding thoughts by suggesting that I try paddle boarding. I gawked at her for a second, then laughed outright. "Um, don't you remember what I klutz I am? I never learned how to surf 'cuz I couldn't manage to stand up on the damn board."

"Come on, just try."

"Uhhh, I dunno." I eyed the paddleboard skeptically, but slowly reached out to touch the board, pulling it towards me as Jonathan let go of it with a grin. "Okay, but you guys don't have to like just stand there and watch me or anything," I said pointedly, then pulled my sunglasses off and handed them over to him. He laughed and took them, then turned around to head back up the beach to lie down on Kylie's towel while she played with Kenny in the shallow part of the water.

I glanced around to make sure that no one was watching, but I spotted a group of red kayaks making their way from Turtle Bay, and I chickened out.

I waited a few minutes until they passed, just hanging my arms across the middle of the board as I floated there like a lily pad. Finally, I looked down at the board and took a deep breath. Okay, I could do this. No prob.

I pushed up with my toes as hard as I could and tried to use the momentum to swing my body onto the board, and embarrassed myself by immediately tipping the board back into me and falling backwards into the water. *Awesome.*

Sputtering water as I resurfaced, I swung my head around to take note of who had seen me fall. Jonathan was sitting up and laughing, Kylie was giggling at me with her hand over her mouth, and even Kenny was smiling at me with his cute chubby cheeks, seeing his auntie fall back into the water like an idiot. I couldn't even manage to get my big body onto the board. *Fantastic.* I knew that I was really out of shape and needed to start hitting the gym more often. I had gotten too comfortable after being with the same guy for such a long time, and I'd grown complacent. It was time for that shit to stop.

Determined to at least get my damn body onto the board, I tried again to mount the board, this time barely succeeding. I lay there for a minute, just clinging to the board, trying desperately not to fall off. After I calmed my breathing, I attempted to sit up slowly, and that went okay as well. Pleased that I hadn't fallen into the water yet, I took another deep breath and leaned forward onto the board, trying to figure out the best way to place my hand to get a good grip to balance my weight against so I could try to draw one knee up onto the board and then put one foot down to start to stand up.

But I was doomed as soon as I even tried to bring my right knee up and immediately flipped myself over into the water. Everyone was in hysterics watching me, and after two more tries, I'd had it. No more for me. I loved a challenge, but I was clearly not in the kind of shape I needed to be to even stand up on a damn paddleboard. Over it, I pushed the board towards the shore until Jonathan took it from me and headed back out by himself. I watched him effortlessly push himself up into a standing position on the board and paddle himself out into the water. *Jerk.*

Shaking my head and muttering to myself, I made my way back to my towel and sat down, grabbing my sunglasses and shoving them onto my face.

Kylie had an amused look on her face as she came back up with Kenny to join me. She pulled out a small yellow bucket and blue shovel and set him to playing in the sand beside us.

"Just shush," I said warningly. "I know I'm out of shape. I can't believe I can't even stand on the friggin' board, but then I've never been able to stand on any kind of board like ever. I have no balance whatsoever. Gravity is not my friend."

She rolled her eyes and smirked at me. "You just have to practice. Keep trying." It was pretty simple advice, but I was already going back to L.A. tomorrow.

"Thanks for asking me to come. I needed to get out of the house and I'm glad I got to spend a little more time with you guys."

"Sure, no worries. I wish you didn't have to go back so soon."

"I know… trust me. I wish I could visit a lot more often, but it is what it is. For now anyway." I gave her a sad smile. I desperately wished I could be here with my family, but there was no way I'd be able to find a job that paid the kind of money I made in L.A., and the cost of living in Hawaii was just as bad if not worse.

I knew I was very fortunate to even be able to visit, so I pushed those thoughts aside and distracted myself by letting my thoughts wander to my cutie from Brooklyn. I checked my phone to see if I had any missed text messages, but there was nothing. Oh well, if it didn't happen, it didn't happen. I wasn't that worried about it. I had my family to spend time with, and that was what was most important anyway. I was just bumming about Mike (the ex) not being there with me and feeling lonely and in need of affirmation that I was still desirable and attractive, but it wasn't the end of the world if I ended up just hanging out with my friends and fam for the remainder of my time.

On our way back to the Tanaka compound—that's how I often referred to it in my head—I shot the new Mike a quick text.

Erin: *Hey you :)*

Mike: *Hey! Sorry, I got caught up at work. Did you still want to meet tonight?*

My lips spread into a huge smile as I texted quickly back that I could.

Mike: *Sweet. Okay, I'm just leaving work and am nowhere near home, so I'm going to need some time.*

Erin: *Sure, no prob. What time are you thinking?*

Mike: *Not sure yet, but probably a few hours. I'll text you in a bit to confirm time.*

Erin: *K. I'm just heading back from the beach so I need time to clean up anyway. Just give me some advance notice, cuz it will take me a bit to get to you.*

Mike: *Okay, will do. I'll text you the address. See you soon. ;)*

Erin: *Cool, see you soon. :)*

My heart felt light and fluttery as I drove back to the villa to get ready to meet Mike, but at the same time I also felt a huge knot forming in the pit of my stomach as waves of nervous energy washed over me. I felt antsy the entire time I was getting ready. I hadn't done something like this in a long time, and I had no clue if it would turn out to be a good gamble or the worst idea ever, but something was spurring me on to take a chance. Maybe it would pay off, maybe it wouldn't, but at least I will have tried instead of waiting around for something to happen to me. At the same time, I was trying not to expect too much. I wasn't setting my expectations that high, because this could undoubtedly turn out to be a one time thing or even a complete waste of our time, but something told me differently. Something told me this could be a really great experience, but all I could do was wait and see how tonight played out.

Chapter THIRTEEN

After I finished getting ready for my date with Mike, I worked on my book for several hours, waiting for him to confirm when I should leave. It was starting to get pretty late when he finally texted and said he'd be ready for me to pick him up in half an hour. After he gave me the address, I put it into my phone and groaned when I saw that it was going to take me a good fifty minutes to get there. Checking myself out in the mirror, I made a few last minute touch-ups to my hair and make-up before nodding approval. *Good job.* I'd managed to make myself look presentable enough, although I could stand to lose a few pounds, and I had a nice golden tan going after all that Hawaiian sunbathing, which added to the cute island girl look I was going for. Hopefully he would dig it. I mean, *I'd* do me and I'm pretty picky, so…

The drive there wasn't bad, but it was raining pretty heavily, and I was stuck on a one-lane highway behind two cars that were moving as slowly as turtles. Grinding my teeth in impatience, I could do nothing but drive at their pace. It was too dark, and the available areas to pass them were too short for me to feel like risking my life just to get to Mike a little sooner. When I got to Wahiawa, I checked Google Maps on my phone and saw that I was still a good forty minutes away, so I texted him an update.

Erin: *FYI – Google Maps says I'm still 40 min away…*

Mike: *Wtf?*

Erin: *I told you it was gonna take me a bit to get to you… I'm staying on the other side of the island.*

Mike: *Geez, I hope I'm worth it.*

Erin: *Me too! Lol ;)*

Mike: *Lmao*

Erin: *You'll make it worth the drive, right? ;)*

Mike: *Absolutely!*

Erin: *Excellent :)*

Mike: *Where are you now?*

Erin: *Just hit the freeway. Should be able to make up some time now.*

Mike: *Actually on the map, does it show the cross streets? Would hate to have Google Maps take you to another island or some shytt.*

Erin: *Yup I already checked.*

Mike: *Damn, you're dumb far from me then.*

To my dismay, even once I hit the freeway, traffic was not moving very quickly. It was getting late and I really wanted to get to him while there was still some nighttime left.

Erin: *Dammit, people! Go faster.*

Mike: *Lol! I fucking hate driving here!*

Erin: *Yeah, not loving this 55 mph BS, either.*

Mike: *Yeah, they either follow it or go under.*

Erin: *Lol, not me!*

Mike: *You want to see me that bad, huh?*

Erin: *Ha, I just don't want to drive anymore right now, but yeah, that too.*

Mike: *Lol*

Erin: *And I kinda hafta pee, too. Had an energy drink.*

Mike: *Lmao! That means you're coming upstairs, huh?*

Erin: *I can go wherever we are going, just need to go soon.*

Mike: *If you come up, you might not make it back down. Gonna lock you up in my room. ;)*

Erin: *Ha, that's not creepy at all.*

Mike: *Lolol! Right. That's exactly what I was thinking. :)*

Erin: *Okay, I'm almost there. Think I'm pulling up right outside your place now.*

Mike: *Cool. I'll be right down.*

While I waited for him, I pulled the visor down and did one last final check, quickly fixing my smudged eyeliner and putting on some lip-gloss. *Gold* by Adventure Club was playing and I turned it up a bit as I glanced up at the apartment building, looking for sign of where Mike might be coming out. A couple more minutes passed and I sat there fidgeting nervously. What the hell was taking him so long? Another couple minutes passed and still no sign of him, so I finally tried calling him, but just as it began to ring, I saw someone coming out the front doors of the building.

My breath caught in my chest as I gathered my courage. It was go time. No turning back now. I gulped as I unlocked the door and reached over to open it for him.

As soon as he got into the car, I knew I was done for. In one picture I'd seen, he'd been wearing a hat, and the other had been taken from the neck down. Now that I had him in person, I could see that he had a shaved head and piercing green eyes, and when I got a whiff as he leaned over to give me a quick kiss, I nearly mauled him but managed to keep myself in check. He smelled just as good as he looked, and I could feel myself getting turned on just being close to him. His sex appeal was literally radiating from him, and I was totally buying his brand.

"Hey, nice to see you," he said as he smiled at me. "Thanks for picking me up."

"No worries. Do you know which theater we're going to?"

"Ah yeah, I looked it up. Ward 16."

"Okie dokie." I plugged the theater name into Google Maps and waited for the directions to pop up and then pulled away from the curb. On the short drive there, we made small talk and learned a little more about each other. He told me he'd done a little modeling for *Abercrombie and Fitch* in his twenties and that he wouldn't mind doing it again, but didn't think it would happen. Work took up all of his time, and that was something he was running out of quickly when it came to how many modeling years he had left. If he wanted to make something happen with that, he needed to do it soon.

"Well, you know L.A. is a great place to be for that, you know," I said innocently, glancing sideways to see how he responded. He grinned and nodded.

"Yup, you're absolutely right. L.A. would be a fantastic place for me to pursue modeling. You're really trying to sell me on living there, huh?"

"Uhh, well, it would be more convenient for us if we want to continue seeing each other. You know…close proximity and all that. And southern California is awesome."

"Haha, I gotcha, I gotcha. Okay pull in right here after that light."

I followed his instructions, pulling into a little parking lot that was across from the theater. When we got out of the car, he pulled me closer for a proper greeting. All my nerves disappeared in a flash. That kiss was everything. After all the months of pent-up frustration with my ex and then with Jesse, I had almost forgotten what it was like to feel something that good again.

Our lips finally broke apart and my chest heaved as I fought to regain my breath. I thought that we would be lucky if we made it through the movie at this rate, but he just kissed my forehead and slid his hand down my arm until he took my hand in his and squeezed.

"I've been looking forward to doing that all day. Come on, let's figure out what movie we want to see."

"Okay," I agreed happily, letting him lead the way across the street and up the escalator to the movie theater.

After perusing our choices for a few minutes, we finally settled on a new action hero spoof that had just come out. Mike moved forward to pay for both of our tickets, making me smile. I knew it was a small gesture, but it still felt nice to have a guy taking me out on a real date for the first time in I couldn't remember when. We bypassed the concession stand and headed straight into our theater, grabbing two seats in the middle.

"So what made you decide to check out Craigslist?" I asked him, making small talk while we waited for the movie to start.

He laughed and shook his head. "You're not gonna believe this, but I've been kinda disappointed in the girls I've met in Hawaii. I thought that there would be so many beautiful girls, but once I got here… I thought, man, they're kinda ugly, you know?"

I almost snorted as I smothered a giggle. "Hey, that's not very nice," I said, trying to keep a straight face, "and it's certainly not true. There are tons of hot girls here."

"Well, I don't know where they've been hiding, 'cuz the girls I've seen here so far have looked pretty whack."

"Ha… so what does that have to do with Craigslist then?"

"I was Googling 'why are the women in Hawaii so ugly' and Craigslist came up as one of the search results, so I was browsing around on there and randomly found your ad."

"I'm not sure if I should be insulted or not. You do know I'm from here, right?"

"Yeah, but you're not Hawaiian, you're what—half Asian, you said?"

"Half Japanese, half German, Scotch-Irish and English. Your basic mutt."

"Sexy mutt," he corrected as he winked at me.

Just then the lights dimmed and the previews began to play. I couldn't remember the last time I enjoyed watching a movie so much. I felt like I was back in junior high or high school, getting to go to the movies with a boy I liked, wondering the whole time whether he would try to hold my hand or not. Well, Mike didn't hold my hand, but he constantly leaned into me at different times during the movie to share a smile or laugh over a funny part of the movie. The whole evening was turning out to be perfect—everything I could have wished for and more.

It was midnight by the time we got out from the movie. Mike asked if I wanted to go back to his place, so we stopped by a convenience store to pick up some wine first. But when we got to the cash register, the cashier said that he couldn't sell the wine to us. I just stood there and blinked at him at first, not quite comprehending what he was telling me. I couldn't believe Hawaii had a curfew for buying liquor. Worse yet, I couldn't believe that I didn't know that they did. Bummed, we left the store empty-handed and headed back to Mike's apartment.

We took a rickety elevator up to the third floor and I followed him down a long, dimly lit hallway until we reached the last door. Holding up a finger to his lips, he smiled as he quietly unlocked the door and gestured for me to go in before him. The apartment was quiet except for what sounded like a TV coming from one of the bedrooms, and I could see a little light under the door. Mike locked the door again and then reached for my hand and led the way to his room.

Being completely sober when you're hanging out with a hot new guy in his bedroom was definitely more nerve-wracking than if you'd had a bit of liquid courage, but Mike put me at ease while making my blood race at the same time. His bedroom was pretty sparse, which befitted him since he'd only moved to Hawaii a few months prior. He explained that he was staying in the second bedroom of an older woman who rented it out for extra cash, and he didn't have a car, so he had to take the bus to work every day. He had planned on buying a car eventually, but Hawaii had not turned out to be what he hoped, so he was already trying to arrange a transfer back to New York. Usually you couldn't request a transfer again for another two years, but his grandmother had gotten sick and was now living with his parents, and his mother had recently experienced a health scare as well, so he wanted to move back to help them. Family was extremely important to him and came before anything else, including himself. I smiled to myself as I listened to him talk, thinking how lucky I was that he'd turned out to be such a great guy.

After we chatted for a bit, he got out his tablet and showed me a *League of Legends* game and then pulled up a bunch of funny YouTube videos. I couldn't remember the last time my belly ached from laughing so hard and my mouth hurt from smiling so much. We were both in hysterics and couldn't keep from giggling and even outright snorting with laughter at moments. It was nice being around someone who shared a similar sense of humor.

As we laid there side by side on his bed, he'd started out with his hand resting casually on my hip, then slid it down to cup and massage my ass firmly yet gently. I snuggled closer to him and marveled in the simple pleasure of feeling his leg pressed closely against mine. We were just starting another video when I glanced over to find him watching me instead with a sexy little smile on his lips. I smiled back at him and turned a bit so I was facing him more. Setting his tablet down, he reached up to gently slide his fingers through my hair, then gripped tightly as he brought his lips to mine.

I was so turned on and ready for him that fireworks went rocketing off in my head as he kissed me for the first time. Our tongues slid together in a sexy little dance, lips kissing and biting as we devoured one another. Shoving my skirt up, he grabbed my ass, pulling me close as he molded my body against his. My heart was pounding wildly as the blood thundered in my ears, and then he grabbed my hand and placed it right on his hard cock. As I wrapped my hand around his bulge, I could feel him throbbing through his jeans, all that hot yummy hardness. I wanted him so badly that I ached, but… the reality was that I was still on my period, and he was probably not going to want to go there. As I reminded myself of this, I groaned out loud.

"Mmm, yeah, baby? You like that?"

"Mmm hmm," was all I could manage, and then I was kissing him again, rubbing myself up and down against that lovely erection. "You know, I almost didn't reply to your email because of that naked bathroom selfie you sent."

He winked at me and laughed. "Yeah, but you liked it, huh? That's the Puerto Rican ass."

Well then, it was official. I was a sucker for Puerto Rican ass.

He might not be down with fucking while I was on the rag, and I was a little too shy to come right out and ask him, but I had felt that big beautiful cock and wanted to see and taste it and make him come so hard that his eyeballs rolled back into his head. I reached for his zipper and began to unfasten his jeans, hearing him gasp as my hand slipped in the waistband of his boxer briefs. I nearly began to drool as my fingers greedily wrapped themselves around his monstrous cock. To my delight, as I grasped his huge throbbing shaft, my fingers didn't even meet. I soaked in the glorious feeling of having such a magnificent cock in my hand, but I wanted so badly to feel him inside me.

Frustrated, I settled for shoving his briefs and jeans down his legs and taking that beautiful penis in my mouth.

"Oh fuck, yeah," he hissed as my lips wrapped themselves tightly around the large head before sliding down further until he hit the back of my throat. I prided myself on my oral skills, loving how I made him groan and shudder as I worked him with my tongue and lips.

I reveled in the pleasure of making him feel so good, caressing him everywhere as I made love to him with my mouth. I sensed that he was getting close to coming when he finally sat up and gripped my head, bringing my lips up to his. After kissing me senseless, he said, "My turn," but I shook my head sadly.

"I can't... I'm on my period right now," I groaned.

"Oh no!" He sounded as bummed as I felt, which was a little comforting at least.

"I know, I'm so sorry," I apologized. "But I can still take care of you?"

"How do you feel about anal?"

My eyes widened as I shook my head. "Mmm, that's okay! No thank you." I glanced down at his beautiful penis and shivered. Yeah right, there was no way that monster was going in my ass. No, sir, not mine!

He chuckled and took my hand and placed it on his hard cock again. "That's too bad, but okay then, I'll take you up on your offer."

For a brief moment I felt a little disappointed as I'd been hoping he was one of those guys who didn't really care and would just put a towel down in case of any mess, or say let's shower together and do it in there so the mess would be washed right away. But it didn't sound like he was interested in that, and I guess I couldn't blame him. I gave pretty amazing head. Why would he want to do any work or have to bother with a mess when he could just have me blow him? Sighing, I shrugged and went back to work, easily rocking his world and making him come within a few minutes.

Once he had finally calmed down from his orgasm, he quickly passed out, so I cuddled close to him and soon drifted off as well. It wasn't long before morning came, and I woke up to the sound of the garbage truck right outside the window and the mynah birds calling their greetings to each other. I glanced over at Mike, who appeared to still be fast asleep, but when I snuggled closer to him, he wrapped his arm around to squeeze me in a hug.

"Morning," he murmured into my hair.

"Morning. Did you sleep well?"

"Mmmhmm," he said, then gasped and bit his lip when my hand found his morning wood.

I stroked him slowly, loving the velvety feel of his hardening thickness in my hand as I listened to the effect I had on his breathing. I'd never been with a guy his size before, and I was fascinated, imagining what he might feel like buried deep inside me. I wanted him to fuck me so badly, but I would settle for rocking his world again. If I worked him well enough, he would probably do almost anything to come visit me in L.A. anytime I wanted. I think I made him come in less than five minutes. Damn was I good.

After he had recovered from his second orgasm, he asked if I wanted to get breakfast, so we cleaned ourselves up a bit and then set off for Zippy's. Breakfast turned out to be a two-hour affair. Over scrambled eggs, Portuguese sausage and rice, we continued getting to know each other. When a little over an hour had passed and we'd finished our breakfast, I sighed regretfully and said we should probably get going, but Mike shrugged and said he was in no hurry and was enjoying talking to me. I was thrilled that he seemed to be enjoying my company, so I settled back to enjoy another cup of coffee and continued our conversation.

I told him about how I had gotten into self-publishing and had chosen romance as my genre, basing my first book on some online dating experiences I'd had in my early twenties. He laughed and suggested that I put him in my next book. I laughed with him and said, "You never know."

He asked if I had any tattoos or any piercings other than my ears, and I shook my head. I told him that I was scared of needles, but that my little sister was a tattoo artist, so I'd probably let her ink me someday. When he told me he used to have his penis pierced and that he wouldn't mind doing it again, I nearly spit my coffee across the table. I had once slept with a guy that had a penis piercing, and it had been amazing. Of course, he had been nowhere near Mike's size, so I was now extremely curious and thinking of ways I could convince him to do it again.

When I dropped him back off at his place, I got out of the car to give him a hug. He gave me a slow, sweet kiss and then wrapped his arms around me in a long hug.

"I had a great time last night," he said before finally pulling back to look at me.

"Me too." And holy shit, what a night! I really didn't want to leave him now, but I had no choice. My plane was leaving with or without me. Just then, thunder rumbled overhead and rain began to sprinkle down.

"Let me know when you get back to the place you're staying so I know you got back safely," he said, giving me another quick kiss before turning to head back inside and out of the rain.

"Okay," I said, waving to him before getting into the car and driving off.

I moved in a haze the rest of the day, a permanent silly smile on my lips. I couldn't wait to see my sexy Puerto Rican again and hoped it was sooner than later. The nice thing was that we continued to text back and forth all day. He told me he was getting his place cleaned up and ready for the lady to show to people so she could rent it out again. He was really doing it. He was moving back to Brooklyn. We talked a little more about him coming to visit me in L.A., but he said he had to wait until he figured out moving back home before he committed to anything. I told him not to worry about it and that we could talk about it later.

I hated packing to go back home after vacation. It was always depressing, and I could never fit everything back in the same way that I had originally packed it. Saying good-bye to my family was tough, and I bravely blinked back the tears as I hugged Kylie and kissed Kenny on his adorable fuzzy head. He smelled like ocean and baby powder, and I nearly lost it right there. I absolutely hated that I was leaving. I wanted to stay longer, but I told everyone I loved them, would miss them, and then I got into my rental car and drove away.

On my way to the airport Jesse called me, and since I was in such a good mood, I felt generous enough to answer. Big mistake. He immediately started yelling at me about talking to some poetry blogger online about him and his family and about the suicide and how he'd come back to life, and that the guy was accusing him of pulling some big scam to gain sympathy from people. I didn't know what the hell he was talking about and told him so, but he kept accusing me of talking about his business. After arguing him for a minute, I gave up trying to talk any sense to him and hung up. He tried to call me back, but I hit ignore. When I got to the rental car agency, I sent him a last text and told him if he ever cared about me, that he would pretend like he'd never met me and just leave me the fuck alone. I so didn't need his shit.

By the time I had gotten through security and sat down at my gate, there was another text from Jesse, apologizing profusely. Apparently the blogger had given him wrong information and he was very sorry. I just ignored him. I wasn't going to waste a single second more on someone who so obviously didn't give a shit about me. I had tried to love him and failed, so I had tried to be his friend instead, and he had done nothing but continue to betray me in return. I was done.

As I sat there all sticky and sweating at my gate, I waited impatiently for them to call my group. I wasn't eager to return to L.A., but I was definitely eager to get out of the heat and humidity. There was still about twenty minutes until time to board, so I decided to go find a cool drink and a snack. After locating a kiosk that sold a plethora of Hawaiian treats and bottled water and sodas, I purchased some water and Japanese rice crackers and headed back to the gate. The airline attendant started speaking into the PA system just as I walked up, announcing that our flight was overbooked and asking for volunteers to give up their seat in exchange for a voucher. She said they would provide a hotel for the night if anyone could possibly fly out the next day. My thoughts immediately started racing. It was Saturday. Technically, I didn't have to work until Monday morning, so there really wasn't any reason I couldn't stay another night.

Grabbing my phone, I tried texting Mike to see if he was free and interested in hanging out if I stayed an additional night. He didn't respond, so I sent another text saying to please let me know ASAP as they were asking for volunteers right then. I paced around while I waited for him to text me back, but my phone stayed silent. Finally I tried calling to see if he would pick up, because you know—maybe he hadn't heard my text messages. I did a mental face palm as I thought about how stupid that sounded, but the phone just rang and rang until it went to voicemail anyway. I briefly explained what the situation was and said if he happened to get the message in the next few minutes, he could try calling me back.

After I hung up, I reasoned that I could just go ahead and volunteer and take the flight and hotel voucher and keep trying to get a hold of him. Either way it was a free additional day in Hawaii, and I could go back to my family's house and visit with them more if nothing else. I considered just going for it, but at the same time I was already starting to feel bummed out that he hadn't answered the phone, and I definitely didn't want to look as desperate as I was starting to feel.

As I sat there staring at my phone, willing it to ring, I argued with myself as I began to overanalyze everything that had occurred in the past forty-eight hours. Maybe I had misinterpreted how good a time he had. Maybe now that he'd gotten as much as he needed from me, he was no longer interested. Yep, logically I knew that I was probably chasing a guy who just wanted a one-night stand and had absolutely zero interest in seeing me again. I had found him on Craigslist after all, but still, I had felt something—a connection. And he'd been the one who wanted to prolong breakfast and chat more. He also could have kicked me out the night before, and he could have said good-bye and not asked me to breakfast. My brain wouldn't shut up as it went back and forth. Finally I sent one last text to him.

Erin: *Never mind... I'm just going to catch my original flight. :) Will let you know when I'm back in L.A.*

They started calling everyone to board, and with a heavy heart, I lifted my chin and joined the group of sweaty tourists who were lining up with their boarding passes. I had gone from cloud nine to cloud zero in the span of a few hours, and my stomach had the biggest knot in it. Had I imagined the special moments we had shared, the way he looked at me, and the way I felt when I was with him? Was it all in my head? Was he just a player? The questions wouldn't stop.

When I was finally settled in my window seat, I leaned my head against the side and stared down at my phone again. I willed him to text me, to at least say something like he was so sorry he'd missed my call, and that he'd had a great time and would miss me. Anything. I desperately needed some validation that the previous night had meant something, but I was to be disappointed. After a few more minutes, the flight attendant announced that all cell phones were to be switched to airplane mode. I obeyed as I popped in my ear buds, turned on some music and leaned back into my seat, trying to relax and fall asleep so the next five hours wouldn't feel as excruciatingly long as I was afraid they might.

Thankfully I managed to sleep for most of the flight, but I couldn't sleep anymore for the last two hours, which felt like the longest two hours of my life. By the time we landed back in L.A., I was a sweaty wreck and could feel a big pimple forming on my chin. I couldn't wait to take a hot shower and then dry off and actually stay dried off. As soon as I turned airplane mode off, a text message came in from Mike.

Mike: *Hey, wow I'm sorry. I was asleep that whole time. Took a nap after all that cleaning. Had no idea you were staying. Wow, and the phone calls. My bad.*

I felt so relieved when I saw his message. He had just been asleep. I wasn't crazy. I texted him back while I waited for the other passengers in front of me to start exiting the plane.

Erin: *I didn't stay. I was going to if you wanted me to, but I figured you* *didn't since you weren't responding, lol. Oh well :) hope you had a good nap. Just landed back in L.A.*

Mike: *Glad you made it safely. It was a good nap.*

Corrine was picking me up since she had let me park in front of her apartment while I was gone, so once I made it to baggage claim and had grabbed my suitcase, I texted to let her know I was on my way outside to the curb. A few minutes later, I was sitting in her passenger seat, showing her Mike's pictures and telling her all about my trip while I happily texted back and forth with him.

Erin: *I'm sitting in traffic with my friend Corinne now. She's a doll and picked me up since the shuttle doesn't start running til 7 am.*

Mike: *Nice!*

Erin: *Ahh home again... I showed her your picture and told her about you. She approves, lol ;)*

Mike: *She better! Thank you for the compliment btw ;)*

Erin: *Lol ;) You're welcome. Yeah, I met Corinne on Craigslist like 12 years ago.*

Mike: *Omg!*

Erin: *I was looking for Justin Timberlake tickets and she emailed me and said she didn't have tickets, but that if I found some and wanted company, she'd love to go with me.*

Mike: *Lmao*

Erin: *And I didn't have anyone to go with me, so I said ok, found tickets, we met up to see a movie first (The Italian Job), and then we went to JT's concert together and had a blast. Best friends ever since. :)*

Mike: *Sweet.*

Erin: *I'm kinda thinking Craigslist is my lucky charm. Never would have met her or you without it. ;)*

Mike: *Yeah, that's pretty uncanny. Hey, I'm going to go back to bed for a bit. Have to show the apartment to some people later today. I'll text you later. xoxo*

Erin: *Okay :) xoxo*

Chapter FOURTEEN

The next Saturday when Mike was due to fly back to NYC, he told me he'd arranged for a long layover in L.A. His work buddies had taken him out drinking the night before as a final farewell, so he was running on no sleep and had a hangover, but he had to be at the airport at the crack of dawn. His brother worked for one of the major airlines, so he was able to travel for free on a buddy pass, but that meant having to fly standby. He texted me and said he'd gone straight from drinking to leaving for the airport. I waited for him to confirm what time he'd be arriving at LAX, but he missed all the morning departures. For some reason, every flight was booked solid. Out of desperation, I started searching for fares myself and found one seat left on a Hawaiian Airlines flight that was leaving in the early afternoon.

I really wanted to see him, so I offered to buy him a plane ticket to L.A. It was going to cost me close to a thousand dollars, but I was pretty sure he was worth it. After first arguing with me and saying he couldn't accept it, he missed yet another flight and then finally relented and let me buy the ticket. The plus side to this happening was that Mike said no one but his brother knew he was coming home, so realistically he said he could stay for the weekend instead of only a few hours. Of course I said yes.

Our weekend together was pure heaven. It was everything I could have hoped for and more. It was evening by the time I picked him up from the airport, and as soon as we got back to my place, we tore each other's clothes off and ravaged each other. The moment he finally entered me was bliss—he felt better than I had even imagined possible. He owned my body with each powerful thrust, his long fingers wrapped tightly around my breasts as he squeezed. I had a feeling I was going to have fingermarks all over my boobs for the next few days, but I secretly loved the fact that I would bear his mark. My legs felt super wobbly when I finally got up to use the restroom and clean myself up, and I couldn't help giggling as I inspected myself in the bathroom mirror. My skin was flushed, my hair was mussed, my lips swollen—I definitely looked like I had just been properly fucked.

The next morning, I took him to my favorite breakfast spot and introduced him to the owner when she came by. She gave me a knowing smile before walking away, which made me giggle. We both ordered omelets and waffles, and Mike inhaled his food, saying it was delicious. After breakfast, it was back to my place for more fantastic sex and snuggles. In between rounds, we lounged around in bed and watched reruns of *Whose Line Is It Anyway*. It was one of the best weekends of my life.

Having to take Mike back to the airport on Monday morning sucked ass. Luckily for me, Jerry was out of town, so nobody was going to care if I was running a little late. I had just had the most incredible weekend, and I was afraid I was never going to see Mike again, but he hugged me tight, gave me a light kiss good-bye and thanked me for everything. I told him to text me when he got home safely, and he promised he would.

Once I finally got to work after dropping him off, the day just dragged by. Kristen came by to let me know she had made an appointment and that Evan had given her money to have the abortion. She looked sad and resigned to the inevitable, and I didn't know what else I could say or do, so I just hugged her tightly and said to let me know if she needed anything. Right after I left work, Mike texted to say he was home and heading straight to bed after a late night dinner. His family was of course thrilled to have him back home again and had sat him down immediately to eat something when he got there. His mom had cried tears of happiness upon seeing her baby boy. It was hard to wish that he was here with me when I knew how much his family needed him right now.

That summer was excruciating for me. All I could think about was seeing Mike again, but now that he was back home in Brooklyn, it sounded like he was working full-time for FedEx and part-time at his family's liquor store. He was exhausted all of the time, and sometimes he went days without answering my texts.

I had known going into this that having a long distance relationship wasn't going to be easy, but there were couples that made it work, so I knew it wasn't impossible, either. We'd had "the talk" a couple of times, and he'd admitted that he didn't think a long distance thing was very realistic, but he'd also said he wasn't saying "No", so we agreed to take one day at a time and just see how things went. One thing I knew for sure is that I wanted to spend more time with him to figure out if we really had something worth fighting for.

He wasn't able to make it back out to spend another weekend with me until mid-July. Although I really wanted to visit him in New York, it made more sense to have him continue to visit me in L.A. where I had my own apartment, which saved us having to spend any money on lodging. If I visited him in Brooklyn, I'd have to get a hotel or vacation rental since he was sleeping on the floor in his parents' basement until he saved up enough for a security deposit on a new apartment. Considering that he was helping them financially at the moment, he had no idea when he'd be able to afford his own place again.

Unsurprisingly, we spent a good chunk of that visit in bed as well, and he even talked me into finally trying anal (which wasn't half as bad as I remembered), but I also took him to a couple more of my favorite restaurants. We even fit in some nerd time and played *Magic the Gathering* and watched some *League of Legends* matches.

Whenever we were together, I had the best time with him. The time in between visits dragged on so slowly, and the lack of communication from him when we weren't about to see each other was beginning to wear on me, but I wasn't ready to give up, yet. I was falling for him hard, and I wanted so badly for things to work out. I was convinced that we could be really good together if he would just give it a chance.

In September, we made plans to meet up in Las Vegas. He'd never been, and I was turning thirty-three, so I proposed that we meet there to celebrate my birthday. While I normally might have lamented turning another year older, this time it didn't bother me one bit. Maybe it was because he had his face buried in my pussy and was making me scream his name when the clock struck midnight and I officially left thirty-two behind. Yep, it might have been that. You kinda tend to stop thinking anything in general when you're exploding from one of the most intense orgasms of your life.

We even ventured out of our hotel room at the Aria to have dinner, play a little Blackjack, and dance the night away at Haze Nightclub. As I suspected, Mike had some nice moves that had me grinning from ear to ear. After downing a few shots we did a little dirty dancing, and before I knew it, he was dragging me back upstairs to our room. We barely made it inside the room before he had his jeans unzipped, and then he spun me around to face the door, shoved my skirt up around my waist, and pulled my panties to one side as he plunged his thick hard cock into my dripping pussy.

"Oh fuck, fuck, fuck!" I panted and moaned as he thrust away. I was so full, and he felt so good.

My legs were shaking as I started to come all over his pulsating shaft, and then he was right there with me, grunting as he slammed into me a few more times. Then I could feel his body tense as his cum began to spurt deep inside me, his orgasm rocking through both of us as he whispered to me, "Happy Birthday, babe."

After cleaning up, we fell onto the bed and curled up together to take a nap, but I couldn't sleep. As he snored softly, I studied his face and traced my fingertips around his eyebrows, down his high cheekbones, across his full lips. He was a beautiful man, and I was completely and totally smitten. If he told me he wanted me to have his babies, I would say, "How many?" I was willing to do just about anything to be with him. I just wasn't sure if he felt the same, yet, or if he ever would. I still didn't know if he was just having fun, or if he really felt something for me. He said he didn't really have time or room for a relationship in his life, but I reasoned that he probably wasn't thinking about the aspect of it being long distance, where the demands on his time wouldn't be as high.

When I woke up the next morning, the bed was empty next to me, but I could hear the shower running. Looking at the clock, I winced when I saw that we both had to be at the airport in less than two hours. I hated how rushed our time always was. It couldn't even be considered a full weekend. I only got to see him from late Friday night until late Sunday morning and then he was leaving me again. Why had I thought this long distance thing was a good idea?

Heading into the bathroom to start getting ready, I got a nice look at his entire profile as he stood there in the shower, the water cascading down his perfectly sculpted body. He was physically perfect from his nicely shaped head to his lean stomach with the sexy "V", and he had an ass that could almost put JLo and Kim Kardashian to shame. And of course, his beautiful, thick penis and perfect big balls that gave me so much pleasure. I could spend a week in bed with him and still want more. Yep, he was definitely worth trying a long distance relationship. The question was whether he thought I was worth it as well, but I was afraid to come right out and ask him. I was afraid his answer might not be what I wanted to hear.

In the cab on our way to the airport, I chattered nervously as I gathered the courage to ask him how he felt about me coming to visit him in NYC. I wanted to visit the east coast so badly, and it was the perfect chance for me to do so while I was dating someone who lived right there.

"I'm glad you came," I said as I leaned into him and smiled.

"Me too." He smiled back and squeezed my leg.

Here goes nothing. "So I was thinking about me coming to New York next, 'cuz you know, I've never been to the east coast before. Just flown through Pittsburgh once, but that doesn't count."

"Seriously? Yeah, you should definitely check it out."

"So that'd be okay with you? I mean, I was thinking I would come for a long weekend, like maybe take a couple days off and make it four days instead of our usual not-quite-two-days. And I would get a vacation rental to stay at while I'm there. I've already been checking out some places on VRBO.com. What do you think?"

"Sure, that sounds doable. When are you thinking?"

"I can check fares and see when a good time would be, but I was thinking maybe in late October or November sometime."

"November would be better. Halloween is a pretty big deal for me and my sister—we always dress up and go out and party."

"Oh okay, sure, no problem. I'll check for dates in early November then and let you know."

"Beast," was all he said, and then he gave me a quick kiss. "You'll have a great time. But to be honest, I won't be able to spend a whole lot of time with you. I still can't take any time off work. I used all my PTO up when I moved to Hawaii and then had to transfer back to New York, and I'm still working on saving it back up again."

"But you'll sleep there with me while I'm there, right?"

"Duh. Well, I still have to work, but I'll be staying over. It just sucks I can't chill with you the whole time."

"It's okay. As long as I get to see you a little bit, I can deal with that. I want to do some sightseeing, so I'll probably just walk around by myself a bunch anyway, take some pictures. I have a few friends who live out here as well, so I might meet up for coffee or lunch or something."

"Awesome, that would be great. Then I won't feel bad for not being able to show you around."

"Aw, don't feel bad, baby. I really just want to be able to spend a little more time with you. These short weekends really don't cut it."

"It is what it is. I told you what my life is like right now." He looked mildly irritated, and I was quick to reassure him.

"Oh I know, I'm sorry. I don't mean to complain. I'm grateful for the time that you give me."

There wasn't any time for me to say more as our cab had just pulled up in front of Mike's terminal. I got out of the car with him to say good-bye.

"Thanks again. I had a great time," he said as he hugged me close. "I hope you had a good birthday."

"Mmm, did I ever," I agreed, humming low in my throat as he kissed me slowly. Reluctantly, I finally pulled back and gave him another hug. "Let me know you got home safe."

"You too."

When I got back home to L.A., the first thing I did was check airfares for November. It was looking like the weekend before Thanksgiving was the cheapest fare, so I checked for available vacation rentals after that and found several that looked pretty decent and were affordable. I plugged all the information into a spreadsheet and emailed it to Mike. He knew the area—I didn't. He would be able to check the addresses and let me know which were good possibilities and which were definite "no's".

I was so excited to visit NYC. I had only seen it as depicted in movies or read about it in books, but I had a feeling I would love it. There was so much culture and history there—how could you *not* love the Big Apple? I couldn't wait to be standing on the streets of Manhattan, sinking my teeth into the hustle and bustle of one of the most famous cities in the world.

Mike got back to me within a couple days to confirm that the weekend before Thanksgiving would work for him too, and then told me which rental units sounded promising. I narrowed it down to a couple of units from there, then finally settled on one in Bushwick. I contacted the owner and put in my request for the dates, then booked my plane ticket online. I was doing it. I was actually going to New York for the first time in my life. I couldn't believe it had taken me over thirty years to finally get my ass to NYC, and it had taken a man to motivate me enough to get it done. I had everything squared away within a matter of a few days, and then began the awful task of waiting. It was going to be a good two months more before I would get to see him again.

Determined to look good for my trip, I started hitting the gym hard. I cut out the carbs as much as possible and I spent almost every day on the treadmill. When I felt like I was going to die, I would imagine the look on Mike's face when he saw me again, looking all trim and lean. It worked. I kept pushing and pushing, and slowly the pounds began to drop. Working out was a great substitute for sex when you couldn't get it, and being that I was only getting it from someone who lived nearly three thousand miles away, I started pretty much living at the gym when I wasn't at work.

By the time mid-November finally rolled around, I was more than ready to go. I had gone shopping and now had a modest winter wardrobe so I wouldn't freeze my ass off in the much colder climate. I had invested in a wool coat and some comfortable looking black Vans, which I figured would be great for doing a lot of walking around the city. I packed and repacked my suitcase until I was satisfied with all my choices. I was so excited and nervous that I could barely sleep the entire week before my trip.

When there were only a couple of days left before my trip, I shot Mike a text to confirm all the last minute details. He hadn't answered the last text I sent him a couple days before, but I assumed everything was still good to go. He would tell me if he had to cancel, right? I really hoped he answered me this time.

Erin: *Hey you… just wanted to confirm everything before I leave.*

Mike: *Hey, I'm sorry, been out of control busy/stressed. Just woke up. Fucking came home and collapsed, lol.*

Erin: *Heh, I heard it snowed for a bit by you yesterday.*

Mike: *It really did. I was like wtf.*

Erin: *I'm sure your job sucks when the weather is bad. :/*

Mike: *Yeah, especially now with my new route. I'm right by the water.*

Erin: *It was like fucking 85 degrees here today. I was dying—like we are in the middle of November. Wtf.*

Mike: *Lolol. That's crazy.*

Erin: *Yeah, I'm ready for some cooler weather, lol.*

Mike: *It dipped into the 20s, so be prepared.*

Erin: *Holy shit. Otay…packing all the warm crap I just got. I had like nothing with long sleeves.*

Mike: *Yeah, it's been stupid, from high 20s to mid 50s.*

Erin: *My closet was definitely strictly California, but I have scarves and my friend made me get a hat. I'll be aight. I used to deal with Nebraska winters.*

Mike: *Yeah, you'll be fine then.*

Erin: *;) You'll keep me warm anyway, right?*

Mike: *Indeed I will.*

Erin: *Hehe :) So I am guessing I won't get to the place I'm staying until maybe 5:30 or so.*

Mike: *Make sure you bring lots of lube.*

Erin: *I just laughed out loud.*

Mike: *Yeah, that sounds good. I'll go home and freshen up first and then head towards you. Why you laughing?*

Erin: *Nothing! Noted...lots of lube. ;)*

Mike: *Lol*

Erin: *Can't wait to jump you ;)*

Mike: *We need a nice anal plug and a vibrator. Then we're all set.*

Erin: *Whaaat? Anal plug?? I can bring my vibrator.*

Mike: *Yeah, anal plug. I'll be fucking both holes.*

Erin: *But anal plug? :p Never tried, but I dunno... sounds interesting, I suppose.*

Mike: *Well, 3 holes really.*

Erin: *3?*

Mike: *Yep, I'll be fucking all 3 holes.*

Erin: *Lol, but not at the same time?*

Mike: *No, just 2.*

Erin: *You miss being in my mouth, huh? ;)*

Mike: *I do. My goal this time is to make you come from your ass.*

Erin: *Really? You think you can do that, hmm?*

Mike: *I know I can. You never even liked it before.*

Erin: *I know. It's so crazy. I was so scared of letting you try, lol. My previous experiences were not good.*

Mike: *I like that you can take me pretty much all the way. Good stuff.*

Erin: *Hehe yeah, with you that is definitely saying something. ;) It was way better than anything I had tried before with that.*

Mike: *See. And I fucked you hard, balls deep.*

Erin: *It felt good, too. ;)*

Mike: *And you took it, no problem. Liked it even.*

Erin: *I know, lol. I was shocked.*

Mike: *Magic!*

Erin: *Indeed. :) I have a surprise for you. It's black and pretty, and it probably won't stay on long, but I hope you like. ;)*

Mike: *Awesome! Send me a pussy and ass pic.*

Erin: *What! No way, lol.*

Mike: *:-\ Fine*

Erin: *Haha, are you going to reciprocate if I do?*

Mike: *Not now*

Erin: *Uh huh, that's what I thought. No way then. But if you ever want to trade, let me know. ;)*

Mike: *No, that's trickery.*

Erin: *Lol, how so?*

Mike: *Cuz you were so against it at first.*

Erin: *Whatever. :p*

Mike: *I gotta get going. Don't forget your vibrator.*

Erin: *I won't! And lots of lube. ;)*

Mike: *Good girl.*

Erin: *I aim to please. ;)*

Mike: *;)*

Chapter FIFTEEN

I made sure to arrive at the airport early the next morning—I wasn't taking any chances on missing my flight. There was no else at the gate when I got there, so I picked a good spot to get settled, popped my ear buds in and cranked up the music before pulling out my laptop to write. I was listening to Kaskade's latest album, and as I glanced at the song title list, I giggled. I hadn't noticed before that the album had a song titled *LAX to JFK*. It was perfect for my NYC Trip playlist.

Erin: *At the airport now, waiting to board. I got what you wanted, by the way. Came in a pack of three sizes, lol.*

Mike: *Oh shytt! Prepare to be stuffed. :P*

Erin: *Mmm ;)*

Mike: *xoxo*

Erin: *Geez, it's like torrential downpour here in L.A. this morning!*

Mike: *Yikes! Is your flight still on time?*

Erin: *Says so.*

Mike: *Awesome.*

Erin: *Just boarded... Virgin America. Pretty nice!*

Mike: *Yeah, I heard they are really good.*

Erin: *Okay, we're boarding now. Turning my phone off. I'll let you know when I land—they said we might even get in a little early. See you soon! xoxo :)*

Mike: *Sweet! Later. Safe trip.*

The flight from LAX to JFK was about five and a half hours, so it was roughly about the same as flying from L.A. to Hawaii. I realized that regardless if he had ended up staying in Hawaii or moved back to Brooklyn, he was about the same distance from me either way. Ugh. Why couldn't he live closer?

I couldn't wait to see Mike. It had been two months since Vegas, and I was feeling pretty sexually frustrated since I hadn't gotten any since the last time I had seen him. But right then as I waited impatiently for the passengers in front of me to exit, I was feeling anything but horny. Someone had brought their pets on board—I counted three dogs total—and it was hot and stuffy in there as we waited for the flight attendants to open the door to the gateway, so you can just imagine what that smelled like. Then once we got off the plane, it took forever for our bags to come out, and I was hot and sweaty by the time I dragged my suitcase, carry-on and other bag outside to wait by the taxis for the car service I had arranged. Why did I love to travel so much?

Finally Tom, the driver who had been assigned to me, found me and picked me up, getting me settled in his mini-van. He was very open and friendly and chatted non-stop as he drove me to Bushwick, telling me interesting little tidbits about the city as we drove through. I shot Mike a text to let him know I had landed and was on my way to the rental place.

Erin: *Hey, I'm here! In the car on my way to the apartment right now.*

Mike: *Sweet! Yeah, I'll be done with work by 6. Let me know how it is when you get there.*

Erin: *Okay, I will. Can't wait to see you. :)*

Mike: *Soon! ;)*

When I got to the apartment, I was pleasantly surprised to find that the unit was spacious and clean. It was quite the contrast to the outside of the building and the surrounding neighborhood, which looked dirty, old and run-down, with graffiti marking the walls around us. It had two beds in two separate bedrooms that were oddly connected right next to each other. You had to walk from the living room through the smaller bedroom into the master bedroom, which included a nice king-sized bed. They had also upgraded the TV in the living room to a flat screen, and the tidy little kitchen was more than adequate for our needs. I didn't anticipate needing to use it much more than to maybe heat something up in the microwave. Relieved, I texted Mike to let him know I was happy with the place.

Mike: *Cool. You ready for me?*

Erin: *Yes, of course. :) When are you going to be here?*

Mike: *Well, I got off work around 6ish, then it'll be 40 min to get home, freshen up, so I should be there before 9 for sure. Send me the address again?*

I sent him the address and told him to let me know when he was out front and I'd come let him in.

Erin: *Hurry up! 9 is a long ways away. :p*

Mike: *Lolol. Np. ;)*

Erin: *;)*

The feeling when he finally walked in the front door was unlike anything I'd ever felt before. I'm sure I probably felt more euphoric than I might have normally because I was in a new city that I'd always dreamed of visiting, and there was a gorgeous man in front of me who knew exactly how to please me, but it was pretty fantastic. It felt a little surreal, being here in Brooklyn in him.

I stepped back to let him come in, momentarily feeling a little unsure of myself. Then those gorgeous green eyes locked on mine and he smiled at me.

"Hey," he said, leaning forward to give me a quick kiss and hug hello before he started peeling off all his layers of clothing.

"Hey," was all I could manage to say.

Oh my God! All of a sudden I felt so awkward, like I couldn't think of anything to say. Think, Erin, think! Don't let the sexy man in front of you think you're a complete fucking moron. Ask him how his day was.

Shushing my brain, I smiled at him and sat down on the couch, patting the cushion next to me. "How was your day?"

He finished stripping down to his boxers and t-shirt and then came over to sit down. "Long as fuck. My route took me longer than it should have. They assigned a really shitty one to me, and the last carrier who worked this route used to cheat on how she did things, so realistically, it's not even possible to meet the quota she was doing in one day. So they're on my ass to do it faster than I have been."

"That's not fair," I said as I pulled his legs over onto my lap and started massaging his calves and kneecaps.

"Nope, but it is what it is, right? I don't really have any other choice at the moment. I gotta take what I can get. Mmm, yeah, that feels good. Keep doing that."

"Totally get it. Just sucks for you." I continued to gently work the muscles in his calves, then swirled my fingertips around his kneecaps. After I had done that for another minute, Mike caught my hand and led it to the large bulge in his boxers. As I grasped him, my eyes widened and my lips parted in anticipation. His size never ceased to amaze me. He was one of those guys that was always big, regardless of whether he was hard or not. And right now, he was quickly on his way to becoming rock hard.

"Show me your new toys," he ordered. "And lose your clothes. You're wearing way too many clothes."

"So are you," I teased before pushing his legs off my lap. I got up and headed straight for the bedroom, stripping my clothes off as I went. Retrieving the toys and lube from where I had stashed them in the nightstand, I placed them on the bed and then moved over to the vanity to light the candle I had brought with me. Then I turned to sit on the edge of the bed and wait for Mike to join me.

I was more than a little nervous, if I was being honest with myself. I eyed the large pink plastic plugs skeptically. The smallest one didn't look too bad, but the largest one was humongous. I wasn't too keen on trying that one. Mike's cock was one thing—a big pink plastic plug was another. It was flesh and blood and much more forgiving than a hunk of plastic.

Mike finally appeared in the door of the bedroom with two wineglasses in hand.

"To help you relax, and to welcome you to New York."

"Haha, thanks. Cheers." I clinked my glass against his and raised it in salute, then immediately started gulping it down.

"Whoa, whoa, babe," he said, quickly extracting the wineglass from my grip and setting it down. "Slow down there."

"No," I said, shaking my head and looking at him with wide, frightened eyes. "More please."

He got a good look at my expression and burst out laughing. "Erin, I'm not going to hurt you. Don't you trust me?"

I bit my lip and nodded slowly. "Yeah, but just—just go really, really slow, kay? You're humongous!"

He chuckled and put his hand over his heart. "I solemnly swear to go slow, babe. Come here." He pulled me close to him and began kissing me, then worked his way over to my ear and neck, lightly nipping at my throat with his lips. He threaded the fingers of one hand through my long hair and then gripped tightly, pulling my head farther back to give him better access to that area. I moaned as he traced his tongue around the sensitive outer shell of my ear, sucked the lobe into his mouth and swirled his tongue around it. He reached forward and caressed his fingers down my stomach and through the small patch of hair at the top of my mound until he reached my clit, already slick with desire for him.

Turning me around, he pushed me forward onto the bed. I felt something cold and hard press against my asshole, making me tighten and freeze up immediately. "That's cold!" I protested.

"Relax," he commanded as he gently stroked my back. Then I could hear the bottle of lube as he squirted some into his hand. Again, I felt something hard press against my anus, only this time it well-lubricated. I groaned as he pushed it in further, muffling myself by pressing my face into the bed. I was so glad I hadn't eaten anything today. I really was not digging this feeling, but I was determined to give it a shot for Mike's sake, so I let him continue to push it into me.

When it was all the way in, he leaned back and palmed himself, getting ready to push into my other waiting hole. But just then the anal plug popped back out of me, making a little "plop" sound. I giggled and he snickered as well.

"I think that one is too small for you. We should try one of the bigger plugs," he said, making my eyebrows shoot up in alarm as my head swung around frantically to look at him.

"That was the smallest one? Are you kidding me?"

"Yeah, that was the smallest one. Let's try the biggest one."

"Are you crazy?" I twisted around to face him and held my hand over my ass as I watched him pick up the biggest plug. "Motherfucker, you *are* crazy. Get that thing away from me," I ordered as I waved him away.

"Babe, it's not any bigger than me, and you took me no problem."

"Yeah, but real penis feels a lot better than a hard anal plug."

"You want the real penis in there?"

Well, no, I really wanted it in my pussy, but he seemed to have this obsession with my ass, so who was I to deny him? "I'd prefer it to that thing, yeah."

"Okay, tell you what, I'll start you off with my cock, but then I'll switch to the butt plug."

"The medium one."

"Fine, the medium one. Don't be such a pussy."

"Do you want me to put the big butt plug in your ass?"

"Hell no!" he exclaimed.

"Well then."

He laughed and shook his head. "Fine. The medium one. Now get your fine ass over here." I could hear the crinkling of a condom wrapper as he unwrapped it and then rolled it onto his shaft.

Grabbing the lube again, he squirted some more into his palm and then spread it around. He helped me back up into the doggy-style position on my knees and then guided his fat cock to my anus and began to press in slowly. I gritted my teeth against the pain as I tried my best not to tense up too much. Finally, he was all the way in and breathing heavily as he thrust hard into me, his big heavy balls slapping against my pussy.

"God, you're so fucking tight," he gasped between gritted teeth. "Yeah, you like that big dick, don't you? You like it fucking your little asshole. You love the way I fuck you with my big fat cock, yeah you do. That's a good girl. Take it deep, all the way. Oh my God, you feel so good, babe."

I wasn't great at dirty talk myself, but I could listen to him talk dirty to me all night long. Coming from him, it was sexy as fuck. He thrust a few more times and then pulled out, then slowly pushed the medium-sized anal plug into my ass. He pulled the condom off and threw it in the small trashcan by the bed, then pulled my hips back, lined the fat head of his throbbing cock up with my pussy and thrust forward.

"Oh my God," I cried as he began to fuck me the way I'd been craving for the past two months. I felt deliciously full with the anal plug in my butt and his thick, rock hard cock thrusting deeply back and forth into my soaking pussy, but the best part of the entire thing was how turned on he was. That made all the pain and discomfort worthwhile. He didn't last too much longer after that, pulling out and coming all over my back. I waited for him to retrieve a towel from the bathroom to clean me up, then rolled over and pulled the covers down so I could crawl into bed. In another minute, he joined me, and I curled up closely next to him as I quickly drifted off to sleep. So far, I really loved New York.

Chapter SIXTEEN

Early the next morning, Mike's cell phone alarm went off, signaling it was time for him to get up for work. I was bummed that he couldn't stay and hang out with me, but he had warned me, so I knew better to complain. After he showered and dressed, I got out of bed and padded over to the front door butt naked to give him a hug and kiss good-bye and to tell him to have a great day and that I'd see him later that night.

Once he left me to my own devices, I started getting ready to go out and play tourist. I was super excited to explore the city, yet more than a little anxious about doing it alone, mostly because I had never used New York's subway system before. Before he left, Mike had told me where I could walk to the nearest station, but after half an hour of trying to work myself up to actually doing it, I had done nothing but psyche myself out. When I was finally all dressed, bundled up and ready to go hunt for some breakfast, Mike texted me.

Mike: *Muggy and rainy outside.*

Erin: *Yay :p I'm almost ready to venture out.*

Mike: *Lol, don't forget if you take the train, you'll need a Metro card. When you purchase one, purchase value—not time. Get like $20 worth. It's $2.50 per ride.*

I couldn't do it. I was trying to get the guts up to just leave the apartment and walk down the street to the nearest subway station, buy a Metro card like Mike had instructed, and be on my way already, but I wimped out and pressed a little icon on my cell phone, then hit accept and texted Mike back.

Erin: *You're gonna yell at me maybe... I chickened out and called Uber just now to come take me into Manhattan. I'm going to try to take the train back, though, I swear.*

Mike: *Uber?*

Erin: *Lol, it's like a taxi service. You have your credit card on file with them, and it's an app on my phone. I press that I want a car, and they show up a few minutes later and take you where you want to go. Autobills to your credit card.*

Mike: *Cool. Where you headed?*

Erin: *Well, I had looked up best breakfast spots in New York and found this one place that sounded really good, so I'm going to try there first.*

The Uber driver pulled up just then and rolled his window down.

"Erin?"

"Yep!" I confirmed, getting in the back seat of the car. "Manhattan please." After I showed him on my map where I was trying to go, we were on our way. It only took about fifteen minutes to get there, and we got to drive over the Williamsburg Bridge, which I snapped a picture of as we drove by.

The Uber driver dropped me off by the Essex Market and then waved before driving off into the rain. I stood there looking around for the restaurant mentioned in the food blog I'd found online, but I couldn't seem to locate it. Frustrated, I sent Mike a text.

Erin: *Well, I just got there and can't find the damn restaurant, so now I'm looking for another one. And then I'm supposed to get coffee with an old co-worker friend around 3 in SoHo.*

Mike: *That's cool. There are lots of great spots. Let me know if you need help finding one.*

I was already Googling away and had found another place that looked promising.

Erin: *Yay! I found a spot. This blog recommended I try the Clinton Street Baking Company because of their banana walnut pancakes. :) And it looks like it is just a short walk from where Uber dropped me off—even better! Hehe :)*

Mike: *Beautiful.*

The restaurant wasn't far at all, and before I knew it, I was walking through the door and putting my name in for one. It was my lucky day, because a single seat opened up a few minutes later. Soon I was seated, tucked snugly in between the door and a small table for two on my right. I was facing so that I was looking right out the window. I had the perfect view. I could see a garbage truck right outside and people walking by, some chatting with each other, some with their head down, looking like they were on a mission to get somewhere quickly.

I took the advice of the food blog and ordered the banana walnut pancakes… and scrambled eggs and country potatoes and locally made hot apple cider. When all my food came, I realized that my eyes had been a lot bigger than my stomach, but I was determined to put away as much of that delicious goodness as I possibly could. Everything was so yummy, and I actually managed to make my way through the eggs, potatoes and half of the pancakes before I gave up. Oh and of course I finished my hot cider as well, which was ridiculously good. After paying the check, I waddled out of the restaurant and texted Mike an update.

Erin: *Oh my God—I am stuffed.*

Mike: *That's what's up. What are you up to now?*

Erin: *Walking. Trying to see how close I can get to the Metropolitan Museum of Art without breaking down and grabbing a cab, lol.*

Mike: *Lmao! Good.*

Erin: *And I need to work off all that breakfast I just inhaled.*

I stopped to send him pictures of the humongous breakfast I just had. They looked like something out of a magazine. I really needed to go back there sometime.

Erin: *I only made it halfway through the pancakes. :-*

Mike: *Weak!*

Erin: *I couldn't fit another bite—seriously. If I tried, I'd probably just head back to the apartment and pass out, lol. But it was delicious. :)*

I walked down the block, thinking to myself how cool it was that I was standing on the street in Manhattan. I took some pictures of the old apartment buildings around me. Everything looked so cute and interesting. I uploaded some pictures to Facebook and soon found myself walking up to Washington Square Park. I loved it there immediately. I sat down on one of the many benches and took pictures of the beautiful park. The leaves on the trees were gold, brown, yellow and red—all the glorious colors of fall.

Some movement in the tree across from me caught my eye, and then I noticed a squirrel scrambling down a branch. Another movement came from the other corner of my eye, and I looked down and saw three squirrels scampering across the grass. As I slowly took in the entire park before me, I saw squirrels everywhere. I raised my phone to take a picture and then looked at it before posting it with the caption, "How many squirrels can you find in this picture?" I counted twelve myself.

I was just finishing posting when I glanced up and saw that one of these squirrels had come all the way up the bench, walked right up to me and touched my arm with his little paw. I yelped and he ran away down the line of benches. Bemused by my encounter with Mr. Squirrel, I texted Mike to tell him.

Erin: *Dude!! I'm sitting on a bench in Washington Square Park, and there are squirrels everywhere! One came up and put its paw on my arm. OMG! I was like, Whoa, wtf? Lol. I have no food for you, little squirrel!*

Mike: *Ha! Oh, you're kinda close to my station. I'm actually not that far from you, either.*

Erin: *I just saw a FedEx truck go by, hehe.*

Mike: *Lol, what are you up to now?*

Erin: *Still just walking around. I love all the fall colors, so gorgeous. :) Union Square looks pretty cool. Think I'll head there next.*

Mike: *Mmmhmm. You'll like it there. Lots of shopping.*

Erin: *Lol, hmm, sounds like you think know me or something.*

Mike: *;)*

When I got to Union Square, I about squealed. They were set up with kiosks everywhere for the holidays. It was a Christmas shopper's paradise.

After spending an hour buying gifts for all my friends and family, I texted my friend to see if he had time to meet me for coffee. He said he could spare fifteen minutes if I came by soon, so I headed down to meet him at the Starbucks by his work.

I was nearly crying by the time I got there. My feet were killing me. Apparently the Vans I had gotten were not the greatest for walking. I met my friend for coffee and we caught up for a bit, shooting the shit about people we used to work with. He couldn't stay long and had to get back to work, so I gave him a hug and thanked him for coming down to say hi. As soon as I left him, I headed straight for the shoe store I had spotted across the street.

I had always made fun of people who wore Uggs, but now I was desperate for a comfortable walking shoe. I knew I needed something of good quality or my tourist time in New York was going to be cut short. After trying on a few pairs, I settled on a black pair that were comfortable and not too crazily priced.

Erin: *OMG, my feet are killing me. The Vans I got SUCK for walking. I just bought some Uggs and my feet are crying in relief. When do you think I should head back?*

Mike: *Whenever you want.*

Erin: *Well, when are you going to be back is what I meant? :p*

Mike: *That'll be a while. Clocking out after 5 for sure, then home to change, then to you.*

Erin: *Sounds good... Oh hey, I just walked by Forbidden Planet.*

Forbidden Planet was a big store in NYC that sold toys, comics, graphic novels and other collectibles. I had remembered Mike telling me about it, saying he usually got his Magic the Gathering cards from there.

Mike: *Nice! Check out the Commander pre-made decks. They are no joke.*

Erin: *Oh, I already left. Too many people in there right now.*

Mike: *Yeah, it's Friday.*

I wandered over to the nearest train station after that and purchased my first Metro card, filling it up with twenty dollars, just as Mike had suggested. I managed to get on the right train to take me back to Bushwick, and when I got off again, I felt exhilarated—like I had just accomplished some big feat. I had attempted and successfully used public transportation in a major city! Check me and my bad self out.

Erin: *Yay, I did it! I took the train back and made it back to the apartment in one piece. :)*

Mike: *Holy shytt! Good job.*

Erin: *Lol ;) ty ty... I feel like I graduated.*

Mike: *How was the train?*

Erin: *Packed! But it was fine. Some guy tripped me out for a minute on my walk back to the apartment, though. He was walking towards me and then stopped right after he passed me, then he started walking in the same direction he had just come from. I thought he was following me for a minute, but he kept walking when I turned. Man, it's dark outside.*

Mike: *Lol! Yeah, it gets dark fast.*

Erin: *I'm going to jump in the shower. Feel icky after walking around all day.*

Mike: *Be careful not to fall.*

Erin: *Lol. Fall? Oh nm...I get it. Haha. :p*

Mike: *Wermp wermp*

After I finished showering and cleaning up, I settled down on the couch to work on my book while I waited for Mike. I texted and asked him what he wanted to do, and of course he wanted to go to the movies, so I checked show times for *The Hunger Games: Catching Fire* at the AMC in Times Square. I was a little surprised that he wanted to see that particular movie, but when I asked him about it, he said, "Yeah, Katniss is the shit!" So that was that.

When he finally got to my place, we headed straight for Times Square. We took the train, but this time I wasn't nervous at all because I could just follow him and not have to worry about whether I was going the right direction or getting on the wrong train. Before going into the movie, we stopped by Five Guys and had some burgers and fries. By the time we sat down in our seats in the theater, Mike was ready to pass out. I felt so bad for him. He was working his ass off to support himself and help out his family, and he was so exhausted, he couldn't even sit through a movie without nodding off. Before the previews started, he excused himself to get something with caffeine from the concessions stand.

We both enjoyed the movie, although Mike did nod off a couple of times towards the end. We took the train back to Bushwick and stumbled into the apartment, pulled off our clothes, then crawled into bed and snuggled up and fell fast asleep. The next morning, he got up before me and got dressed, then leaned over to give me a kiss.

"Hey, I'm going to walk down the street and get us some breakfast, okay?"

"Mmm, sounds good," I murmured, still half asleep and snuggled up in bed.

I went back to sleep when he left, then heard someone at the door about twenty minutes later. Assuming it was Mike, I popped up out of bed and ran to the front door to open it for him. Only it wasn't him. When I opened the door and cracked it open, I saw a man I didn't recognize standing there. I eeped and closed the door in his face.

"I'm so sorry! Just give me a second!"

"Okay. It's the landlord. I came by to check on the heater for you."

"Oh! Okay, I'll be right there."

Running to the bedroom, I grabbed some jeans and pulled them on, hopping around comically as I tried to fasten them. Then I threw on a sweatshirt and returned to the front door.

"Sorry about that!" I apologized and opened the door for him to come him. "So yeah, the heater works really well, and it's just been a little warmer in here than it needs to be. I wasn't sure how to turn it down."

"Sure, no problem," he said, moving to the kitchen and then to the master bedroom to adjust the heat. "Everything else okay here?" he asked before taking off again. I nodded and thanked him for coming by, then showed him to the door.

Mike returned a few minutes later with breakfast from McDonalds— my favorite. I told him about me greeting the landlord in the nude, which he laughed and shook his head at. "I thought it was you," I exclaimed. "Not like I was trying to give anyone else a show."

"Maybe check through the peephole first next time before you open the door."

"Yeah, yeah, yeah. So hey, I was thinking about what I'm going to do for my Christmas vacation this year. My work gives us two weeks off, so I was kinda thinking about coming back here to spend some more time with you. What do you think?"

Mike shook his head. "I dunno about that. I have mad family coming into town for the holidays. Why don't you spend it in Hawaii with your family?"

That was not the answer I'd been hoping to hear. "Because I'd rather spend time with you? I don't have to come for Christmas—I could just come the day after Christmas and stay here for like a week or week and a half."

He seemed to think about this for a minute, then nodded his head thoughtfully. "Day after Christmas? That could work."

"Yeah, and it's not like you have to see me every day while I'm here. I get that you're busy. I can use the time to write and hang out with my friends, do some shopping, etc."

"Aight, it's up to you."

Ecstatic that he agreed, after we finished breakfast, I started to search for affordable airfares and lodging for the holidays while Mike headed in to his family's liquor store to work. Unfortunately, I wasn't finding anything very promising. Almost everything affordable and decent had already been booked for the holidays. I would look more later, but I had plans to meet up with an old family friend who used to babysit me when I was a little girl in Hawaii, so I jumped in the shower and got ready to meet up with Carol and her two girls, Ashlee and Roxy.

It was nice having someone else to sightsee with, and I hadn't seen Carol since I was in grade school. We walked through Central Park, did some shopping on Fifth Avenue, had coffee inside the Trump Tower, oohed and aahed over the jewelry counters at the infamous Tiffany's, had lunch at Serendipity and bought ourselves some sweets from Dylan's Candy Store. I got a big box of assorted fudge to give to Mike for his family and then treated myself to some Belgian chocolate-covered Oreos, which were ridiculously good. Our last stop was FAO Schwarz, the biggest toy store I'd ever seen. When I told Mike where we were, he asked me to get him a toy. I asked what he wanted, but he just told me to surprise him. Gambling on the fact that he was a gamer nerd and hoping that he'd like my choice, I crossed my fingers and got him a figurine of Yoshi, my favorite *Super Mario Bros.* character. I got myself a beautiful FAO Christmas ornament of a court jester's face.

After I exchanged hugs with Carol and the girls and said good-bye, I headed back to Times Square to do some more shopping and sightseeing. I wandered by some theaters and saw that *Phantom of the Opera* was playing, and immediately hurried inside to see if tickets were still available. *Phantom* was my favorite musical and had gotten me interested in singing and acting when I was a teenager, but I'd never gotten to see it performed on stage before. I decided to splurge and got myself a seat right in the Orchestra section, then texted Mike to gush.

Erin: *I'm so fucking excited, you have no idea! Lol :) I just treated myself to a really good seat to see Phantom of the Opera. I'm in the 8th row! I'm finally getting to see Phantom. Hurray! :)*

Mike: *Very nice. Congrats!*

Erin: *So I'm not sure what time I'll be home from the show.*

Mike: *That's okay. Take your time and enjoy yourself. I'll head over when you get home.*

Erin: *Okay! So excited! :)*

Phantom was everything I hoped it would be and more. It was literally a dream come true. In fact, the only complaint I had was that the infamous chandelier in the Opera House was suspended from the ceiling by these thin-looking cables, and it was right above my head. Those cables didn't look that sturdy to me. I mean, I knew they had to be, of course, but that didn't keep me from constantly glancing upwards to make sure that shit was not about to fall on my head.

I called Uber to pick me up once the show was over and made my way back outside where snow was now falling, ever so lightly. Then began the worst Uber ride of my life as I struggled to communicate with the driver who had a very heavy accent. He couldn't seem to figure out where I was, and being that I wasn't from this city, I had no clue where I was. Twenty minutes later, I was finally in the back seat of the car and fuming, and the ridiculous traffic we encountered the entire way home only served to infuriate me more. I had wanted desperately to see *Phantom*, but not at the cost of losing precious time with Mike. There were very few hours I actually got to spend with him, and now I was wasting one of them sitting in this stupid car that was going nowhere. I decided that Manhattan traffic was just as bad as L.A.'s, if not worse.

By the time I finally got back to the apartment, Mike was there waiting for me. He had made himself comfortable on the couch, thank goodness, and was chillin' and watching TV. I was relieved he hadn't passed out already. It was too late to go anywhere for dinner, so I just ordered a pizza for us, then cuddled up next to him on the couch to watch *The Big Bang Theory*. It was in a simple moment like this that I could lose myself, imagining what it would be like if I lived here, and this was my apartment, and he was really able to come over and just hang out, and watch TV. It felt so good. How could I not want to hang onto something that felt so good?

As I sat there on the couch with his legs draped over my lap, I breathed in and closed my eyes for a moment, trying to memorize every note of his scent. He smelled like Armani Code and laundry detergent, and it took every bit of my willpower to not tear his clothes off. I knew how exhausted he was, though, and I didn't want to make him feel like all I wanted from him was sex. It just sucked that we had so little time together, period.

Remembering the toy I'd gotten him, I tapped his legs and motioned for him to move and said I'd be right back. I scampered into the bedroom and pulled Yoshi out of my bag, then put him behind my back as I came back out into the living room.

"I hope you like it," I said shyly as I brought Yoshi out from behind me and handed it to him.

His eyes lit up and he flashed me the biggest grin as he examined his gift. "Yoshi!" he exclaimed, then pulled me back down to give him a kiss. "I love it."

"I thought you might." Sitting back down, I had the biggest smile of satisfaction on my face as I pulled his legs back onto my lap. I loved making him smile. I felt like he sacrificed so much for his family, and all I wanted was to offer him some small comfort in the time we spent together. I just wanted to take his worries and cares away and love him.

On my last day in New York, I spent the first half of the day holed up in the apartment, not wanting to go out into the cold. I wished I didn't have to leave so soon. The apartment was actually quite cozy, and I could see myself staying there for a few weeks, just writing, going out to sightsee and do a little shopping, spending the evenings with Mike. If only I didn't have a day job waiting for me back in L.A.

A little after lunchtime, I finally ventured out and took the train back to Union Square so I could do a little more Christmas shopping. I found the most charming Christmas ornaments for both myself and friends and family. One kiosk was selling little rag dolls made of all organic materials, so I bought a little stuffed bunny for Hannah, my friend Greta's two-year-old daughter. I didn't have any nieces or nephews to spoil, so my friend's children made for good substitutes.

It was another late night for us, with Mike not getting to the apartment until almost midnight. Too beat to do anything else, we heated up leftover pizza and watched some more episodes of *The Big Bang Theory*. When we finished eating, he wanted to take a shower, so I decided to start packing while I waited for him to finish so we could go to bed. As I folded clothes and put them in my suitcase, I came across the black negligee I had brought to surprise him. I had completely forgotten all about it.

Stripping quickly, I put it on and then turned my curling iron on. I wanted to look nice for him when he came to bed. I must have tried sitting and standing in a dozen different positions before he finally came back out of the bathroom. I finally settled on leaning casually in the doorframe of the bedroom. When he walked out of the bathroom into the living room, he just glanced at me and then went to turn the TV off. I bit my lip and stood there uncertainly for a moment, then turned and went into the master bedroom. He turned the lights off as he came through the second bedroom and then we were in pitch darkness. Sighing, I crawled under the covers. Guess he either didn't notice or didn't care.

At least he wasn't too tired to fuck. And fuck me he did, deeply, slowly and thoroughly, but it was still over way too soon, and then he was fast asleep. It was our last night together before I had to go back to L.A., and he was already passed out. Morning would come all too soon, and he would have to get up super early and leave for work, and then I'd have to finish packing and wait for Tom to pick me back up and take me to the airport. I didn't want to go. I didn't want it to be over already. Why was he already sleeping? He didn't even cuddle or snuggle up to me. How could he just go to sleep and not want to cherish every second that we had left together before I had to go? I knew he was tired and overworked. I knew he simply did not have the energy to stay awake any longer, but that didn't make it hurt any less.

Silently I cried, the tears wetting my pillow as I lay there facing him, just watching his profile in the dimness of the light that shone through the windows from the street. I willed him to wake and tell me he was going to miss me, but he was fast asleep. It wasn't until an hour later that I finally drifted off to sleep out of pure exhaustion with my hand tucked around his belly and my tear-streaked face snuggled against his arm.

When his cell phone alarm went off a few hours later, I wanted to murder it. I wanted to kill it dead. I wanted to stomp and smash it into itty bitty pieces. But doing that wouldn't change the time or the fact that he had to get his ass moving and out the door or he was going to be late for his train. I got out of the warm bed and pulled on some clothes so I could keep him company for a few minutes more while he got ready for work. The time flew by too quickly as usual, and before I knew it, he was hugging me good-bye.

"I had a great time this weekend," he said, pulling back from the hug to give me a smooch.

"Good. Are you glad I came?"

"Definitely." He kissed me again, then turned to open the door. "I have to get going. Hit me up when you get home."

"Okay. Have a good day." As the door closed and he vanished from my sight, my lips trembled and the tears began falling again. I wasn't ready for him to go, yet. I sat there sniffling on my couch for a while, feeling sorry for myself. Then I looked at the clock and realized I didn't have a lot of time left if I wanted to do anything else before it was time to leave for the airport.

As I gathered up the items I had left to pack last, I realized that Mike had forgotten his phone charger.

Erin: *Oh shit. You forgot your phone charger and your ear buds. Do you want to meet up somewhere so I can give it to you before I leave for the airport, or should I just mail it to you?*

Mike: *OMG! Yes, please!*

Erin: *Which? Mail or meet up?*

Mike: *Meet up.*

Erin: *Okay. Where and when? I have to be back here by 2 to leave for the airport.*

Mike: *Take the 1 to Canal Street.*

Erin: *Okay… making my way to the L train shortly.*

Mike: *Okay.*

Dressing warmly, I got ready to leave to meet Mike. I took the L Train and tried to figure out how to get to Canal Street myself using the Subway app I had installed on my phone, but I ended up going one stop too far in the wrong direction and had to turn around and come back. I finally made it to my destination, thanks to a kind fellow passenger who told me which train to take. I wasn't sure how New Yorkers had gotten their bad reputation, but the people I'd met here so far had been super nice.

Getting to meet up with Mike one last time was a bonus, and I savored every second of getting to see him out in the sunlight for a change. He thanked me for bringing his charger and ear buds and gave me another kiss before he had to return back to work. I smiled all the way back to the apartment, then finished getting my things ready to leave for the airport. As I listened to Tom chatter to me during the drive back to JFK, I watched the city pass by. It had been a great trip. Not long enough, but great all the same, and I couldn't wait to come back after Christmas.

Chapter SEVENTEEN

The next weekend, I flew up to San Jose to spend Thanksgiving with Allison and Brian. We'd spent a handful of Thanksgivings together in the past, and I loved it every time I got to go. We would have our traditional trip to The Cheesecake Factory, do some shopping at New York and Company, eat lots of yummy Thanksgiving food, play Texas Hold'em, and some of her family smoked weed even if she didn't, so there was usually a pipe being passed around after dinner. It was my favorite place to spend the holidays.

Allison picked me up from the airport, and I texted with Mike on our way back to her place, letting him know I had arrived safely.

Erin: *Just got to San Jose. In the car catching up with Allison right now. :)*

Mike: *Cool, tell her I said hi.*

I giggled and relayed his message to Allison who smirked and rolled her eyes. "Well, tell him I said 'hi' back."

Nodding, I texted him back.

Erin: *She says hi back. :) Happy Thanksgiving, btw!*

Mike: *Happy Thanksgiving!*

Erin: *You working right now?*

Mike: *Yeah.*

Erin: *Aw, hope it goes by quickly.*

Mike: *Thanks.*

I tried not to over-analyze his text messages, but it was hard when one second he sounded like he gave a shit, and the next he was so distant. I knew he was busy, I just didn't know exactly how busy. I didn't know if he truly had no time to pay much attention at all to me, or if maybe he just wasn't interested enough to make time for me and didn't know how to tell me without hurting my feelings. I knew he was a good guy. If I didn't feel he was, I wouldn't have wasted my time on him, but I still wasn't sure of his intentions.

As much as I hoped things would get better, they just started to get worse. Mike was answering my texts less frequently, sometimes completely ignoring them. I was tired of sounding like a nagging girlfriend, so if he didn't answer a question, I didn't ask him about it—I just let it go. I was trying to make plans for my next visit, but it was like trying to talk to a brick wall. As we got closer to Christmas, he became more and more distant until it got to the point where I wasn't even sure he wanted me to come anymore.

I drove to Vegas the weekend before Christmas for our holiday party. I had originally planned to fly, but there were so many things I needed to take with me to make swag bags for the party that I decided it was better to drive than stress over trying to fit everything into two suitcases. I texted Mike to let him know of my change of plans, but he didn't respond. Valiantly, I resolved to push him from my mind and focus on throwing the biggest and best party of my life.

The Mad Hatter theme turned out to be a smashing success, and everything went perfectly according to plan. Jerry congratulated me on a job well done within minutes of the party starting, and I took that as a green light to knock a few back and enjoy myself a bit. It was an amazing night, filled with lots of drinking, good food and laughter. I danced the night away with Kristen and some of the other girls and saved her from making a fool out of herself when she got a little too tipsy and tried to confront Evan, who was there with his wife. I barely managed to steer her away from them before it was too late, but I gave him a steely glare when I caught his eye, making him adjust his collar uncomfortably. As far as I knew, he didn't know that I knew, but I'm sure he now had his suspicions after I had given him the stink eye.

Waking up the next morning was pure torture. I was so sore, and my feet were a wreck. I could barely stand up from the bed and hobble to the bathroom. After I had relieved myself, I caught a glimpse of myself in the mirror and shuddered. Yikes. I needed a shower, stat.

Remembering that I had drunk texted Mike the night before, I grabbed my phone and saw that he had texted me back around four-thirty in the morning. Quickly I scrolled through the texts. He had texted me only once in the past week, and that had been a simple, "You as well", when I told him I hoped he had a good day. So apparently I had decided to confront him about it while I was drunk at the party.

Erin: *Did I do something? Are you just busy or are you upset with me for some reason? Haven't really heard back from you all week and not sure what's up. :(*

Mike: *Hey, I'm sorry I haven't gotten back to you. My grandmother is in the hospital again and my family is going nuts. I'll hit you up again on my lunch break today.*

Only he didn't. I texted him back immediately, telling him how sorry I was and that I was sending all my positive thoughts and prayers her way, and then I waited and waited for him to text or call me again so I could apologize for bugging him when he was going through hell with his family. But he never called. With a heavy heart, I packed up my car and started the long drive home.

I tried texting him the next morning. Thankfully he answered this time.

Erin: *How's your grandma doing?*

Mike: *Hey...not well. She's still in the hospital. :-*

Erin: *:(What happened?*

Mike: *She caught a dizzy spell and fell and hit her head.*

Erin: *Oh no :(Concussion?*

Mike: *She's not doing good... that plus the amnesia amplified a bit cuz of it. Now my mom is crazy stressed. Blood pressure in her chest is killing her.*

Erin: *Ugh, I can imagine. :-\ I'm so sorry. I wish there was something I could do. *sending a big hug your way**

Mike: *Aww, thanks, babe. Shytt is so hectic over here. I'm so fucking stressed out.*

Erin: *I bet. :-\ Aww, I feel so bad for you. Want to help take the stress away. Ugh why do I have to be so far away right now? Could I send her flowers for you or something?*

I sent him a Jeff Thomas cartoon I'd found online. The little cartoon guy was hugging the air and the caption said, "I'll just pretend to hug you until you get here." It made me smile, and I hope it did the same for him.

Erin: *Until "I" get there, but yeah...*

Mike: *Lolol, that's awesome. :)*

Erin: *:)*

Mike: *Don't worry about sending anything. It's fine.*

Erin: *Okay. Just let me know if there's anything at all I can do. I'm here for you.*

Mike: *Thanks*

So at least now I knew why he hadn't responded much lately. I knew how much his family meant to him, so if his grandmother and mother were both in poor health, I could only imagine how freaked out and stressed he must be. I tried to make myself be understanding and patient, but as the countdown to my departure ticked down and he ignored text after text, became more and more nervous. Should I cancel my trip? Was it not a good idea for me to even be there right now? I wanted to be supportive—not add more stress to his life.

Corrine came over a couple days before Christmas so we could exchange our gifts. She gave me a couple of framed Linkin Park posters, which I thought were awesome and the perfect gift for me. Knowing Mike would appreciate them since he loved LP as much as I did, I snapped a couple photos after hanging them up in my living room. Unsurprisingly, he didn't respond.

Early the next morning, he texted at six-fifteen, waking me up.

Mike: *Nice! Hey I'm sorry, things are still hectic around here. Mad family over for the holidays. When are you arriving again?*

Well, at least he was still planning on me visiting. I had begun to wonder.

Erin: *Thursday afternoon. Leaving back to L.A. on Sunday the 5th. Supposed to meet up with a couple of my friends while I'm there.*

Mike: *Sweet. I hope you planned things out this time.*

Erin: *Lol, why do I have to have a plan? I had fun just doing whatever whenever. :p But I'm planning to hit up some of the places I missed last time,* *but also want to spend a good chunk of time writing. I just finished my beta edits on my book and need to get started on the second half, yay!*

Mike: *Oh sweet, congrats.*

Later in the day, I texted him the address for the new vacation rental property I was staying at—this time in Park Slope. He thanked me and said he would look the address up.

The next day was Christmas, so I texted him in the morning and wished him a Merry Christmas. He responded and thanked me, wishing me a Merry Christmas as well, but to my disappointment, that was all I heard from him that day. I consoled myself with the knowledge that I would see him the next night when I got to New York.

At the airport the next morning, I told him I was boarding my flight in a bit and asked if I would see him tonight. "Mmmhmm" was all he said, but at least it wasn't "no". At this point, I would take what I could get from him, but I was getting dangerously close to putting my foot down and confronting him once in and for all. I hadn't yet because I was still afraid that if I gave him an ultimatum, he would choose to move on without me.

JFK didn't seem as big and scary to me now that I'd been here once before. Tom was there to pick me up again. He was so friendly and warm that I couldn't imagine having anyone else drive me to and from the airport when I was in town. I let Mike know I had arrived and for once, he responded quickly.

Erin: *I'm hereee…*

Mike: *Nice!*

Erin: *:)*

Mike: *At your place or just touched down?*

Erin: *My driver just picked me up from the airport. Heading to Park Slope now.*

Mike: *Copy*

Erin: *What time are you coming over?*

Mike: *After work.*

Erin: *Lol, that's not vague at all. :) Okay, well just give me a heads up when you're heading my way in case I'm out and about.*

Mike: *Okay, no prob.*

The rest of the drive to the apartment went quickly as Tom caught me up on everything that had been going on with him and his family the past month. The place looked cute from the outside, but once I finally got inside, I was bitterly disappointed. The apartment was old, outdated and reeked of cleaning supplies, like someone had literally *just* cleaned it and left without opening any windows. I felt sick to my stomach as I tried to breathe.

Wandering into the bathroom, I saw that the showerhead was placed in an odd position. It was on the largest wall facing out instead of on one of the smaller walls facing sideways like a normal shower in a tub would. I wasn't quite sure how that was supposed to work without spraying water everywhere, but I supposed the shower curtain must catch the spray. When I looked down into the drain, I wished I hadn't. It was full of hair, fuzz and other gunk. I grabbed a piece of toilet paper and wiped it clean. Gross!

Erin: *Trying to get a hold of the landlord. Not too happy with this place. Might check into a hotel down the street if I can't get something figured out. I'll keep you posted. Found all kinds of gunk in the shower drain. Nasty. :-*

Mike: *Wow, I'm sorry. That sucks. Make sure you take pictures.*

Rationally, I knew that getting upset wouldn't make anything better, but that didn't really help me in the moment. I still felt stressed out and panicked by the entire ordeal, and now I was worried I was going to be stuck paying for an apartment that, in my opinion, wasn't fit to have someone inhabit in its current condition. I kept trying the landlord's number as well as the back-up "emergency number" he had given me, but neither picked up, ratcheting my anxiety up by another notch.

Finally the landlord called me back and apologized, saying he was at dinner. I explained everything to him, but all he could offer was to have someone else come clean the apartment again the following day. I said that wasn't good enough and asked if he had another unit available that he could swap. He avoided my question and again offered to have the place cleaned again the next day. I told him again that I either wanted a full refund or a different unit completely. He told me he would have to get back to me and hung up. Frustrated, exhausted from traveling all day and close to tears, I sent Mike an update.

Erin: *Ugh, landlord was at dinner, but he called me back finally. He doesn't want to refund me anything and is only offering to re-clean the place tomorrow. I told him I want a full refund or a different unit, so I'm waiting to hear back from him. I'm going to the Nu Hotel at Atlantic and Smith for tonight at least, and I'll figure out what I'm going to do tomorrow after I've had some sleep. This fucking blows. Let me know when you get there and I'll give you the room number.*

Mike: *Leaving now.*

As upset as I was, it all melted away as soon as I opened my hotel room door and saw Mike standing there, looking all kinds of delicious. I almost cried with relief when he hugged and kissed me hello. It had been a stressful evening, and I was only too happy to forget everything and snuggle up with my honey. I had brought my laptop and plugged it into the hotel's flat screen TV with an HDMI cable, so snuggled into the comfy hotel bed and surfed through the available movies until we settled on *The Host*. We made it through more than half of the movie before we started feeling each other up, which quickly turned to stripping our clothes off and getting busy.

Fifteen minutes later, we were both sprawled across the bed, sweaty and panting for breath. The sex was as amazing as it always was when we were together. Since we had missed a good chunk of the movie, I rewound it to where we'd stopped paying attention so we could finish watching. As soon as it ended, I flipped the TV off and we settled down to sleep.

It was a nice feeling, knowing that I still had over a week left in New York when I kissed Mike good-bye the next morning.

"See you later."

"Have a great day," I almost sang to him, smiling broadly. "Oh wait. Do you maybe want to see a movie tonight? We could see Anchorman 2 or something else. My co-workers gave me some AMC gift cards for Christmas."

"Sounds like a plan."

Although I didn't want to deal with my current lodging situation and just wanted to snuggle back into bed and stay in the hotel the rest of the time without another thought, I knew I had to face the music this morning. Groaning, I headed for the shower, pausing for a moment to start making a cup of coffee in the Keurig machine they'd provided. After I finished getting ready, I left the hotel and started walking towards the apartment. It was only about a fifteen-minute walk, and the weather was chilly, but it wasn't freezing.

The apartment looked exactly the same as I had left it, so I knew the landlord hadn't sent anyone over to re-clean it. I opened the trashcan in the bathroom and looked for the wadded up toilet paper I had thrown away with the gunk from the shower drain. Propping it up on the lid of the trashcan, I took a picture. Moving around the rest of the apartment, I took more pictures of a wadded up tissue left on the floor of the closet, cracks in the ceiling, bits of leaves and crumbs on the dining room table, an old stained mini fridge that smelled like something had died in it, and the stains on the carpet. As I took these pictures, I marveled at how well the owners had been able to disguise the poor condition of the apartment in the pictures they had posted online.

Once I was safely back in my warm, clean, pleasant smelling hotel room, I typed up a detailed email to the vacation rental website and to the landlord and attached the pictures I had taken. Then I sat back to wait. Mike checked in with me around lunchtime and I filled him in. I told him I'd found hotel rooms for the rest of my stay, but that the one I was currently staying in wasn't available for the entire time. The good news was that they were all cancellable without penalty as long as I gave twenty-four hours advance notice. If the guy refused to refund my money, I was going to contact my credit card company and dispute the charge.

Mike: *Sweet! Fuck that dude.*

Erin: *Seriously. What pisses me off is that he acted like he was this really nice guy, but when it came down to it, he looks like a real scumbag. I wonder how he'd like his first review on this website to be a shitty one.*

Mike: *Hey listen, think we can move tonight to Sunday? It's the busiest*

week in the year for us, and we're looking to close around midnight. Sunday
will be regular time again.

Erin: *Sure. Does that mean I'm not going to see you until Sunday?*

Mike: *Unfortunately, yes.*

Erin: *Aight :-*

Mike: *It's just too busy right now.*

Erin: *Yeah...understood. Sucks, but I get it. Sorry, just been a shitty couple*
of days. I'll see you Sunday.

Mike: *I know, you got shytted on pretty hard with the rental. And the dude*
isn't even trying to help.

Erin: *Yeah. :-\ I just needed a hug, heh. Sorry everything is so crazy for*
you right now. I'm probably just making it worse. Am I going to get to spend
NYE with you?

Mike: *No, I'm spending it with my family, you should already know that.*

Excuse me? Come again, sir? I sat there, staring at my phone. I should
already know that? Furious, I typed back to him. Anytime I had tried to make
plans with him for this trip, he had been MIA. He claimed it was because of his
grandmother, but had he just been avoiding making any concrete plans with
me, period?

Erin: *Uh, no. I didn't know that. I asked you about NYE a while back and*
you never responded. Why are you being mean about it? :(I didn't know it was
a family occasion.

Mike: *Lol, hold on. How am I being mean?*

Erin: *"You should already know that."*

Mike: *I'm a family man, sorry.*

Erin: *Okay, I get that, but what am I to you?*

Mike: *Not family.*

Was he freaking serious right now? Ouch. Like really, ouch. If he had
stuck a dagger in my stomach just then, it would have been less painful than
his response. More than anything in the world, I wanted a little family of my
own. I had dreamed of marrying into a large family, and all these months

of knowing him as I had been admiring what a stand-up guy he was, a real family man, all this time, apparently I was not good enough to bring around his family. I couldn't believe what was happening. Why the fuck had I come all this way to visit someone who felt this way, and how could I have been so blind as to not realize how he really felt?

Erin: *You know, you could have saved me some time and heartache by just responding to me before when I asked you about it. Did you even want me to come?*

Mike: Wow, really. You're going to put this on me?

Erin: *I have no idea what's going on in your head about us. You barely talk to me. And I get it. Life's been busy and crazy and your family comes first.*

Mike: *Why are you acting like this?*

Erin: *Because I asked you a simple question, and you replied in what came off to me as kind of mean. Like I should've known better than to even ask. I flew across the continent to see you, because I wanted to spend time with you. And hoped we could have a serious conversation before I left. But then you say things like you're a family man. So if you're just having a good time and that's all this is to you, then just tell me. But I was starting to feel more.*

Mike: *Okay, I'm really sorry things aren't going the way you planned.*

Erin: *That's not what I'm saying.*

Mike: *I never meant to hurt you. At all. That wasn't my intention.*

Erin: *Then what's going on? Just tell me what you want from me.*

Mike: *I don't want anything from you. We're friends. Why do I need to want something from you?*

And now he has just twisted the dagger in further and yanked it viciously to the side. "*I don't want anything from you. We're friends. Why do I need to want something from you?*" His words echoed over and over inside my mind. So that was it. There was the truth at last. All he saw me as was a friend... a fuck buddy. Someone he could just have fun with and casually toss aside when he was done.

Erin: *I see. I meant did you want this to go anywhere, or did you have no* *intention of it going anywhere? Man, I did not think I was going to have this conversation via text message. This blows.*

Mike: *I never NOT wanted it, but I haven't the time for it, as you can see.*

Erin: *I know.*

Mike: *Well, listen, I'm sorry I don't have a great fucking job with awesome vacation. This is what my life is currently.*

Erin: *I get it.*

Mike: *I can't afford not to work both these jobs.*

Erin: *Babe, I didn't even realize that you were working at the liquor store during the week, too. I'm sorry, I do understand. I don't come from money, you know. This trip is on a credit card that I'll still have to pay off, but I did see potential with us and had wanted to talk to you about the possibility of me relocating eventually. But I didn't even feel right bringing it up, because I know how busy you are and don't have time for it. And I didn't want to freak you out. :-*

Mike: *Yeah, I work all fucking day. That's why every time you've seen me, I've been chugging energy drinks just to stay awake.*

Erin: *I know. I just thought you were working late/double shifts at FedEx during the week. And it meant a lot to me that you were trying so hard to stay up a little later just to see me. Don't think I didn't recognize or appreciate that. I feel like I've made you angry by wanting to be with you or something. I dunno what to do anymore. I love being with you. I honestly didn't expect to like you this much when we first started talking. I guess it was unrealistic to begin with, but I'm still a romantic at heart. But if this is too much for you right now in your life, I understand. I'm sorry I put more pressure on you and added more stress to your life. That was never my intention. All I ever wanted to do was make you smile when I could, because you make me smile and laugh whenever you're with me, and I know life's been hard for you lately. But it seems I've been selfish in wanting more from you.*

Mike: *Sigh... why you write so good? Lol...*

Erin: *Lol, uh well, I am a writer...*

Mike: *Give me a sec, it got hella busy here.*

I waited and waited, but he didn't text me back again. Miserable and with no clue what to do next, I couldn't stop crying. This trip had been nothing but a total disaster from the very beginning, and right now, all I wanted was to go home to L.A. and curl into a ball in my own bed and cry my heart out. Instead, I was stuck in this hotel room in Brooklyn with no friends or family nearby. I was too sad to do anything but sit there despondently in my hotel room, replaying every detail of the past several months over and over in my head. What had I said? What had I done? We'd had "the talk". I'd given him an out more than once. Why was he acting like this now? Why didn't he bail a long time ago? I just didn't get it.

It was starting to get late when I finally sent him a text.

Erin: *Alrighty, well I guess a lot of people are buying alcohol tonight, but I know that's a good thing for you. You left your umbrella and boxers here, by the way. It'd be nice to see you before I leave. I'm going to sleep on it tonight, but it seems it may be best for me to just go home. I care about you. A whole lot. I'm sorry for everything.*

I'm not really sure how I finally got to sleep that night, but at some point, I stopped crying and fall asleep. In the morning when I woke up, I had an email waiting for me, letting me know that the landlord had begrudgingly refunded my money, saying he didn't have to, but that he would. Damn straight!

Erin: *Got my money back.*

Mike: *G'morning, Erin. That's good news to wake up to.*

Erin: *Yeah, minus the website's service fee, which was like $150 or something, but at this point I don't even care.*

Mike: *I'm sorry about that night. I crashed as soon as I got in.*

Erin: *I figured you would. It's okay. I just don't know what to do right now. Contemplating getting my flight changed to go back home soon. What are your thoughts on that?*

Mike: *I'm glad they refunded the money. They should keep their businesses clean. Like wtf? Anyhow, I'll call you before I head in.*

But he didn't call. I waited and waited, I checked the flights back home for the following day. I was so sick to my stomach about the whole thing that I couldn't bring myself to venture out for food or even just order in room service. I had no appetite. The whole reason I had come to New York was quickly going down the drain.

He finally checked in with me later that afternoon, acting like nothing was wrong.

Mike: *Hey what's up?*

Erin: *Nothing really... an author friend of mine just introduced me to a friend of hers who lives in Long Island. She's trying to convince me to come visit, but I was waiting for you to call me back.*

Mike: *Oh yeah, sorry. That was my bad. I was going to call you on my way to work, but I ended up having to go out and get my grandma some breakfast 'cuz she was fighting with my mom and wouldn't eat any food we had in the house.*

I felt bad for he and his mother having to deal with his grandmother, I really did. But right then, it was the last thing I wanted to listen to. I just wanted him to tell me if he wanted me to stay or go so I could make up my mind about what to do next.

Erin: *Okay. What do you want me to do, Mike? Do you want me to go home or do you want me to stay? I just need to know so I can figure out what the hell I'm doing. I'm tired of crying, and if you don't want me here, I'd rather go home.*

Mike: *Wow, I didn't think you were so serious. If that's the case, then I think it's best you go home.*

My heart sank and I felt ill as my face grew hot and my head began to throb. Just like that? It was so easy to tell me to just go home just like that?

Erin: *You didn't think that I was so serious? Are you kidding me? I flew across the continent to see you. How is that not serious?? You really hurt me with what you said last night.*

Mike: *Okay, you need to take a step back for a sec. People travel to go fuck and have fun. I didn't know you were getting serious. I'm sorry for hurting you. Honestly.*

Erin: *Wow.*

Mike: *But I'm guessing we were both on different pages.*

I couldn't believe the nerve of him! Did he really think I was so desperate and hard up for sex that I had to travel across the fucking United States just to get some? Was he completely delusional? I had never been so insulted in my life.

Erin: *You thought I was just coming out here just to fuck you? I could have found a friend with benefits in L.A. if that's all I wanted. I wanted to talk to you after this trip to see if you wanted to get more serious, because I was trying to give us more time to spend together. Yeah, obviously I wanted more. I wouldn't have bothered coming out here either time if I didn't. That last time I tried to talk to you about it, you said no matter how cool I seemed or how much fun we had together, the fact remained that we had only spent a few days together. So I tried to give us the opportunity to spend more time together.*

Mike: *I understand, but I haven't the time for anyone at the moment. I did tell you that.*

Erin: *Yeah, I just didn't know how long you would be too busy for anyone. And the family comment hurt. This family that invited me to spend the day with them in Long Island? They don't know me at all, and they welcomed me into their home.*

Mike: *I'm prioritizing my family and me. It's nothing towards you whatsoever. And your point is? That family is nice. Big deal.*

Wow, could he not hear himself? *That family is nice. Big deal.* They didn't even know me, and they were willing to "be nice" to me. I'd been dating him—or so I thought—for the past several months, and he couldn't even bring me by his family's house for New Year's Eve because I happened to be in town? I had casual acquaintances who treated me better than that. Even if we weren't officially together, wasn't I still a friend? Apparently, I was good enough to fuck, but not good enough to bring home to his family—even as just a friend. I was horrified to realize exactly what he thought of me.

Erin: *Obviously you don't want me to meet your family, regardless if we are just friends or more. I was willing to consider moving out here. I can't believe*

I'm such an idiot. If you didn't have any time for me, you should have ended this—whatever this is—a long time ago. Did you really think I just wanted to fuck you? Give yourself more credit than that. I genuinely liked you for you. I could have gone to see my family in Hawaii for the holidays instead of coming here. I said I'd rather see you. That didn't give you a clue I was serious?

Mike: *Okay, I see your point. And again, I'm sorry.*

Erin: *I'm sorry I didn't realize the extent of your unavailability or your disinterest in pursuing anything serious with me ever. I would have walked away a long time ago. Just shook hands and said it's been real*

Mike: *I saw things differently and went about them the wrong way.*

Erin: *Yeah, and now I'm here and alone and heartbroken, but whatever, right?*

Mike: *You also said that you enjoyed NY and wanted to see more of it besides having friends to hang with. And you also said you were coming out here to work on your book.*

Erin: *Yeah! So you wouldn't feel bad for not being able to spend more time with me! I didn't even want to say something crazy like, "Hey, what do you think about me moving here," until I had seen NY for myself and could figure out if I could be happy here. I was thrilled when I found that I loved it here.*

Mike: *Then that's on you. I thought you understood my current situation with work and my family. If you didn't say any of those things, then I would have told you not to come then.*

Erin: *I was going to try to talk to you last time, but I thought things were going so well, so I thought, I'll save it for next time. My mistake. I understood that you'd be busy. I didn't expect you to even see me every night while I was here. But I was under the mistaken impression that maybe you were starting to feel more for me, too. Like I said, I'm an idiot. I was feeling something that I'd never felt before, but I guess it was one-sided. Too bad I didn't realize it before deciding to come here. And yeah, I know. That's on me. I guess I'm going home. I dunno what else to do with your umbrella and boxers. I'll probably leave them at the front desk for you, and you can come get them. I'm sorry I misread everything and inconvenienced you.*

I waited for him to respond, but he said nothing. After waiting for an hour for him to say something, I finally gave up and booked the next ticket I could find back to L.A.

Erin: *I'm leaving tomorrow morning. My flight leaves at 9:22 AM. Can I ask you one question? Because now I'm a little concerned. Did you sleep with anyone else between seeing me? I only ask because we weren't using protection. I had assumed at the very least, you were probably too busy for that anyway, but I need to know if I have a reason to be worried.*

Mike: *No reason to be worried whatsoever.*

Hmpf. At least he hadn't kept me waiting long for a response this time. That would've sucked monkey balls.

Erin: *Great, thanks.*

Chapter EIGHTEEN

It was a little humiliating to have to pack my bags and return to L.A. the next day. Here I had come to New York with big dreams of pursuing love and living happily ever after with the sexiest man I'd ever been with, and he wanted nothing to do with me. I was angry with him for leading me on, knowingly or not, but I was furious with myself for not being able to pull out of the current funk I was in and just enjoy the rest of my time in the city. Here I was on vacation in NYC, and I was holed up in my hotel room doing nothing but crying and feeling sorry for myself. It was a waste of time, energy and money, and I knew it was time to admit defeat, cut my losses and just go home.

Once I had calmed down, I decided to send an olive branch and offer to part on good terms. Life was too short, and there was no reason for us to waste time being angry with each other. We had obviously misunderstood each other's intentions. If I was being honest, I should have known and probably did know deep down inside that he didn't want anything serious. I was just so enamored by him and our chemistry together that I chose to turn a blind eye and a deaf ear to all the warning signs that told me I was way more into him than he was into me.

Erin: *Listen, I don't want to leave this on a bad note with us. I'm sorry for misunderstanding. I should have known better. I still think you're a good guy, and I wish you nothing but happiness and success in your life. I hope you will smile when you remember the good times we shared and not think of me as some crazy chick that got too attached, lol. Anyways...take care of yourself. I know your family is your first priority, but don't forget to live for yourself, too.*

I shouldn't have been surprised and hurt that he didn't respond, but I was. I had given him the chance to still look like a good guy and take the high road and part as friends. If he gave a shit about me even a little, why wouldn't he have responded and simply said, "You're right. I'm sorry it didn't work out. No hard feelings. Peace be with you, my friend." Whatever! But he said nothing. I was worth nothing to him. Wow, did that hurt.

Sitting at my gate waiting to board, I couldn't refrain from sending one last text.

Erin: *It's kinda tough to realize that I mean so little to you that you can't even tell me good-bye. I was hoping we could at least part as friends, but I guess you don't even want that from me. *sigh* Well, nothing more I can say. Good luck and farewell.*

When I got home to L.A., I wallowed in misery on my couch for one day, and then I started writing… and I didn't stop writing until I finished my second book. I may have come home an entire week early from New York, but I made good use of my time. And during all that time, I heard nothing from Mike. Not a single word. I felt devastated to have him gone from my life all of a sudden, like he'd never been there to begin with. I missed him. Hoping against hope that he would answer and at least say good-bye, I tried one more time.

Erin: *I've been trying not to message you again, but I can't stop thinking about you and wishing I had handled things differently. I was so happy being with you that I pushed for more when you didn't have more to give. I wish we could at least still be friends. :(I wish you would talk to me. I'm reaching out one last time and asking if that's possible. I won't bother you again if you don't reply. So this is me, holding out my hand in offer of friendship with no expectations or demands. I just didn't want to walk away forever without trying one more time to save a friendship with someone I genuinely care about.*

No answer came again, and I had to finally accept that I would probably never hear from him again. It saddened me, but there was nothing I could do about it.

By the time I started back to work on Monday, I had pulled myself together again. I knew life would go on. I had faced some of the biggest disappointments this past year and gone through some major changes in my life, and I was still standing. One thing I had learned about myself was that I was a survivor. I would keep fighting no matter what I encountered, and I wouldn't settle until I found someone who deserved all the love I could give.

Thinking it was the perfect time for a girl's night out, I instant messaged Kristen and asked her if she was free. I knew she was probably in need of cheering up and could use a girl's night as well. It didn't take much convincing on my part. I only had to offer to buy the first round of drinks and she was in.

After floating back three double kamikaze shots, I got up to sing my first song, *You Oughta Know* by Alanis. I wasn't bitter and angry or anything, nah.

The rest of the evening was filled with more Alanis, some Evanescence and Linkin Park. I took my aggression and frustration out on the microphone, and surprisingly after all was said and done, I did feel a little better. Singing always did that for me, though.

I'd just sat down after killing *One Last Breath* by Evanescence when one of my old karaoke buddies spotted me and came over to pull up a chair to our table. Dani had been coming to the same bar as me for over ten years, but we'd only recently connected and started coming together occasionally. I loved her raspy, soulful voice, especially when she sang her favorite song, *Stereo Hearts* by Gym Class Heroes. I introduced her to Kristen and asked if she had just gotten there.

"Guess what!" she exclaimed, obviously excited about something.

"What?"

"I just heard that there's a new reality TV talent competition that is holding auditions, and they're coming to L.A.!"

"Shut up—is it a singing competition?"

"Singing, dancing, acrobats, comedians, magicians, you name it."

"Sounds kind of like *America's Got Talent*, no?"

"Yep, like that, but the grand prize for this show is *five* million dollars. It's called *The Next American Superstar.*" She said *Superstar* like Molly Shannon, making us giggle.

"And *America's Got Talent* is only one million?"

"Yup," she said, nodding. "How sick is that shit?"

"That is pretty dope," I agreed. "Are you going to audition?"

"Fuck yeah! You wanna go with me?"

"Oh, me? Ha… I dunno. I've already tried out for *American Idol* a couple of times, remember, and that went absolutely nowhere."

"Well, you gotta keep trying, right?"

I nodded thoughtfully. "Right… I just don't know if it's something I want to pursue right now. I mean, I'm writing now, and that sucks up most of my spare time. If I auditioned and happened to make it on the show, that would mean I'd have to quit my job and put my writing to the side and focus on the show instead. And if it doesn't work out, what do I have to show for it? No job and the little fan base I have as an indie author will have probably disappeared because I'll have become irrelevant."

"Your mouth is moving, but all I'm hearing is excuses."

Smirking at her, I nodded. "Okay fine. I'll go. Think it's probably a waste of time, but I'm no quitter."

"Yes!" she said, pumping her fist triumphantly. "Now I don't have to stand in line by myself."

"Haha."

"I have absolutely no talent, but I can come and stand in line with you guys and be your groupie," Kristen offered. Dani and I both laughed and nodded in agreement.

"Deal!" we said in unison.

"Awesome! Time for more shots?" Kristen suggested.

"Definitely."

"Yep, let's do it," Dani said, waving the waitress over to take our order.

In spite of my pessimism, I had a good feeling about this talent competition. It was the perfect thing to get my mind off of Mike and my broken heart. "I think we should come to karaoke every single night between now and the auditions," I proposed as our shots arrived, grabbing a glass and raising it to make a toast.

"I'm in," Dani agreed, taking a glass and handing one to Kristen before taking the other and raising it to complete the toast.

"I don't think I can come every night, but I will definitely come at least one more time, and I will be there to cheer you guys on in line!" Kristen promised.

"To being badass singers! Let's represent for L.A."

"Fuckin' A, man," Dani exclaimed. Then we all tossed back our shots in unison, making equally awful faces as the alcohol hit our tastebuds.

"Ugh, tequila," I moaned. "I almost puked just now. That shit is so nasty. I can't believe you made me shoot that."

"Stop being a baby," Kristen ordered, raising her hand to wave the waitress over for another round, but I pushed her arm back down.

"No more shots. I still gotta make it home in one piece, you know. And you rode with me."

"Fine! What about you, Dani? One more shot?"

"Fuck yeah, I'm not driving tonight. I took Uber here, and then my buddy is gonna give me a ride home. So tomorrow night, we'll meet here at nine?"

"You know it," I agreed.

Staying true to our word, we both showed up every single night until the day of the L.A. auditions arrived a couple of weeks later. Dani didn't own a car, so I swung by her apartment in Venice first with Starbucks coffee in hand. She offered to play navigator and plugged the address into Google Maps for me, then we were on our way to Hollywood. We thought we were going to be early, getting there at seven in the morning, but there was already a huge line in place by the time we got there.

I'd already been through two auditions like this before when I had tried out for *American Idol*, so I had an idea of what to expect, but that didn't really make me any less nervous. Did I really want to go through all of this stress and pressure just to be rejected again? Dani and I killed time by starting up an acapella sing-a-long with some other singers who were standing in line near us. We were just ramping up on our version of *No Diggity* when the line started to move again, bringing us to the front.

This was it. In a matter of minutes, I would be standing in front of producers for the third time in my life, trying not to make a fool of myself. I had to sing my fucking heart out, and I couldn't hold anything back. Could I get my nerves under control this time? Could I do this? I'd always loved to sing, but I wasn't sure if I was cut out to do it professionally. It was my biggest dream, but after all the years of rejection, I wasn't sure it was meant to be. So far, it hadn't seemed to be in the cards for me, but that's never stopped me from wanting it. Sometimes if I let myself think about it for too long, I started wanting it so badly again I could taste it. There was just something about singing that made me feel better than anything else. It's like when I sang I felt more in tune with my body and soul.

Then it was our turn, and after our release waivers were collected, we were led to a roomful of producers. All of a sudden my palms began to sweat, and my cheeks began to warm until they felt like they were on fire. I was *so* nervous. It had been a few years since the last time I'd done something like this, and aside from the occasional night at karaoke, I hadn't really been training for this. That didn't mean I wasn't going to give it my all, but I was having a difficult time breathing, and my face still felt like it was flaming hot. I was sure it was bright red to everyone there, but I couldn't help it.

"Good morning, ladies. Alright, I want everyone to just take a big, deep breath and try to relax. Ha, I know—easier said than done, right? Okay, so we're going to start with number 405 and then 406 will go next and on down the line. I'll hold up my hand when we've heard enough, and then we'll go right to the next person. Everyone got it? Okay, great. Number 405, anytime you're ready."

I could hear the girl next to me gulp hard, but she looked down at the floor, took a few deep breaths, looked up again and started singing. And it was impeccable. She did a totally unique version of *It's a New Day* by Nina Simone, and it was spot on and completely breathtaking. I couldn't believe I had to follow that. Fuck me.

Before I could catch my breath, the guy who I assumed was the head producer held up his hand and it was my turn. I needed to get a grip of myself and fast. This was it. No turning back now. No changing my mind. I could either do this shit, or I could look like a fucking idiot and not open my mouth at all. I could chickenshit out.

But I wasn't born to do that. No way. This was my time. I could literally feel it pulsing in my veins in the mere seconds that passed when the first girl stopped singing and I started. I'd chosen a bluesy rendition of *I Can't Dance* by Genesis, and it was, in my opinion, the most unique translation of a song that I'd done to date. And I kinda really loved it. With the richness of my alto voice, the sound of my vocals was deep and sexy.

Every other time I'd auditioned for something like this, I hadn't been satisfied with my song choice, and I'd end up second-guessing myself every freaking time. This was the first time I'd chosen a song I knew in and out. A song I'd been singing since I was a kid. You really had to be comfortable with what you're performing when you audition for something like this, especially when you're already battling your own nerves. I mean, maybe some people are made out of steel, but I am not one of them. I've struggled with self-confidence and public speaking all my life. I still wonder how I got through years of acting in community theatre when I had such stage fright now at this point in my life. Regardless, it was go time; it was do or die. So here I was singing my heart out and laying it all down, and this time it felt different. This time it felt good. And the head producer dude didn't stop me after only ten seconds! He let me go on for a good forty-five or so. I started with the second verse because I was hoping I could get to the bridge before he cut me off, which turned out to be a very good decision.

Everything after that was kind of a blur. I remember Dani singing after me, doing one of her all-time favorite karaoke songs, *Talking to the Moon* by Bruno Mars. I thought she did great, but the guy cut her off after only twenty seconds. So either she'd pretty impressed the shit out of him in that little bit of time or he wasn't interested. The last girl started singing *Before He Cheats* by Carrie Underwood, and I was yet again blown away by the level of talent we were going up against. However, the poor girl stopped singing right after she got out of the chorus, but the guy hadn't raised his hand for her to stop, yet. She had forgotten the lyrics: every singer's worst nightmare. She couldn't remember what came next and just stood there, shaking her head before saying, "I'm so sorry," and bursting into tears. Oh boy.

Dani patted the girl on the back and murmured to her in a consoling tone. I couldn't breathe as we waited for the producers to huddle together and come to their decision. Had I done enough this time? The first time I'd ever auditioned for a show like this, I felt like my voice had just disappeared when I opened my mouth. Did my voice really sound that quiet and weak? What seemed like an eternity passed before they finally broke their huddle as the head producer cleared his throat in preparation to deliver the verdict.

"Numbers 405 406, you are on to our next round. Numbers 407 and 408, thank you so much for coming in to sing for us today, but you're not quite what we're looking for."

Oh no. Even as I rejoiced that I had finally made it farther than the first round, my heart sank. I was moving on this time, but Dani wasn't. This was terrible. I knew how good she was, and I felt like they weren't giving her a fair chance, but there was nothing I could do. She was a good sport about it and gave me a tight hug.

"I'll Uber it home, no worries," she said, winking at me. "You're doing great, Erin. Knock 'em dead, okay?"

"Thanks, girl," I said, pulling her back to hug again as I whispered in her ear, "You did just as great, though. Fuck what they think."

As she pulled back, she smiled and then turned to leave. There was barely any time for me to dwell on Dani's departure as one of the female producers started speaking.

"Okay, ladies. Please report back here later this afternoon by four PM. Don't be late."

We both thanked the producers and then followed a guy with a clipboard and headset out of the room. After being given specific instructions on where to report when we returned, we were released.

Oh my God. I'd done it. I'd really, finally done it. I still had to get past at least one more round before I made it to the finals, but just making it this far was the big confidence boost I desperately needed. I could do this. I needed to do this for me. After all the shit I'd gone through this year with my love life, I needed to refocus on what was important. I needed to learn how to put myself first before any guy or relationship, and giving my singing career another shot when I'd already given up was a good way to start.

Deciding it was best if I stayed in the immediate area, I found a small café down the street. After eating a small salad and a cup of minestrone, I sat back to enjoy a hot cup of tea as I reflected on how lucky I felt. Even if I didn't win, even if I didn't make it past the next round, I had still done better than I'd done before. I figured that was still something to be proud of.

My sister Regan was the only person I texted to say I'd made it to the next round. She called immediately, freaking out as she congratulated me. After demanding to hear all the details, she told me how proud she was of me and said to keep her posted. I thanked her and told her I would for sure.

For a few minutes I debated calling my parents. I really didn't want to tell them anything until I made it farther along. I don't think either one of them took my singing or acting seriously, so I didn't want them to see me fail again. I only wanted them to see me succeed this time, so they'd know that I really was meant to do something creative with my life and that it wasn't "just a hobby". In the end, I decided against calling. I'd wait until I made it to the finals before I said anything.

I reported back half an hour early, not wanting to chance being late and missing my callback. Eventually I was led to another roomful of producers, all of them sitting there quietly watching me as I walked into the room. There were more of them this time, and I recognized the head producer from the first round. I'd been told to introduce myself, say where I was from and why I thought I was the *Next American Superstar*, so I took a deep breath and went for it.

"Hi, I'm Erin Tanaka and I'm originally from Hawaii, but I've been in L.A. for about fifteen years. I think I'm the *Next American Superstar* because music is my passion and something I feel I was born to do. I am happiest and feel most whole when I'm singing, and I think I have something special to offer the world with my music."

A woman with wavy brown hair thanked me and said I was welcome to start whenever I was ready. I'd chosen a song that was the hidden track on Alanis' *Jagged Little Pill* album. *Your House* was done acapella on the album, and it was one of my favorite songs to sing. To my disbelief, they let me sing the entire song. When I finished, the room was silent. Then the woman thanked me for coming and said someone would be in touch within the next week to notify me whether I had made it to the finals in New York City.

That week was the longest week of my life as I waited to hear whether I would be returning to NYC or not. I was at work and about to leave for the day when I finally received my call. The man who called introduced himself as Lee Inman of Starway Productions and said the producers had really been impressed with my audition and would be thrilled if I would join them in New York for the finals in a few months time. I was speechless. This was everything I had been dreaming of since the first time I sang on a stage. This was really happening. Someone else recognized my talent and wanted to give me a shot. Were they crazy for believing in me? Maybe. But I would take the chance and give it my best. After all, third time's a charm, right?

Chapter NINETEEN

Three months later it was time for me to head to NYC with Keri, one of my other karaoke buddies. Determined to get as much practice in as I could, I'd invited her to karaoke and explained I'd be going there a lot more frequently now. When I told her I'd auditioned for *The Next American Superstar* and was heading to New York for the finals, her jaw dropped open, then she told me she'd also auditioned and gotten through to the finals.

It was a huge relief to me that I'd know someone there. I was using up every bit of my vacation time in order to do this, and I was hoping it was worth the gamble. I only had three weeks before I had to report back to work or I'd have to ask them to take a leave of absence. If they said no, I'd have to quit my job. There was no one for me to fall back on and I didn't have much in savings, so if I failed, I could be royally screwed.

Keri and I went to karaoke five days a week, taking a break every few days to rest our vocal chords. I tried to broaden my range by choosing songs that I'd heard many times but never tried to sing. Everything from Stevie Nicks to Rihanna to Tina Turner went into my new repertoire. I was preparing for battle... musical battle.

Keri: *Hey lady, we're on our way. Be there in a few minutes.*

Keri's boyfriend, Jerome, had agreed to drive us to the airport, so they were swinging by to pick me up. I did a last check around my apartment to make sure I'd packed everything I'd need for possibly the next several months. This was crazy—I had never done anything like this before. If I made it past the first week, I would sublet my apartment until I returned, but I still had other bills to pay in the meantime. I had a few credit cards I could use to float myself for a while, but it was a huge gamble. Or my boss might take pity on me and hire me back if he couldn't find a decent replacement while I was gone. I was crossing my fingers for that, but I knew I couldn't rely on it no matter how good at my job I might be. Taking a deep breath, I gathered all my things and locked the door. No turning back now.

It was still super early in the morning before rush hour, so we made good time getting to the airport. When Jerome finished unloading all of our baggage from the car, Keri and I exchanged glasses and burst into giggles. We had six pieces of luggage between the two of us, but we only had to get to the ticketing counter with them, so it wasn't that bad. Keri and Jerome said their good-byes to each other, exchanging a hug and a long, passionate kiss that had me coughing and turning away to give them a moment of privacy.

The line at the ticketing counter was short and getting through the TSA security check didn't take long either, so in no time at all, we were walking to our gate.

"Oh hey, I know her," Keri said, pointing at a beautiful girl with brown hair who was sitting near our gate. Her eyes were closed and she was wearing ear buds, nodding her head in time to the music she was listening to. "She was at the auditions with me. Let's go say hi."

"Okay," I said as I followed her.

Giggling, Keri nudged the girl's foot. Eyes popping open, she looked up at us with a startled expression and then pulled the ear buds out.

"Hey, girl. Remember me?" Keri asked, grinning down at her.

"Hey! Keri, right?" she asked, returning the smile.

"Yep, good memory! Annie, right?"

"Yep, good memory for you, too."

"Haha, thanks. And this is my friend, Erin. We go to the same karaoke bar. Bumped into each other one night while we were both out celebrating our birthdays, and we've been karaoke buddies ever since! I had no idea she even auditioned until we were talking about it while we were out for a karaoke night recently, and we found out that not only did we both audition, but we both made it to the finals!"

"Oh that's awesome!" Annie exclaimed. "Great to meet you, Erin," she said as she offered her hand to me. I shook it and smiled warmly at her. I had a good feeling about this chick already. She had a good vibe about her. "Do you guys wanna sit here?" she asked, waving at two empty seats next to her.

Keri nodded and dumped her luggage on the seat next to Annie. "Sure, I'm going to grab some coffee, but I'll be right back. Do you guys mind watching my bags?" "Not at all," Annie said, then asked if Keri could grab her a cup as well, handing her some money. After Keri left, Annie turned to me. "So are you excited? Nervous? Both?"

I laughed and nodded as I sat down. "Definitely both. You?"

"Yup, same. This is my first time going to New York, too."

"Oh yeah? It's pretty cool. I just went for the first time last year, like the weekend before Thanksgiving." I felt a pang as I thought about how great that first weekend in New York with Mike had been.

"Nice! What did you go for? Vacation? Visit family?"

"My family lives in Hawaii. I went to see a boy," I said, turning a little red with my admission.

"Oh really?" Annie didn't tease me, but just smiled warmly. "Long distance relationship?"

"Well, I was willing to give it a shot, but him, not so much."

"Aww, that sucks. How did you meet him?"

"I was home visiting my family in Hawaii and I posted an ad on Craigslist."

Annie started laughing, making me blush again. "Haha, I love that I'm not the only one crazy enough to post on Craigslist."

Well that was not what I was expecting her to say.

"Oh, you've tried it as well? How's your luck been?"

Looking thoughtful, Annie smiled wistfully and shook her head. "Not the best, but I've definitely met some interesting men."

"Yeah, same here. The guy I met in Hawaii seemed like a keeper. We had so much in common right away. I'm a huge gamer nerd, and he is as well. Not to mention he's a total hottie." I gave a little sigh as I thought about how amazing he had looked in my bed.

"How'd it go down?"

"He responded to my ad and sent me a couple of pictures. I almost didn't respond, because one of the pictures he sent was of him pretty much naked. Like he was standing in front of a bathroom mirror doing a profile shot, only holding a towel in front of his junk."

Annie snickered. "Yeah, I've gotten my share of those types of pics. So you responded anyway and?"

"Yeah, I mean, I normally wouldn't respond to someone who sent a picture like that…but he's pretty damn fine, so I couldn't resist."

"Nice. Did you guys go out to dinner?"

"No, he said he had to work kind of late, so he asked if I wanted to see a movie with him. But he lived in Waikiki and didn't have a car, so I had to drive my rental all the way from the house I was staying at on North Shore to pick him up. It took me almost an hour to get there. He couldn't believe how far away I was. I told him I was staying on the other side of the island, but turned out he'd only moved there from Brooklyn a couple months prior for work, and he'd pretty much stuck to his immediate area, so he had no idea how long it took to get around the island."

"Brooklyn? Damn, he's a long ways from home."

I nodded and shrugged my shoulders. "Yeah, he said transferred to Hawaii for the warmer climate, but once he got there, he hated it."

"What the hell? Who hates Hawaii?"

"I know…that should have been my first red flag for him. Anyways, when I finally arrived and he got in my car—oh my God, girl. He smelled so good." I closed my eyes for a moment and smiled as I remembered how delicious his scent was.

"Oh yeah?"

"Yeah, and he looked amazing. I was so nervous, but at the same time, I felt so comfortable around him. We went to see this action hero spoof, and we laughed and joked around and had a great time together. Like everything seemed so perfect. We didn't hold hands during the movie, but he would do that thing where he'd lean into me during certain parts of the movie and laugh. The chemistry was so electric. I didn't want the night to end."

"Aww, that sounds great! So what happened after that?" I almost laughed out loud. Annie was on the edge of her seat as she listened to me tell my Mike story.

"Are you sure I'm not boring you?" I asked skeptically.

"Of course not! I love hearing stories like these. Keep going."

Grinning, I nodded and continued. "Okay, if you're sure…so we decided to go pick up some wine from a convenience store to take back to his place. He suggested we have a drink and watch some *League of Legends* games."

"Oh, I think I've heard of that game. It's like *World of Warcraft*, isn't it?"

"Kind of. Just as addicting anyway. I hadn't played the game before at that point, but I didn't really care what we did together. I just knew I didn't want to leave him, yet. I mean, I was already heading back to California the next evening, so that was my only chance to spend time with him before going back home. But when we got to the store, they told us that they weren't allowed to sell us any alcohol, because it was already fifteen minutes past midnight."

Annie looked surprised. "They have a curfew on alcohol in Hawaii?"

"Yep, apparently they aren't allowed to sell alcohol after midnight. I mean, if you go to a bar, you can still get a drink a little later than that, but you can't go to a store and buy alcohol after midnight."

"That blows. So what'd you do after that?"

"Yeah, I could have used a drink right then, too. I was still so nervous. But we just laughed about it and headed back to his place anyway. We cuddled up on his bed and watched a little bit of a *League of Legends* game, but then he took pity on me and found all these funny videos to show me. Oh my God, we laughed so much! My mouth hurt from smiling, and he would slide his hand up my leg and squeeze my ass a little every now and then. It was so sexy." And it had been sexy… extremely so. It made me sad to think that I'd never get to hang out with him again.

"Nice, nice. So did you seal the deal?"

Annie's frank question made me blush yet again.

"Sorry, you probably don't want to tell a complete stranger that," Annie said apologetically, but I just laughed and shook my head.

"Oh no, it's fine. I'm pretty much an open book. But no, we didn't 'seal the deal', or not technically anyway. I was kind of on my period…"

"Oh no," Annie groaned. "That sucks so bad."

You're telling me.

"I know, and honestly, I would've been down to do it anyway. I mean, he slid my hand over his crotch, and I was very pleasantly surprised by what I found, so I was totally bummed that I was on the rag. But after I went down on him, he tried to reciprocate, and I had to tell him. All he said in response to that was, 'How do you feel about anal?', so that was the end of that!"

Annie made a face and shook her head. "Gah, what is it about men and butt sex?"

"I don't know, but they all seem to be obsessed. And he was huge! There was no way in hell I was going to let him fuck me up the ass." Wincing, I paused for a moment and apologized. "Sorry—I have a pretty bad potty mouth."

"Please, it can't be any worse than mine. I think you and I are going to be great friends."

I grinned at Annie, happy to have found a kindred spirit in her. "You're pretty awesome. I'm glad Keri introduced us."

"Same here, and speaking of the devil, here she comes with my coffee."

Keri walked up to us just then, carrying a large cup of coffee in each hand. "Highway robbery, people! Seven dollars for a freaking latte," she complained, handing Annie's coffee and change to her.

"Geez," Annie said. "Glad I stuck to regular coffee."

"Seriously. I don't think I can afford my frou frou coffee habits at these prices."

"It's just as bad in New York," I cautioned, "if not worse."

"Are you serious?" Keri sputtered as she took a sip of her coffee.

I nodded. "Yep. Everything is a lot more expensive in NYC."

"Erin was just telling me about the boy from Brooklyn that she met in Hawaii last year."

"Oh yeah, that's a great story. Did she show you a picture of him, yet?"

"No! Let me see," Annie demanded.

Happy to comply, I started scrolling through my phone for a picture, then finally turned it around for Annie and Keri to see.

"Hubba hubba! He is fine!" Annie said in frank admiration. "I like his shaved head. What is he?"

"So when I commented on his naked pic and how I almost didn't respond because he sent it, but still told him he had a nice ass, his response was, 'Yeah, but you liked it, huh? That's the Puerto Rican ass.' Can you believe that smile? And those abs?"

"Yeah, the abs are super nice. And the shaved head is definitely working for him. Has he ever modeled?"

Glancing at the picture on my phone again, I nodded. "Yeah, he said he did a little modeling for *Abercrombie & Fitch* back in the day. He sent me one of the pics. Here it is," she said as she found it and turned the phone towards them again.

"Damn, girl. I want me a piece of that."

"I know, right?" I said, sighing heavily.

"Did she tell you about the trip to New York, yet?" Keri asked Annie as she wiggled her eyebrows.

"Not yet, but it's almost time to board our plane. I want to hear all about it soon, though."

I exchanged numbers with Annie and then we got up to join the other passengers who were getting ready to board. After checking our tickets, we saw that Annie was sitting towards the front of the plane while Keri and I were sitting together towards the back. As the airline attendant began to call Annie's group to board, she turned to say good-bye, giving us each a quick hug.

"It was great chatting with you, Erin. Great seeing you again, Keri. See you on the other side." Annie waved to us as she joined the line to board the plane.

By the time we arrived in New York, I couldn't feel my ass. It had gone numb from sitting for five hours straight. While we waited for the other passengers in front of us to exit the plane, I turned my cell phone back on and checked my email. On a whim, I suddenly decided to text Mike. I had no idea if he'd want to hear from me ever again, but I was in NYC, so I had to give it a shot. Keri and I were making our way to the baggage claim carousel when we spotted Annie and a tall, hunky guy with blondish hair and very nice arms standing next to her.

"Hi, Annie. How are you, Casey?" Keri asked as she walked up to them, flashing a big smile at the guy I assumed was Casey. From the look on Annie's face, it didn't seem like she appreciated Keri's blatant flirting, but she seemed to shrug it off and instead started talking to me.

"Hey, Erin. How was the flight for you?"

"Ugh, I wasn't all that bad, but I started thinking about Mike—you know the guy from Brooklyn slash Hawaii? And yeah, it was a little depressing. I may have texted him just now."

"What?" Keri whirled around and smacked my arm. "Tell me you're joking, lady. You did no such thing."

Wincing, I rubbed my arm. "I couldn't help it."

"Yes, you could! Girl, he is nothing but bad news. He was such an asshole to you the last time you were here. Why on earth would you want to put yourself through that again? Are you crazy loco?" Keri waved her hands about as she scolded me.

Annie just looked at me sympathetically. She understood what it was like to be attracted to assholes who only thought of themselves first. Casey moved away from us, looking like he just wanted to avoid getting involved in any boy/girl drama.

"I just have to make a quick phone call, okay? I'll be right over here," he told Annie, then moved over to the side.

"So what'd you text him?" Keri asked in a resigned voice.

I handed my phone over to her, and she read the text out loud.

Erin: *I don't know if you'd want to see me, but I'm in town this weekend. Hope all is well with you and your family.*

"Oh, Erin. You are worth so much more than that scumbag," Keri said.

I nodded in agreement with her. "I know I am. I can't help it. He has a beautiful penis, what can I say?"

Annie's eyes widened as she burst out giggling, slapping a hand over her mouth to stifle the laughter. "Sorry! A beautiful penis, you say?"

"Yes, wanna see?" I asked as I started to look through my phone for one of the pictures he'd sent me.

"No!" Keri said, slapping my arm. "We don't need to see his penis."

"Well it's not his actual penis. I mean it is, but it's just the outline of his penis. He's wearing underwear," I explained. Like I would show them a picture of his naked penis!

Keri eyed me skeptically, then finally nodded her consent. "Alright, fine, show us this beautiful penis that has rendered you a complete fucking idiot."

All three of us burst into giggles at that point, then I looked through my phone for the picture I wanted to show them, zoomed in on his crotch, then showed it to the other girls. An attractive Puerto-Rican guy with a shaved head who looked to be in his late twenties had taken a selfie holding his phone in front of a mirror. He had a toned six-pack and was wearing boxer briefs that showed the impressive outline of his semi-flaccid penis.

"And that's mostly soft."

Keri let out a low whistle and Annie nodded her head in agreement.

"Nice," she said.

"Beautiful man," Keri said admiringly.

"Beautiful penis," I said mournfully.

"But not a penis worth getting your heart broken for again," Keri snapped back at me.

"I dunno…it might be worth it." Just then, my phone vibrated, and I glanced down to see who had texted me. When I saw who it was, I started bouncing up and down excitedly. "Oh my God, he just texted me back."

"What'd he say?"

I read the text out loud to them.

Mike: *What time are you landing and how long are you staying?*

Keri groaned and shook her head at me just as the baggage carousel light flashed, signaling that our bags were finally on their way out to us. Casey rejoined us shortly after, and Annie grinned as she leaned up to give him a kiss.

"So are you going to see him tonight?" Annie asked as she scanned the bags.

"I don't know. Tonight's really my only chance to see him before everything starts. I guess if it works out."

"Right. Well, keep me posted. I hope it all works out for you."

"I will, and thanks. I really hope I get to see him."

"Oh there's mine," Annie said as she spotted her bag, but before she could step forward to grab it, Casey beat her to it and easily lifted it away from the carousel and set it down next to her.

"Jesus, what'd you pack? Everything in your closet?" he complained.

Annie smirked at him. "What are you complaining about? You just lifted my bag like it was nothing. I may pack heavy, but that's cuz I know I have a man who can handle it."

"Is that so?" he asked, smirking back at her.

"Yep. Hey, is that your bag?" she said, pointing at the carousel. Looking where she pointed, Casey nodded and moved to get the bag. Moments later, Keri and I had our suitcases as well, and all four of us headed outside to join the taxi line.

We ended up taking separate cars since we had to fit in our luggage along with ourselves. After checking in at our hotel, Keri and I decided to grab dinner together. We spent an hour freshening up before meeting downstairs in the lobby, then walked to a little Italian restaurant that I'd found nearby on Yelp. We didn't stay out too late, but went back to the hotel straight after dinner. A good night's sleep was needed before the final auditions the next morning. Falling asleep that night was a little harder for me than usual, but I did my best to calm my mind and finally after about an hour went by, I drifted off into a deep sleep.

Early the next morning the alarm on my cell phone went off, waking me up instantly. This was it. This was the day. Was I ready for this? Probably not. But you know what they say. "Fake it 'til you make it."

I took an hour to get ready, going through some vocal warm-ups as I did my make-up and hair. Keri texted me, asking if I wanted to meet for breakfast downstairs. I texted her back and said I'd be ready in a few more minutes. Doing a final check in the mirror, I decided that it was as good as it was gonna get. I grabbed my purse and made sure I had my room keycard before heading down to the hotel restaurant for breakfast.

Keri was already waiting when I arrived. She looked super cute in her black skinny jeans and a skin-tight purple top paired with a short black leather jacket. Her black strappy heels were at least four inches, and as I watched her work them with seemingly effortless grace, I wondered how I would fare in shoes like those.

After going through the breakfast buffet, we found a table and sat down to enjoy our meal. I had gotten some oatmeal and fresh fruit while Keri had gone for an egg white omelet and some Greek yogurt. Once we'd eaten, Keri said she needed to stop by the ladies' room before heading into the auditorium. We found seats toward the front, and she texted Annie to let her know where we were sitting.

It was probably another fifteen minutes before Annie finally joined us, looking a little flustered. She seemed to be just as nervous about the audition as Keri and I were. As she sat down and glanced over at me where I was sitting on the opposite side of Keri, I gave her a shy smile and a little wave. She smiled and waved back and I felt happy to have made a new friend. I was definitely going to need one in the days ahead. This competition was sure to break some people down, and for all I knew, I could be one of them.

Just then, a cute guy with blonde hair who was sporting a nice suit walked to center stage and spoke into a microphone that was waiting there.

"Welcome, ladies and gentlemen, to the first season of *The Next American Superstar.* I am your host, Kyle Atkinson. I know many of you have traveled a long ways to get here, and we are very happy to have you here with us in The Big Apple. Now we have a lot of acts to get through today, so I'm just going to give everyone a brief run-down of today's schedule and then we'll get started. When you checked into your hotel, you were given a badge with a number. Does everybody have their badge? Great. Okay, we are not going to pass out a schedule for today. Look for your badge number on the schedule. That is the approximate time you are performing today. Please make sure you are ready to go half an hour prior to that. If you do not see your badge number on the schedule, congratulations. Your previous audition has guaranteed you a pass into the next round tomorrow. You may, however, choose to stick around… and I'd recommend it. Check out your competition. All of this is being recoded, and per the waivers you signed, any and all film can be used, so please remember that this is a family show, people. Keep it clean. Okay, that's about it. I don't know about you, everybody, but I know I'm excited. Are you excited?"

Wow, that had been quite a long speech. I cheered along with everyone else, excited that the time had finally come for me to prove myself. After everyone had quieted down, Kyle said, "Alright then, we will start in half an hour. Thank you." When he left the stage, ushers began to move around the auditorium, passing out schedules to everyone. I looked at the schedule and found my badge number. I was on at nine forty-five. Annie said she was on after me at ten. Man, why did I have to go first?

"I heard that there are a lot of vocalists and they're making all of them sing today, and they are only going to keep four girls and four guys," Keri said as she picked up her bag and stood up. Annie and I exchanged glances before picking up our bags and following Keri out of the auditorium. Once backstage, we headed into the ladies' room and started prepping for our auditions. I got my curling iron out and turned it on to heat, then dug out my make-up bag and proceeded to touch up my face.

When the iron had finished heating, I picked it up and began to fix some of the pieces that had lost their curl. In my head I ran over the lyrics to my song.

I'd decided to do *Back to Black* by Amy Winehouse, one of my favorite songs. I was pretty confident that I could do it justice, and I was comfortable singing it, so I thought it was a good choice.

A young guy with a clipboard took us back to the greenroom along with some of the other contestants where we waited for half an hour. Then they called the first four girls up to wait "on deck", which included Annie and myself. There was one girl in front of me, so at least I wasn't the very first to go, but that still wasn't much comfort to me. I'd never gotten this far before. What was I doing here? Who was I fooling? I couldn't do this.

Calm down, I ordered myself. *Now just take a deep fucking breath and relax. Wooosaaahh.*

"Hey," Annie said, getting my attention, then she gave me a tight hug and wished me luck.

"You as well, girlie girl. You knock 'em dead."

And just like that, they were telling me to go. It was my turn. Taking a deep breath, I started to walk out on stage until I reached the microphone.

"Hello, everyone. My name is Erin Tanaka, and although I've lived in Los Angeles for the past several years, I am originally from Hawaii. I've been singing ever since I was a little girl, and it's been my biggest dream to sing on a stage like this. Thank you for having me here today."

My heart felt like it was pounding out of my chest as I waited for the music to start, but as soon as I heard the familiar notes, my nervousness began to melt away and I began to sing my heart out. It was a feeling unlike any I had ever experienced before... a feeling of pure bliss as I let my voice just soar through the chorus. When the last note had played, applause broke out from the audience, and I nearly sagged with relief at hearing their approval.

I'm not quite sure how I made it backstage again, but somehow I managed to. Then I waited to listen to Annie's performance before returning to the greenroom. She'd chosen *Always Be My Baby* by Mariah Carey, and she was killing it. That girl had been born to sing. You could tell she had a real gift, and she completely commanded the stage throughout her entire performance.

When she had finished and returned backstage, I gave her a big hug, happy tears flowing freely down both our faces. We went to the ladies' room to freshen up before rejoining everyone in the auditorium.

Keri came on later in the afternoon, and we cheered ourselves hoarse for her. She'd chosen to do *Fuckin' Perfect* by Pink, but had edited out the bad words since it was a family show. It was one of her favorite songs to do at karaoke, so I knew she would kill it, and indeed she did do a great job. However, the audience didn't applaud as loudly as they had for Annie and myself.

When the results were hung in the hallways at the end of the day, we all swarmed around the lists to look for our badge numbers. I found my number first and my heart stopped for a moment, then I started shrieking and jumping up and down. Annie pointed right below my finger and sure enough, her number was right there as well. She started jumping up and down and shrieking along with me. This was the best day of my life. I couldn't believe I was going on to the next round.

But in the midst of my happiness, I heard a sob catch in Keri's throat as she stood there beside us, scanning the lists for her badge number and not finding anything. Annie and I stood there in dismay, then gave her an awkward hug and pat on the back. As thrilled as I was to move on, it still sucked to see our friends get sent home.

After saying our good-byes to Keri, we were informed that the remaining contestants would need to report at seven the next morning. Now that my dinner buddy was gone, I wasn't sure what to do next. I knew Annie had her man Casey here, so she'd probably want to have dinner with him. I was about to excuse myself to go back up to my room and just order room service, but Annie told me to hang on a minute as she texted furiously away. Then finally she looked up from her phone.

"Feel like venturing out and finding something to eat?" she asked with a hopeful look on her face.

Oh thank God, I wouldn't have to be a loser and eat alone in my room after all. I smiled and nodded.

"I totally do. Let's go to Times Square. You ready for your first subway experience?"

Annie grinned nervously and nodded. "Um, yeah sure. Why not? I'll have you there to protect me."

I laughed. She was so cute. "It's really not as bad as you think. Don't worry. I was terrified my first time, but by the third, I felt like a pro. And New Yorkers really aren't as rude as the movies make them out to be."

"Really? That's cool. Yeah, I've always thought the people in New York are supposed to be really rude. Especially the cab drivers."

I shook my head. It was a common misconception. "Every single person I asked for help when I got lost a couple of times was really nice. I asked my friend who lives here about that, and he said, 'Yeah, just don't get in our way when we're in a hurry to get somewhere, and we're actually very nice.' Now cab drivers, I can't say. I use Uber, and all that drivers were great."

"Oh my God, don't you freaking love Uber?"

"I do. They are the best! Did you want to just Uber it instead?"

Annie shook her head. "Nah, fuck it. When in Rome, right? Let's take the subway."

I laughed. "Haha, okay."

I looked up the nearest subway station using the app on my phone, then we headed out. As we walked the short distance, Annie cleared her throat.

"Okay, now I hope that you won't get angry with me for what I'm about to tell you, but please know I only had your best interests at heart."

What the hell? What was she talking about? I gave her a confused smile and said, "Okay?"

Taking a deep breath, she started explaining herself.

"So this morning I went outside to get some fresh air before I joined you and Keri in the auditorium. I happened to bump into someone you know. It was Mike, the guy you met in Hawaii. He was dressed in his FedEx uniform, so it was easy to recognize him from the picture you'd shown me. Anyhow, he was hoping to see you, but he had to get back to work. I wanted to tell you right away, but I didn't know if it would upset you, and I didn't want to fuck up your concentration before your audition."

I didn't say anything for a moment as we stood there on the platform. Mike had come by to see me? He hadn't texted me back to arrange to meet up, yet, but I had told him where I'd be that day. I opened my mouth to respond finally, but just then the next train arrived, interrupting my train of thought. We climbed on board, but there were no empty seats, so Annie and I each grabbed a hold of the overhead bar and were forcibly squished together by the other passengers on the train.

Once the train lurched forward, I finally spoke. "I'm still in shock that he came. I just told him where I was going to be today and asked if he wanted to grab dinner after he got off work. I didn't think he'd actually come to the theater."

"Well, girl, now I understand why you're so gah gah over this guy."

"Right? I don't know what it is about him. He's just... yummy."

Yep, he had been deliciously yummy, but that was all in the past now. He'd made it pretty obvious he didn't want to be with me. So why couldn't I just hate him already? It'd be so much better than just pining away after him.

"He definitely has a certain charm about him," Annie agreed. "And those green eyes of his are fuckin' sexy as hell."

I nodded. "I know. They're pretty boy eyes, but he's so masculine. Like he just knows what he wants in bed and takes it. It's so—yeah. I have no words. It's a huge turn on. He just makes me go 'rawr' big-time. But I don't think he wants to try the long distance thing."

Annie groaned. "Long distance relationships are the worst. I mean, technically I've never had a long distance relationship, but my high school boyfriend wouldn't even try it. He broke up with me before he left for college in Boston. And Casey lives in L.A., but he's touring around the country right now, so I only see him every few weeks or so."

"So I should text him now, right?" I asked hesitantly.

Nodding, Annie shrugged. "Sure. See if he can do dinner tomorrow instead."

Now it was my turn to groan. "It might be my last supper here in NYC if I don't do well with tomorrow's audition."

"Girl, you killed it today! What makes you think you can't do it again tomorrow/'"

"Oh we're talking about who killed what not, Miss 'I make Mariah Carey sound like a karaoke singer'?" I shot back, giving her a teasing smile.

Turning bright red, she beamed back at me. "That is the nicest thing anyone's ever said to me."

"I only speak the truth, lady. Your voice is ridic. Fair warning—I'm thinking about putting Ex-lax in your coffee tomorrow morning." I wouldn't really ever do that to someone, but I had to admit it was funny to think about.

Laughing, Annie shook her head as the train came to a stop. "I don't think you have anything to be worried about. Your song was amazing. I adore Amy Winehouse."

"She was one of the best for sure," I agreed, leading the way off the train and up the stairs. We came out right by Times Square. We continued to chat as we walked around a bit to check out our different options. After seeing long lines outside all of the nicer restaurants, we decided to just go to Five Guys for burgers and fries. I sent Mike a text and tried not to feel sad again as I remembered back to the night when we'd gone to the movies at the theater across the street and stopped by Five Guys for dinner first. That night had been the first time I'd really started to see what it might be like if Mike and I actually lived in the same city and could be together and go on fun dates.

After dinner we walked around Times Square, shopping for souvenirs. We took some pictures of each other to send back to our families, then decided to head back to the hotel. Mike finally responded when we were almost back.

Mike: *Hey, sorry I missed you today.*

Erin: *It's okay. My friend Annie said she saw you outside the theater.*

Mike: *Yeah, I came by for a minute, but I couldn't stay. And I didn't want to interrupt your concentration, either.*

Erin: *Well, thanks... so are you free for dinner tomorrow night?*

Mike: *I actually have plans with my family already, but I might be free the night after that.*

Erin: *Okay, sounds good. Let me know.*

As we approached the elevators, Annie gave me a hug and said she was heading to bed.

"Hang in there, okay? And keep me posted on Mike."

"I will. Get some good sleeps. And thanks for inviting me out tonight."

"Of course! It was fun. See you in the morning."

Chapter TWENTY

The next morning, I met up with Annie for breakfast before we wandered over to the auditorium and found seats towards center front. After checking the schedule, we saw that the dance groups were going first, and the vocalists wouldn't be called until the end of the day.

Annie twisted around in her seat next to me, getting a good look around the theater. Nudging me, she cocked her head towards the seats behind us. Swiveling around, I saw the most adorable little girl with curly brown pigtails sitting between her parents, an attractive looking young couple. She was wearing a cute little white dress and had the sweetest smile. Annie and I chatted with the little girl and her parents, learning that her name was Lara and that she was there to sing as well.

A few minutes later, Kyle Atkinson took the stage and the crowd cheered. He briefly explained that the next round of eliminations was about to begin. First up was a dance crew from SoCal called the East LA Dance Crew, and they were amazing. Casey's crew might be in trouble. I glanced over at Annie who had a worried expression on her face as she looked back at me.

"Wow. That's going to be a tough act to follow," I said honestly. "They were really good."

"I know…"

I felt a little pang of guilt as Annie sighed heavily and her shoulders slumped. Maybe I shouldn't have been so honest. "But hey, you said Casey and his crew are awesome, right?"

"I said Casey is awesome, but I've only seen him dancing backup for Kayla. I've never seen him perform with his crew. I mean, I'm assuming that they're amazing or they wouldn't have gotten this far, right?"

I laughed and put up my hands in defense. "Whoa, girl, I'm not dissing your boy or his crew. No need to get defensive. All I said was that the ELADC is going to be a tough act to follow… for anyone, though. But I'm sure your man's got skills or he wouldn't have gotten this far, like you said."

Annie hung her head, looking slightly embarrassed. "Sorry, I'm just nervous for him. I want so badly for him to wi—" She stopped herself as I gave her a pointed look. "For him to do well."

I shook my head. "Girl, I don't envy you at all. I don't know if I could compete against the man I love. But you're here, which tells me you want this. So go big or go home, chick, but don't give him the crown before this shit has even started. If he's meant to win, if you're meant to win—it doesn't matter. You make him earn it either way."

Giving me the biggest smile, Annie cocked her head to the side. "You're pretty awesome yourself, you know? And I'm not even talking about your vocal talent, girl, which you've got in spades."

Uncomfortable being praised by someone whose vocal skills kicked my vocal skills' ass, I said, "Aww, are we having a mushy girlie girl moment?" as I scrunched up my nose at her.

She laughed and shook her head. "We were, but don't worry. It's over now, I promise. You've fulfilled your quota for the day."

"Oh yay," I said. Just then the lights flickered, indicating that another performance was about to start. We watched a quartet of sisters dance to *The Nutcracker*, and then it was time for Casey's crew, Pure Flow, to perform. They'd chosen to do a Michael Jackson and Justin Timberlake medley, and thankfully, they were absolutely on point and amazing. I was just relieved because Annie had seemed so nervous for him and she had enough stress to deal with on her own without taking more on for him as well.

That night both my and Annie's performances were probably the best we'd heard so far overall. She'd gone with a classic and done *Georgia on My Mind* by Ray Charles while I had chosen another kind of classic and gone with *Uninvited* by Alanis Morissette. While we waited for our food, my phone buzzed. I fished it out of my pocket and looked to see who had texted me. To my surprise it was Mike.

Mike: *Hey, what's up?*

Erin: *Just hanging with friends at a diner in Park Slope. About to eat some dinner.*

Mike: *Cool. I'm actually not too far from there right now. Want me to roll by?*

My pulse started to race. Did he actually just offer to come hang out? Before he could change his mind, my trembling fingers texted back as quickly as I could.

Erin: *Sure. I'll send you the address. Just give me a sec.*

Belatedly, I remembered that I should probably check with Annie first, considering we were hanging out with her boyfriend and his crew. Tapping her on the shoulder, I showed her the texts from Mike. She smiled and nodded.

"Sure, no problem. He's more than welcome to join us."

"Okay cool, thank you so much."

"No worries."

I Googled the diner to find the address and then texted it back to Mike.

Mike: *Oh okay. I know where that's at. I'll be there in fifteen.*

Erin: *Okay, see you soon.*

About fifteen minutes later, Mike walked into the diner and came over to where we were sitting. I got up and gave him a hug, then sat back down and scooted over to make room for him next to me. He smelled really good and I had a hard time concentrating on the group conversation. I was surprised that he had shown up but even more surprised that he hung out with us for the next couple of hours before walking us back to the hotel.

I was about to turn and give Annie a hug and say good night, but then Mike said, "Well, I'd better get going."

I swung back around as I said, "What?" a little too loudly. Then more quietly, "You're leaving? You don't want to come up for a bit?"

"Nah, I've gotta be up early tomorrow for work, so I'd better head home."

Was he seriously leaving? I thought he had agreed to come hang out because he wanted to fuck. Why was he leaving?

"But you could stay here with me tonight?" I suggested, trying to keep the desperate tone from my voice.

"Nah, you know, I've got a meeting early in the morning before my shift starts, and I haven't been feeling well lately. I need to get home and get some rest. Is that cool?"

No, it wasn't cool. Was he kidding me? This could be our only chance to get together if I didn't make it to the next round. I could be going home to L.A. very soon, and who knew when I'd ever get the chance to come back to NYC again. But I couldn't say that, so I just nodded dumbly, feeling a little shell-shocked. He smiled at me and leaned forward to kiss my cheek and hug me good-bye. I hugged him back and waved weakly as he walked out of the hotel.

"What the hell just happened?" I exclaimed out loud as I watched him walk away down the street and out of my life once again.

"Um, I'm not too sure," Annie said.

"Like why wouldn't he stay? Why did he even bother coming if he was just going to hang out for a couple of hours and then bail? I wasn't even going to grill him over what happened the last time I was here. I was just going to fuck him and that was that. Like for old time's sake."

Annie shrugged. "Yeah, I dunno, dude."

I shook my head, feeling bewildered. "Did he not think I have my own room? Did he think you were staying with me? I should text him."

Sighing, Annie shook her head at me, but I had already whipped my phone back out and started texting and then paced around the lobby as I waited for him to respond. After a few minutes, I finally paced my way back over to Annie.

"Ugh, I texted him, but he didn't answer. Let me try calling him." She started to say something, but I waved my hand to shush her. "Sorry, just wait one second. I just want to try calling him before he gets on the subway." Waiting as the phone rang but no one picked up, I chewed nervously on my lip. Finally it went to voicemail, so I ended the call and looked at Annie sadly.

"He didn't answer. I can't believe he came and hung out and waked us back here and then just left like that."

"I know, it's crazy," she agreed with me, shaking her head.

"Why would he bother walking me back to the hotel?" I wondered out loud, unable to let it go just yet.

Annie shrugged. "I dunno. You said he's a good guy, right? That's what you like him about him?"

I nodded. "Yeah."

"Well, then he has to uphold that image, you know? The good guy."

"That's such bullshit," I retorted.

She just shrugged again. "It is what it is."

Sighing, I leaned forward to give Annie a hug. "Alright, well since I'm not getting laid tonight, I'd better get to bed. You'd better head there, too." "Yeah, except I might be getting laid tonight," Annie said, winking. I smacked her arm in response.

"Bitch. I hate you."

"That's okay. I feel your pain. I'll see you in the morning."

"Okay. I'm still probably going to hate you in the morning."

"What if I bring you caffeine?"

"I might hate you a little less… especially if it comes in the form of a large Vanilla latte with almond coconut milk."

"Deal," Annie said.

"Deal," I echoed.

We said our goodnights and headed off to our rooms. Once I was alone, I started feeling really sad. I still couldn't understand how Mike could come and hang out and then just leave like that. Like why did he even want to? Every other time we'd seen each other, we'd always fucked, but this time he just left. I felt rejected. What was wrong with me? Did he suddenly gain a conscience and feel bad that he'd been using me all that time? Who knew, but he was gone now and there was nothing I could do about it. I was left with these stupid unresolved feelings. All I wanted to do was forget about him, but it was the last thing I could seem to do right now.

I was so glad we had Saturday off while the judges debated on who was going to make it into the next round. Annie texted to see if I wanted to hang out, but in my state of depression, I knew I wouldn't be great company and didn't want to inflict my misery on her. I just needed a day to mope and I'd be good as new again… hopefully. I ventured downstairs to find some coffee and a Danish and then went right back to my room. Trying to take advantage of my whacked feelings, I pulled out my laptop and tried to get some writing done, but it was hard for me to concentrate.

I ended up watching season one of *The Big Bang Theory* on my laptop and napping throughout the rest of the day. By the time Sunday morning rolled around, I was well rested and felt better equipped to take on the world. If Mike didn't recognize what kind of woman he had in me, then he wasn't worth my time. I needed to move on.

After I showered and changed into my clothes for the day, I headed downstairs with Annie to check the result boards. There were already small groups of people gathered around the boards when we arrived, some of them rejoicing and some of them not. I waited for a space to clear, then moved towards the board to see for myself. What was my fate? Would I be moving on or would I be going home?

Holding my breath, I scanned the lists, looking for the vocalist results. There was Annie's name, and there was mine! Oh my God! We'd actually done it. We were moving on to the next round, the live performances. We would be filmed live and nationally televised. Shit was getting real fast.

"We made it!" I squealed excitedly, bouncing up and down next to Annie as I tugged on her arm. "We made it into the next round!"

"Yay, go us!" Annie squealed along with me, bouncing up and down. We were like a couple of school kids right now, but we didn't care. We'd made it. But we did need to get out of the way of the other contestants who were trying to get closer to the boards to find their names. I grabbed Annie's elbow and steered her to the side and out of the way.

"Where's your man?" I asked. "It looks like Pure Flow made the cut as well!"

Annie groaned and began to relay the events of the previous night. Apparently she and Casey had gotten into a fight and he hadn't come back to their room. I shook my head as I listened to her. This relationship was not healthy for her right now. I wish she'd just break it off and focus on herself right now, but like I was one to talk. I couldn't stop thinking about a guy who didn't even want to be with me.

"Speaking of the devil," I said as I spotted Casey walking up to us.

"Hey, Erin," he said as he leaned down to greet me with a quick hug and kiss on the cheek. For a moment, I got a whiff of his aftershave and cologne and envied my friend. She had such a great guy who was crazy for her, not to mention extremely attractive, even if he was distracting her from focusing on winning. I wanted so badly for someone to be just as crazy about me. "Do you mind if I steal Annie for a minute?"

"Not at all," I said. "I need to use the little girl's room anyway."

Excusing myself, I left them alone and headed for the restrooms.

The week before the live performances were spent in rehearsal for the first show. Annie and I agreed to help each other practice, so we met every day and sang and memorized lyrics for hours. When Tuesday night rolled around, I was so nervous I was convinced I was going to lose the little food I'd been able to eat. Annie seemed to be even worse off than I was, though. She kept pacing around the green room, and her nervous energy started to get to me. I counted slowly to ten, but she kept walking around and it was driving me crazy. Finally I snapped.

"Annie, stop. You're making me nervous. Sit down for a minute and relax."

Shaking her head vehemently, she refused. "I can't. I can't sit. I can't relax. I think I'm gonna puke."

Oh no, if she puked, then I was gonna puke. This had to remain a puke-free zone for both our sakes and for the sakes of all the other contestants packed into the green room with us.

"Do not puke. That's an order, lady." I pointed my finger and gave her a steely look.

"Okay," she said, swallowing hard. Then she smiled. "I'm good, I'm good."

"Uh huh. Not buying it," I said. "You need to breathe. Like seriously. I think you may be turning purple."

She stuck her tongue out at me "Shut up. And I am breathing."

"Breathe more," I insisted.

"You're making it worse."

"Shut up, sit down, and breathe, bitch."

She glared at me, then sniffed before sitting down next to me on the sofa, taking an exaggerated big breath, then another, then another. I smiled smugly as her face started to relax. I'd succeeded in distracting her and now she was starting to calm down.

"See? Isn't that better?" I asked.

Like a five-year-old, she stuck her tongue out at me, making me smirk back at her. "Shut up."

Just then I saw the stage manager waving. "Oh, I think you're up, sweetie. The stage manager is waving you over."

"Fuck me," she muttered as she got to her feet.

"Tempting, but I prefer men," I said dryly, getting to my feet to give her a hug. "Knock 'em dead, lady."

"Thanks! See you on the other side. Break a leg!"

I watched her walk out to center stage and take her place in front of the microphone. Then the chords to *Impossible* by Shontelle began to play. I'd heard her practice this song over and over again in the past week, and I knew she was going to do well. And indeed she did. By the time her performance was over, all three judges were on their feet and the audience was chanting her name. I was so proud of her. She'd done an amazing job. Kyle Atkinson led her over to do their little interview where he asked her questions about where she was from and what she'd been doing with her life before the show.

The stage manager came up to me and asked if I was ready to go. I nodded and gulped hard, taking that last minute to close my eyes and try to center myself. I breathed slowly and deeply until I felt a hand at my elbow. Opening my eyes, I saw the stage manager nod for me to enter onto the stage. Here goes nothing.

I'd decided to go with *What's Love Got to Do With It* by Tina Turner this time. It wasn't the hardest song, but I knew it front to back and it was important for me to be comfortable the first time I'd be performing on camera. It was also very fitting for my life right now. Who needed a heart when it could be broken? I was tired of having my heart broken.

I left it all out there on the stage. Every bit of emotion I'd been feeling and struggling with over the past year, I poured into my performance. And it paid off. The crowd seemed to love it, the judges enjoyed it—I was feeling good about myself.

When the show was over, I headed to a bar with Annie, Casey and his crew. When we got there, Annie turned and grabbed my hand tightly and pulled me behind her through the crowd until we reached the bar. Chris, one of the guys from Casey's crew, ordered Fireball shots for everyone and in another moment I had cinnamon whiskey running down my throat like red hot fire.

"Woo!" Annie exclaimed, slamming her empty shot glass back down on the bar.

"Yeah? You like that?" Chris teased Annie, grinning at her.

"Yeah, not bad. You're right. It tastes just like a red hot."

I nodded in agreement. It was actually a pretty tasty shot—I was surprised to find out it was whiskey.

"Told ya!" Chris crowed. "You ready for another?"

Annie glanced at Casey first, seeming to ask him for permission. This irritated me for some reason, making me roll my eyes, but he just smiled back at her and she turned back to Chris and nodded. "Bring it on!"

As we waited for the bartender to pour the next round, Annie congratulated some of the other dance crew members on their amazing performance. The bartender asked what she was congratulating them for, so she explained that we were all in a talent competition together.

"Oh that's fuckin' awesome. Congrats to all of you!" he said. "Tell you what. This round's on me."

We all gaped at him incredulously. Had he just offered to buy a round of shots for all of us? That was really nice of him.

"No way! Seriously?" Chris exclaimed in surprise.

"Are you sure that's okay? Do you need to clear it with your boss first or anything? We don't want to get you into trouble," Annie protested, but I nudged her. If the guy wanted to buy us a round of shots, shush already! She elbowed me back and continued on. "Hi, I'm Annie, by the way, and this is my boyfriend, Casey. His dance crew is competing as well as myself and Erin, but Erin and I are both solo artists."

"Nice to meet you all. I'm Avery, and I co-own this bar. So yeah, no sweat, guys. This round's on the house. Just tell all your friends to check out our bar sometime while they're in town for the show."

"Oh for sure," Annie agreed and we all nodded. "I'm not even a huge fan of bars, but I really love this place. Cool name, too!"

"Thanks, glad you like it. Well, let me know if I can get you anything else."

"Um yeah, we'll do this one," she said and then glanced at me. "And then one more round." She winked and I grinned back at her. It was time to party.

"You got it, princess," Avery said with another wink, then started pouring out another round for us.

I grinned at the look on Casey's face when Avery said that. I knew that was his pet nickname for Annie, so that probably hadn't sat well with him. Annie giggled and told him the bartender could call her whatever he wanted if he was going to give them free shots. I wholeheartedly agreed.

I had turned around and was talking to one of the other dance crew members, getting ready to do my third shot when Annie yelled my name. She had climbed on top of the bar and was shaking her ass, crooking a finger at me. Oh lord help us.

Shaking my head, I mouthed back, "No fucking way," but Casey, the sneaky bastard, slipped another shot into my hand just then. I glared at him for a moment, then shrugged and rolled my eyes, taking the shot glass and tossing it back.

"Here goes nothing," I muttered as I hoisted myself up onto the bar beside Annie. The whiskey was doing its work and had loosened me up quite a bit. *Get Low* by Lil Jon and the East Side Boyz came on and the entire bar was singing and dancing along as we danced, shimmied and gyrated above them. We pointed in one direction as everyone sang, "to the window," and then pointed in the other direction as everyone sang, "to the wall". Casey and his boys were waving one dollar bills up at us, making us giggle as we grabbed the bills and stuffed them in our shirts. California Love by Tupac came on next and the crowd went crazy again, but Annie and I were pooped. She hopped off the bar first and I followed closely behind.

"That was fun!" I gushed as I panted, trying to catch my breath.

Avery poured Annie two cups of ice water and she turned to hand one to me, already gulping hers down. "So fun!" she agreed, then her eyes widened, making me glance at the guy who had just come up to me. He was standing close... very close. I took him in slowly from head to toe, appreciating how attractive he was with his blond hair and warm hazel eyes. He was wearing a pair of black skinny jeans and a black button-down shirt with rolled up sleeves.

"Hey," was all he said out loud at first, but his eyes spoke volumes as he gazed at me with an appreciative smile on his face. He might as well have been Joey from *Friends* saying, "How *you* doin'?"

I almost giggled at him, but bit my lip and gave him the same kind of frank, admiring gaze. "Hey," I said nonchalantly.

"What's your name?" he asked, his eyes never leaving mine.

"Erin. What's yours?"

"Traver."

Traver... that was a little different—kinda like Trevor and Travis mixed together—but I liked it. "Do you come here often?" I asked.

He glanced around the bar, then grinned as he looked at me again. "Well, yeah. I just started working here kind of recently, so I've been spending a good chunk of my time here."

"Oh, that's cool. Are you one of the bartenders?"

"Yep. About to relieve my boss from duty, but I still have a few minutes. Can I buy you a drink?"

Was he seriously asking to buy me a drink? Guys never hit on me... not guys I was attracted to anyway, and he was actually offering to buy me a drink. He had come up to me.

"Um, sure, if you'd like," I said hesitantly.

He reached for my empty shot glass and sniffed it once, then set it back down. "Another shot of Fireball for you?"

I grinned. "Know your liquor, do you?"

Grinning back, he nodded. "Hard to miss that scent."

"Sure, I'll take another shot. Can you have one with me, or is that against the rules?"

Turning toward the bar, Traver quirked a questioning eyebrow at his boss. Avery answered by setting out three shot glasses and pouring Fireball into them. Then he nudged two of the glasses towards us and picked up the third, raising it in a salute.

"Does that answer your question?" he asked with a wry grin before tossing back his shot.

I drank my shot as well and winced as the smooth liquid burned down my throat. "You have a cool boss."

"Oh, I know it. Both of the guys who own this place are pretty awesome bosses, all in all. I consider myself fortunate to be working for them. They're fair and pay good money. So what brings you to Halo tonight? You out celebrating or just unwinding after a long day at the office?"

Oh no. I didn't want to have to tell him I didn't actually live here in NYC, yet. "We're actually here celebrating the success of our first live recorded show... it's for this talent competition we're all in. Tomorrow night is the results show, but we're partying it up tonight. I think we're all feeling pretty good about the way the results show will go."

"That's awesome. Do you live here, or are you only in town for the show?"

And dammit, there was the question. Well, no choice but to be honest with him. Byebye, Traver.

"I'm just here for the show, but I'm not sure how long I'll be here. It could be weeks, or I could be gone tomorrow. You never know how the audience will vote."

I waited for him to excuse himself and get back to work now that he knew I didn't live here, but he surprised me.

"Well, here. I'm going to give you my number. If you feel like doing something fun and spontaneous sometime, give me a buzz. For now, I gotta get to work before my boss gets upset. He's cool, but I don't like to push my luck. May I?" he asked, pointing at my iPhone.

He wanted my phone? Okay! "Oh yeah, sure. Go for it," I said, handing it over to him. He entered his his name and number into my contacts, then handed the phone back to me.

"Bye for now, Erin. I hope we get to hang out soon," he said, taking my hand in his and squeezing it before letting go and turning to disappear behind the Employees Only door.

"Shut the front door. Oh. My. God." Annie said, smacking my arm.

"Christ on a cracker," I exclaimed. "Did a gorgeous man just come up to me out of nowhere and put his name and number in my phone? Did that shit really just happen?"

Annie raised an eyebrow at me and smirked. "Did you really just say 'Christ on a cracker'?"

"Shut it. Focus, lady. Hot bartender just gave me his digits. What the hell am I supposed to do next?"

"Well, play it cool obviously. If you look too interested, he's going to lose interest fast. You have to keep things interesting and play a little hard to get."

"That's just it. I don't have time for playing games right now."

"Doesn't matter, trust me. You have to play the game. Everybody does, so you have to, too."

I sighed, grumbling under my breath. "Fine, but that doesn't mean I like it." But I did like Traver, so if I needed to play some stupid games to see him again, so be it.

Chapter TWENTY-ONE

The day of the results show, I was so scared that I was going to be sent home. I had no clue if I'd done enough to guarantee my way into the next round. All I could do was hope and pray.

I was trying to force some food down for lunch when my phone buzzed. It was Traver! I had texted him my phone number last night, but he hadn't messaged me until now. I'd almost begun to think he'd changed his mind.

Traver: *Hey, it's Traver.*

Erin: *Hey, how are you?*

Traver: *Pretty good. Just wanted to wish you luck tonight.*

Erin: *Aww, thank you.*

Traver: *Sure. I think it's great that you're pursuing your dream. Have a lot of respect for anyone who puts themselves out there like that.*

Erin: *Yeah, same. So is it your dream to bartend, or are you just doing that to pay the bills and pursuing something else on the side?*

Traver: *Ha, definitely not my dream to bartend. It's just a good way to earn cash. I used to play basketball, but now I'm trying to get into acting and modeling.*

Why was I not surprised? He definitely looked like he could be an actor or model, and he had the personality to go with it.

Erin: *That's cool. How long have you been doing that?*

Traver: *I just moved here a couple years ago from Detroit, so pretty much since then.*

Erin: *Nice.*

Traver: *Where are you from?*

Erin: *I was born and raised in Hawaii, but I've lived in Los Angeles all my adult life.*

Traver: *L.A., huh? Nice.*

Erin: *Yeah, but I spent my junior high and high school years in Nebraska.*

Traver: *Oh no shit. That's quite the change. Must have been a bit of culture shock for you, moving there from Hawaii.*

Erin: *Uh yeah, that's putting it mildly. I definitely felt different from everyone I went to school with. I was super tan and talked with a pidgin English accent. Everybody thought I was kind of weird.*

Traver: *Lol, did they tell you that?*

Erin: *What? That they thought I was kind of weird?*

Traver: *Yeah.*

Erin: *No, but they didn't have to.*

Traver: *Aw, I think you're being a little hard on yourself.*

Erin: *Maybe. So what made you get into acting and modeling?*

Traver: *Nice redirect.*

Erin: *Thanks! :)*

Traver: *Lol. Well, for modeling, someone said I'd be good at it, so I said yes. And for acting, I like discovering myself and putting myself into different characters. Satisfies my need for change. And in both of those I am in front of a camera, and I am very comfortable in front of cameras and embrace the limelight.*

Erin: *That's cool. I love to perform. I did children's theater for a few years when I lived in Nebraska, and my one year of college was spent studying musical theater. Those were some of the best days of my life. I miss it so much.*

Traver: *Oh awesome. Do you still act?*

Erin: *Nah, I gave that up a long time ago. It was difficult to pursue an acting career while I had to work full-time just to pay the bills and make ends meet.*

Traver: *That's too bad. Have you ever thought about getting back into it?*

Erin: *Sure, I think about it all the time, but that doesn't mean I'm going to do anything about it. I don't know how I used to be so fearless when I was* *younger, but these days I'm not sure I could handle performing on stage. Not acting anyway. Singing, yeah.*

Traver: *You shouldn't give it up if you really love it.*

Erin: *I know, I've just found other creative areas to pursue instead. There just isn't enough time in the day to do everything I want to do.*

Traver: *Ain't that the truth? Lol*

Erin: *Unfortunately. :) And as much as I wish I was SuperWoman, I'm just not. I'm only human.*

Traver: *And a beautiful one at that.*

Oh wow, did he just say that? My heart fluttered a little as I texted back.

Erin: *Thanks :)*

Traver: *You're welcome. Hey, I have to bounce, but I'll hit you up later, okay?*

Erin: *Sure, talk to you soon.*

I was floating on cloud nine the rest of the day. It helped take my mind off of things so I didn't feel as anxious about the results show.

That night I wasn't up until last, and they had paired me against a male vocalist from Seattle. I had the biggest lump in my throat as I stood there waiting to hear the verdict. Finally, after what I thought was a way longer than necessary pause, Kyle announced that I would be moving on to the next round. I don't think I've ever felt so relieved in my life. I felt myself begin to breathe again as I walked offstage. Now I just had to choose another great song. No sweat.

And choose another great song I did. This time I wanted to give a nod to the first American Idol and do *The Trouble With Love* by Miss Kelly Clarkson. It was soulful and from the soundtrack of one of my all-time favorite movies, *Love Actually.* I felt like I did the song justice.

After the show I looked around for Annie and finally found her arguing with Casey in the lobby. I was too far away to make out what they were saying, but they both looked really angry at each other. Then she gasped when he turned and walked away from her.

I watched Annie watch Casey walk over to a gorgeous short blonde who looked vaguely familiar. His face was apologetic as he spoke to her and waved towards where Annie was standing. When the blonde responded to him and shook her head, I started towards Annie, recognizing the beautiful face of Kayla Miles. I could almost see the steam coming out of Annie's ears as she glared at them. Someone came up to talk to Casey and he turned away to answer. As soon as he did so, Kayla smiled sugar sweetly at Annie and then proceeded to give her the finger.

There was barely enough time for me to slip my arm through one of Annie's to catch her and hold her fast before she launched herself across the room at the singer.

"Whoa, lady. Where do you think you're going? You look like you're about to go all *Kill Bill* on someone, and I'm guessing it might be Miss Kayla Miles."

Annie gave me a withering look. "What tipped you off?" she asked sarcastically, shrugging my hand off her arm.

"She isn't worth getting kicked out of here or worse, off the show."

She sighed as her shoulders slumped in defeat. "Ugh, I know. You're right. But I'd still love to rearrange her face. You should have seen the smile she gave me after he said something to her, and I'm dying to know exactly what that was."

"So ask him later. You need to get out of here now. Let's go. I'll buy you a drink." And maybe we'd bump into Traver.

"Fine," she snapped, turning to storm out of the room.

Rolling my eyes, I fished out my phone to press the Uber app and call a driver to take us to Halo.

At Annie's insistence, we did a few shots of Fireball, one right after the other. Then she decided to drunk dial Alex, her gay BFF in L.A. I listened to her beg him to come to New York and bring their friend, Katie, and by the time she hung up, it sounded like she might have succeeded in convincing him.

Already feeling pretty tipsy after three shots, I pushed a fourth towards Annie and then raised my shot glass as I made a toast. "To best friends who are always there for each other."

"Cheers," Annie replied, lifting her glass up to meet mine. Then we both pounded our fourth shot.

She quizzed me about Traver, asking how things were progressing. I told her that we'd only exchanged the most basic of information so far, but that I was trying to play it cool.

"That's cool. Are you going to try to hang out with him soon?" she asked.

I nodded. "Probably, but I'm kinda getting over Mike still, so I dunno."

"Well, what better way to get over him than to distract yourself with a yummy guy like Traver?"

She had a point. I nodded and grinned. "Totally, I know. You're right. How is this even a question?" I grabbed my phone and started typing a text to Traver. I didn't have to wait very long for a response. He texted right back.

"What'd he say?" Annie demanded impatiently.

"He said he's working tonight and tomorrow, but he's free on Thursday."

"Perfect. What are you going to do?"

I continued texting as I talked. "I'm asking him if he wants to grab coffee after I get done with rehearsal."

"Nice. Just take it slow."

"Yes, Mom."

"Hey!" Annie protested. I'm just looking out for you."

"I know—I'm just giving you shit," I said, sticking my tongue out at her. Just then, Traver appeared over Annie's shoulder. I turned beet red as I clapped a hand over my mouth. I probably looked like I was about ten-years-old, sticking my tongue out like that.

"Hi, ladies," he drawled with a little smirk on his face as he winked at me. Leaning over, he greeted Annie with a cheek kiss, then did the same to me. I felt all flustered as he got close to me. Oh my God, he smelled so good. I was afraid I might start drooling in front of him. "When you said you were having drinks, I didn't realize you were here. You like this place, huh?"

"Yep, it's great! Excuse me a minute—I have to use the restroom. Be right back," Annie said as she hopped off her barstool and scurried off towards the ladies' room. I was gonna kill her later.

"She did that on purpose, right?" he asked as we watched her disappear.

"Um, yep. Sorry about that."

He laughed and shook his head. "No worries, no need to apologize. Hey so, tomorrow night."

"Right. I have the results show, but I should be done by eight, I'm guessing."

"How about I pick you up for a late dinner around nine then?"

I smiled widely at him, unable to remember the last time I'd been legitimately asked on a real date. "That sounds perfect."

We chatted for a couple more minutes before Annie returned from using the restroom and he excused himself, saying he had to get back to his shift.

"So how's Traver doing?" she asked in a singsong voice as she lifted an expectant eyebrow at me.

"Good," I replied, grinning smugly. "Oh my God, that man smells like sin. And he looks like sin dipped in chocolate. And he's so nice. Like what the fuck? Where the hell has he been hiding all my life?"

"Maybe he's been waiting for you to be ready for him," Annie suggested, smiling just as smugly back at me.

"I feel like I've been ready for a while. The extra years of torture were completely unnecessary, in my opinion."

"What doesn't kill you makes you stronger."

"Yeah, yeah, yeah," I said, waving her off.

"Just sayin'."

"I know. You ready to blow this popsicle stand?"

She nodded and gathered her things. "Yeah, I want to get some decent sleep tonight. Have you seen the bags under my eyes?"

"Have you seen the bags under mine?" I asked, a yawn cracking my jaw as I stretched. Then I caught Traver watching me again. Dammit, why did that guy always happen to catch me looking unattractive? "Okay great, Hottie has now seen my oh-so-attractive yawning. He's probably thinking I'm old, yawning at a bar when it's not even midnight."

"More like he's thinking about the fact that you have a big mouth and can accommodate his big packaged when you give him a blowjob," Annie said blandly, making me choke on the water I had just started to take a drink of.

Sputtering and glancing around to see if anyone had heard, I complained, "Oh my God, say it a little louder, why don't you?"

"Nobody heard me. Stop being paranoid."

"How can I when I have to deal with your big mouth shooting off all the time?"

"Hey now," she protested.

"Sorry. Come on, it's late. Let's get out of here. I don't want Traver to think I'm lingering around just because he works here."

Annie nodded and picked up her drink to finish draining it.

"Good call," I said. "Let me just close out my tab."

"Oh yeah, we kinda have to pay for our drinks, huh?" I said before I burst into giggles.

"You lush. How much did you have to drink? I thought we had the same amount."

"Um, well… I didn't just drink." I fidgeted nervously, not sure if I should reveal my secret vice.

"Huh? What do you mean?" Annie asked, then her eyebrows shot up in understanding. "Are you on drugs? What'd you take?"

"Shhh, say it a little louder—geez, Annie." I looked around, checking to make sure no one had heard her outburst.

"What'd you take?" she demanded again.

"I just have my vape pen. Calm down."

Her eyes widened and then she started laughing. I first tensed up when she started laughing, but then gradually I started to relax.

"You blaze? Yes! I love it."

Shocked, I looked at her again. "Wait, you smoke herb?" I asked in surprise.

"What? I don't seem the type?" she asked defensively.

"Well," I said, trailing off.

"Fuck you. And you do?"

Laughing, I shook my head. "I'm sorry! I didn't know. I would have offered you some earlier if I knew you smoked. Here, you want to hit this?" I asked, pulling my vape pen out of my purse.

"Fuck yeah. Let's walk back to the hotel and smoke on the way."

"Okay!" I agreed.

After we finished closing out our checks, we started the long walk back to the hotel, passing my vape pen back and forth between us. Needless to say, I slept like a baby as soon as my head hit the pillow that night.

The next night was another results show, and for once, I wasn't feeling that nervous. I knew I had given the performance of a lifetime. Casey's crew, Pure Flow, and I were the first contestants to make it into the next round, but Annie joined us soon after.

When Traver picked me up for dinner after the show, I felt like I was floating. There was only one more round until the top ten—I was so close I could taste it. He took me to a little restaurant he said he'd discovered when he first moved to NYC, and he loved it so much, he kept coming back.

"So what made you decide to become a bartender?" I asked.

"Well, it seemed like it might be fun and fit into my schedule for acting, and at the same time, it satisfies my need to go out. I like being out and about, and I might as well make money while I'm doing it. And this way, the people come to me. I mean, when you bartend, you're usually out in front of a lot of beautiful women, and I can't lie—that's where I love to be. Most women are attracted to someone who is not trying to impress them and will just have a conversation with them, so they'll come to my bar to be served or to get away from some other dude or situation. So they are coming to me for a need, and I can fulfill it, or at least try to." He started laughing and looked mildly embarrassed. "Wow that sounds bad, but it's basic science or economics."

I smirked at him. At least he was honest.

"So did you introduce yourself to me because you thought I might be trying to get away from some other dude or situation, or did you have different reasons?" I asked with a raised eyebrow.

He laughed again and shook his head as he flashed a brilliant smile at me. Whoa, be still my heart! A guy who looked like he did should be careful when he threw around panty-dropping smiles like that!

"I introduced myself because I think you're beautiful, and there's just something about you that makes me want to get to know you."

"Good answer," I said, giving him an approving smile.

Annie's friends, Alex and Katie, flew into NYC that weekend and we spent the next few days doing touristy shit with them. I loved them both and we had so much fun. We all exchanged numbers and promised to hang out once we got back to L.A. Then I found out that Annie had some ex-boyfriend with a dick piercing who was flying out to NYC for the next performance. I demanded to know more details and the three of them did their best to fill me in.

When I wasn't hanging out with my new SoCal buddies that weekend, I was texting with Traver or practicing my next song, *Next Plane Out* by Celine Dion. He was unable to get the night off for my next performance, but I got him a ticket to the results show the following night so he could come see me.

My hands were clammy and my teeth were practically chattering as I waited for the show to start, but when Kyle Atkinson called my name and then Annie's, my heart stopped beating for a few moments. Oh no, this was the last thing I wanted to happen. Why did they have to put me up against the girl who in only a short amount of time had become my best friend? But I was pretty sure I already knew what the outcome would be. I may love singing, but Annie was born to sing. I knew it, and I hope America and the judges recognized it.

As we both approached center stage, I saw that Annie's face mirrored my own. We'd been almost inseparable since we had gotten to New York, and now we neared the end of our journey together. This is where we had to part ways. This is when we determine who would go on, and who would go home. And although we both knew this day was coming, I knew neither of us was happy that it had to come to this.

We stood there facing the audience, grasping each other's hand tightly, tears streaming down both our faces as we waited for Kyle to read the verdict out loud. He fumbled with the envelope, finally getting it open.

"And the person leaving us tonight is…"

I leaned a little closer to Annie and whispered," I love you girl, you deserve this."

"Erin Tanaka!" Kyle finished. "That means you are safe again this week, Annie Chang. Congratulations, you can exit the stage that way. Thank you. Okay, and Erin, thank you so much for being with us on the show and sharing your amazing talent with us. Let's take a quick look at your journey here on *The Next American Superstar.*"

I did my very best to hold it together through the video clip they played. Unsurprisingly, Annie was in a lot of the footage. As I watched the clip play and saw how close Annie and I had become, more tears came. I had made a new best friend, and if she took this thing all the way to the end and won, she'd be moving to Las Vegas. I consoled myself with the fact that Las Vegas was only a few hours' drive away from L.A.

Valiantly I wiped away the tears as I heard Annie yell, "I love you, Erin! You fucking rock!" I turned and blew a kiss to my bestie, waiving before turning back to the audience. Then I took a bow and turned to leave the stage as the applause started to die down.

Traver found me after the show. He'd brought a big bouquet of red roses to surprise me, which definitely helped perk my spirits up quite a bit. I may have lost *The Next American Superstar*, but I had met a great guy who seemed to like me just as much as I liked him. But the fact that he liked to bartend so he could be around beautiful women all the time bothered me a bit. He didn't really sound like someone who wanted to settle down, even if he had been the one to approach me.

"Hey, don't be sad," he said as he hugged me tight. "You gave it your best shot, and look how far you came."

"I know. I just always dreamed that someday I would get to sing professionally, but I think I should probably take this as a sign that I'm just not cut out for this."

"Hey, just because this door closes doesn't mean another window won't open somewhere else."

I nodded and sniffed, wiping away a stray tear. "I know, you're probably right. But I don't have to do music. I just really want to do something creative, so maybe I should stick to my writing."

"Nothing wrong with that," he said.

He waited for me to change and then took me to another late dinner.

I told him a little about how I'd gotten into self-publishing, which he seemed to take a keen interest in. Then I jokingly said he should be the cover on my new book, and he said okay. I hadn't really been serious at first, but the more I thought about it, the more my idea appealed to me.

"You know, I should try to book a photo shoot with you now before I go back to L.A."

He nodded thoughtfully. "I have a photographer who I work with who would probably give you a good deal."

"That'd be awesome," I said excitedly, then paused. "Except we don't have a female model to pose with you."

"Why don't you pose with me?"

I looked at him like he'd grown two heads. "Are you serious? I can't pose for my own book."

"Sure you can, babe. You're beautiful, and you'll look even better next to me," he said with a wink.

I smirked back at him. "Modest much?"

He threw his head back and laughed. "I left modesty behind a long, long time ago," he said with a twinkle in his eye.

"Still, I don't know that I am the right choice to pose with you for my cover."

"Well, I can try to get someone on short notice, but I can't promise anything."

"Alright, I'll agree to be the back-up, but can you please try to get someone else?" I smiled pleadingly at him.

I had nothing to lose really. Why not have an impromptu book cover photo shoot in NYC? I was looking better now than I ever had in my life, but I'd never really modeled before. But I wasn't left with a choice as Traver was unable to find another female model on such short notice, so I ended up agreeing to pose for the shoot with him.

Surprisingly enough, at the photo shoot Traver immediately put me at my ease, and in no time at all, we had some great shots to choose from. Later that day we went over all of the pictures, one by one, selecting our favorites and narrowing them down. We stayed up until the wee hours of the morning figuring out which one was the very best. By the time we picked one, it was six o'clock in the morning and we were lounging on my hotel bed, curled up together in a spooning position with him behind me.

"I don't want to go back to LA."

"I wish you didn't have to go, either."

I sighed. "But I have to. I called my boss and told him what happened and he said the temp they hired for him is "god-awful" and he'd love for me to come back. I lucked out this time."

"I get it," he said, making me shiver as he gently nuzzled my neck.

We hadn't slept together, yet. After being burnt by so many men in the past year, I was a little hesitant to get physical too fast, especially when I liked him so much. But I responded by wiggling my butt back into him. To my delight, I felt him hardening against me. I was tempted to go further, but I really didn't have enough time. My flight was leaving early afternoon and I still had to finish packing.

Traver had offered to drive me to the airport, which I had gratefully accepted. When he pulled up to the Virgin America curb and got out to hug me, I had a hard time letting him go.

"I'm coming to L.A. to shoot a commercial soon," he said as he pulled back. "What!" I yelped in surprise. "When?"

"My agent just texted me. I'm flying there in a couple of weeks."

"Oh that's awesome." I hesitated before offering the next, not sure how he'd take the invitation. "Well, you know you're welcome to stay with me while you're in town if you want."

"Really? That wouldn't be too much trouble?" he asked, his eyes lighting up.

"Not at all. I can probably come pick you up from the airport as well, depending on what time your flight gets in."

"Okay, as soon as I book my flights, I'll let you know."

"Sounds good. Well, I'd better get in there and get checked in."

"Right, okay. Well, text me when you get back home safely, okay?"

I smiled, nodded and hugged him again, then gave him a hard kiss before pulling back and grabbing my suitcase to head into the terminal. I didn't look back. I didn't think I could handle seeing his handsome face so sad as I walked away, but I was really looking forward to seeing that same face light up with a smile when he came to visit me in L.A. in a couple of weeks. Maybe everything does happen for a reason. Maybe I did find love in NYC. I didn't know if we could make a bi-coastal relationship work, and after seeing how little effort Mike wanted to put into one, I was paranoid that Traver would be the same. But I didn't want to think about that right now. For now, I wanted to live in the moment and enjoy every experience as it came my way.

THE END

Turn to the end for an excerpt from
Angels and Whiskey
by Kimberly Knight!

Acknowledgements

A lot of hard work, blood, sweat and tears went into finishing the first installment of the Love in NYC series, but I am happy with the finished product. Thanks to all my friends and family for continuing to give me moral support.

A big thanks goes out to Tyler White, who I bumped into while he was bartending in a club in Hollywood. About fifteen minutes after meeting him for the first time ever, I asked him to be on the cover of my new book for my Love in NYC series. Not only is he gorgeous and droolworthy, but he is one of the nicest, most down-to-earth people I've ever met, and I consider myself fortunate to have met him and partnered up on this cover. Tyler, thank you so much for everything. You've been great to work with, but you've been an even better friend. Thanks for all your encouragement and support.

Thank you to Catherine Gontran (aka _coryvegas) for agreeing to pose with Tyler for this cover. You are breathtakingly beautiful and have portrayed Erin just as I see her in my head. You, like Tyler, are one of the nicest, warmest people, and I am happy to have gotten the chance to work with you as well.

To Magdalena Bleu, my photographer, thank you for this beautiful shot. It was great working with you! Thanks for finding me a location with an NYC vibe in L.A.!

To Kimberly Knight, my BFFL, thank you for continuing to be my friend and inspiring me with all you've done and accomplished, and I'm not just talking about the book stuff. You have gone through hell and back, lady, and I greatly respect and admire you for pushing through all of the pain and stress and always trying to remain positive. I love you!

About the AUTHOR

Audrey Harte was born and raised on the North Shore of Oahu in Hawaii until she and her family moved to Nebraska where she attended junior high, high school and college. During her time in Nebraska, she pursued her love of the arts, acting and singing in several local theater productions as well as writing poems, plays and musicals in her spare time.

In 1998, she moved to Los Angeles, California, where she has lived ever since. Her main interests are reading (primarily romance, erotica and fantasy, although she has been known to read the occasional thriller), writing (obviously), karaoke, finger crocheting blankets and hangers for friends and family (she doesn't use a hook), watching her favorite TV shows and hanging out with friends. She is a serious reality TV show addict. Really, she may need an intervention at some point. Before writing started consuming all of her time, she used to play *World of Warcraft* with Kimberly Knight, who is one of her best friends.

http://audreyharte.com

http://www.facebook.com/authoraudreyharte

http://audreyharte.wordpress.com

http://twitter.com/audrey_harte

http://www.goodreads.com/author/show/6869140.Audrey_Harte

http://www.instagram.com/audreyharteauthor

About the COVER MODELS

The models featured on the cover of this book are Tyler White and Catherine Gontran, and they portray the characters of Traver and Erin.

Tyler is an actor/model who formerly played for the Washington Generals and Harlem Globetrotters. He has a couple of projects in post production, which are still to be released at a later time, but he was most recently featured in the *Irresistible* music video with Fall Out Boy, playing a pick-up game of basketball with the band. And yes, ladies, his shirt comes off in the video! Check it out on YouTube! He also has a short film out titled Super Zero, where he plays a zombie killer. This short can also be found on YouTube (just search Super Hero – badass zombie apocalypse short film). The biggest of the projects Tyler is currently working on is *Where Does the Maiden Lie*. He has already shot the trailer for it and is in the process of fundraising for it on Indiegogo. Filming starts in August 2015 with an estimated worldwide release date in Spring 2016. Tyler is very excited about this as it would be a huge step for his career and definitely a test of his acting chops, but he can't wait to show you what he can do.

Website: http://www.tyler-white.com
Film Website: http://www.wheredoesthemaidenlie.com
Fundraising Website: http://www.indiegogo.com
Instagram: http://instagram.com/tylerdashwhite
Twitter: http://twitter.com/tylerdashwhite

Catherine is a good friend of Tyler's who he met bartending some years ago, and she kindly agreed to do the cover as a favor to do him. She is a successful fitness model and was most recently seen in a New Balance ad in Times Square in New York. Follow her on Instagram! And you never know! She might make an appearance at one of my book signings!

http://instagram.com/_coryvegas

NOTE FROM THE AUTHOR

Thank you for taking the time to read *Say Anything,* the first book in my Love in NYC series. I hope you have enjoyed getting to know Erin and the men in her life.

Please take a moment to leave a review on the website of purchase and on Goodreads. Reviews help other readers decide whether to try a book, so they are invaluable to authors.

I have yet to announce a release date for my next book. It will most likely be book 2 of the Love in NYC series, but you never know! I might decide to take a break and writing something completely different. But I won't be announcing a new release date for a while.

Keep an eye on my Facebook fan page for more news on upcoming books, and you can always check the Events tab on my website to see what book signings I will be at. I love to meet my fans, so please don't be shy. Come say hi to me at any signing! I look forward to meeting you.

Some of these songs are specifically mentioned in the book, and some are just songs that inspired certain parts of the book. My playlist is available on Spotify. I hope you enjoy!

http://bit.ly/1yExgfs

Waves (Robin Schulz Remix) – Mr. Probz

Human - Krewella

When I Was Your Man – Bruno Mars

Gold – Adventure Club, featuring Yuna

Say My Name – Odesza, featuring Zyra

Without You (Vindata Remix) - Odesza

Habits (Stay High) – Tove Lo

La La La – Naughty Boy, featuring Sam Smith

Fantasy – Alina Baraz, featuring Galimatias

LAX to JFK - Kaskade

Clair de Lune – Flight Facilities, featuring Christine Hoberg

No Diggity – Chet Faker

Bridges - Broods

Latch – Disclosure, featuring Sam Smith

Prayer in C (Robin Schulz Radio Mix) – Lily Wood and The Prick, featuring Robin Schulz

The Way – Ariana Grande, featuring Mac Miller

Uninvited – Alanis Morissette

What's Love Got To Do With It? – Tina Turner

The Trouble With Love Is – Kelly Clarkson

Next Plane Out – Celine Dion

Angels & Whiskey

By Kimberly Knight

PROLOGUE

March 9th
Gabe

I never thought I'd see a day where my world was more consumed by one person than by serving my country.

My life was set to follow in my grandfather's footsteps. It was my destiny. I'd forgotten he'd met my grandmother while serving in Vietnam, so I should have known I would meet my future wife while serving in Afghanistan.

"You gotta girl back home we don't know about, Cap?"

I glanced from the computer screen to First Lieutenant Paul Jackson as he spoke and then to Cochran, who was sitting across the room. The moment I'd laid eyes on Cochran when she joined my crew, I had no idea she'd become my first love.

For a few seconds, I watched as Cochran laughed with Stone, her fellow medic. "Something like that," I murmured, turning back to the website on the computer that was allowing me to *secretly* design an engagement ring for her. I was Specialist Cochran's Captain, and because of military regulations, no one could know we had been dating for nine months and that I wanted to make her my wife.

My life's plan had always been to work my way through the ranks until I was no longer breathing. But now I wanted to be with Cochran and spend the rest of my life making her happy. It was hard not being able to kiss her whenever I wanted—to touch her as she walked by or hold her hand. I felt like a stalker; always secretly watching her.

"Why are you designing an engagement ring?" he asked, interrupting my thoughts.

I looked over my right shoulder at him. "Are you a moron, LT?" I chuckled.

"I just didn't know you gotta girl is all." He shrugged, still peering over my shoulder and looking at the computer screen.

"Well, I do." I glanced to Cochran again and then back to the computer before Jackson noticed. "Get out of my hair and go check your gear before Major Dick rips you a new asshole."

"You don't have any." He laughed, looking at my bald head.

"I like it that way, Lieutenant. Now fuck off." I ran my hand over my bald head. I'd been losing my hair for a few years, so I finally said fuck it and shaved it all off. Cochran thought it looked sexy on me. I was his Captain, but we were like brothers and even had that brotherly banter. Honestly, he was the closest friend I had on base, so it was no wonder he was questioning me about my love life.

"You know I'm going to get you to show me naked pictures of her."

"In your dreams, P.J. Now really, fuck off."

"All right," he huffed. "By the way, the gear's good, Cap. But I feel ya. I'll leave you to your girly shit." He laughed again then slapped me on the back and left to join the rest of the crew. They were binge watching *Lost* while we waited for any MEDEVAC (medical evacuation) calls.

I was tired of the war. I never thought I'd say that. For as long as I could remember, I'd wanted to be an American hero. Not anymore.

I'd already completed two tours and as soon as my third was done, so was I. I didn't want to be in the sand anymore. I didn't want to hear gunfire in the distance twenty-four-seven. I didn't want to have that sinking feeling in the pit of my stomach on a MEDEVAC call as we potentially stepped into the line of fire.

I wanted Alyssa Cochran—on a beach in Hawaii.

I wanted to wake up next to her and see her blue eyes sparkle while the sun rose.

I wanted to see her blonde hair fanned across my pillow.

I wanted to be with her openly.

I wanted her as my wife.

Cochran rose from her seat on the couch and I minimized the computer screen. I glanced at her a few times as she made her way across the room, trying not to be obvious that I was watching her. She brushed her finger along the bridge of her nose. *Our sign.* I tried to hide my smile as I saved my design in my online account on the computer, then erased my browser history and closed the window. I couldn't wait to have her in my arms.

I made my way down the hall, pretending to need the latrine. I looked over my shoulder and when I saw no eyes on me, made my way through the door across the hall where Cochran was waiting.

"Have I ever told you that I love a man in uniform?" she whispered, grabbing my arm and pulling me into a vacant room.

I closed the door behind me. "I'll make sure to keep my uniform after this tour." I wrapped her in my arms, holding her as if it were our last day together. I hated the whole situation: the sneaking around, not being able to kiss her whenever I wanted, not being able to cuddle on the couch and watch a movie.

"Good." She smiled as I leaned down and kissed her soft lips enjoying the faint taste of cherry Chapstick.

Taking her hand, I led her to one of the cots and sat in the center, pulling her down to sit on my lap. Her arms wrapped around my neck and she leaned into me. "What were you and Stone laughing about earlier?" I asked, then took a breath of her scent. She always smelled like vanilla … warm vanilla sugar.

She leaned her head back and gave me a wicked smirk. "I can't tell you. You're my Captain."

"Alys—"

"We were playing Fuck, Marry, Kill," she blurted.

My jaw clenched. I didn't want to hear who she wanted to fuck, but curiosity won. "Who'd you pick?"

After a few beats, she finally spoke. "You can't get mad, Gabe. It was just for shits and giggles."

"All right, I won't. Tell me." I brushed a piece of her hair behind her ear that had fallen from her bun.

"Well, of course, I'd marry you—I love you. And Stone and I both want to kill Major Dick even though he's not bad on the eyes." She paused and took a deep breath before continuing. "Now this is the part you can't get mad at—"

"Just tell me, babe." I knew I couldn't get mad over a silly game, but it was just like when you had a dream and someone pissed you off in it; you'd wake up mad at them for no reason. And that's how I was feeling. I wanted to know who my *competition* was.

"I'd ... I'd fuck Jackson."

My back straightened and my arms wrapped tighter around her. Yeah, I wanted to throttle him even if he was my best friend.

"It's just a game C.H." I smiled. CH stood for Captain Hottie. I knew she used my nickname to lighten the mood. "I only want to fuck you—and *do* only fuck you."

"I know, babe. But my best friend?"

"Just a game, C.H. Just a game."

"I need to come up with my own list." I grinned at her. Two could play this game.

She slapped my arm playfully. "Don't you dare!"

"All right, I won't. But I hope these next six months go by fast. I want Jackson to know you're mine." I brushed my hand under the hem of her army green T-shirt, feeling her smooth belly and needing to feel her soft, warm skin.

She gave a tight smile. "Me too."

"Maybe..." I paused for a moment before continuing to make sure I wanted to suggest this. "Maybe we *should* tell Jackson and Stone? I trust them and they can be our lookout people."

"You want to risk them telling?"

My hands had worked Alyssa's T-shirt from her pants without me knowing. I wanted her and at that moment, I didn't care if my whole crew knew. If someone ran and told Major Dick, I'd deal with it. I'd risk getting kicked out of the army just to be with her and a chance to kick Major Dick's ass. Major Dick wasn't his real name, but he sure as shit earned it, and I'd leave with the respect of everyone in the army because no one liked *Dick*.

"I'd risk anything for you."

"Okay, let's tell them. I trust them. Stone's my best friend too."

"Good." I agreed and began to lift her shirt over her head until there was a knock on the door. We both stilled, me holding my breath.

"Cap, we gotta Dustoff," Jackson called out behind the closed door. While I wanted to spend the rest of the day with Cochran on my lap, we had a ME-DIVAC call we had to go to.

"Shit, he already knows," Alyssa whispered, her eyes wide with concern then scurried off my lap.

I watched her, not saying anything while she tucked her shirt into her pants. Jackson knocked on the women's door. He knew I was in there with her.

"How many?" I asked while Alyssa righted herself.

"Two."

"How bad?"

"Urgent. No enemies in the area."

I rushed to the door, swung it open with Alyssa on my heels. "You know nothing." I pointed a finger in his face in warning.

He smiled. "I found you in the shitter. I don't know what you're talking about."

"Good. We'll be right behind you." I grabbed Alyssa's hand and halted her as Jackson continued walking down the hall. "One down and one to go." I smiled and kissed her cherry lips.

"Stone won't be a problem. Tonight I'll show you how happy I am to finally tell people."

"I like the sound of that. But real quick … Since you want to marry me, what shape of diamonds do you like?"

"What?" she asked, scrunching her eyebrows.

"In your game of Fuck, Marry, Kill, what ring would you hope I'd give you?"

She laughed. "You're silly."

"Just tell me. We don't have time for you to question me."

"I don't know. I'd never really given it much thought. I'd like any ring you'd give me."

"All right. Good to know. Let's go so we can get back and tell Jackson and Stone. Then I can take my time tasting you and not have to worry about anyone catching us." I kissed her again before we joined the rest of the crew.

The crew chatted about what was happening in the current episode of *Lost* as we made our way to our coordinates. My thoughts were only of Alyssa. I couldn't wait for tonight so I could take my time making love to her somewhere other than a supply closet.

I stared at her as she laughed with Stone, the desert sand behind her, and I envisioned her in a bikini laying on the beach in Hawaii. I hated Afghanistan. I wanted to be back on American soil with the Pacific Ocean in the distance.

When we finally touched down, the helicopter caused the sand to blow around us. Every day I found sand in places on my body it didn't belong. It felt as if I could never be one hundred percent clean no matter how hard I scrubbed.

The popping of gunfire could be heard in the distance as we made our way from the bird. Heads down, gear in hand, we made it to the soldiers that were covered in crimson blood. After Cochran and Stone had patched up the bullet holes on each soldier with enough gauze so we could transport them back to base, the crew and I strapped them on the gurneys. I faintly heard the gunfire getting closer as we stood.

Pop. Pop. Pop.

"I thought you said dispatch radioed there were no enemy troops in the area?" I asked Jackson.

"That's what the 9-Line said."

Usually dispatch was correct when they'd called in a 9-Line MEDEVAC request for us. They'd tell us where the location was, how many patients, if we needed special equipment … Nine items to prepare us. Obviously they were wrong this time.

"We need to move. They're getting closer."

The wind kicked up, blowing the rough sand in the air and making it hard to see our own hands in front of our eyes. I fucking hated Afghanistan.

The gunfire got louder.

Pop. Pop. Pop.

"Let's move!"

Jackson radioed base. "Charlie Tango, this is Delta Sky. We have enemy fire and we're being ambushed. Send backup, stat."

My crew and I picked up the two gurneys and began running toward the helicopter. The gunfire was close as we slid one gurney in.

Pop. Pop. Pop.

"Cap!" Jackson yelled.

I looked back seeing enemy troops in the distance, the wind dying down enough to see them crouch and take aim.

Before we could pull our weapons, they fired.

"Get this gurney in!" I snapped, drawing my gun and covering my crew.

Instinct took over as I aimed, firing my gun and praying we didn't get hit with bullets as we stood in the open desert with nothing to hide behind. As we fired back, Cochran and Stone tended to our downed soldiers.

"Heads down, keep firing!" I barked.

Pop. Pop. Pop.

"Watch Cochran's and Stone's six, Woodring!"

Pop.

"Move, move, move!"

Pop. Pop.

We continued to fire. I didn't know how many enemy troops there were. I couldn't see with all the sand in the air, but we kept firing until the wind wasn't blowing and we saw all of the enemies down.

"Everyone good?" I asked. I turned around to see one of my medics down. I couldn't tell who, but my heart stopped.

"Jackson!" I hollered as I ran to the downed medic.

When I reached her, I fell to my knees, flipping her over—Cochran.

"No!" I yelled, my heart pounding so hard that I thought it would beat out of my chest. Alyssa wasn't moving and blood started to seep and stain her uniform.

"Fuck!" Jackson shouted, kneeling beside me.

"No!" I yelled again. This couldn't be happening. This was Alyssa, the love of my life. She was part of my crew. The crew I was trained to protect and the one person I wanted to protect the most was down, her chest covered in dark red blood and not moving.

"Cap, we gotta get her in the bird. More enemies could be coming," Jackson affirmed.

I was numb, unable to move. Alyssa was in my arms still not moving and barely breathing. I held her asking her to open her eyes …

But she didn't.

"Open your eyes, Cochran." I could feel the tightness in my throat as I fought off the tears that were building. Everything around me didn't matter anymore. I only cared for Alyssa and she was shot—shot on my watch.

"Cap, we gotta move," Jackson persisted.

"Put her in the bird so I can stop the bleeding," Stone begged.

I hesitated for a minute, still looking at Alyssa. The severity of the situation hadn't hit yet.

"Cap—"

"All right!" I picked her body off the ground, placing her inside the helicopter. We piled in and I removed her helmet. Her beautiful blue eyes didn't stare back at me. Her smile wasn't spread across her face like it had been thirty minutes prior.

Tears rolled down my cheeks. No one had seen me cry before. I was a soldier. I was an American hero. I was a fucking captain—I didn't cry. But as my worst fear came crashing down around me, I lost it.

Tears trickled down my cheeks and onto Alyssa as she lay in my arms, her breathing diminishing every second. I didn't care anymore. This was real and she was the love of my life. I wanted to go back to thirty minutes ago and prepare everyone for the ambush. I wanted to be the one in front of the bullet—not Alyssa. I wanted to save her.

We started to fly back to base, the tears still rolling down my face. No one said anything. Stone and Jackson worked on Alyssa while my other crew members tended to the original soldiers the best they could since they weren't medics.

Alyssa started to cough up blood and then before I knew it, she stopped.

"Stay with me, babe," I pleaded, brushing my fingers down her cheek.

I looked up to see Stone's eyes fill with tears as she listened through a stethoscope, then she shook her head at Jackson, advising my gaze.

"No!" This couldn't be happening. Alyssa wasn't dead. We were going to get married. She was going to take my last name. I was going to wake up next to her every morning—I was counting on forever.

But we weren't.

Alyssa died in my arms on the way back to base and worst of all …

I didn't get to tell her how much I loved her.

Made in the USA
Charleston, SC
08 April 2015